Sovereign Risk

A Mallard Melodrama

Book 3

R J Williams

For Mrs Daniels, my form teacher,
who introduced me to the world of literature.

Other books by R J Williams

A Fitting End

Death in Earnest

Chapter 1

January 1896

What should have been a triumph ended in disaster. Leander Starr Jameson held his head high as he trudged along the dusty road in Doornkop. The bitterness of defeat weighed on him, but he did his best not to let it show.

His plan, devised with such care, had failed. It had all seemed so achievable - crossing the border and making a lightning dash to Johannesburg to join his allies, Uitlanders as the Boers called them, Britons and Americans mostly, frustrated by the onerous restrictions forced on them by the Boer government. The South African Republic would be overthrown. Transvaal would be theirs and Jameson would have the pleasure of declaring victory to the Prime Minister of the Cape Colony, Cecil Rhodes.

He crossed from Bechuanaland with six hundred men, but soon encountered Boer forces and found the road to Johannesburg blocked. In the skirmishes that followed, he lost men and horses. The initiative lay with the enemy and on the second day of January 1896, four days after his column set out, he faced the grim reality that his position was untenable. Surrender was the only option.

Surrounded by Boer soldiers, with his hands manacled, he was brought before their Commandant, Piet Cronjé.

The man surveyed his captives. A bleak smile of triumph spread across his heavily bearded face. He spoke in Afrikaans, pausing at intervals to allow the man standing at his side to translate.

'So, Englishman, what is to be done? You must know your situation is grave. The Uitlander conspirators in Johannesburg will face the full force of the law. We know who they are. What have you to say?'

'The responsibility for this action is mine alone. My men have acted on my orders, as was their duty. They are disarmed and pose no threat. I urge you to allow them to return.'

Cronjé waited for his translator to finish. He looked at Jameson's men, surrounded by his own soldiers. 'I have a simple view of justice,' he began. 'You came here to kill and spread terror in our peaceful Republic. You are not soldiers, merely brigands, and should be treated as such.' He paused while the translator spoke in English. A murmur rose among Jameson's men. Jameson himself kept silent, staring defiantly back at his captor.

Cronjé raised his voice. 'I would have no hesitation in executing every last one of you.' The murmur grew louder, with voices raised in anger as they heard the translation. Their guards looked around nervously and levelled their weapons at the prisoners.

'But,' Cronjé continued, holding up his right hand. 'The decision does not rest with me. I will send you to Pretoria. President Kruger will decide what to do with you.' He turned on his heel and walked away.

Chapter 2

In Berlin, a flurry of snow descended in the dim light of the late afternoon. The figure at the window watched the flakes settling on the balustrade. Outwardly, he seemed impassive, lost in thought. He showed nothing of the turmoil in his head, save perhaps for the whitening of the knuckles gripping the hilt of his sword. The British - it was always the British that got under his skin. So smug. So condescending. He was the eldest of the old Queen's grandchildren, a king and emperor in his own right, and yet, who would know it from the way his royal relatives in England treated him? And worst of all was the Prince of Wales - Bertie, his uncle. That old peacock, as he thought of him. A stout, preposterous old fellow, given up to debauchery. He still smarted at the memory of how Bertie had kept him waiting when he'd visited Cowes the previous summer. He, a reigning monarch, left to cool his heels for forty-five minutes.

Great Britain and that empire of theirs. The fruits of three hundred years of conquest and double-dealing. Well, that was history. New powers were stirring. The German Reich would have its place in the sun. He'd rejected Bismarck's oh-so-calculated approach to diplomacy. That was no way for a great power to behave. He, Kaiser Wilhelm II, had charted a fresh course.

He would not allow Germany to be hemmed-in by the old powers. France and Russia looked to one another to counter him. But Britain held aloof, preserving its haughty policy of isolation, confident in the dominant power of its navy. Sea power – that was the key. Germany must have a powerful fleet, fit to challenge the British. German shipyards were already producing the cruisers and battleships he needed. More would follow. The days of Rule Britannia were numbered.

When news of the Jameson Raid first reached Berlin, Wilhelm was incandescent with rage. His deep-seated suspicion of the British and his barely concealed animosity toward the British Empire had him fulminating at what he called, "this vile example of British treachery."

It had taken a mighty effort by his ministers to dissuade him from ordering a cruiser with a contingent of marines to be dispatched to southern Africa to aid the Boer Government in Pretoria. The Kaiser had even proposed declaring the Transvaal a German protectorate.

His War Minister violently opposed him. His Chancellor even threatened to resign.

Finally, they arrived at a compromise. Grudgingly, the Kaiser gave his approval to the Foreign Office's suggestion that they should only send a telegram of support. It read –

> *I express to you my sincere congratulations that you and your people, without appealing to the help of friendly powers, have succeeded, by your own energetic action against the armed bands which invaded your country as disturbers of the peace, in restoring peace and in maintaining the independence of the country against attack from without.*

It was addressed to President Kruger, but its message would be obvious to the British. Germany stood ready to help protect the independence of the Transvaal. The gloves were off.

Abruptly, he turned to face his audience. The three men sitting at the table waited expectantly.

Wilhelm took his seat at the head of the table and regarded his three onlookers. Hohenlohe looked his age. The receding grey hair, the sunken cheeks, the bags under his eyes, and his air of weariness made Wilhelm wonder whether he'd made the right choice in appointing the man as his Chancellor. The future he envisioned for Germany called for a man of greater energy, more sympathetic to the Kaiser's imperial ambitions.

Next to him sat von Bieberstein, the State Secretary of the Foreign Office, the man behind the text of the telegram that lay before them on the table. Wilhelm eyed him with distaste. While Hohenlohe was largely a passive player, von Bieberstein was too often inclined to dilute the Kaiser's influence on foreign policy. No doubt he felt a sense of satisfaction at watering down Wilhelm's perfectly justified desire to provide material assistance to the Boers. Wilhelm wondered when it would be opportune to dismiss him.

The third man was Philipp, Prince of Eulenburg. Wilhelm caught his eye and smiled. Philipp was his confidant and loyal friend – perhaps his only true friend. Philipp returned his smile and inclined his head in acknowledgement.

Wilhelm took up the pen lying on the table and signed the text of the telegram. 'Thank you, Chancellor, State Secretary. I trust you are both satisfied,' he said dryly. 'You may both leave.' Hohenlohe got stiffly to his feet while von Bieberstein reached across the table to retrieve the telegram. Both men bowed and left the room.

'Well, have I done right?' Wilhelm asked.

'Your instincts were no doubt correct,' Eulenburg replied. 'A gunboat would have been a fitting retort to British arrogance, but perhaps it's better to keep your powder dry. The time will come for a direct military challenge but, for now, I think the telegram will be a sufficient indication of Germany's stance. Some will say that even that is an unnecessary provocation to British sensibilities. Did you see the look on Bieberstein's face? He will cross you once too often and then you can appoint someone more worthy of the position.'

Wilhelm leaned across and patted his friend's hand. 'Yes, dear friend, you advise me well, and faithfully, as always. Let the British take offence. After all, it is they who meddle where they are not wanted.'

'And yet, imagine what could be achieved if Britain could be made to see the advantages of an understanding with Germany.'

'Pah, you jest Eulenburg. You cannot seriously suppose that I would countenance an accommodation with them.'

'Well, of course, you have good reason to dislike the thought. They have always treated you with scant regard. But just suppose that a way might be found to convince them that their future interests would be best served by aligning with the Reich. Is it so outlandish a proposal? They are not natural allies of either France or Russia. France and Britain have conflicting interests in Africa and Russia is an ever-present threat to British control in India.'

'Hmm, all very interesting Eulenburg but never forget that Germany's place in the world will be secured by German will, German steel, and German blood if need be. If the British are ever to give us the respect we deserve, it will be because they recognise our strength. Yes, and fear it, by God.'

The fierce glint in Wilhelm's eyes warned Philipp that it would be prudent to change the subject. He was forestalled by the Kaiser, who abruptly rose to his feet and left without a word.

Eulenburg watched him go, then produced a small notebook from his coat pocket and started writing.

Chapter 3

February 1897

'Ma chérie, come in from the garden now. I have something to show you.'

'Oui, Maman. Qu'est que c'est?'

'In English, please, dear. Remember, today is…?'

'English, mama. Today we speak English,' the little girl replied with a shrug of her shoulders.

Verity smiled and led Jaqueline along the passage to the drawing room.

In the six months she'd spent at Montvalon, Verity Mallard had watched her daughter with a mixture of delight and aching regret. Delight, in seeing the girl so absorbed in childhood's innocent enjoyments, and regret in the knowledge that this fleeting idyll would soon draw to a close.

Verity saw herself in miniature in Jaqueline's blond hair and blue eyes, but her mouth and the set of her head when she spoke were a poignant reminder of Antoine.

'Come over to the table, Jaqueline. What do you see, my dear?'

'I see… I see a…' - the child looked at Verity, who mouthed the word she sought. 'A box?'

'That's right, and what a pretty box it is. Would you like to open it?'

Jaqueline nodded and climbed onto a chair to reach out and touch the object. It was covered in purple silk. Her fingers moved to the clasp. For a moment she puzzled how to undo it, then she slipped it open and lifted the lid.

'Ooh.'

There, cushioned in crimson velvet, lay a brooch. In its centre was a large ruby set in a silver mount, chased with images of mythical creatures and with small pearls around its circumference.

Jaqueline looked enquiringly at Verity.

'It belonged to Grand-mère Ninette, *chérie*. Is it not beautiful?'

The child nodded and extended her hand tentatively to touch it.

Verity remembered the times she'd seen the brooch decorating her mother's dress. It had been a family heirloom for generations, acquired in Russia by her ancestor, Guy Roland, a member of Napoleon's staff, and a survivor of the disastrous retreat from Moscow. Verity herself had worn it on the night of a ball seven years ago, here at Montvalon. The night she met Antoine.

Montvalon was her mother's house then, her parents' retreat during those endless French summers of her youth. Her favourite place in the whole world, and now it was hers, bequeathed to her after her mother's tragic death, and the place she had chosen to be Jaqueline's home.

How different her life had been then. A young woman with so much ahead of her and all the advantages of her family's place in society. They never pushed her towards marriage or made her feel that she must follow some preordained course. She received nothing but support when she declared her intention to study at the University of London. And, as one of the few women to obtain a Bachelor of Arts degree, they applauded her ambition to become a journalist.

That ball changed everything. The crazy few weeks with Antoine, when all she could think of was the excitement of the moment. The shock and panic of discovering that she was pregnant. And then the final hammer blow. A mild fever foretold the grim diagnosis of typhoid. In five days, Antoine was dead.

Grief and despair claimed her.

Had she the misfortune of having parents that lacked the good sense and compassion of Sir Stanmore and Lady Ninette, her despair might have been well founded. But they, and her wonderful aunt Claudette, had given her their love and support. Being in France made it all so much easier. In England, society would consider her predicament an indelible disgrace. But here, people tolerated and understood the consequences of human nature. She spent her pregnancy under her aunt's care and gave birth to a healthy baby girl.

She knew the reality of her situation. The child must be a secret known only to her parents, her aunt, and her brother, Mortimer. She would have to endure the painful reality that Claudette would bring Jaqueline up. And so it had turned out. In England, she single-mindedly pursued her career, slowly and persistently forging a path in journalism. Twice a year, she visited her daughter. She and Claudette made sure that Jaqueline understood from an early age that Verity was her mother. Mercifully, she seemed to accept it without qualms, showing maturity beyond her years.

'You must keep it safe Jaqueline, tante Claudette will show you where,' she said, closing the box.

Tomorrow she would return to London. It had been a tumultuous year. One that almost cost the life of her dear friend, Mary, and exposed them both to a side of life that they never thought could intrude upon their ordered world. They'd met with violence, depravity, and murder, and survived. She, Mortimer, Mary, and long-suffering private detective George Benson, had forged a close bond of trust. So close that she'd admitted Mary and George to the secret of Jaqueline's existence.

Chapter 4

April 1897

'Miss Forbes, I've heard so much about you. It's such a pleasure to meet you, at last,' Mary Phillips said cheerfully, savouring the pleasure of finding herself once again in the drawing room at Thorneycroft. In the months that had passed since she'd last stood there, she'd resumed her work in the theatre. Her memories of the dark events that had, so recently, almost cost her life, weighed much less upon her, but they would never be forgotten.

Mary willed herself to concentrate on the here and now; the presence of her dear friends and the joyous occasion that brought them together again. Verity stood smiling at her side, while Verity's brother, Sir Mortimer, dear Mortie, beamed at her with his arm around his fiancée's waist. Mary recalled Verity's description of her brother's betrothed: quite tall, slender and with a warm, open temperament. She had light brown hair and a small face with a few prominent freckles on her cheeks, making her seem younger than her twenty-four years....

'Miss Phillips, the pleasure is all mine, I assure you. I am a great lover of the stage and it's such a thrill for me to meet an accomplished actress. Do let us dispense with formality and be Olivia and Mary. There's so much I would like to ask you about the theatre.'

'Certainly, I'll be happy to oblige, but no doubt you both have other matters to occupy you with the wedding just two days away.'

'Our lives are consumed by little else,' said Mortimer. Mary thought he'd filled out a little since they'd last met. He looked and sounded very much the master of his domain: the baronetcy, which he'd inherited on his father's death less than twelve months ago, the estate and, of course, the house, Thorneycroft Hall. 'By the way, George Benson arrives tomorrow afternoon. He'll be on the same train as Gilbert Johnson, my best man.'

George Benson, the man to whom Mary owed her life. It was he who discovered the vital information that led to her deliverance from her abductors. She would always feel an overwhelming sense of gratitude to him.

'Ah, it will be wonderful to see George again,' she replied, 'and for all of us to be reunited on such a happy occasion. And the wedding itself. Is it to be a very grand affair?'

'No, we both feel that it should be an occasion for our nearest and dearest rather than a social gathering for the county,' Mortimer said. Olivia nodded in agreement.

'Who will officiate?' Mary asked. 'Is there a new rector? I assume the ceremony will be at Holy Trinity in Flaxminster.'

'Yes, it will. Reverend Mason is the new rector. You may remember him. He conducted Father's funeral.'

'And Mr Timmins, dare I ask. Is he still curate?'

'Let me set your mind at rest there, Mary. Timmins has left the parish.'

'Really. Was there some scandal?'

'Ha. No. He has gone to a higher calling. Timmins is in Norchester, where he attends upon the new bishop. It seems that our erstwhile curate is a second cousin of the bishop's wife.'

'My word. I hope for his sake that he mends his ways,' Mary recalled with a shudder the curate's distinctly ungentlemanly behaviour when she had last been in his company.

'Well, as the good book says, the Lord giveth, and the Lord taketh away. He has given Timmins to the bishop and taken him away from us. Blessed be the name of the Lord,' Mortimer pronounced with a satisfied smile.

After luncheon, Mary and Verity donned their winter overcoats and ventured outside. Winter still held Thorneycroft in its grip. The lawn and the lake beyond had a dreary look. Mary remembered how they'd sat on a bench at the edge of the lake when she had still been raw with the shock of her abduction. She saw the bench in the distance and shivered at the awful associations it represented. Verity sensed her dismay and turned away along a path that led to the stables. 'I know. We'll look in on Tanglefoot. He's a new chestnut gelding that Mortie bought for Olivia. I'm sure she'd let you ride him if you wanted.'

Mary allowed herself to be led into the relative warmth of the stables. Young Bernard Morris, the groom, lifted his cap as they passed the tack room and asked if he could do anything for them.

'How is Tanglefoot settling in?' asked Verity.

'He's doing well, Miss. No trouble, but he's a lively one. Took him out this morning and gave him his head.'

'Good. Has Miss Forbes ridden him yet?'

'Not yet, Miss. To tell the truth, she don't seem to have a great deal of interest in 'orses. Not in ridin' them leastways.'

'Oh. I dare say she'll take an interest after the wedding. Thank you, Bernard, we won't keep you.'

Bernard returned to the tack room. Verity led Mary out of the stables and along a path flanked by rhododendrons leading to the kitchen garden and the greenhouses. Beyond was Mortimer's croquet lawn. The two women walked arm in arm, skirting the edge of the lawn.

A sharp gust of wind rustled the branches of the nearby trees, bringing with it some drops of icy rain. Verity looked up at the ugly black clouds barrelling in from the west.

'Quick, Mary, over there,' she urged, propelling her friend towards a wooden summer house fifty feet away.

'Goodness, just in time,' she gasped as they stepped through the door at the very instant that the heavens opened. 'What a frightful soaking we'd have had if we'd been caught right out in the open. Oh well, it will pass eventually. May as well make ourselves at home here for now.'

They sat side by side on a pair of wicker chairs. Rivulets of water cascaded down the windows, reducing the scene outside to a silvery blur.

Mary hadn't spoken since they'd left the house. Verity saw that her friend was troubled. The anguish that Mary suffered during and after her abduction still surfaced from time to time.

'Mary dear, I haven't yet heard how your stage career is progressing,' Verity said brightly to lighten the mood.

'Mary, are you quite well?' she added when Mary didn't respond.

'What?' Mary turned to Verity blankly and shook her head as though waking from a dream. 'Oh, I'm sorry, I was miles away. How rude you must think me.'

'Not a bit. I was asking about your acting. Was your tour with Phillip Aspinall a success?'

'Oh yes. It was such an enjoyable tour. South Coast - Brighton, Hastings, then Dover. Phillip was wonderful, quite the impresario. The play was *The Rivals*, do you know it?'

'Of course, and I need hardly guess your character – the female lead?'

'Yes,' Mary replied with obvious pride. 'Lydia Languish, I simply adored playing her.'

'And Edward Crawford?'

'He was Sir Lucius O'Trigger. You should have heard his Irish accent — most convincing. He sends his regards, by the way.'

'How kind. Do remember me to him. Look, the rain's stopped. Shall we go back indoors before the next shower?'

Mary nodded. 'Thank you for humouring me. I allow dark memories to get the better of me now and then.'

They found Mortimer in the drawing room. 'Hello, you two. Escaped a drenching, I see.'

'By the skin of our teeth,' Verity replied. 'Has Olivia left already?'

'Yes, she's gone back to the George Hotel. She's taking tea with her parents. The next time I see her will be at the altar.'

'And a whole new chapter in your life will begin,' Verity said, approaching her brother and squeezing his arm. 'You deserve every happiness,' she added in a whisper, lightly kissing his cheek.

He blinked at his sister's endearment and felt a little shy in front of Mary. After a brief silence, he cleared his throat. 'Oh, by the way, Olivia and I are both adamant that you should remain at Montagu Square, at least for the next six months or so.'

Their family townhouse in London had been Verity's home since she embarked on her career as a journalist. On their father's death, its ownership passed to Mortimer, and she fully expected to vacate the premises following his marriage. Indeed, she'd already viewed a set of rooms in Belgravia, which looked quite suitable.

'Really, it's kind of you both, but I'm more than willing to find somewhere of my own. Please don't feel that you should deny yourselves the use of the place on my account.'

'There's no question of that. Let's just say that it will keep until we have a reason to need it,' he said, reddening slightly.

'Ah – yes, you mean when there's a new member of the family in the offing,' Verity grinned and winked at Mary. 'The patter of tiny feet and all that. No need to be so coy about it, Mortimer. I fully expect you to do your duty to keep the line going. Look, I'm happy to stay on for the time being. Let's just say that I shan't make myself too comfortable.' Verity viewed her brother's obvious embarrassment with amusement.

'Good, good, that's settled then,' Mortimer muttered, heading for the door. 'I'll see you both at dinner,' he added over his shoulder. The sound of the two women's laughter followed him out into the hall.

'Verity?' Mary said hesitantly.

'Yes?'

'I… I didn't get around to it earlier. Not with others present…'

'What do you mean, dear?'

'France. Your time in France. Your daughter,' Mary whispered, glancing nervously over her shoulder.

'Oh, Mary. You needn't whisper. It's not some shameful secret. At least not here at Thorneycroft. That's not to say that it's a matter of public knowledge, of course. But Olivia knows. She's a sensible, level-headed sort. Anyway, Jaqueline is very well and such a joy.'

'You must have found it a dreadful wrench to leave her.'

'Of course, but social sensibilities being what they are, I have no alternative. Her great-aunt takes the most marvellous care of her and Jaqueline has such a grown-up attitude. For a six-year-old, she has an understanding of the world far beyond her years.'

'When will you see her again?'

Verity leaned across to whisper in her friend's ear. 'Between you and me, I'm planning to bring her over to England for a visit.'

'Goodness, Verity. When…?'

'Shush, dear. All in good time. Now, why don't I ring for tea?'

'Did I hear you mention tea?'

Mary giggled and turned her head. That deep baritone, the theatrical intonation, could only be …

'Ambrose,' she exclaimed. 'Where have you been hiding?'

'Ah… can it be? Yes, it is. Miss Mary Phillips, as I live and breathe. The greatest actress of her age. Yet she speaks to me. What grace, what condescension, what…'

'Yes, Ambrose,' Verity interrupted. 'You may spare us the full panegyric, deserving though it may be. You should answer Mary's question.'

'Ah – well, as you can see from my clothes, I am dressed for the country, a man of the great outdoors, an adventurer roaming the wilds of the estate. Friend to the fish, fowl, and fauna within and foe to vermin and trespassers alike.'

Mary looked him up and down, noting the thick tweed suit, the gaiters and stout boots and, of course, his headgear – a deer stalker, naturally.

'Ambrose has appointed himself our unofficial gamekeeper, though we keep no game. He roams the grounds and pops up quite unexpectedly as the mood takes him,' Verity commented. 'At least it keeps him out of the house. Come along Ambrose, you're welcome to join us for tea.'

'Most kind. Miss Phillips can tell me all about her triumphs on the stage. Ah, would that I had followed my heart and become a thespian. What a loss for the theatre.'

Verity shook her head in despair and rang the bell for tea.

Chapter 5

'Now then boys, quietly if you please.' Joseph Maguire stood in front of the blackboard as his class got to their feet and started shuffling towards the door. 'Quiet, I said – yes, you Ellis. I'll have no talking until you're out in the schoolyard. And don't forget, I want your essays on Monday morning. No – you can all stop that groaning. You've got all the weekend to work on them.'

As the boys' boots clattered along the corridor, he turned to clean the board, erasing his summary of the founding of the Roman Empire. The greatest empire of the ancient world, as he'd explained to the class.

'But, sir – surely the greatest empire of all is ours,' Andrews had called out. 'Yes, sir,' one of his classmates echoed. 'The map shows it in pink. No one owns as much of the world as we do. Isn't that right, sir?'

He glanced at the map on the wall. Yes, the British Empire spanned the globe. Africa, the sub-continent, Australasia, Canada and the rest – all under the dominion of the Queen Empress. But the Roman Empire fell in time. His eyes came to rest on that one small patch of land that meant so much to him. The place that had borne the weight of oppression for centuries. His homeland. So much blood spilt. And it would take more blood before it was finished.

But the end must come soon. He felt it, viscerally. Ireland would be free, even if he did not live to see it.

The staffroom was almost empty when he entered. Most of the masters had left already, as eager as their pupils to escape the confines of the school for the weekend. Joseph edged towards his cupboard and removed his gown, hoping to slip away without being noticed. In the eighteen months since he'd taken up the post of history master, he'd avoided forming any friendships. He made excuses when any of his colleagues suggested meeting socially: a drink, a football match, or going fishing. He was always congenial. He'd no wish to appear standoffish, but he could not risk compromising his mission.

'Anything planned for the weekend, old man?' It was Jenkins – young fellow - English and Geography.

'What? Eh, no, not much…'

'Oh well, Simpson and I are going to the Arsenal match tomorrow. You're welcome to come along if you like.'

'Ah, that's very kind of you. When I said I've not got much on – I should have mentioned that my cousin is visiting from Dublin.'

'Bring him along too, the more the merrier.'

'It's she, actually. I can't see Dolores cheering from the terraces. She's quite the shy type. But thanks all the same.'

He smiled and turned for the door to forestall any further chit-chat. It hadn't been a complete fabrication. He had a cousin called Dolores, but she was a nun in Limerick.

Thirty minutes later, Joseph shook the water off his umbrella and felt in his pocket for the front door key to the house on Despard Road, just a few steps from busy Holloway Road. Its anonymous redbrick exterior attracted no attention and provided no clue as to its purpose as one of several places of refuge on the British mainland for those dedicated to the Irish Republican cause.

The smell of cooking welcomed him as he crossed the threshold. Mrs O'Leary had his dinner on the stove. The rich aroma stimulated his appetite. Lamb stew and dumplings. One of Mrs O'Leary's favourites and most welcome on a cold, wet evening. He called out to her, 'I'm home, Edna,' hearing her muffled response from behind the kitchen door as he trudged up the stairs.

In his bedroom at the back of the house, he opened the envelope that had been waiting for him on the hall table. Inside was a piece of a playing card cut diagonally. Joseph placed it on his washstand and crossed the room to a small bookcase next to his bed. He picked out a slim volume of poetry and opened the cover. The fragment of playing card within fitted perfectly with its mate to make a complete two of clubs.

'That smells delicious, Edna,' he said as he entered the kitchen. 'Would I be right in thinking it could stretch to feed three?'

His caller arrived twenty minutes later. Edna knew better than to ask questions. She'd only speak when spoken to. She served the meal and sat quietly while they ate. Their visitor made polite small talk about the weather and a recent visit he'd made to Dublin – what he'd seen at the theatre - a race meeting at the Curragh. She was relieved when the two men got up and left for the front parlour, leaving her to clear the table and wash up. She was all for the cause, but she knew her place.

Sean O'Brien was a cautious man. Not that he went by that name, not here leastways. Joseph knew of him as Carter. No Christian name – just Carter. That's all he needed to know. Joseph placed a bottle of whiskey and two glasses on the table between them and poured.

A clink of glasses. 'Sláinte!'

Carter made an unlikely soldier. The wisps of dark hair, the watery eyes behind pince-nez, the toothbrush moustache, and the scrawny neck emerging from his wing collar, gave him the air of a country solicitor, which, in another life, is exactly what he was. But Carter was every inch the soldier, a commander at that.

'How've you been, Joseph?' he said.

'Oh, well enough?'

'How long has it been now? Two years, isn't it?'

Joseph nodded. Two years and two months, to be precise, since he'd joined the cause. His father drowned at sea when he was just a year old. It was his grandfather, Daniel Maguire, that became the father figure in his young life. And it was through him that Joseph developed a fierce passion for a free Ireland. As a young man, Daniel had taken part in the Young Irelander Rebellion of 1848. That short-lived revolt was quickly suppressed, and the ringleaders sentenced to transportation. Daniel was small-fry. He slipped away without attracting the attention of the authorities, but his zeal was undiminished.

In 1867, at fifty-one years of age, Daniel was a proud member of the Irish Republican Brotherhood when a new uprising took place. Together with their Fenian brothers in the United States, the Brotherhood prosecuted a widespread campaign of insurrection in Ireland, which spilled over into England. Daniel spoke with both pride and bitterness of a battle at Ballyhurst near Tipperary against the British Army. His close friend was killed that day and many comrades were wounded. But his charmed life continued. He evaded capture and made his way to Dublin. The Brotherhood's dream of achieving a free Ireland by military means had failed, and the organisation turned its attention to gaining power through parliamentary rather than military means. But for Daniel, the war would never be over.

It was not long after he'd started as a pupil at the Catholic University School that Joseph experienced what he described as 'his awakening'. Daniel's tales had been a feature of his life since he was an infant. He'd treated them as simple adventure stories, tales of times gone by, exciting but distant. Now, they affected him differently. He felt them emotionally – felt them personally. The burning sense of injustice that had gnawed at Daniel for decades, gnawed at him. He immersed himself in the history of his nation, discovering how time and again his ancestors had been ground down by their neighbours across the water. But somehow their spirit was never crushed. He didn't know it then, but soon there would be another upswell of Irish militancy, more savage and uncompromising than the events that had swept his grandfather along.

The Invincibles, they called themselves. What a brash, confident, brave ring that had to it. They were a radical splinter group of the Irish Republican Brotherhood who set out to strike at the very heart of the British administration in Ireland. On May 16th, 1882, Chief Secretary for Ireland, Lord Frederick Cavendish and his Permanent Under-Secretary, Thomas Henry Burke, were murdered in Dublin's Phoenix Park. The brutal stabbing of the two men brought widespread condemnation, both from Britain and moderate Irish Republicans. But to young Joseph, it seemed a fitting act of retribution. The subsequent conviction and execution of the murderers only hardened his sense of grievance.

It didn't end there. Between 1881 and 1885, Fenians pursued a dynamiting campaign. They attacked barracks and public buildings in England, Scotland, and Ireland. Taking the fight to the British establishment, they even bombed the House of Commons itself.

Joseph read of their exploits with growing excitement. Dynamitards, they called themselves. He applauded their successes and felt nothing but satisfaction in the destruction and injuries they caused. He cared for nothing more than to become a Dynamitard himself one day.

'Have you come with orders?' he asked Carter.

Carter nodded at his empty glass. Joseph filled it. 'Have you?' He persisted.

'Well now. I have, but...'

'But what? Haven't I been waiting for long enough? It's action I want, man. Why would I not be happy to strike a blow for the cause? It's why I'm here.'

'My orders are for you to keep standing by, just for...'

Joseph snorted dismissively. 'Stand by. Stand by, you say. Bejesus, is this what you call fighting for the cause, sitting on my arse week in and week out? You're wasting my time, Carter.'

'It's Captain Carter to you, and don't you forget it.' Carter said sharply. 'Now, you listen to me. I don't give a tinker's cuss about what you think. So, you're tired of waiting, are you? Well, I've been a soldier for Ireland for twenty years and more and I don't need the likes of you to tell me my business.' Carter paused to take a slug of his whiskey. 'I had a fellow like you under my command in Cork. Always itching for action, he was. I warned him often enough, but he wouldn't listen. Went off at half-cock and got two of my best men arrested because he wouldn't do as he was told. He realised the error of his ways in the end. Do you know how?'

Joseph's belligerence cooled under the force of Carter's onslaught. He shuffled uncomfortably in his seat and shook his head.

Carter reached inside his tweed jacket. He placed his Webley Mk 1 service revolver on the table with its muzzle pointed at Joseph and looked him in the eye. 'I put this to his head and blew his brains out, and he's not the only one. There are three police informers lying in shallow graves in Ireland that I've accounted for and one that I took care of here in London just this last week. Fools and traitors. It's all one to me. Have I made myself clear?'

Joseph's mouth felt suddenly dry. He nodded. 'Yes.'

'Yes, what?'

'Yes, Captain,' Joseph replied meekly.

Carter held Joseph in his gaze. He reached for his gun and replaced it in his shoulder holster. 'Right, now that we understand each other, there's something else I have to tell you. You've not handled explosives before, have you?'

Joseph shook his head.

'When the time is right, you'll be taught to use them. Now, what I'm going to tell you next must remain secret on pain of death. You will get your chance of action and it will be the greatest blow of our campaign. If you'd let me finish just now, I was going to say that you need to stand by for just a little longer.'

Fifteen minutes later, Carter produced a playing card from his pocket. A five of clubs. Joseph went to the sideboard and found a pair of scissors that he used to cut the card diagonally into two. Carter pocketed one half and got to his feet.

When he'd left, Joseph filled his glass and emptied it in one gulp. 'Here's to you, Granddaddy Daniel,' he murmured.

Chapter 6

George Benson leaned back in his chair with his feet on the desk, savouring a well-earned cigar. It had been a rewarding week. He'd just deposited two handsome cheques at his bank. And a lucrative fresh case had come his way – an insurance fraud investigation, just the sort of thing he enjoyed sinking his teeth into.

He thought back to that momentous day in the autumn of the previous year when Mortimer Mallard called on him. He was just plain Mister Mallard then, a junior lawyer seeking George's services in connection with a divorce. Had George known where it would lead, he'd have run a mile. It started a chain of events which involved George in the discovery and disposal of the most notorious murderer of the age. Henry Powell, the killer known universally as Jack the Ripper.

If only it had stopped there. But somehow Mortimer and Verity had drawn him into an adventure which could have cost the lives of all three of them. Only the intervention of the authorities, in the shape of a Colonel Quilter of the Home Office, saved them.

Still, that was behind him now. He'd settled back into his old life as a simple private investigator. From now on, it would be straightforward, bread-and-butter investigative work. He was happy to be invited to Mortimer's wedding, but after that, he'd be content if he never set eyes on the Mallards again. Tomorrow, he'd travel to Thorneycroft, then after the wedding, he'd get straight back to London. Goodbye Mallards once and for all.

Could our thoughts tempt fate? George had reason to think they might when a silhouette appeared beyond the frosted glass panel of his office door, accompanied by the sharp tap of a cane. His caller was a tall man in a top hat by the shape of his outline. George put his cigar to one side and got to his feet. 'Come in,' he called.

The door swung open. 'Oh,' said George, as the man entered the room. 'It's you.'

'Not the most effusive of welcomes,' his visitor said in clipped military fashion. 'No doubt, you hoped you'd seen the last of me after that affair at Larkford Grange.'

George viewed Colonel Quilter with foreboding. The man could make his life very difficult if he chose. 'What do you want?'

The Colonel ignored his question, walking in and taking a seat by the window. George sat back down and glared at him. The Colonel occupied himself by placing his hat and cane and a leather despatch case on the floor at his feet and slowly removing his gloves. 'Well, Mister Benson, I am here to seek your help.'

'Do you wish to become a client? What is it? Divorce case? Think your wife is being unfaithful,' George said defiantly.

Quilter gave him a sharp look. 'Do you think it's quite wise to adopt that tone? Look, Benson, when I say I need your assistance, I'm speaking in an official capacity. It's not a personal matter.'

'Go on.'

'You were a Pinkerton man, I gather.'

George nodded.

'And quite a resourceful one, my inquiries tell me. You did a lot of clandestine work, is that right?'

George shrugged.

'Military experience too. Sergeant in the King's Royal Rifle Corps. I've looked into your military record. An honourable discharge and the Distinguished Conduct Medal.'

'So, you know something about me.'

'I know a great deal about you. It's my business to do so.'

'Well, why don't you get to the point? What sort of assistance and on what terms?'

Colonel Quilter paused, removing his monocle and polishing it with his pocket-handkerchief. Having replaced it, he drew his chair closer to George Benson's desk.

'What I'm about to tell you is highly confidential. It concerns a matter of national importance involving the safety of the realm.'

George nodded.

'Have you heard of the Irish Republican Brotherhood?'

'Fenians? Yes, of course. They played merry hell a few years back - assassinations and bombings. They seem to have gone quiet since. I haven't heard much about them of late.'

'No, there haven't been outrages such as we saw in the eighties, it's true. However, that does not mean that their ambition to establish an independent Irish Republic has diminished. There are men here in London planning to commit violent crimes. The failure of their previous campaigns only motivates the more fanatical members to continue their pursuit of an independent Ireland by force. I am determined to thwart them.'

'Aren't the police keeping an eye on them? The Special Branch, isn't that their job?'

'They have their role to play, certainly, but when the threat is so serious as to threaten the very fabric of the state, then it goes beyond a policing matter.'

'You still haven't told me why you need my help.'

Quilter gave a thin smile. 'What you need to understand is that if I tell you any more, you will have no choice but to agree. You will be bound by the Official Secrets Act.'

George stared at the Colonel in disbelief. He laughed at the absurdity of it. 'You seriously expect me to sit here and listen to any more of this? I'm a private investigator, not a civil servant. I choose the work that I'm prepared to undertake and I do so on my terms. How could you possibly assume that I'd agree to be caught up in whatever game it is that you're playing?'

Quilter shrugged. 'Perhaps I thought I could rely on your sense of public duty, but if that is not the case, I must ask you to cast your mind back to the time we last met.'

George said nothing, waiting for the Colonel to continue.

'On the night that I and my men extricated you from a very sticky situation, you and your associates were facing a group of ruthless criminals. Some, if not all, of you, would have been killed.'

'So you're appealing to my sense of gratitude, and I am grateful, but it doesn't mean that I'm obligated to you.'

'Very well. Then consider this. After our intervention, we found three dead bodies. One was the unfortunate Miss Cynthia Grant, murdered by a member of the Bishopsgate

Mob called Jackie O'Doyle. The others were O'Doyle himself and the leader of the Bishopsgate Mob, Bert Figgis. You and your colleagues maintained that you had no idea how those two men died. But we both know that's not the truth. I'll get straight to the point, shall I? Someone in your party must have killed them. One with a short blade, and the other, rather exotically, by a poison dart. Perhaps those cockney associates of yours were responsible, they're no angels. But it could equally be someone else. Who does that leave? Yourself? Then there's Sir Mortimer and Miss Verity Mallard and that eccentric relative of theirs, with a shady past – Ambrose Mallard.'

George sighed. 'You've no evidence, nothing to…'

'Let's stop playing games, Mr Benson. You're a realist. You know full well that I could put you out of business. I could also gravely damage the reputations of the Mallards without recourse to the law courts.'

There was no point in further argument. George knew he must either refuse and take the consequences or acquiesce. 'You can hardly expect me to work for you without payment. I have a living to earn.'

The Colonel's stern expression softened. 'Ah, bravo Mr Benson - George,' he said brightly. 'Let's talk terms by all means. Of course, Her Majesty's government will compensate you for your services. You'll be paid a fee for the work that I instruct you to undertake, plus associated expenses. My assignments will take precedence over your other work and, in return, I will authorise a twenty per cent premium above your normal fee.'

'Thirty per cent.'

'Twenty-five. Now let's move on, shall we?'

Chapter 7

A perfect day, everyone said so. Early clouds soon cleared, revealing a vivid blue sky. Sunlight streamed through the windows of Holy Trinity as Mortimer and Olivia exchanged vows.

Later, as the shadows lengthened, Verity, Mary, and George stood together in the doorway at Thorneycroft. They waved at the carriage bearing the newlyweds as they left on their honeymoon until it rounded a bend and disappeared.

George tipped his hat to the two women. 'I'd better be on my way. Duty calls,' he said sheepishly, hoping to slip away quietly. He knew it was a shabby way to behave, but he had a well-founded fear of becoming caught in Verity's orbit. Bitter experience taught him to be wary of her powers of persuasion. He would be happy to pass the time of day with Mary. Indeed, he was genuinely interested to see how well she'd recovered from the ordeal of her abduction. But Verity would inevitably dominate any conversation between the three of them.

'But George, we've hardly had an opportunity to talk,' Verity protested. 'Surely, your business can't be so pressing that you would deny Mary and me your company for a few minutes.'

'Um – well…'

'Oh, George,' Mary joined in. 'It's been such a long time since we last met. I had so looked forward to the three of us having some time together. We've been through so much. Would you really prefer that we just go our separate ways without another word?'

George felt himself wavering. 'No, please don't think that. It's just that…'

'Well, if you simply cannot remain, George,' Verity cut in. 'At least you could agree to meet Mary and me in London. Dinner next week? Mary, when would suit you?'

'Oh, that's a splendid idea. I only have rehearsals, so any evening would be convenient. Do say you'll come, George?' Mary pleaded.

'There George, Mary and I are at your disposal. Dinner at Montagu Square. Pick your evening. Far be it from us to curtail your busy schedule. When might you fit us in?'

George cursed inwardly. She'd outmanoeuvred him again. 'Wednesday,' he answered wearily. 'How about Wednesday?'

'Splendid. Montagu Square, seven o'clock sharp. Do have a pleasant journey back to London,' Verity said crisply, taking Mary by the arm and re-entering the house.

***

The only other occupant of the compartment was an old lady sitting in the corner by the window. She and George exchanged a few pleasantries as the train left Bicester station, but within ten minutes, she was asleep. George settled into his seat at the opposite end of the compartment. The irritation he'd felt at Thorneycroft had passed. Was dinner with two intelligent and attractive women an unappealing prospect? Not normally. But Verity always had a motive. There'd be a price to pay. Anyway, he'd accepted Verity's invitation, so that was that.

He tried to free his mind by gazing vacantly out of the window, but dusk soon gave way to night so that all he saw was his own reflection.

He couldn't keep thoughts of Quilter's visit at bay.

Like a pact with the devil, he'd reluctantly signed the paper that the Colonel placed on his desk. A declaration under the Official Secrets Act of 1889. He listened uneasily as Quilter outlined the business in which he was about to become entangled.

One of the Colonel's men was dead. Two municipal gardeners came across his body in Finsbury Park. He'd been missing for three days. How and why?

George remembered the conversation word for word.

'A man of yours, you say? Cause of death? Not natural causes, I'm guessing.'

'Someone stabbed him and cut his throat.'

'And you think Fenians did it?'

'He was following a suspected Fenian. Keeping him under observation, hoping that he would lead us to others. They are organised in small cells, circles as they call them, operating discretely from one another.'

'So, this suspect killed him? Is that what you're getting to?'

'That's possible, but, if so, it was one of the last things he did on this earth.'

'Go on.'

'Paul Crotty's body was found in a back alley at Crouch End. He'd been shot in the head.'

'Suicide - a fit of remorse?'

'Suicides don't usually manage a second shot, Benson. Whoever did it left nothing to chance. They put two rounds into his brain. My suspicion, and it's no more than that, is that Crotty killed my agent and that his Fenian comrades got rid of him.'

'Why? Why kill one of their own?'

'Come on, Benson. You call yourself a detective. Why do you think they did it?'

'He'd been compromised.'

'Precisely. They're ruthless.'

George considered his position with growing unease. He was being drawn into a situation in which two men had met violent deaths. He eyed the Colonel warily.

'I'll not beat about the bush, Benson. You can see where this is leading. I need someone to take over from… I won't say his name. Better that you don't know it. He was a good man, that's enough.'

'So you would force me to step into the shoes of a murdered man? And you call the Fenians ruthless.'

Quilter's reply was clinical. 'I will do whatever is necessary to preserve the safety of the realm. And I can assure you that I've never asked any man to do something that I have not done myself. The reason I've come to you is that I'm confident that you have the grit and intelligence to succeed.'

'And you're asking me to believe that none of the other men under your command is up to the task? Never mind your fine words about grit and intelligence. Why me?'

Quilter sat back and withdrew a silver cigarette case from his jacket. George took the proffered Sobranie and accepted a light from the Colonel. They sat smoking silently for a few moments. 'Well?' George persisted.

Quilter tilted his head back and blew a smoke ring towards the ceiling. 'Someone within my organisation is a Fenian sympathiser. A traitor. This murder occurred because that someone betrayed us, betrayed a colleague, a man that they would have known, talked to, shared a joke with perhaps. Smoked with, as we are doing now. Don't ask me who it is. If I knew, we would not be having this conversation. That's why I can't risk exposing any of my men. I need an outsider, someone that the traitor will be unaware of. A man known to me alone. I need you, George.'

'But how the devil do you expect me to take up where your man left off? The Fenian he was following is dead. Where would I start? I mean, if I could pass myself off as an Irishman, then I suppose I could frequent their meeting places, pubs and the like. But they'd see through me in no time. I'd end up dead in an alley myself.'

'You disappoint me, George. I like to think I'm a sound judge of a man's character. I don't believe I've been mistaken in you. Now, let me suggest a course of action.'

Chapter 8

Philipp zu Eulenburg played the last bars of a Beethoven sonata. Consulting his pocket watch, he stepped away from the piano and took a seat near the fire. He surveyed his surroundings with satisfaction. Since his appointment as ambassador to Austria-Hungary, his aesthetic sensibilities had been nourished by the tasteful opulence of the embassy. Here, in his private apartments, he was surrounded by paintings, books and exquisite *objets d'art*.

Lensch was due in five minutes.

Eulenburg recalled the day, almost a year and a half ago, when he'd first conceived of his plan to engineer a rapprochement between Britain and Germany. The Kaiser was dismissive, of course, still raging over the Jameson Raid. His telegram to President Kruger stirred up a hornet's nest. The British were outraged. Diplomatic relations, while not especially cordial at the best of times, became strained. The British press trumpeted anti-German sentiment and even German-owned businesses were attacked.

The Reich Foreign Office urged conciliation. Eulenburg used his influence as the Kaiser's closest confidant to persuade Wilhelm to repair the rift. Eventually, he agreed and wrote to Queen Victoria, assuring her that he had not intended the telegram as a threat to British interests.

A calm of sorts was restored. Eulenburg put his plan aside for a time, but the more thought he gave to it, the more he became convinced that it might work. It was risky, and he had no illusions about how difficult it would be to accomplish. But if it succeeded? If Britain aligned with Germany? The prize was incalculable. It needed precise planning, flawless execution and a great deal of nerve. And the Kaiser must not be told. Not until success was assured. Perhaps not even then. Let the change in Britain's posture come as a welcome surprise.

'Enter,' he called out in response to a tap on the door. 'Come in, Lensch,' he said, gesturing towards a chair on the opposite side of the fire.

Major Erich von Lensch bowed and took a seat. Eulenburg regarded him silently. He could hardly imagine a less convincing example of the German officer class. A short, portly man, balding, with protuberant eyes peering owlishly behind thick spectacle lenses. His uniform did his figure no favours and his smooth, pink cheeks showed no sign of a duelling scar. But Lensch was a fixer. He got things done.

'How was London, Lensch?'

'Wet and foggy, Excellency, as it often is when I visit.'

'And our man - Orpheus, is fully briefed?'

'As you ordered, I've told him what he needs to know.'

'Are you sure he can handle it?'

'If the Irish business is anything to go by, then yes. Colonel Quilter's attempt to infiltrate the New Invincibles has failed thanks to Orpheus.'

'The New Invincibles?'

'That's the name this group of breakaway Fenians chose. It's a reference to an earlier band of assassins.'

Orpheus was Eulenburg's trump card. A spy at the heart of the British establishment, a senior man at the Home Office with an impeccable background.

He was in contact with the most radical group of Irish revolutionaries, the New Invincibles. Germany could not publicly support them. But, behind the scenes, the prospect of a renewed Irish insurrection was welcome. A shipment of German explosives had been supplied in readiness for a bombing campaign on the British mainland. It would soon begin.

'And Orpheus will be on the alert for signs that the British have any knowledge of Operation Geck?'

'Of course. He will be our eyes and ears in the British Home Office.'

'Very good. Will you join me in a glass of schnapps, Lensch?'

The Major nodded. 'Thank you, Excellency.'

Eulenburg turned to the table at his elbow and poured two glasses of kirschwasser.

'Prosit!'

Eulenburg savoured the cherry-flavoured spirit, his favourite schnapps.

'So, what of Riemann?'

'He has his instructions, and he has the funds.'

'You impressed on him that von Hatzfeldt is to be kept out of this? The less our ambassador in London knows, the better.'

'I did. Riemann knows what he has to do and that everything must be in place by June.'

'The twenty-second of June, to be exact,' Eulenburg added, draining the remains of his schnapps.

Operation Geck. Eulenburg congratulated himself for coming up with that name. The Kaiser liked to refer disparagingly to his royal uncle, Bertie, the Prince of Wales, as "the old peacock". He'd thought of naming it Operation Pfau, meaning literally a peacock. But Geck was better – meaning fop, dandy, popinjay - the strutting self-regarding creature that was Bertie in Wilhelm's eyes.

Operation Geck would shock the British to the core and the finger of blame would point firmly at Russia. Germany would express outrage and offer its support, and Wilhelm would show his solidarity.

'Hmm – you realise that we have a problem on our hands, Lensch?'

'How so, Excellency? We will have Fenians running riot throughout Britain while Operation Geck is underway. They will distract the British authorities.'

'But that's it, Lensch. On the one hand, we're helping these Fenians to cause mayhem for the British, but if Operation Geck succeeds, we'll be Britain's allies. There is a contradiction there, is there not? This Fenian business is all very well, but the prospect of bringing Britain and Germany together is much the greater prize.'

'I'm confused, Excellency. Are you now suggesting that we cease supporting the Irish revolutionaries?'

'Not yet. Just be aware that the Irish business is secondary. I will have no hesitation in abandoning them if necessary. In the meantime, you will oversee Riemann and keep me fully informed of progress. That is all for now, Lensch.'

'Excellency.' Lensch levered himself out of his chair.

As Major von Lensch closed the door behind him, Eulenburg returned to the piano. Something Russian. He flexed his fingers. The opening bars of Tchaikovsky's Grand Piano Sonata sounded faintly as Lensch left the building.

Chapter 9

Verity answered the door herself. 'George, I'm so glad you could come,' she said effusively, offering her cheek. Taken aback, he hesitated, then brushed it with his lips. She'd not treated him with such familiarity before. He couldn't decide whether he should feel flattered or suspicious.

'Come along into the drawing room. Mary's already here and I have a little surprise. Well, two surprises actually,' she continued, flashing a mischievous smile. George flinched inwardly. He'd overcome his qualms about Verity's dinner invitation by reminding himself that it would only be the three of them. But, typically, she'd found a way to put him at a disadvantage. At least that's how it felt.

He followed her, feeling like a condemned man. Mary's beaming face was the first thing he registered on entering the room. She blew him a kiss and inclined her head towards the figure standing next to her.

'Hello, old man,' Edward Crawford said in his characteristic louche drawl. 'Don't suppose you expected to see me again.'

'Edward. No, I didn't imagine our paths would cross again. I'm not much of a theatregoer. But never mind that. It's good to see you,' George replied, shaking the actor's hand.

'Edward is playing opposite me in our latest play. It's my first really serious role. Ibsen, one can hardly find a more serious playwright. I must confess I'm rather petrified,' Mary gushed.

'Isn't that marvellous, George?' Verity interjected. 'It's Hedda Gabler. I'm so looking forward to seeing it.'

George was little the wiser. Ibsen sounded vaguely familiar. 'So you're playing this Hedda Gabler, are you, Mary?'

'Oh good lord, no. It's flattering of you to think so. I play a character called Thea Elvsted. This is Hedda,' Mary gestured to a woman sitting quietly in the corner. George had noticed her from the corner of his eye. He turned to face her.

'Mister Benson, I am pleased to make your acquaintance,' she said, crossing the room. Half a head taller than he, exquisitely dressed, she exuded an air of confidence that even put Verity in the shade.

George was uncertain when she extended her hand whether he should kiss or shake it. She observed him with amusement as he took her fingers awkwardly in his. So much about her seemed larger than life. Her dark eyes had such intensity. Her mouth was wide and generous, set in a mocking smile that George found unsettling. Jet-black hair fell in curls around her shoulders, giving her an untamed, bohemian look. Half gypsy, half duchess, he thought. And that accent?

'I am Anna Jesenska. I see you look puzzled, Mister Benson. Where does this woman come from you ask yourself? I am from many places. But I was born in Prague.'

Bohemian in more than her appearance, Benson reflected.

'Anna is a rare talent, George,' Verity said, asserting her role as hostess. 'She has graced the stages of most of the leading theatres of Europe. We are fortunate indeed that she's consented to spend some time here in London.'

'You are too kind, Verity,' Anna responded. 'You know, London is my favourite city after Vienna. I only regret that I have not spent more time here before now. But that is enough about me. I see you are old acquaintances with much to talk about. I am content to sit back and enjoy your company.'

When they went through to dinner, George found himself seated between Verity and Mary. Anna proved to be as good as her word, speaking only occasionally to answer a question or make a light-hearted comment. By the end of the evening, he'd learnt little about her.

As usual, Verity steered the conversation. They all listened politely while she held forth on votes for women. 'You men cannot continue to deny us our rights,' she looked accusingly at George and Edward. 'Do you realise that New Zealand has extended the franchise to women? So has the Colony of South Australia. Now, if the colonies can do so, what possible justification can there be for the so-called mother of parliaments to deny us?'

Edward looked down at his plate, clearly uncomfortable. Verity was undeterred, warming to her theme. 'I'll tell you now that the time is coming when women will rebel. There are brave committed women for whom words will no longer be enough. If they continue to be ignored, they will act. You'll see then what a determined woman can do.'

George held his peace, waiting for the storm to blow itself out. Mary shuffled uneasily at his elbow. Across the table, he saw Anna looking on with just the hint of a smile.

Elsie's appearance with dessert saved the day, obliging Verity to pause while it was served.

Mary seized the opportunity to change the subject. She'd consumed a little more wine than she was accustomed to.

'Tell me, George. Are you walking out with anyone? You're such a private person. Don't tell me you have not formed an attachment?' Verity and Edward looked at her with astonishment. It seemed very much out of character. Unabashed, she ploughed on. 'You're not getting any younger, you know,' she added, raising her glass to her lips. Verity considered whether to interrupt, but held back. She was as curious as Mary to discover something of George's private life.

George felt like a cornered fox. He half turned towards Verity, hoping she might intercede, but only received a blank look in return. If *she'd* posed such a question, he'd have felt justified in politely telling her to mind her own business. But not Mary. He knew she would have no ulterior motive. It was simply curiosity, fuelled by a little too much wine.

'An attachment? Nothing to speak of at present, Mary,' he replied, hoping to leave it at that.

Mary regarded him through narrowed eyes. She was obviously tipsy. 'Goodness, George, you're a… I mean, women would not consider you unattractive. I would even go so far as to say quite handsome,' she said, trying but failing to suppress a hiccough. 'Don't tell me there's been no one…'

George decided it would be safer to say something rather than allow Mary to embarrass herself. 'Well, since you ask, I was once engaged. In America. She was called Louisa. We met in Boston.'

'Louisa?'

'She left me. Took up with a lawyer.' George braced himself for further questions. His salvation came unexpectedly from Anna Jesenska.

'Well my dears, it's time I went home. It's been such an interesting evening, Verity. And George, such a pleasure to make your acquaintance. We have a day of rehearsals tomorrow before the play opens next week. Do please come and see it, both of you.'

She rose from her seat and gave Edward a meaningful look. 'Ah yes,' he agreed, taking his cue. 'Best to get a good night's sleep. We can all share a cab. Mary, are you ready?'

'Oh, very well.' Mary attempted to rise. George steadied her and passed her arm to Edward, who helped her to walk to the door.

'I suppose I'd better be on my way too,' he said, nodding to Verity. 'Thank you. It's been a pleasure to see you all again and to meet you, Miss Jesenska.'

'Oh well, if you must all depart, I'll see you to the door,' Verity announced. 'George, would you kindly stay behind for a few minutes? I'd appreciate your advice,' she added quietly.

George waited uneasily while Verity said goodbye to the others. He knew she hadn't invited him for the pleasure of his company. Not Verity. She always had a motive where he was concerned. A favour to ask.

Her footsteps echoed in the hall. 'Come through to the drawing room, George.'

She showed him to a seat. 'Scotch?' He nodded.

She poured two glasses and sat opposite him.

'I had a caller yesterday.'

He shrugged resentfully. Here it comes, he thought. What does she want this time?

'Not a welcome caller. Someone we both know.'

George sipped his scotch, determined not to show any interest. Whatever she wanted, she'd have to work at it.

His truculence had no effect on Verity. She ploughed on.

'Colonel Quilter.'

George gave her a sharp look and put his glass down.

'There, I see I have your attention.'

'What did he want?' George said despite himself.

'I'm not sure. You see, he wasn't specific.'

'Why are you telling me this? What makes you think I'm interested in what Quilter wants?'

'Because he's visited you too, George. Please don't try to deny it. He told me as much. He didn't tell me what transpired between you, only that he thought we both have talents that he can use.'

'Did you tell him to go to hell? I can't imagine you allowing your talents to be used by anyone. Didn't you send him packing, Verity?'

She shook her head. He saw the anxiety in her eyes.

'He threatened you, didn't he? What was it? Did he accuse you of killing O'Doyle?'

'He implied it. That wasn't the worst of it, though. He said, "How is your daughter?" He knows about her, knows her name, knows that she lives in France.' She rubbed her hands together nervously.

George leaned across and placed his hand on hers. 'Surely he didn't threaten her.'

Verity shook her head. 'No, not her. He threatened to disclose the fact that I have a daughter to… the world, I suppose. The publications I write for. Friends, acquaintances, and society in general. I needn't tell you what that would mean, George.'

'The man's a…' George restrained himself from uttering a string of barrack-room expletives. 'What does he want from you?'

'He said that when he has a need for me, he'll be in touch. He said it as though I am simply a thing, an instrument to be used as he sees fit. I feel so powerless, George.'

'Does Mortimer know?'

'No. He and Olivia must be kept out of it. This is our burden and our secret. We must bear it together. There, I've told you everything. Will you tell me what he demanded of you?'

'I can't, Verity. It's gone too far for that. I'm bound by the Official Secrets Act, for one thing, and I don't doubt that he'd use it against me if I divulged anything. But more than that, the business he's involving me in is dangerous. I won't place you at risk by speaking about it. I know you too well. You have a habit of becoming involved,' he said, smiling.

She returned his smile, acknowledging her tendency to meet trouble head on. 'Look, George, let's at least agree to keep in touch. You may neither want nor need my help, but I need yours. When Colonel Quilter calls again, I'd like to know that whatever he asks of me, I'll have your support if I need it. I console myself with the thought that it's my intelligence and feminine qualities that he values, if that doesn't sound too conceited. I can't imagine that he intends to put me in physical danger.'

'No, I'm sure you're right,' George agreed, masking the doubts he felt.

Out in the street, George filled his lungs with the fresh night air. He'd digest what Verity had told him later. Now he needed to take his mind off it. He chuckled at Mary's awkward attempt to probe his private life. How would she react if he told her the truth? That for the past two years, he'd enjoyed a relationship of mutual convenience with Mrs Effie Davenport.

Thirty years of age and widowed, she made a comfortable living as a florist with her own premises in Clapham. A loose arrangement of occasional evenings together at her house and weekends away every month or two suited them admirably. And tonight he knew she'd be at home.

Chapter 10

Seven Sisters Road was choked with traffic. A mild collision between a rag-and-bone man's cart and an omnibus created a logjam of horse-drawn vehicles. George picked his way between them, avoiding the occasional pile of manure. His eyes adjusted to the gloom as he entered the public bar of the Bedford Arms. George no longer - he took on the mannerisms, accent and persona of Brendan Hogan.

It was Quilter's idea. 'You say that you cannot pass yourself off as an Irishman, George. But there's no need to adopt an Irish brogue. Where would you find a large population of Irish, other than in the Emerald Isle itself? America, of course.'

George knew where this was heading.

'You spent how long in America, George? Three years wasn't it? They say it's a difficult accent to resist if you spend time there. And, as a Pinkerton man, I'll wager you passed yourself off as a home-grown Yankee from time to time. Isn't that right?'

'From time to time,' George confessed reluctantly.

'Splendid. There you are then. You can present yourself as an Irish American, a Republican sympathiser.'

He took a large envelope from his despatch case and placed it on George's desk. 'This is your brief, George.

Study it well. Your life may depend on it. You will become Brendan Hogan. You will master every detail of his life. And you will know a great deal about the Fenians and their movement. I gather that you spent time in Boston, so that is where Brendan hails from.'

'You just said it yourself. My life may depend on it. You have no qualms about risking my life to do your dirty work?'

'George, George, or should I say Brendan? You do yourself an injustice. You are most certainly capable of bringing this off. And please don't try appealing to my better nature. You'll find that when it comes to doing my job, I don't have one. Now, open that envelope and we'll go through your brief together.'

This was George's third visit to the Bedford Arms. With a generous financial contribution from the Colonel, he'd established himself as a bluff Irish American, keen to stand his countrymen a drink and enjoy some craic about the old country.

He took care not to overstate his Republican sympathies. But whenever the conversation touched on the subject, he showed his support for the cause. If all went to plan, word would get around that Brendan Hogan was a well-to-do patriot, with a passion for a free Ireland and a healthy American disdain for all things British.

He surveyed the bar. There were a few familiar faces, regulars who patronised the place most days. A hand waved from a table in the far corner. James Mulcahy was a writer of sorts. He earned a crust, as he put it, contributing articles to expatriate Irish journals and newspapers, but fancied himself as a poet and something of an intellectual. On his first visit to the Bedford Arms, George had found himself standing next to Mulcahy at the bar and an exchange of the usual pleasantries had turned into an evening of lively conversation lubricated by pints of stout and whiskey chasers.

Brendan Hogan's accent had piqued his interest. 'You wouldn't be from New York now, would you?' he'd asked. 'My uncle Eamon has a gentleman's outfitter's there. Left the old country twenty years ago with hardly a penny to his name and now he's got a fine house, a wife, and a brood of cousins of mine. Ah, it's a grand country for a man with ideas and the urge to get on, so I'm told.'

'I'm from Boston.'

'Another fine place. Do they still throw those tea parties there, Brendan?' Mulcahy clapped him on the back, laughing at his own witticism.

More questions had followed, and he allowed himself to satisfy Mulcahy's curiosity. Gradually, his story emerged. His family emigrated when he was just a small boy. He retained no memory of Ireland, but he'd been raised on his parents' romanticised recollections of it. Yes, he agreed, a man could do very well for himself in the States. He was living proof that hard work, a talent for self-promotion, and a dose of good luck brought big rewards. 'I'm an investor, James. Railroads and shipping, mostly. Made a decent pile at it and thought I'd spend a bit on myself. So here I am in London. I heard that this bar was a good place to soak up a bit of the atmosphere of old Ireland.'

Mulcahy's eyes narrowed. 'But would you not be better doing that in Ireland itself, Brendan? If you're so keen to experience something of the old country, you'd be better doing it in Dublin than here, man?'

'Yes, of course, James, and I will be doing exactly that on my way back to Boston. A few more evenings in this place and perhaps I'll sound as though I've lived in Dublin all my life. What do you think?'

'Aye, and so you might,' Mulcahy agreed, laughing. 'Now, let's get these glasses filled and I'll introduce you to a few of my friends and acquaintances.' When he left the pub that night, George felt quietly confident in his new identity.

Now Mulcahy got up and wandered over with a near-empty glass of stout.

'James, looks like the tide's going out there. Let me buy you another,' George offered.

'Why, that's mighty generous of you, Brendan,' Mulcahy responded, affecting surprise.

A small crowd of Mulcahy's cronies gathered round, all eager to take advantage of the American's generosity. Soon the conversation turned to Irish independence, with the occasional Republican song thrown in. Brendan sang along with them. He eventually got away, after promising to return, with his newfound friends' farewells ringing in his ears.

Outside on the pavement, he stopped to light a cigarette. The man emerging from the pub a few paces behind him stood and looked uncertainly at him for a moment before turning away. With the match still in his hand, George watched from the corner of his eye as the fellow sauntered along and stopped to look in a shop window. Following people discreetly was second nature to George. The next few moments would tell whether he was about to be followed himself.

A hansom cab pulled up at the kerb in response to his outstretched arm. 'Savoy Hotel,' he shouted to the cabbie. He put his foot on the step of the cab and pretended to tie his shoelace. Glancing sideways, he grunted with satisfaction at the sight of another cab coming to a halt twenty feet away.

Confident that he was being followed, he sat and gazed idly at the streetscape as his cab made its way towards the Strand.

The façade of the Savoy Hotel blazed with electric light as his cab entered the forecourt. He alighted quickly, paid the cabbie, and walked with a hint of a swagger past the doorman. As his cab turned and drove off, the clatter of another replaced it. He turned back to the doorman. 'Is it far to Westminster Abbey?' he asked, playing the tourist.

As the man answered, George spotted a head emerging from the side of the arriving cab. It looked in his direction for a moment, then disappeared, and the cab turned around and returned to the Strand.

George thanked the doorman and crossed the vestibule. A sensitive divorce case involving a member of the House of Lords, two years earlier, had required him to play the part of a hotel porter at the Savoy. Now his knowledge of the back stairs and corridors enabled him to emerge unseen from a rear service entrance and make his way home. In his sitting room, he wrote a brief report of the night's events and a description of the man who'd followed him: slight build, thinning dark hair, a toothbrush moustache and a pair of pince-nez.

Chapter 11

Major von Lensch liked St James's Park. He liked the oak trees, the lake and its bird life, and the well-tended lawns. It had a sense of order and tranquillity that appealed to him. Most of all, he liked its proximity to the centres of British power. To his right was Buckingham Palace, with the Royal Standard billowing in the afternoon breeze. The roofs of the Foreign Office and the Treasury were visible to his left, and hidden away beyond them, Downing Street. And here, on a park bench in their midst, sat Lensch, a servant of quite another power.

His watch showed he had five minutes to wait for his next rendezvous. As a pair of geese floated by, he thought about his meeting with Orpheus that morning.

Lyons tea shop in Piccadilly somehow epitomised the cultural peculiarities of the British. To Lensch, steeped in the cosmopolitan grandeur of the coffeehouses of Berlin and Vienna, it was gauche and provincial. Orpheus was a sophisticated man. That he had chosen this place for them to meet was surely a sign of a perverse sense of humour.

He viewed the display of cakes, pies, and tarts on the countertop with a shudder. The coffee he'd ordered for appearance's sake remained untasted, cooling on the table in front of him. He placed a neatly folded copy of the Times next to it.

The door to the street jingled as Orpheus entered. Over six feet, clean-shaven, with a shock of fair hair greying at the temples, he struck Lensch as the archetype of the British ruling caste. Giles Friedrich Temple-Swift was the scion of an old family of landed gentry. After Charterhouse and Brasenose College, Oxford, he spent a year at Heidelberg University. A deep nick in his left ear served as a reminder of his membership in the Corps Rhenania Heidelberg, one of the oldest German student fraternities, in which he'd practised Schläger, the art of academic duelling. The Corps' culture attracted him. It appealed to that part of his heritage inherited from his mother, Magda von Meyer.

It was also at Heidelberg that he'd met a young man named Erich von Lensch. Erich took no interest in the Corps. He considered its emphasis on tolerance and free thinking to be naïve and insufficiently committed to the interests of the German Reich.

It was at Erich's invitation that he came into the orbit of a group of students and academics inspired by patriotic ideas. Through them, he found himself attracted to the notion of German exceptionalism. He learned to place a higher value on his German rather than his British heritage. When he announced to Erich that he'd decided not to return to England but to stay and serve the Reich, it astonished him to receive a cool reception.

'But Erich, you encouraged me to see that my destiny lies with Germany,' he protested. 'The Reich is the future. We both know it. The British Empire has reached its high-water mark. It can only decline, but Germany is full of vigour. Why would you not welcome me with open arms?'

'Because, my friend, there is more than one way of showing your loyalty. You have gifts that will be of enormous benefit to the Reich. I can see that you are ready to prove yourself. In three days' time, I'm going to Berlin. I would like you to accompany me.'

The few days that he spent at the centre of the German state changed everything. It was here at the *Auswärtiges Amt*, the German Foreign Office, that he was persuaded that his loyalty to the Reich would best be served by returning to Britain. They gave him the codename Orpheus.

He entered the Civil Service, serving firstly at the Board of Trade. In a service blessed with many talented men, he established himself among the highest of flyers. A transfer to the Home Office followed. At thirty-eight, he was an undersecretary, and widely thought of as a future department head.

Early in his career, he'd fretted about proving his worth to his masters in Berlin. But they were patient men who regarded Orpheus as a long-term investment. Now, his value was beyond question. As the Home Office representative on the Committee of Imperial Security, he was privy to some of the most closely guarded secrets of the Empire. He also had visibility of the activities of one Colonel Quilter.

Erich von Lensch was his handler from the outset. And he, in turn, answered to one of the most influential men in Germany - Philipp, Prince of Eulenburg.

Orpheus' entry in Who's Who gives his interests as fencing and mountaineering. His club memberships include the Alpine Club, the Marlborough and the Traveller's.

His marriage to the Honourable Beatrice Chater has produced two sons and a daughter. They often spend their summer holidays in Germany, having a particular fondness for the Bavarian Alps.

Orpheus ignored some empty tables near the door and headed for the far side of the café. He held his hat in his right hand. In his left, he gripped an umbrella, with a folded newspaper wedged under his arm. Lensch deliberately looked away as he approached.

At the moment Orpheus passed Lensch's table, the umbrella slipped from his grasp, clattering against the table and spilling the German's coffee.

Two women at a nearby table turned to see what the commotion was about. The small boy sitting with them laughed and pointed until a sharp word from his mother made him return his attention to the half-eaten chocolate éclair on his plate.

'I say, old man, terribly sorry, how clumsy of me,' Orpheus blurted out, placing his newspaper on the table and stooping to retrieve his umbrella. 'Oh dear, please let me buy you another coffee,' he offered.

Lensch waved him away. 'No, there's no need for that. You should take more care.'

Orpheus whispered another apology, picked up his newspaper, and walked off. Lensch didn't turn round. He heard Orpheus ordering a pot of tea at a table some distance away, then made his way to the cash desk and out into the street.

Later, in the privacy of his hotel room, he unfolded *The Times*. Concealed within was a map and several sheets of coded handwriting. As he consulted his code book, half a mile away, in a private room at the Traveller's Club, Orpheus was likewise engaged.

In St James's Park, the geese took off, flapping their wings rhythmically over the surface of the lake until they lifted clear of the water and flew purposefully to the west. Lensch returned to the present. His watch said three pm and, exactly on time, a man took a seat next to him.

'Punctual as always, Riemann,' Lensch said without turning his head.

'Thank you, Major.' Klaus Riemann was a taciturn man. He received orders and carried them out precisely to the letter. Tall and angular, his cropped head and the way he held himself, with his head up and his back straight, marked him out as a soldier. An old soldier. After thirty years in the army, Klaus had risen to the rank of *Feldwebel*, the German equivalent of Sergeant-Major. Now he occupied a civilian post at the German Embassy, a clerk to the military attaché. But his real master was Lensch.

'Your report?'

'The Dutchman. He will do it.'

'How can you be sure?'

'How can one be sure of anything, Major? All being well, the sun will rise tomorrow. Beyond that, who can say that anything is sure?'

Lensch looked amused.

'Very well, Riemann. Let's not get into a philosophical discourse.'

'He will do it for two reasons, Major. First, he believes in his cause.'

'And the second reason?'

'Five thousand pounds is as good a reason as most men would require.'

'How good are his sharpshooting skills?'

'He has a marksman's eye, and enough patience, I think. And I have the weapon.'

The weapon was a Russian Mosin-Nagant M1891 bolt-action rifle with a 5-round magazine, fitted with a telescopic sight. It had an effective range of 800 metres. His man, the Dutchman, was already proficient with the Mauser Model 1895. But for this job, the rifle must be Russian.

'It will be vital to pick the best firing point,' Lensch continued. 'And now, I have something for you that will make that task a much simpler one. Earlier today, I received details of the procession route, not only that but the order of march and the timing. Here they are.'

Lensch reached into a leather satchel at his side and produced a sheaf of paper. 'You must secure a room on the route. The procession will return through south London, the poorer districts. Borough High Street, and St George's Circus. I suggest you look there. Study the map. You will take the Dutchman there on the day before, no earlier. That will be all.'

Riemann pocketed the papers, nodded and walked away. Lensch returned his gaze to the lake. Orpheus had done well. No, he'd done brilliantly. Queen Victoria's Diamond Jubilee would be an event of supreme significance, not only to Britain but to the whole Empire. The sixtieth anniversary of her accession to the throne. The longest reign of any British Monarch. It would be a celebration of massive proportions.

Only one thought clouded his moment of reflection. The Irish question. Germany's secret support of the most militant of the Irish Republican factions was a valuable thorn in the flesh of the British. Germany provided them with arms and encouragement, and Orpheus did whatever he could to hamper the British authorities' attempts to contain and counter the Fenian threat. For now, it was expedient to continue supporting the Irish nationalists. But, as Eulenburg had warned, the day might come when that support might have to cease. If Britain and Germany became allies, the Irish would be a liability.

Chapter 12

Three days had passed since George Benson last visited the Bedford Arms. He had plenty of other work to do and he thought it best not to appear too eager to spend time there.

Colonel Quilter had called earlier. He listened as George described his last visit to the pub. His mention of Mulcahy's name received a cursory nod. 'He's a known sympathiser,' Quilter said matter-of-factly. 'But not a threat in himself. He has a strong romantic attachment to the cause, but he's not a man of action. Is that all you have to tell me?'

The Colonel's dismissive tone rankled. George considered whether to say nothing about the man who'd followed him. If Quilter thought he was failing to obtain useful information, perhaps he'd leave him alone.

Quilter seemed to read his mind. 'Don't think of leaving anything out, George. You'll find that I have an uncanny ability to know when I'm being deceived. If there's more, and I sense there must be, you'll tell me now.'

George shrugged. 'There was another man. He followed me when I left the pub. Don't worry, I led him to the Savoy, then he went away. As far as he knows. I'm the rich Irish-American with Republican sympathies that I pretended to be.'

'Is that it? Did he speak to you at the Bedford Arms?'

'No, he just appeared behind me as I left. He must have been inside, but I didn't notice him before. I can only tell you what he looked like.'

George's description of the fellow clearly piqued Quilter's interest.

'Describe him to me again, would you?'

George complied.

'I wonder?' Quilter murmured pensively.

'Wonder what?'

'Oh, I can't be sure. But your man could be Sean O'Brien. Not that he goes by that name. He calls himself Captain Carter. He's wanted in Dublin for three murders. Don't be fooled. He may look innocuous, but he's dangerous. The last I heard of him, he'd gone to ground in Ireland.'

'So what now?'

'Now you get back to the Bedford Arms, of course. Continue to play the part. Keep your eyes peeled for O'Brien. I want to know what he's doing here, where he goes, who he associates with. This is important, George. You will give it your full attention, half-measures will not do.'

After the Colonel left, George cursed him roundly. He was furious that he was expected to set everything else aside to become Quilter's spy. Not only that, but there were practical difficulties to consider. How could one man keep tabs on this Captain Carter character day in and day out, possibly around the clock?

There was nothing for it. He needed help from someone he could trust, and that meant the Cotton brothers.

The Bedford Arms was quiet when he arrived at six-thirty. He nodded to a couple of drinkers he recognised and took a seat near the door. There was no sign of Mulcahy, or the man who'd followed him, O'Brien, or Captain Carter, if Quilter was right. He was halfway through his pint of stout when the door to the snug opened. James Mulcahy appeared, took two paces into the public bar, halted, and turned sharply on his heel, closing the snug door behind him. Though Mulcahy had tried not to show it, George could tell that it was the sight of him that had sent the Irishman scurrying back inside the snug.

Two minutes later, the door opened again. Mulcahy stood there, beckoning. George played dumb. Mulcahy gestured again, impatiently. 'Me?' George mouthed, pointing to himself. Mulcahy nodded emphatically.

He picked up his glass and ambled across the bar, taking his time. Mulcahy was almost hopping up and down with irritation by the time he reached the snug door. 'Inside, man. Now,' Mulcahy hissed.

The door snapped shut behind him. George's eyes adjusted to the gloom. A haze of tobacco smoke hung in the air. It felt close and oppressive.

Two men sat at a table in the centre of the room. Their eyes turned towards him. There wasn't a word of greeting from either, just cold, brutish stares - a crude form of intimidation.

'What's this, James?' he said to Mulcahy, who remained standing with his back to the door. 'Some sort of private card school? How 'bout introducing your friends? I like to know who I'm playing with.'

'It's not a game we're playing, Mister Hogan.'

George turned to face the speaker.

'Sit down.'

George approached the table and took the one remaining chair. The man who'd addressed him took out a handkerchief and polished his pince-nez. 'James there tells me you're from Boston,' he continued, still polishing his spectacles.

'That's right, Mister…?'

The man replaced his pince-nez. 'You've no need to know my name. You see, Brendan, when a strange man who says he's an American turns up professing to be a Republican and waxing lyrical about the old country, I wonder if he's all he says he is. It's all very well to stand out there in the bar singing Republican songs with men whose passion for a free Ireland lasts only as long as the drink is coursing through their veins. Ireland's freedom will be won by those of us prepared to spill blood. The blood of our English oppressors. Aye, and our own blood, too.'

George stayed silent. Quilter had urged him to look out for Captain Carter. However, it appeared that Carter was looking out for him. He did his best to disguise his unease. His safety hung in the balance. He was in for an interrogation. How well he could maintain his cover would determine whether he walked out of there or ended up in an alley with a bullet in his brain.

Carter spoke again. 'You hail from Boston, you say. That's good. You'll be pleased to meet a fellow Bostonian, I fancy. William here,' he said, indicating the man on his left, 'spent some time there. No doubt you could share some reminiscences of that fair city?'

'Be happy to. When were you there, William?'

George was reassured by William's response. The man had stayed there for six months in 1892, just a year before

George was based there for Pinkerton. His familiarity with the city was likely to be historical, reducing the chances of him quizzing George on recent events.

George handled the man's questions deftly. They were mostly straightforward, concerning places, prominent people and events. Dramas they'd attended at the Boston Museum Theatre made one lively topic. They spoke of public meetings at Faneuil Hall and the locations of several well-known landmarks along Tremont Street. George easily dealt with a ham-fisted attempt to catch him out on the name of the Governor of Massachusetts, and William's attempted interrogation soon petered out into inconsequential chit-chat.

Carter, who had studied George's face throughout the process, interrupted to call it to a halt. 'Thank you, William, you can leave,' he said, nodding towards the door. Mulcahy held it open for him.

'Now then, Brendan,' Carter began. George forestalled him. 'Hold your horses there, Mister whoever you are. Let's get a few things straight. I don't know what Mulcahy here has told you about me, but I don't take kindly to being accused of being some spy for the British. And don't make the mistake of treating me like some damn fool with romantic ideas who's just playing at being a Republican. I didn't make my money by being pushed around and I'll tell you now, some people I've had to deal with over the years make your attempts at intimidation look pretty puny.'

Carter didn't blink. He sat back in his chair and unbuttoned his jacket, allowing George a glimpse of the pistol resting in his shoulder holster. George thought about producing his own revolver. He thought better of it, but took comfort in feeling its weight in his pocket.

'James, stop skulking there by the door,' he called over his shoulder. 'Come over here where I can see you.'

Carter looked over George's shoulder and nodded to Mulcahy, who took William's seat.

'Now then, why don't we start again?' George suggested.

Carter gave a cold, thin-lipped smile. 'All right, Brendan, why not? James, here tells me you're keen to help the cause.'

George nodded. 'If you have something in mind. It would be easy for me to pledge some financial support, but I've got a mind to do something of a more practical sort, get my hands dirty, so to speak.'

'What practical help could a man like you provide us, Brendan? You're a businessman, not a soldier,' Carter scoffed. 'Ever killed a man?'

George shook his head.

'Anyway, how long are you planning to stay in London? No point in you offering your services if you're just about to return to Boston.'

'I've no firm plans. I'm prepared to stay on here for a while.'

'To be any use to me, you'll need to stay on until the end of June. That's another month.'

'Yes, okay, I could do that.'

'A month at the Savoy. That will cost a pretty penny, even for a man of your means,' Carter said.

'The Savoy? Did I say anything about the Savoy? How did you know that I was staying at the Savoy?' George asked, feigning surprise.

Carter shrugged. 'Still, it's a grand place, right enough. How about you showing us around sometime? Dinner at the Savoy, eh, James?' he laughed, nudging Mulcahy in the ribs.

George thought fast. In the back of his mind, he'd worried that his pretence of staying at the Savoy might be put to the test, but hadn't acted on it. That was careless.

He laughed along with Carter.

'Well, they do a fine steak there, I must say. But I moved out just a couple of days ago. Fancied somewhere more… homely, I guess.'

'Is that so, Brendan, and where would this homely place be situated?'

What could he say? It would be foolish to use his home address. In desperation, he said, 'Montagu Square, I've taken rooms there.' He had to come up with something, but he had no idea how he would explain it to Verity.

'All right, here's what I want you to do, Brendan. Go back to Montagu Square. Spend a few days looking around London, if you like. In two weeks from today, you will come to this pub at two o'clock. That's all. Now get on with you.'

George resented Carter's patronising tone, but played his part. He got up, nodded to James Mulcahy and left the snug. Out in the street, he stopped to buy an evening newspaper from a vendor standing on the corner. They exchanged a few words as George rummaged in his pocket for some loose change. With his newspaper in hand, George set off along Seven Sisters Road and hailed a passing cab at the next street corner.

Meanwhile, Carter sat alone brooding while James Mulcahy went to the bar, returning with a bottle of whiskey and two glasses.

'Is he any use, do you suppose?' James asked.

O'Brien blew out his cheeks. 'Well, I can't see him with a gun or a stick of dynamite in his hand, can you?'

Sometime later, Carter stepped out into the night. The light was fading, though a pleasant warmth remained in the air.

'Newspaper, sir?' He glanced briefly at the newspaper vendor on the corner and shook his head.

He thought of hailing a cab, but favoured a walk instead, setting off towards Camden Town.

Alfie Cotton removed his cap and scarf, putting them in the newspaper bag at his feet and taking out his brown bowler. Setting it on his head, he walked casually after the Irishman.

***

George was at a loss. Sitting in the cab, he'd tried to prepare himself for the inevitable. It could hardly be said that Verity's bark was worse than her bite. They were equally devastating. When he arrived at the house in Montagu Square, it was Elsie who answered his knock. He waited anxiously in the drawing room while she went to find the mistress.

'Hello, George,' she said briskly. 'Whatever brings you here? Do keep it brief. I've got a splitting headache and was just about to take to my bed.'

Perhaps it was the fact that she felt unwell that accounted for it, but instead of the tirade he'd expected, she heard him out calmly.

'You want to stay here for how long?'

'A month?'

'And this is on account of the work you're doing for Colonel Quilter?'

George nodded.

'The work that you said you couldn't talk about?'

'Yes.'

'Well, my dear George, if you want my help, you must share your dark secrets. Either you explain exactly what is going on or I'll get Elsie to show you out. Do I make myself clear?' Her tone was civil enough, but George knew she meant it.

'Sit down, George,' she continued.

Verity heard him out without interruption.

'That's it,' he said at last. 'You've got the entire story.' He waited nervously for her reaction.

'The last time we sat in this room, I was the one asking for help,' Verity pronounced with a hint of a smile. 'And now it seems the tables have turned. How satisfying. What was it you called yourself – Brendan Hogan from Boston? Tell me, should we keep up the pretence among ourselves, I'm quite partial to an American accent.' She was laughing at him now.

'It's a serious business, Verity.'

'Yes, it is, George. Deadly serious perhaps. Did it occur to you that coming here would put me in danger? How do you know that some murderous Fenian isn't lurking outside at this very instant?'

'Yes, of course, and I'm so sorry. It was an absurd idea. I don't know what I must have been thinking. I'll leave, of course, right away.'

'Now that would be truly absurd. You can't change your story now. That would only raise their suspicions. What exactly did you tell them?'

'That I wanted somewhere more homely than the Savoy.'

'That sounds rather twee. Did they accept it?'

'Seemed to.'

'So, you want me to play the part of some woman who takes in lodgers, do you? It's not really me, is it? What if they see me coming and going? It won't look convincing.'

'So, what are you suggesting?'

'If they press you on the matter, admit that I'm your mistress.'

'What!'

'Not the little kept woman variety of mistress, George. A rather fast society lady who has taken a fancy to a visiting American gentleman. A summer dalliance, if you will. You needn't look so shocked, George. It will be fun. All pretence, of course. I promise I'll not take advantage of you. Oh, George, you should see your face. Do you know - my headache has quite gone.'

Elsie accepted Verity's instruction to get a guest bedroom ready for George, with just the hint of a raised eyebrow. 'It doesn't have the most stimulating view, I'm afraid, George,' Verity said. 'But you'll find it quite comfortable. What will you do about clothes and so on?'

'Ah – I was thinking about that. Um, would you mind running an errand for me tomorrow?'

'I'm to be your errand boy as well, am I? Do you expect me to collect your clothes? Really, George, there is a limit.'

'No, that's not what I'm leading to. It's a little awkward, but there's nothing else for it. I'd like you to call at a florist for me. I'd go myself, but I wouldn't want to risk her being seen with me, if the Fenians are watching.'

'Her, George? Who is this female for whom you have such regard? It doesn't matter that you have dragged me into this risky adventure, but it seems we must ensure the safety of this mysterious woman. I'm all curiosity.'

George squirmed. Verity was enjoying herself.

'Mrs Davenport, Effie is…'

'I'll spare your blushes. You needn't spell it out. Let's just say that she ranks highly in your esteem. Is that correct?'

'Yes, Verity, she does. I'll write a letter. She has a key to my rooms. She can pack my trunk and have it sent round by carrier. Thankfully, she's very level-headed. I'll explain as best I can why I'm staying here, for now. Would you mind delivering it? It shouldn't raise anyone's suspicions for you to call at a florist.'

'Oh, George, what a tangled web you weave. She may well be level-headed, as you say, but it will surely come as a shock when some strange woman calls bearing a letter from you.'

George could only nod and give her a rueful smile. He was tired, mentally drained. His shoulders slumped.

'There's pen and paper in the bureau,' Verity said. 'You look all in George, when you've written your letter, you'd best get to bed. Good night.' Verity turned and walked away, then stopped. 'Oh, by the way. I should mention that we'll have company in a few days. Jaqueline is coming for a visit. My daughter, George, remember? She can be our chaperone.'

Chapter 13

After two tense days, cautiously on the lookout for signs that Verity's house was being watched, George relaxed a little. He worried about Effie. She'd done as he asked. A trunk containing clothes, personal possessions and certain of his business ledgers, arrived by carrier, together with a note expressing her surprise and dismay at this sudden change in his living arrangements.

Verity assured him that she'd made clear to Effie that her relationship with George was in no sense a romantic one. But the poor woman could hardly be blamed for having doubts. His letter to her explained that it was all due to a professional matter arising from one of his private investigations, but said nothing about his involvement with Fenians. His determination was to ensure that she was not exposed to any danger.

***

George kept up his guard as he crossed the city by cab, alert for any sign of being followed, but saw nothing untoward. At Covent Garden, he alighted, pushed his way through the crowded market and along a narrow passage to the Lamb and Flag. A couple of costermongers stood at the bar, puffing on pipes and passing the time of day.

The cramped, gloomy back room was empty. There was no sign of the man he'd hoped to find. He took a seat in a narrow corner booth, uncertain whether to stay or look elsewhere. Deciding to wait a little longer, he retrieved a discarded morning newspaper from an adjacent table and scanned the front page. The words made little impression. He had too many things on his mind, including what to say to Colonel Quilter.

'Mine's a pint of bitter, Mr Benson.' Alfie Cotton's sudden appearance took him by surprise. 'I called round at your office first thing, guv. Thought you must be out on a job.'

'Ah, Alfie, hoped I'd find you here. Get us two pints, would you?' said George, flicking Alfie a coin and putting the newspaper to one side.

'Tell me about the other night,' George said when Alfie returned.

'Well, I followed him, like you said. He's a wily cove. Had to 'ave me wits about me and no mistake. A couple of times he turned back on himself, you know, to see if someone was following. Then he ducks into an alleyway all of a sudden. Well, I knew that was a dead end, so I didn't follow him, just waited out of sight and sure enough, out he comes after a minute.'

'And then?'

'He turned into Greenland Road. Halfway along he stops at an 'ouse, takes a key out of his pocket and goes in. Saw him at the front window, then he draws the curtains. Must be where he's living.'

'Good. Have you discovered anything else?'

'I figured he was at home for the evening, so I didn't 'ang about. Got Dick to keep an eye on the place the next morning,' Alfie explained, referring to his younger brother.

'And?'

'Dick says he almost caught his death when it poured with rain. But anyway, out comes our man at nine o'clock. Walks off down Camden High Street and stops at an undertaker.'

'An undertaker?'

'Well, he didn't go into the undertaker's itself. There's a door at the side leading to the premises above, you see. There's offices and such in there according to the nameplates outside. A watch mender, Dick says, and a secretarial agency, and a third nameplate for Carter.'

'Did it say, so and so, Carter or just the word Carter?' George asked.

Alfie shrugged. 'Dick didn't say.'

'How long did he stay there?'

'About an hour.'

'Did anyone else arrive?'

'Dick said there was a bit of coming and going, mainly to the undertakers. Never short of custom in that line of business, eh guv.'

'Suppose not. But next door? Anyone who might have called on our man?'

'There was a couple of young ladies,' Dick told me, 'and later on a gent went in there. Proper gent, according to Dick. Posh type, more your Mayfair sort that Camden High Street.'

'Anything else?'

'The posh bloke comes out again after twenty minutes. Hailed a cab but Dick wasn't close enough to hear the address he gave the cabbie. Sorry, Mister Benson.'

'Can't be helped,' Alfie. 'What about our man?'

'He comes out half an hour later. Dick tailed him back to 'is 'ouse and hung around for a couple of hours, but he didn't come out again. What now, Mister Benson? Do you want us to keep tabs on him tomorrow? I only ask 'cos we're a bit pressed for time this week.'

George thought about it. The new information he'd discovered, courtesy of Alfie and Dick, should be enough to satisfy Quilter for now. Anyway, he didn't want to push his luck. Carter was no fool. If he realised he was being followed, who knows what might happen?

'That will do for now, Alfie. Thank Dick for me, and here's something for your trouble.' George pushed an envelope across the table.

Alfie drained his drink and stuffed the envelope into his pocket. 'Ta guv, see you around.'

Chapter 14

Orpheus was impatient. Not that anyone would have known. Outwardly, he was his calm, urbane self, but he was fretting to get away. He needed space to think. Drat the man, why now, of all times and over such a trivial issue? Sir Matthew Ridley droned on. The Home Secretary was warming to his theme. Orpheus had hurried along in answer to his summons. He'd nodded to two other undersecretaries as he took his seat around the table, noting the presence of several more junior civil servants.

What was it this time? Prison Reform? The Metropolitan Police? Criminal Statistics? No, it was not. The topic which occupied the holder of one of the Great Offices of State was – bicyclists. The burning issue on which the Home Secretary required urgent advice was the worrying incidence of collisions and injuries to pedestrians caused by errant bicyclists. A matter made all the more vexing by the recent running down of the Honourable Member for Essex.

Carter's demeanour when Orpheus met him in Camden Town that morning worried him. When they'd met previously, Carter had been a supplicant, asking for weapons and explosives and touting an ambitious campaign of bombings in England, mimicking the earlier Fenian campaign of the 1880s. Orpheus passed his requests to Lensch, and a consignment of dynamite was secretly handed over to Carter and his associates in March.

But this time, he was guarded. When Orpheus asked when the campaign would commence, Carter merely smiled and shrugged.

Orpheus pressed him. 'Captain Carter, I do not seek to know precisely when and where the bombings will take place. But, my masters are surely entitled to have some idea of when their contribution to your cause will bear fruit. Our continued support is naturally contingent on results. It would assist me in advocating such support if you could provide me with some indication of your plans.'

'And my masters will hold me accountable if word should leak out,' Carter replied bluntly.

'No doubt, Captain. But bear in mind that your ability to live and operate here in London depends on my protection.'

'You told us about that Home Office spy. Aye, I'll grant you that.'

'And do you suppose the matter ends there? The authorities will redouble their efforts. They already are. Without me and my unique ability to forestall them, your campaign hasn't a chance in hell. Now then, what do you say?'

'In one month, you'll know what we've done with your dynamite. The whole stinking British Empire will know. There, that's enough. We've no need to meet again before then,' Carter said defiantly. 'Take it or leave it. You'll get nothing more.'

At last. Saved by the division bell. The Home Secretary stopped in mid-sentence and hurried out. 'I would appreciate your advice within the week, gentlemen,' he called out.

'Serve him right, if he got run over by a bicycle crossing Parliament Square,' some wag muttered.

Orpheus emerged into King Charles Street and set off along Horse Guards Road towards the Traveller's Club.

Chapter 15

George walked back to Verity's house, mulling over what he should tell Quilter. Not only what, but how? The Colonel had always come to him, turning up at his office. But now it would hardly be prudent for George to go back there. He had no idea how to contact Quilter, so what could he do?

It still worried him as he arrived at Montagu Square and let himself in with the key Verity had given him. Perhaps she'd know how to get hold of the Colonel. A slim chance, but he may as well ask. He caught sight of her through the drawing-room door, sitting near the fireplace.

'You wouldn't know how to…' he began.

'Know what, George?'

'Oh. You're here.'

The Colonel lounged opposite Verity with his legs outstretched as though he owned the place.

'Having failed on two occasions to find any sign of you at your office, I came to enquire if Miss Mallard had any knowledge of your whereabouts. She has enlightened me as to your current domestic situation,' Quilter said stiffly.

'Well, I…'

'Save your explanations, George. Miss Mallard has already told me why you entered into this unorthodox arrangement. And, in doing so, It is obvious that you have divulged confidential information to her. Despite being bound by the Official Secrets Act, you have seen fit to… '

'Oh, for heaven's sake. Enough of this nonsense,' Verity erupted. 'You are in my house, Colonel, and I will not allow you to behave in this boorish, overbearing manner. No, hear me out. You may issue all the threats you like. I defy you. Whatever hold you may think you have over George and me, we can cause you a great deal of trouble. Anthony Spencer's convenient escape from Larkford Grange was orchestrated by you to protect the reputation of someone in high places. If you act against either of us, then I will go to the press.'

Quilter heard her out, stony faced. 'Madam, if you have quite finished, I hesitate to call into question the fierce independence of the British press, but there are certain areas of extreme sensitivity into which newspaper editors and owners intrude at their peril. I can assure you that a word in the right quarters will ensure that what may or may not have occurred at Larkford Grange will never see the light of day.'

'I see,' said Verity.

'I'm glad that you do.' Quilter replied.

'However, Colonel, you and Her Majesty's government do not hold sway over the foreign press. Your implied threats, the last time you called on me, led me to take out a form of insurance. A letter accusing the Government of connivance at Spencer's disappearance is held by my attorney in France. If necessary, he will release it to the French press, who would no doubt delight in publishing its contents.'

George observed the exchange with amazement. He had to admire her. Her attack had clearly discomfited the

Colonel, who glared at her but seemed temporarily lost for words. George seized the moment. 'If you were not so intent on browbeating us, Colonel, you might realise that Verity and I are both loyal British subjects. Now that you've involved us in this Fenian business, do you suppose we are indifferent to the threat they pose? Yes, I was resentful at the way that you press-ganged me into working for you, but I'd be failing in my duty to the country if I did not play my part in defeating them. Is that too idealistic for you?'

Now it was Verity's turn to be amazed. George wasn't given to high-flown rhetoric and surely he knew he was taking a risk in including her in his statement. Normally, she'd slap down such presumption, but the Colonel's attitude riled her a great deal more. 'There, Colonel,' she said, 'if you'd rein in your cynical attempt to treat us as your minions, perhaps you would appreciate that in us you have two intelligent and resourceful allies. Together, we can accomplish great things. But as equals. Doesn't that sound more satisfactory than a relationship founded on crude compulsion?'

George emitted a low whistle of admiration.

Twenty minutes later, the front door closed behind the Colonel. A tactical withdrawal was the phrase that came most readily to George's mind.

Some ground rules had been established. 'You will not call at this house again, Colonel, unless I invite you,' Verity declared. 'If you wish to meet either or both of us, please send a telegram to this address. We must also know how to get in touch with you. The Colonel gave an address in Hammersmith. 'You can send a telegram there,' he said. 'It will reach me within the hour. We can meet at that same address.'

George recounted his audience with Carter at the Bedford Arms. 'He's ordered me to return on Monday week. Looks like he's planning to use me in whatever he's scheming.'

Quilter said nothing, still smarting from the indignity of having the tables turned on him. He was interested, though, no longer slouching but leaning forward in his chair.

'There's more,' said George, mentioning the house in Greenland Road and the premises in Camden High Street. 'Is that enough to be going on with, Colonel?' he added.

'Yes, it is, George,' Quilter replied meekly. 'It's a great deal. More than I expected. Thank you.'

'It's good to be appreciated,' said George, with a hint of condescension. He couldn't help enjoying the moment.

'What now?' Verity interjected. 'You know where he lives. Why not arrest the man and we can resume our normal lives?'

'Arrest him? Yes, I could do that. But he'll not talk,' said Quilter, his voice regaining some of its authority. 'I need to know what the Fenians are plotting. His arrest might disturb their plans, but there's always someone else ready to step into the breach. And I must find the traitor in the Home Office. When the time's right, I will arrest Carter and anyone associated with him. Until then, George, I must ask you to continue to pose as Brendan Hogan. Attend this next meeting with him and then you might learn what's afoot.'

'And me? What am I to do?' asked Verity.

'I think for now, allowing George to stay here is enough, Miss Mallard. I dare say the opportunity may arise for you to play a more active part. I appreciate that you have a range of talents to offer, even if I have not said as much.'

'Very well. Thank you for that vote of confidence, and for pity's sake, let's drop the formality. Call me Verity and I assume you have a Christian name…?'

'Oh… yes. It's Clarence.'

'Well, Clarence, let me show you out. George and I will be in touch after his meeting at the Bedford Arms. Until then, *au revoir.*'

A glass of sherry, I think? Said Verity when she returned to the drawing room. 'Bravo, George, you were formidable.'

'Oh, I only spoke up when you already had him on the run. That threat to involve the press was brilliant. How did you come up with that on the spur of the moment?'

'I didn't come up with anything, George. The letter exists. It really is with my attorney in France. I was damned if I'd allow Quilter to have a hold on us. He certainly seemed chastened by it. But we'd be fools to trust him. It's funny though.'

'What is?'

'I would never have thought of him as a Clarence. Would you?'

'Not a bit,' George chuckled.

'Now George, to change the subject, can I assume that you are not engaged this coming Saturday evening?'

'Engaged. Well, I won't be seeing Effie as things stand. Why do you ask?'

Verity went to the mantelpiece and returned with a card - a printed invitation. 'There's a reception at the Russian Embassy. I'm invited to attend with a guest. Mary has one too – she's taking Edward Crawford.'

'Really. I didn't know that either of you had connections at the Russian Embassy?'

'We haven't. The invitation comes courtesy of Anna Jesenska. She has the connection.'

'Well, I thought that there was something intriguing about that woman.'

'You certainly spent enough time admiring her, George,' Verity teased.

Chapter 16

'A most satisfactory meeting, was it not your Royal Highness? The day will be a dazzling success,' Sir Francis Knollys enthused, collecting a sheaf of papers from the table. The Diamond Jubilee Committee meeting, chaired by Edward the Prince of Wales, had just concluded at Marlborough House. Bertie, as he was known to the Royal Family, was determined to create a spectacle worthy of his mother's unprecedented reign of sixty years.

He regarded his private secretary through rheumy eyes while setting a match to his cigar and drawing on it until he'd achieved a satisfying red glow. He exhaled lazily, adding to the grey fug hanging in the air. Dazzling, yes, it would be that alright. It was his brainchild. His drive and determination had harnessed the talents of a host of subjects, from the most powerful in the land to the humblest, to celebrate a reign in which the British Empire had swelled to encompass a quarter of the population of the globe.

On the twenty-second of June, a vast glittering procession would pass through the great city of London. A celebration of the Empire, featuring the leaders and the troops of the Colonies and Dominions. The reigning kings and queens of the European powers were not invited. The day was dedicated to only one monarch, Her Majesty

Queen Victoria. And crowds, such as London had never witnessed before, would proclaim their love for their sovereign as she passed by. It would be a day that would live on in people's memories, but also one that could be shared with people all over the world through the modern marvel of the cinematograph.

'Can't command the weather, of course,' Bertie remarked laconically, 'but we will simply have to trust in providence that the sun is as keen to witness the procession as Her Majesty's subjects.'

'Indeed, sir. Will you be requiring me for anything further?'

'No, Francis. I'll stay and finish my cigar. I will be taking tea at Great Cumberland Street, by the way. I shan't require you until the morning.'

Only a few weeks remained until the Jubilee. Sixty years, surpassing that of George III. It couldn't last much longer. Bertie's relationship with his mother had never been easy. She had always viewed him with disappointment and made no secret of the fact. It made his childhood and youth a misery. Now, at the age of fifty-five, the once distant prospect of the succession was close. He had tried to share in his mother's official duties, to take on some of the burden as well as to prepare himself for the future, but she repeatedly rebuffed him.

No matter, he would ensure that she was properly honoured on the occasion of the Jubilee. It would be the last great public occasion of her life. Knollys was right. It would be dazzling. Everything was going to plan. Only one small cloud of irritation marred his feeling of satisfaction. Its source was all too familiar. His nephew, Wilhelm.

While all the other European monarchs respected the decision not to invite them and were content to send representatives in their stead, not so Kaiser Wilhelm II. He even went so far as to complain to the Queen. *'To be the first and eldest of your grandchildren and yet to be precluded from taking part in this unique fête… is deeply mortifying,'* he wrote - to no avail.

Bertie put it out of his mind, stubbing out the thought as he stubbed out his cigar. The clock on the mantelpiece struck five. He rose and left the room with a spring in his step. In half an hour, he would be comfortably ensconced at 35a Great Cumberland Street, Jennie Churchill's smart London address. Ah, dear Jennie Churchill. Her American *joie de vivre*, her spurning of stuffy British convention, had attracted him since he'd first known her. He'd had a hand in smoothing her path to marriage with Lord Randolph Churchill, overcoming the objections of his parents, the Duke and Duchess of Marlborough. And all despite Randolph's disgraceful attempt to involve him in a scandal swirling around his friend, Lord Aylesford, and his wife Edith, whose affair with Randolph's older brother, Lord Blandford had rocked polite society.

Theirs had been a chequered history, but Randolph and he had, in time, become reconciled and Jennie came once more into his orbit. More than his orbit. They'd become lovers.

Randolph died in 1895. Now Bertie found pleasure in Jennie's company over tea, rather than in her bed. There was flirtation, certainly, but Jennie had more than enough lovers - younger ones.

Chapter 17

A sudden shower freshened the air as Verity and George's cab made its way to the Russian Embassy in Chesham Square. It soon passed, and George, unaccustomed to the strictures of formal evening dress, appreciated the cool breeze playing over his cheek through the open window. Verity sat stiffly upright at his side, obeying the dictates of her corset. Her sleeveless ball gown of lace and sapphire-blue taffeta was complemented by a cape of black velvet with gold embroidery. Her fair hair was drawn up in a knot, topped by a simple *aigrette*. A choker of pearls with matching earrings completed the ensemble. While frequently scornful of the fancies of *haute couture*, tonight was an exception.

The cab joined a procession of carriages approaching the entrance to the embassy, stopping and starting, until a liveried footman opened the door and assisted Verity to the pavement. George swiftly joined her and extended an arm as they ascended the embassy steps. In the fading daylight, a glittering array of chandeliers, powered by electricity, shone dazzlingly through the open doorway ahead.

'Miss Verity Mallard and Mr George Benson,' the major-domo announced in a stentorian Slavic bass.

It was only after Verity had dispatched an RSVP accepting the invitation on behalf of herself and Mr George

Benson that it occurred to them that George was now carrying two identities. In the unlikely event that Captain Carter or one of his associates was also present, his deception would be discovered. It worried him.

'It's hardly likely that one of your Fenians will be there, is it George?' Verity said dismissively. 'Anyhow, Mary and Edward will be there. It would hardly do for you to turn up under an assumed name and have them asking awkward questions.'

They passed down the line of embassy dignitaries, receiving polite words of welcome from the ambassador, His Excellency George de Staal, and his wife, and nods of acknowledgment from various secretaries and attachés.

The wildly ostentatious dress uniforms of the military attachés stood out. A pride of strutting peacocks, Verity thought to herself, as though to suppress the thrill that they evoked at first glance.

Pausing to take a glass of champagne from a footman's silver tray, Verity swept along with George at her side. From the corner of her eye, a figure waving an ostrich-feather fan caught her attention.

Mary and Edward crossed the floor. 'My word, you've certainly pulled the stops out,' said Mary, looking Verity up and down. 'All the other women here will hate you by the end of the evening. You look very smart too, George,' she added, flashing him a smile.

Verity brushed off Mary's remark, disguising the pleasure she felt. 'You look lovely too, dear. And you'll put most of the men to shame, Edward.' She meant it. Edward always dressed with a certain style and panache. He looked like a younger version of Oscar Wilde and the resemblance did not end there. Hopefully Edward had now learnt the value of discretion in his personal life, she thought.

They chatted inconsequentially until the major-domo's booming voice called everyone to order. The Ambassador walked unsteadily to a dais. The gathering listened politely, while he extended an official greeting, giving a rambling speech about the warm and enduring relationship between the two great imperial powers of Russia and Great Britain. It concluded with toasts to their imperial majesties, Nicholas II and Victoria.

'He doesn't look terribly well,' Mary whispered.

'I dare say a new ambassador will be presenting his credentials before long,' Verity remarked.

A string quartet struck up a jaunty tune, and the hubbub of conversation resumed. Verity was about to suggest to George that they should circulate when a female voice at her elbow had her turning to face the speaker.

'Anna, there you are,' Verity exclaimed. 'I wondered where you were…' her voice trailed off as she took in the tall figure standing at Anna Jesenska's side. Resplendent in his red tunic with a mass of gold braid, she had passed the man earlier in the line of military attachés. While his uniform was no more flamboyant than the others, his height and, she had to admit, his looks, captured her attention. Not a young man, but with a youthful face and bearing. Fair and clean-shaven, with a pronounced twinkle in his eye.

'Allow me to present, General Dmitri Cherkasov,' said Anna. The General bowed and, introductions having been made, polite conversation followed.

Verity dexterously drew the General to one side.

'Have you been in London long, General?'

'A week only, Miss Mallard. I have had the pleasure of visiting several times in the past,' he replied in barely accented English.

'Shall you be staying long?'

'A few weeks, then I will return to Saint Petersburg.'

'Ah, how I should love to visit Russia one day. Saint Petersburg. It conjures up such romantic images.'

The General nodded. 'I'm sure you would find it a fascinating experience. It would be my pleasure to be your guide, should you decide to visit. I would be delighted to translate your romantic notions into reality.'

Verity wondered what he meant. Was it flirtation or just an innocent turn of phrase? She thought it best to change the subject.

'Oh, well, I dare say that it's most unlikely. I have never ventured further than France, and…'

'May I ask you a question?' the General interrupted.

'A question? Well, yes. What is it?' Verity replied, uncertainly.

'Your name.'

'Yes?'

'I know that name. I mean, I knew someone with that name?'

'I see, and what is your question?'

'Do you know a man named Ambrose Mallard?'

'Good Lord. Ambrose? Why, yes. He's my uncle, well, my late father's cousin, to be exact, but I think of him as an uncle. How remarkable. How is it you know him?'

The General smiled. 'Oh, it was many years ago and far away. In the mountains of the Karakoram. We played for opposing teams, you might say. Is he in good health?'

'Goodness, such an amazing coincidence. Yes, he's in rude good health. Quite irrepressible. I knew he'd spent many years in India, but he only ever talked about being in business there. What a dark horse.'

'Where is he now, may I ask?'

'Here in England. At my family home in Oxfordshire.'

'Not in London? A pity. Would you please send him my best wishes?'

'Of course. And what on earth did you two get up to in the wilds of Central Asia?'

'Ah, that would take too long in the telling. Regrettably, duty calls. I must circulate among our other guests. It has been a pleasure speaking with you, Miss Mallard. *Au revoir.*' The General bowed and turned away.

Verity had lost track of her surroundings. Mary and Edward had drifted off and joined a group of guests crowded around the ambassador.

She smiled to herself at the sight of George with Anna. There was definitely an attraction there on his part. However, it was the person next to them that intrigued her. Tall, debonair and awfully English, she thought. A fellow guest, not an embassy official. As she stepped over to join them, the stranger walked away with Anna on his arm. Curiouser and curiouser, thought Verity.

George looked stranded and a little put out. She noticed his disappointment. 'George, how are you enjoying the evening?' she said brightly. 'Quite an occasion, isn't it?'

'Oh, there you are, Verity.'

'Yes, my Russian Hussar has deserted me, I'm afraid. It looks as though you and I are in the same boat.'

'What do you mean?'

'That we've been abandoned, George. Anna looks to be as thick as thieves with that fellow she walked off with. Who on earth is he?'

George shrugged. 'Some civil servant, I gather.'

'Does he have a name? You have to admit he cuts a bit of a dash.'

'Really? A bit flashy, I thought.'

'Oh, George, don't be so put-out. Just because he intruded on your little tête-à-tête with Anna. Who is he?'

'His name is Giles Temple-Swift, if you must know.'

'Oh well, never mind that. You'll never guess what I discovered talking to that Russian General. He's acquainted with Ambrose. There, that got your attention. Our Ambrose.'

'No,' George laughed. 'How the devil would he and this Russian know each other? Ambrose spent most of his time in India. Can't recall him saying he was ever in Russia.'

'Apparently, it was in the Karakoram mountain ranges. That's just to the north of India, isn't it? Who knows what Ambrose got up to there? Anyway, the General holds him in high regard. I must let Ambrose know. I'll write to him tomorrow.'

Chapter 18

General Cherkasov looked down from the gallery at the sea of heads below. He was a soldier, not a diplomat. The protocol of such occasions bored him. Diplomatic niceties and small-talk were best left to others. He excused himself from the reception after an hour.

From his vantage point, he scanned the assembly until he spied Verity speaking with one of the embassy staff. What an astounding coincidence that she should be related to Ambrose Mallard. He'd often wondered what happened to the brash Englishman he'd encountered all those years ago in the wild territories north of Kashmir. The Great Game, as it was dubbed, pitted Russian and British imperial ambitions against one another. The game was already decades in the playing, when circumstances brought the young Lieutenant Cherkasov and an adventurer named Ambrose Mallard together.

Russia's steady advance into Central Asia had already swallowed the cities of Samarkand, Bokhara and Khiva. It would not end there. But the mountain ranges of the Pamirs, Hindu Kush, and Karakoram, presented a formidable natural barrier to any Russian expansion to the south, and the jewel in the crown of the British Empire — India. This dangerous, forbidding landscape, with its complex mishmash of tribal loyalties, was a magnet for courageous and ambitious men from both sides.

General Constantin Kaufman, the Governor General of Turkestan, dispatched Cherkasov, to spy out the mountain passes for routes that would enable the passage of an invading army. Accompanied by a small detachment of Cossacks and a motley gang of hired tribesmen, he left Samarkand and disappeared into the mountainous hinterland. His party skirted the cities and larger settlements, wearing tribal garb where necessary, seeking to avoid the attentions of Yakub Beg, the wily and ruthless ruler of a large swathe of Central Asia, called Kashgaria.

They lived on their wits, constantly alert for danger, loath to take anyone or anything on trust, including their native guides and servants. Ambush in the desolate high passes was an ever-present threat. Twice, they fought off attacks, at the cost of two wounded Cossacks. At other times, Cherkasov resorted to bribery, buying safe passage from local chiefs and warlords.

In the high country below the Chang Lung Pass, his luck ran out. His party spent an uncomfortable night encamped at the edge of a straggling village of stone houses. Cherkasov endured an awkward evening as guest of the village chief, eating goat meat and dried fruit with the man's extended family, with one of his guides as interpreter. The headman made a poor job of disguising his intentions. Cherkasov could see the calculation behind his gaze. The valuable prize that his horses, mules, guns and silver would represent to such a man.

Next morning, the crisp, clear, pre-dawn air filled the Russians' lungs, its freshness helping to revive their cramped limbs. The Cossacks readied their horses.

Cherkasov supervised the loading of the pack mules, whispering orders, urging the muleteers to make haste. They'd breakfast later. Several of the servants muttered their displeasure and dragged their feet.

He'd sensed resentment building among some of them for several days. His head guide warned him that all was not well. He offered a small increase in pay, but still they muttered oaths and looked askance at him. At least he could rely on his Cossacks. They had no illusions about their situation. Their survival rested on maintaining discipline and trusting in his leadership.

They left the village, descending along a rugged path, picking their way cautiously at first and increasing their pace as the sun rose. They skirted high rock walls, nerves taut in anticipation of an ambush. It was the perfect place. But after an hour, Cherkasov took some comfort in being a healthy distance from the village. The terrain ahead looked more promising, opening out into a wide plateau, a suitable place to have their delayed breakfast.

His contingent of Cossacks deployed onto the plateau, and Cherkasov urged the mule train after them. Only four remained. They'd stopped fifty paces back. Irritated by the delay, he called to the two men with them, gesturing impatiently. They ignored him.

Damn their impudence. He set off towards them at a brisk trot, bellowing at them to get a move on. At first he thought the muleteers were pointing at him until a clatter of falling stones made him turn in the saddle to see what had caught their attention. A stream of loose scree slid down the cliff face, but as he watched it became an avalanche of rocks and boulders, thundering down the scarp, blocking the road, cutting him off from his Cossacks.

The sound was deafening. Enough to mask the gunfire from above. It was the puffs of earth and the stone splinters flying about as projectiles struck the path nearby that revealed he was under attack. He looked desperately for cover, spying a narrow defile running parallel to the path. Pulling sharply on the reins, he turned his horse's head and kicked hard with his heels, urging it into a gallop, bending low over its neck.

The horse stumbled down a shallow slope of loose rock and gravel into the defile. Cherkasov slid out of the saddle. The depression in which he found himself was barely deep enough to offer protection to his crouching figure. Unburdened of its rider and disturbed by the steady crackle of gunfire, the horse tore itself free of Cherkasov's grip on its bridle and galloped away along the gully. He cursed, realising that his rifle remained in its saddle holster. His only weapon now was his revolver.

Cherkasov moved to his left until he found sufficient cover to stand and hazard raising his head to assess the situation. His thoughts turned to his Cossacks. They would have been taken by surprise, as he was. He could rely on Ivan, his under-officer, to take charge in his absence and organise a counter-attack. But his first duty would be to get his mounts safely out of range. It would take time. Cherkasov was on his own.

He surveyed the cliffs. The enemy were hard to spot, betrayed only by the occasional puff of smoke from their jezails, the long-barrelled muskets ubiquitous to the region, and deadly accurate in the right hands.

The two muleteers dropped to their knees on the path, abandoning their mules, which trotted away, seemingly unconcerned by the surrounding commotion.

They called out, waving their arms at the attackers. 'Bastards,' Cherkasov muttered, 'they're in league with them.' As though to confirm his suspicions, two of the attacking tribesmen clambered down the rocks on to the path. The muleteers ran to them, gesturing in supplication. Cherkasov watched helplessly as the first of them was cut down by the tribesmen's curved swords. His companion screamed and ran for his life, only to be winged by musket fire from the cliff. The tribesmen calmly walked over to him and finished the job.

Absorbed by the horror of the scene, he'd unwittingly exposed himself. A musket ball ricocheted from the rocky ground, mere inches from his head. He ducked and moved further along the defile. A ragged volley of shots struck nearby. Excited shouts sounded from the cliffs, echoed immediately by the two tribesmen on the path. He needed no interpreter to realise that they were being ordered to advance on him.

Despite the gunfire, he was compelled to raise his head again. A glance was enough. The two men were running in opposite directions, slanting away from the path. Their intention was plain. While gunfire pinned him down, they would come at him from left and right.

He drew his revolver. The six rounds in the chamber were all the defence he had. It had gone quiet. The gunmen on the cliffs were not wasting their ammunition. He gathered his thoughts. The gully did not run straight. He could see fifteen paces along it in one direction, half as far in the other. If his assailants ran at him simultaneously, he'd be hard pressed to shoot both of them.

Needing to seize the initiative, he ducked down, moving to his right. Rather than be caught like a rat in a trap, he'd go on the attack. His two assailants might expect him to have remained where he was, he reasoned. If he could surprise one and kill him, he'd have a fighting chance of dealing with his comrade as well.

His reasoning was flawed. Rather than descend into the gully, his attackers stayed on the surface, creeping along the lip of the defile, to leap down on him. A man's shadow gave Cherkasov a moment's warning before he collapsed, winded, under the fellow's weight. The revolver fell from his grip. He could recall to this day the panic he'd felt, pinioned under his assailant with the man's beard pressed against his face, expecting powerful hands to grip his throat. Desperation gave him strength, convulsive strength, a survival reflex. Somehow, he found himself looking down at the man beneath him, their positions reversed, his hands around the tribesman's throat. It was the blank eyes that told him, then the bloody ink blot spreading across the floor of the gully.

The realisation that the fellow had been shot had barely formed in his mind when a deafening war cry directly above him proclaimed the presence of the dead man's companion. Murderous rage contorted his face as he stood on the lip of the gully, sword raised. Cherkasov scrambled to his feet, overwhelmed by the fear of imminent death.

This time, he heard the shot. The boom of a large-calibre weapon. The projectile burst through the tribesman's torso in a welter of blood and flesh, flinging him face forward into the gully at Cherkasov's feet.

He struggled to order his thoughts. Could both of the attackers be accidental victims of their compatriots' gunfire? Surely not. The shot he heard came from the other side of the valley. Had his Cossacks come to the rescue?

Not possible in so short a time. And that was not the report of a Russian army rifle.

Then came a shout. Not a tribesman. Not Russian. English? Cherkasov stood on tiptoe, looking over the edge of the defile. Two arms waved at him from the rocks, a hundred paces distant. More shouting. Definitely English. 'Over here. Run, man. Over here.' the voice grew more urgent. A quick glance behind told him why.

Half a dozen tribesmen had descended from the cliff top. Two of them levelled their Jezails, and he ducked to avoid the musket balls coming his way. Pausing only to retrieve his pistol, he hoisted himself out of the gully and ran, crouching low, zig-zagging. Shots pecked the ground close by.

His rescuer exhorted him to run faster. He could see him now, just twenty paces away. Crouching among the rocks. A young fellow, about his own age, with a wild mop of red hair and a fearsome firearm in his hand. He had a companion, too. A Sikh.

Cherkasov threw himself behind the rocks, gasping for breath.

'Ambrose Mallard' the man said, extending a hand.

'Lieutenant Cherkasov, Dmitri.'

'Russian, eh? Well, Dmitri, it looks like we're in for some hot work. Thakur, here, bagged the first one, and I potted the second one with this,' Mallard said, brandishing a heavy express rifle. 'A Gibbs-Farquarson, fresh out from England. That's enough talk. Thakur will give you our spare rifle. Time for some target practice.'

The Sikh pointed to a Snider-Enfield carbine propped against the rock next to him. Cherkasov pocketed a handful of cartridges from Thakur's ammunition pouch and took up a firing position alongside.

More tribesmen had descended from the cliffs. They advanced in a ragged skirmishing line, kneeling to fire, then running forward a few paces, to crouch behind whatever sparse cover they could find, to reload. One screamed and fell to a shot from the Englishman's gun as Cherkasov examined the unfamiliar rifle in his hand. He stole a glance at Thakur and copied his action, cocking the hammer, opening the breechblock, and inserting a cartridge. His first two shots were ineffective. He steadied his rifle and sighted it on a rock forty paces away. A tribesman, distinguished by his elaborate purple and gold headdress, had taken cover there. Cherkasov exhaled slowly, his finger exerting a light pressure on the trigger. The long barrel of the tribesman's weapon came into view as the man levelled it and raised his head to take aim.

The crack of Cherkasov's rifle coincided with a puff of smoke as the Jezail discharged its musket ball. The colourful headdress flew off the tribesman's head together with the top of his skull and at the same instant a splinter of rock gashed Cherkasov's ear. Had the tribesman fired a split-second earlier, it could be Cherkasov's brain spattered on the barren ground.

They added two more tribesmen to the tally before the attack faltered. One by one, the skirmishers fell back, occasionally aiming a parting shot.

Mallard held up his hand. 'They've had enough. Better save our ammunition,' he said. 'Well done, Dmitri, fine shooting.'

Cherkasov nodded. 'Thank you, but it is your shooting that deserves praise. You saved my bacon. Isn't that the correct English expression?'

'My word, your English is a damned sight better than my Russian.'

'I had a tutor as a boy. He was Scottish.'

'He did a good job. Now, while our friends on the cliffs are licking their wounds, let me introduce you to my good friend Thakur Singh.'

The Sikh put his rifle down and stood up. 'Lieutenant Cherkasov, how nice of you to pop in on us,' he said, flashing a smile. '

He stopped and cupped his ear. An eruption of gunfire in the distance captured their attention.

'Your men?' Mallard asked the Russian.

'My Cossacks. They're mounting an attack. I should be with them.'

'By the sound of things, they're managing without you.'

The three men listened as the rifle fire reached a crescendo. The occasional sound of an answering Jezail trailed off. A brief silence was followed by a bugle call.

'It's over,' Cherkasov announced. 'Thank you again. I must join them.' He handed back his rifle and turned away, but stopped after a few paces. 'May I request a favour?'

'Favour, Lieutenant?'

Cherkasov shuffled. 'I've no right to ask, especially after you've saved my life, but I would be grateful if this episode could be kept to ourselves. You see…'

Ambrose smiled at the Russian's obvious discomfort. 'Lieutenant, let me stop you there. You would rather that your activities in these parts went unnoticed, is that right?' No, don't explain. Your countrymen and mine have been spying out the land for years. Just like you, Thakur and I also have our reasons for keeping a low profile. If you keep our presence here to yourself, we're happy to reciprocate.'

That was the last Cherkasov saw of Ambrose Mallard, but he had never forgotten the red-haired Englishman.

His Cossacks had cleared some of the fallen rocks away by the time he walked back to the foot of the cliffs. A dozen tribesmen were killed in the attack, the rest slipped away to fight another day. Ivan saluted and reported three men lightly wounded, but one young horseman would never return to Berdyansk.

***

The reception drew to a close.

Edward escorted Mary back to her lodgings and took the cab on to a discreet address in Bermondsey, catering for gentlemen with unconventional tastes.

Verity and George discussed their impressions of the evening as they were driven back to Montagu Square.

In a Bloomsbury bedroom, Orpheus kicked off his shoes and reclined languidly on the edge of the bed, enjoying a cigar and the sight of Anna Jesenska stepping out of her dress.

In Vienna, Eulenburg read the dispatch from Lensch for the second time. The good humour he'd felt after returning from the opera evaporated. His misgivings about the Fenians were proving to be well founded. He took up his pen. Ten minutes later, he folded the sheets of paper and placed them in an envelope, carefully sealing it and marking it most urgent. Lensch took pride in his abilities as a fixer. Now, Eulenburg would put those abilities fully to the test. Failure was neither to be contemplated nor forgiven.

Chapter 19

George sat in Verity's drawing room, scanning *The Illustrated London News*, nervously awaiting her return. He had little experience with children, save for the occasional visit to his sister's place in Portsmouth. Her brood of three, two girls and a boy, ranged from eight to twelve and took little notice of their uncle, once they'd pocketed the sixpences he always handed out.

He'd twice looked out of the window at the sound of cabs drawing up, but they were false alarms. He took out his cigarette case but stifled the urge to smoke. Verity tolerated a cigarette or even a cigar after dinner but insisted on George going out to the back garden at all other times.

Perhaps the train from Dover had been delayed.

Verity had schooled him on what to say and how to behave. Elsie and the other servants were the problem. Modern woman, though she thought herself to be, Verity was hardly going to entrust them with her secret. To them and the world at large, Jaqueline was the daughter of a French cousin, come to visit and improve her English. George would have to play along with the deception.

This time it *was* them. George put his newspaper down and tramped through the hall to open the door. He crossed the pavement to take Jaqueline's portmanteau from the cabbie and gave the little girl a warm smile and words of greeting. 'Thank you, Mister Benson, I am very happy to be here,' Jaqueline pronounced slowly and deliberately and dipped a curtsey to Verity's obvious delight.

George gave Verity an enquiring look. 'I thought your aunt was accompanying her? She didn't travel from France on her own, did she?'

'No, of course not. Claudette's husband, Gaston, has taken ill. She's gone straight back to France. Actually, I think it's for the better. Not that Gaston is unwell, I mean. But she will be spared the need to keep up pretences where the servants are concerned. Now then, *chérie*, let's get you inside,' she said, taking her daughter's hand.

***

Ambrose Mallard wiped the mud from his boots and hung his hat on the hallstand. After Mortimer and Olivia's wedding, he'd vacated his room at Thorneycroft Hall and taken up residence at the lodge. It suited him perfectly, enabling him to come and go as he pleased, with just the services of a cook/housekeeper to ensure his comfort. Whereas once he'd explored every nook and cranny of the big house, delighting in roaming the attics and investigating its hidden places, he now spent much of his time outdoors, tramping to the farthest corners of the estate with a notebook and a pair of binoculars, taking pleasure in its flora and fauna. He felt better than he had for years. It invigorated him.

Mrs Elkins came bustling from the kitchen, wiping her hands on her apron. 'Ah. There you are Mister Mallard. Just look at you. Get out of that damp coat. You don't want to be catching a chill now, do you?'

Ambrose let her fuss over him, handing over his coat and accepting her offer of a 'nice cup of tea'.

'Postman just called,' she said, returning with the tea tray. 'Left this letter for you.'

Ambrose squinted at the envelope. Letters were a rare event. Fumbling in his pocket, he retrieved his spectacles and balanced them on the bridge of his nose. His frown of concentration became a smile as the writing on the envelope came into focus. 'Ah, it's Verity. Now then, where's the letter opener?'

'It's there on the tray,' Mrs Elkins replied, turning on her heel and returning to the kitchen.

Ambrose studied the letter. His hands shook a little as he read. More than a quarter of a century had passed since he'd braved the lawless grandeur of the Karakoram. The letter brought it all back to him.

His years in India resembled a game of snakes and ladders. Good times would suddenly be overtaken by misfortune. He played his luck as best he could. A shipping clerk in Bombay, a tea planter in Assam, murky dealings running contraband, even an enterprise managing a string of bordellos, which he preferred not to recollect too clearly.

He was kicking his heels in Simla as a clerk in the colonial administration when opportunity knocked. He'd performed some favours for an enterprising and highly persuasive businessman named Thakur Singh. One or two lucrative contracts went the Sikh's way, and he duly showed his gratitude.

Always with an eye to the main chance, Thakur Singh appeared at Ambrose's modest bungalow one evening with a bottle of single malt and a cheery smile. Ambrose savoured his whisky, listening to the Sikh's seemingly endless fund of anecdotes and gossip until he finally disclosed the purpose of his visit.

'What can you tell me about the expedition to Kashgar?'

Ambrose had heard of Kashgar, the city far away to the north, beyond Kashmir and the wild mountain ranges of Central Asia. It was the capital of the area known as Kashgaria, carved out by conquest in a few short years by a ruthless adventurer named Yakub Beg. Its strategic position, between British India and Russia's expanding border, made it the subject of diplomatic overtures from both imperial powers. Reluctant to commit himself to either side, Yakub Beg played them along. Having granted a trading agreement to a Russian delegation, he deemed it prudent to assuage British concerns about Russian influence by inviting a British mission to Kashgar.

'Of course. Forsyth's mission is the talk of the town. The Viceroy's ordered it and everyone's rushing around making preparations. It's a big affair.'

'How big?'

'Enormous. There's all sorts of people: political officers, surveyors, interpreters, secretaries. And a military escort, of course.'

'So, what does the Viceroy wish to achieve from this enormous mission?'

'To counter Russian influence, I suppose. Then there's trade.'

'Yes, trade, and let's suppose that an enterprising trader was to be part of the mission. Just think of the advantages such a person might gain. In on the ground floor, isn't that the right expression?'

Ambrose recalled the Sikh's sparkling grin that night as he leaned over to pour another measure of whisky into

Ambrose's glass. The bag of gold coins he placed next to it clinched the deal.

A month later, Ambrose rode out as a junior member of the secretariat. A small cog in a party of 350 officials and servants supported by over 500 baggage animals. Somewhere up ahead rode Thakur Singh, now engaged as an official interpreter.

Ambrose embraced the adventure of it. A refreshing contrast with his humdrum existence in Simla. The inevitable privations of the journey were not too vexatious for a young man in good health, and along with many of his British compatriots, he relished the opportunity to hunt. The hills teemed with game. His newly acquired hunting rifle took pride of place in his baggage.

They marched for weeks, traversing high passes and fast flowing watercourses. At pains to disguise the connection between them, he and Thakur kept their distance, only occasionally exchanging a few words. The Sikh formed a friendship of sorts with three of the baggage train drovers. Riding alongside them and taking tea with them now and then.

Ambrose often wondered how different his life might have been if he'd not allowed his head to be turned. What if he'd ignored the note that Thakur Singh surreptitiously pressed into his hand?

But he hadn't.

The expedition paused for a couple of days before pushing on towards the Karakoram pass and the high country beyond. Ambrose wrapped himself in his sheepskin lined chogah and rode out, waving at two sepoys from the Corps of Guides and brandishing his hunting rifle. They returned his wave. 'Good hunting, sahib,' one called out. Relieved that his bulging saddle bags had gone unnoticed, he trotted around a fold in the hills.

A thin column of smoke led him to a small copse of ragged trees where Thakur was waiting. The Sikh's grand design to establish himself as a trader with the Kashgarians had not survived his discovery that among the baggage train were cases of gifts to be presented to Yakub Beg and other dignitaries. Jewelled timepieces, ornate swords, daggers and firearms, and a host of fine objects carefully packed for the journey.

Four pack mules and a spare mount stood tethered among the trees. Thakur explained that two of the mules carried crates of gifts. The others were loaded with supplies of food and camping equipment.

'Weapons?'

'Two rifles and two hundred cartridges,' Thakur replied, clapping Ambrose on the back. 'Time we disappeared, my friend.'

They made the best progress they could, heading south, anxious to put some distance between themselves and the expedition. They'd be missed, though not immediately, they hoped. And the expedition leaders would surely be anxious to press on rather than waste precious time searching for two junior members of the party.

Ambrose's hunting rifle proved its worth. Antelope were plentiful and a welcome supplement to their rations. It also took care of the odd wolf.

They had camped north east of Leh, secure in the knowledge that they were well clear of the expedition. Ambrose and Thakur Singh sat around a small fire drinking tea from tin mugs when the thud of hoofbeats and raised voices caught their attention. Thakur immediately stamped out the flames while Ambrose searched in his knapsack for his binoculars.

'I'll be damned,' Ambrose muttered. 'Russkis, Thakur. Cossacks by the look of them.'

They stayed low, hidden by rocks, and passed the binoculars back and forth.

It was Thakur who saw the tribesmen first, catching a flash of reflected sunlight from a sword blade, high on the cliffs above the Russians. The sword swung down, followed by the rumble of cascading rocks. As the dust settled, the grim tableau of the muleteers' murder and Cherkasov's desperate bid to escape played out in front of them.

Ambrose poured himself a cup of tea. His hand still shook, spilling some of the dark brown liquid into the saucer. His memory of that day was sharp. The recoil of his gun against his shoulder, the sharp crack and the reek of powder. The fear in the pit of his stomach and the sweat trickling down his spine. Not that he let it show. Stoicism and a stiff upper lip were the very essence of the code he lived by. Him and any self-respecting British gentleman.

Cherkasov, eh? In London. He put his cup down and crossed the room to his writing desk.

Chapter 20

George was at a loose end. His next visit to the Bedford Arms was still a few days away. Verity had dedicated herself to showing Jaqueline the sights of London. She'd already taken the child to look at Buckingham Palace and enjoy a walk in St James's Park. George scrutinised the long list of attractions she'd drawn up to visit during Jaqueline's stay.

'The poor child will be worn out within a week.'

'Nonsense, George. She'll be thrilled. Were you never young yourself? Everything seems so much brighter and exciting through a child's eyes.'

'I think some of these places on your list are more for your interest than hers. I mean, the National Gallery?'

'Just because you're a philistine yourself, don't assume that Jaqueline won't appreciate it.'

George raised his eyebrows.

'Very well, I concede that I'm looking forward to visiting some of these places. But what about Madame Tussauds? She's bound to love that. And the Zoo, we're going there on Friday. Come with us, George, better than moping around here.'

'Oh, I don't know, I was thinking of…'

'Save your lame excuses. I would very much like you to accompany me and my daughter to the Zoo.'

'Good afternoon, sir.'

Orpheus looked up from his armchair and gave a nod of acknowledgement.

'There's a letter for you,' the Traveller's Club servant said, extending a silver tray. 'Came by hand, sir.'

Orpheus picked it up. 'Thank you, Chivers. Bring me a scotch and soda, would you?'

'Certainly, sir.'

Orpheus scrutinised the envelope. He knew the handwriting. It unsettled him. He'd reported his unsatisfactory meeting with Carter to Lensch. His coded letter was sent on to Eulenburg in the diplomatic bag. This was Lensch's response.

The envelope remained unopened until Chivers returned with his drink. 'Thank you,' Orpheus muttered. When the servant left, he rose and stretched, twisting his neck from side to side as though to overcome some stiffness. The room was almost empty, he noted, save for two members in conversation at the far end, and old Sir Harley Fitzgibbon snoring gently in his seat by the fireplace. He opened the letter and produced a small black-leather code book from his inside jacket pocket.

Five minutes later, he studied the decoded message, then consulted his pocket watch. Two hours. Ample time to take a bath and compose his thoughts. At least there'd be no domestic complications to deal with. No need to concoct a tale as to why he had to go out that evening. Beatrice was in Sussex visiting her parents. The boys were at boarding school and she'd taken their daughter Florence with her. 'I may as well stay at the club while you're away,' he'd told her. 'There's a devil of a lot going on at work at the moment. It would save me having to go to and fro from Hampstead.'

She'd seemed to accept his reasoning, not suspecting that it would make it all the easier for him to be with Anna. No scandalous overnight absences for the servants to gossip about.

Lensch had chosen a very discreet private dining room in Mayfair for their rendezvous. The head waiter showed Orpheus in and closed the door after him. Lensch beckoned for him to take a seat and poured two glasses from the bottle of Dom Pérignon resting in an ice bucket beside them. 'I've ordered Dover sole to start and roast beef to follow. Good old English fare, eh Giles?'

Orpheus smiled and sipped his champagne.

He listened politely while Lensch prattled away about Berlin and a holiday he'd taken with his wife to Warnemünde on the Baltic coast. When the roast beef was served, Lensch got down to business.

'This difficulty with the Fenians that you reported. Why do you suppose that Carter was reluctant to tell you what he's planning?'

'It was more than reluctance. The man was downright aggressive.'

'But he said we'd know all about it in one month.'

'The whole stinking British Empire would know, is how he put it.'

Lensch concentrated on his beef for a few moments, chewing appreciatively and taking a gulp of his claret.

'He disclosed more than he intended to,' he said.

Orpheus nodded. 'That's why I had to contact you. It's the Jubilee. Carter and his Fenians plan to attack the Jubilee procession. That must be it.'

'Hmm. Unfortunate. That would upset our plans, of course. The details you supplied to me of the procession route and so on, could Carter also have obtained that information?' von Lensch asked, putting his knife and fork down and looking pointedly at Orpheus.

'Eh? What? You mean did I give them to him? What the devil are you suggesting, Erich?'

Lensch raised his eyebrows.

'No, of course, I damned well didn't. Why would you even consider the possibility?' Orpheus spluttered.

Lensch returned to his beef, leaving Orpheus to fume silently across the table.

'Giles, I'm not calling your loyalty into question,' he said at last, pushing his empty plate to one side.

Well, it certainly felt like it, Orpheus thought, but said nothing.

'It's a complication, of course, but in another sense it makes things simpler,' Lensch continued.

'How so?' Orpheus snapped, still smarting.

'It solves our dilemma about supporting the Fenians. Operation Geck cannot succeed if the Fenians go ahead. It matters not if the old Queen is blown to pieces or shot, but Russia must be implicated.'

'So the Irish plot must be stopped?' I've put my neck on the line to keep the authorities at bay and now what?' Orpheus demanded. 'What do you expect me to do now? Find a way of informing Quilter of the plot?'

'I think not. You will take no part in what must follow. Your value to the Reich is too great to have your position compromised. Carry on as normal. Carter doesn't expect to see you again, so keep away from him.' Lensch stopped abruptly as the door opened.

'Ah, here's our dessert, or should I say pudding?' he enthused, grinning at the waiter.

Plum duff was a step too far for Orpheus. He admitted defeat, leaving it half eaten. The champagne and the very acceptable Bordeaux they'd consumed produced a pleasant sheen of light-headedness, but it failed to mask the misgivings that he felt.

They went their separate ways on the doorstep. Lensch walked briskly towards his hotel. The Traveller's lay in the opposite direction, a walkable distance, but after rounding the street corner, Orpheus spied a cab.

'Where to, guv'nor?'

'Leicester Square.'

He needed time to think. The Fenian business didn't bother him. Let Lensch deal with it. It was this Operation Geck. If it succeeded. If everything went to plan. Britain and Germany would be allies. It was inconceivable. His life, everything he'd worked for since he was a student in Heidelberg, was for the Reich. To gain its rightful place as the pre-eminent world power. He'd picked his cause - scorned any allegiance to Britain, the land of his birth. And now there was the prospect of an alliance. He tasted the bitterness of disillusion.

He'd dreamt of victory, Germany ascendant and Britain humbled. Emerging on the winning side. Heaped with honours. Invited to Berlin. Now what? More time-serving at the Home Office. The distant prospect of a knighthood if he played the game. What had it all been for?

The cab slowed to a halt. He paid the cabbie and threaded through the crowd on the pavement. The performance had just finished. He ducked round to the stage-door. 'Oh. it's you, sir,' the doorman said, standing to one side.

He slid quietly into her dressing room, watching Anna change from her costume. She caught sight of him in the mirror and turned. Her face lit up, and Orpheus felt his mood lift. For a few scant hours, he'd evade his dark thoughts.

But they'd be back.

Chapter 21

'Look, Jaqueline, the chimpanzees, aren't they comical?' Verity called her daughter over to the primate enclosure. 'See how they leap about?'

The child skipped across and stood entranced, giving little squeals of pleasure, then recoiling in alarm when one of the creatures came too close.

'It's alright, *chérie*, it can't hurt you. Look, it's just being curious,' Verity reassured her, taking her hand.

George looked on. He'd enjoyed this outing despite himself. Jaqueline was unperturbed by his presence, immersing herself in the sights and sounds of the zoo. Verity seemed to be almost as enchanted as her daughter. He'd not seen this side of her nature.

At last, Jaqueline admitted that she was feeling tired and begged for an ice cream.

Outside the zoo entrance, they found an ice cream cart. 'Don't be such a stick in the mud,' Verity scolded him when he tried to decline the offer of a cornet.

They found a bench nearby and sat in companionable silence. To the casual passer-by, they looked like any married couple enjoying a day out with their daughter.

George gazed into the middle distance, letting his mind wander. He'd managed to avoid spilling the melting ice cream on his waistcoat. As he popped the last of the cornet into his mouth, a violent outbreak of barking and snarling jolted him out of his introspection.

Across the road, a Staffordshire terrier took strong exception to a passing dalmatian. The terrier let fly with staccato, high-pitched barks, straining at its leash, paws scrabbling on the pavement. The object of its fury, bemused by the aggressive flurry of the smaller dog, took a step back and looked up at its owner for reassurance.

The terrier took the dalmatian's hesitation as a sign of weakness and sprang forward only to be half-throttled when its owner, a solid young man, tugged hard on its lead, cursing. The dalmatian, gaining confidence in the knowledge that its would-be assailant was restrained, gave a low growl and started barking itself. Its deeper notes, combining with the increasingly frenzied yelps of the terrier, attracted the attention of everyone within earshot. A small crowd of onlookers started to gather, only to disperse when the dalmatian's keeper, a tall, bespectacled fellow, dragged it away and walked off muttering angrily. The terrier barked a few parting shots until it, too, was brought to heel and marched away.

Jaqueline clung to her mother as the scene unfolded. George was about to suggest that they move away when something else drew his attention. Beyond the dogs, leaning against the outer wall of the zoo, was a lanky young chap in a crumpled grey suit with a dark cloth cap sitting high on his forehead. At first it was the fellow's posture that struck a chord, then George took in the thin, sharp face and sunken cheeks. He'd seen him before, propping up the bar in the Bedford Arms, joining in with the Republican marching songs.

George cursed inwardly. He'd let his guard down. There could be no doubt about it. That was one of Carter's men. Had he been under observation from the moment he'd left Carter at the pub?

He kept the knowledge to himself. 'Is it time to take Jaqueline home?' he asked. Verity nodded, bending to wipe a smear of ice cream from the child's cheek with her handkerchief.

At Montagu Square, Verity opened her front door and Jaqueline scampered down the hall towards the kitchen. 'It's Elsie's baking day,' Verity explained to George. 'There are bowls and spoons to lick.'

'Go through to the drawing room, George. I'll ring for Elsie to bring tea and some of that delicious cake I can smell.' Verity followed, scooping up a letter from the hall table.

'Ah, it's from Ambrose.'

***

He put down the cloth and examined his boots with satisfaction. His grandfather was a stickler for a clean pair of boots. 'You must polish them until you can see your face in them, Joseph,' he'd instructed his young grandson. 'You can tell a sound man by the shine of his boots, so you can.'

Another week of chalk dust and grumbling schoolboys lay behind him. Another week that brought him closer to the action he craved. He put the boots aside and reached into his jacket pocket, extracting the playing card, a five of hearts, cut diagonally in half. A white envelope with the other half of the card inside was waiting on the hallstand when he'd arrived home. So, the Captain would be calling. And surely this time there'd be no talk of standing by.'

Edna O'Leary had called at the fishmongers near the Archway. She didn't always adhere to the church's strictures for fish on Fridays, but today she fancied a bit of cod. The white envelope that she'd found on the doormat meant that there'd be an extra one for supper that night.

Carter seemed more than usually preoccupied. She served the fish with parsley sauce, some tender new potatoes and garden peas. The two men ate quickly, with hardly a word, anxious to get down to business. With a mumbled thank you, Carter pushed his empty plate to·one side and waited in silence while Joseph mopped up the last of the sauce with a piece of potato.

Their footsteps retreated along the passage to the front parlour. Edna cleared the plates and stacked them on the draining board. The washing up wouldn't take long once the kettle had boiled. Then she could have a cup of tea and do a spot of darning.

She was just contemplating a second cup when she heard the scrabbling. Putting the half-darned sock to one side, she shuffled to the back door. 'Come on in then, Ajax.'

The ginger tomcat gave a gruff miaow and sauntered past her, tail up. 'I've got some nice little scraps of cod here for you,' Edna said, opening the larder door and reaching for the old chipped saucer she used for the cat's food.

Ajax looked up and sniffed as Edna lowered the saucer to the floor. She'd just settled back down again when the cat licked up the last of the fish and scampered off along the passage to the front door, where it set about scratching furiously at the paintwork.

'Drat that cat,' Edna muttered under her breath. She'd taken pity on the pathetic creature when it turned up thin and bedraggled on her doorstep, six months past. It was Joseph that called it Ajax. Ajax, indeed. Ungrateful nuisance, more like it, was Edna's verdict.

She let the cat out and turned back to the kitchen. The parlour door was open a crack. She didn't know why she did it. She knew full well what brought Carter to the house. Fenian business. She was a proud Irishwoman herself and happy to be doing something useful for the cause, but she'd always kept well away when the men were talking. It's not as if she set out to eavesdrop. She'd only stood there for a few moments.

Carter's voice was little more than a whisper. She only made out a few phrases before she tip-toed quietly back along the passage. 'It's time… tell the school… here is the place… say nothing to Edna, mind – just that you're going back to Dublin.'

Chapter 22

'I think that's him now,' said Mortimer. Olivia put down her novel and smoothed her skirt.

'Hello, Ambrose, we're here in the parlour,' Mortimer called out.

'My, what a fine evening. Isn't new mown grass the most exquisite smell? Sorry if I'm a bit late. Stopped on the drive to watch a murmuration of starlings. What a spectacle. Quite enchanting.' Ambrose entered breezily, shaking Mortimer's hand and bending to kiss Olivia's cheek. 'You look more beautiful every time I see you, my dear.'

'And you look very sprightly, Ambrose. It must be all that time you spend outdoors. There can't be a square inch of the estate that you haven't traversed. Only last week I saw you over at Carson's spinney when I was exercising Tanglefoot.'

'Ah, there's life in the old dog yet,' Ambrose chuckled. 'I say, Mortimer, the old throat's a bit dry.'

'I have just the very thing.'

Mortimer crossed to the sideboard. Olivia rose and stood next to Ambrose. They watched expectantly as he lifted the bottle of champagne resting in a silver ice bucket, grinning at one another in anticipation and applauding the satisfying pop of the cork.

Mortimer poured and handed the glasses round.

Ambrose narrowed his eyes. 'Celebration?'

Mortimer's smile said it all.

'Ambrose, you are the first to know that Olivia and I are expecting a child.'

For the first time that Mortimer could remember, Ambrose was almost lost for words.

'Oh… g-good Lord. Marvellous, simply marvellous. Congratulations, heartiest congratulations to you both,' he chortled, hugging Olivia and pumping Mortimer's hand furiously.

'Steady, old chap,' Mortimer warned. 'Let's not spill the champagne before we've drunk a toast. Now then, here's to a healthy young Mallard.'

The gong signalled dinner.

'And I'm the first to know? What an honour,' said Ambrose, taking his place at the table.

'We'll write to Olivia's parents and Verity tomorrow, of course, but we couldn't keep the news to ourselves any longer.'

The evening passed in a flash. Buoyed by the excitement of the occasion, in no time, it seemed, the plates were being cleared away. Ambrose had partaken liberally of Mortimer's wine, which only served to boost his good mood. Olivia wished him a good night and squeezed his hand. 'Time I retired.'

The men stood as she left the room. 'One for the road?' Ambrose ventured.

'Very well,' Mortimer said warily. 'But only one. I have estate business to deal with in the morning.'

They settled into armchairs. Ambrose took an appreciative sip of his port and put the glass down. 'I've some news of my own, as a matter of fact.'

Mortimer listened in astonishment as Ambrose informed him of the letter he'd received from Verity and recounted the tale of how he'd 'come across this Russki fellow', in the treacherous, breathtaking wilderness of the Karakoram ranges. Ambrose always took a certain delight in romanticising his time in India. Truth and fantasy were cunningly interwoven and Mortimer had long given up trying to distinguish one from another.

This story was of a different order, however, and, because Verity had met the Russki in question, there must be more than a grain of truth to it.

'What a remarkable coincidence. This Cherkasov being in London and meeting Verity,' said Mortimer.

'Could have knocked me down with a feather when I read Verity's letter. I can't leave it at that, you know. I'm going up to London to see the fellow. Not every day you save someone's life. Creates a sort of bond, I suppose.'

'Yes, I dare say, it does. When are you leaving?'

'Monday. Strike while the iron's hot, eh?'

'You could stay with Verity. Jaqueline's there with her, I gather. You'll have a chance to meet her.'

'Ah. I'll put up at a hotel. It seems Verity has a bit of a houseful at the moment, what with Jaqueline *and* George.'

'George. What the devil is George doing there?'

'Oh, I assumed you knew. Verity said in her letter that George was staying at Montagu Square. Didn't say why, old chap.'

'No, it's the first I've heard about it. Seems as if her brother is the last person she chooses to confide in,'

Mortimer grumbled. 'Well, can you call by and deliver a letter to her? About the baby. At least Olivia and I do not harbour secrets,' he added irritably.

***

On the express to Paddington, Ambrose shared a compartment with a group of clergymen, all gaiters and frock coats, attending an ecclesiastical gathering at Lambeth Palace. Having what he regarded as a healthy disdain for organised religion, Ambrose produced a rather racy novel he'd taken to pass the time and buried his nose in it to discourage the reverends from engaging him in conversation.

He'd only managed half a page before his thoughts drifted back to the extraordinary events of 1873. He and Thakur Singh kept their word and made no mention of their encounter with Lieutenant Cherkasov and his troop of Cossacks. It was less a matter of honour than one of self- preservation. Their only concern was to get safely over the Kashmir border and lie low.

They had no idea whether a connection had been made between their sudden absence from the expedition and the disappearance of a quantity of valuables, but they took no chances. They stayed for a month in Srinagar with a cousin of Thakur's, then made their way by degrees to Bombay. At no time did they disclose their involvement with Sir Douglas Forsyth's expedition to Kashgar.

And then, it had all gone wrong. Thakur set about selling the items they'd stolen, boasting of his many business connections. At first, all seemed well. Two precious artefacts made a decent sum, which they shared fifty-fifty. And then nothing. Thakur disappeared with the rest of the treasure and, to add insult to injury, he also purloined Ambrose's treasured Gibbs-Farquarson.

His hopes of having enough money to set himself up in some style were dashed. He sank back into the precarious way of life that characterised the whole of his time in India.

Cherkasov must have done well for himself, however. A General, according to Verity's letter. Oh well, good for him.

When he alighted from the train at Paddington, he realised that the whole carriage must have been occupied by clergy. They milled about on the platform with their luggage, obliging the other passengers to thread their way past. Ambrose found his path blocked by an awkward black-clad fellow whose suitcase appeared to have fallen open, strewing items of clothing onto the floor. He stood by while the cleric scrabbled about clumsily, frustrating his efforts to step around the man.

'Excuse me, could I just squeeze past?' Ambrose asked politely.

There was no response until Ambrose tapped him on the shoulder and he looked up.

The clergyman scrambled to his feet. 'You,' he said accusingly.

Ambrose hadn't seen the Reverend Wilfred Timmins, erstwhile curate at Holy Trinity in Flaxminton, since he'd left the parish several months earlier, much to the satisfaction of the Mallard family. Timmins' disgraceful behaviour towards Mary Phillips two Christmases ago had neither been forgotten nor forgiven.

His unprepossessing appearance and his disconcerting habit of bobbing his head up and down and fidgeting from foot to foot were just as Ambrose remembered them. He also remembered with satisfaction the way he'd humiliated the odious fellow while performing his Christmas party piece, accidentally knocking the curate to the ground in front of the whole Mallard household.

'You,' Timmins repeated agitatedly, spittle flying from his mouth.

Ambrose had the perfect response to hand. 'Jabberwock!' he blared into the man's face, shouldering him aside and setting off down the platform, beaming. My word, won't Verity have a jolly good laugh when I tell her?

Chapter 23

While Ambrose passed through the ticket barrier at Paddington, George kept his appointment with Carter at the Bedford Arms. It was two thirty when he pushed open the door to the public bar, half an hour after the appointed time, deliberately calculated to show Carter he wasn't intimidated.

The barman swivelled his eyes in the direction of the snug and George headed that way, acknowledging the greetings of one or two of the patrons that he'd drunk with on previous visits. He hesitated for a moment at the door, took a deep breath and stepped inside, closing it behind him.

He remembered how gloomy the place had been on his last visit, but now it was even more forbidding. Curtains covered the snug's windows. The gaslights on the wall were unlit; the only source of illumination was an oil lamp on the table where he'd faced Carter previously. He hesitated by the door while his eyes adjusted to the semi-darkness.

There were three of them. Stern. Silent. Their faces, reflected in the yellow lamplight, looked strangely disembodied. No Mulchay, George noted. He recognised Carter by the glint of his pince-nez. The two men on his right shared similar features. Fair hair in thick curls, and ruddy cheeks. Though their bodies were in shadow, the thickness of their necks bespoke strength and bulk.

'Do you not possess a watch, Brendan?' Carter broke the silence.

'More traffic than I allowed for,' George replied.

'Do you suppose that we have nothing better to do than to sit here waiting for you?'

George didn't respond. He left the door and approached the table, taking a seat facing Carter and his henchmen. 'Look…' he began. The last thing he knew was the click of Carter's fingers and the sharp explosion of light in his brain before his limp body keeled over onto the floorboards.

'Is he out cold, Dermot?' Carter asked. Dermot took the oil lamp and held it close to George's face. 'Aye, he's out alright. Still breathing, though,' he replied, grinning.

'Now then you two,' Carter ordered the curly-haired pair next to him, 'get him gagged and bound, then help Dermot to carry him out to the cart. I'll go on ahead.'

***

George had no idea of how long it had been since someone had bludgeoned him. The cloth gag between his teeth cut into the sides of his mouth but didn't cause as much discomfort as the cords that bound his hands behind his back and tied his ankles together.

Cart wheels rumbled on the cobbled road. His cheek juddered against the rough timber floor of the conveyance, and his nostrils were filled with the pungency of the oilcloth covering him. An attempt to roll-over to relieve the stiffness in his legs was rewarded with a sharp kick in the ribs. Twin emotions contended with one another: fear, and a visceral hatred of the man who had put him in such peril. Not Carter. Quilter.

George's anger sustained him until the cart reached its destination. It must still be evening, according to the tiny chinks of light showing at the edges of the oilcloth. He was still somewhere in London, he calculated.

He blinked as the oilcloth was pulled to one side. Strong hands grabbed his ankles and hauled him towards the rear of the cart. He knew that face, the same one he'd seen outside the zoo. Other hands grasped his arms on either side and helped to place him on his feet. It was the curly-headed duo from the Bedford Arms.

The horse and cart stood in a courtyard enclosed by high, soot-stained red brick walls. The gate through which they'd entered was shut and barred. He swivelled his head. The three-story building behind him must be a warehouse, he thought, noting the openings on the upper floors and the pulley mounted under the roof with a metal hook dangling from it.

The flash of a knife almost unmanned him. His heart pounded as the zoo man approached, then knelt to cut the rope from his ankles. His hands remained bound as his captors pushed and prodded him to the warehouse door.

Inside was a cavernous expanse of stone floor with rough timber beams supporting the floor above. He saw a staircase, grimy brick walls and an oblong wooden table standing in the centre with three chairs ranged behind it, and a single chair facing it, ten paces away.

'Hold him here, Dermot,' said one of the curly-headed pair. 'We'll go up and get the Captain.'

Dermot roughly untied the gag. He pointed to the solitary chair and shoved his captive towards it. 'Dermot, eh?' said George. 'I hope you know what you're getting into here.'

'Just sit.'

George complied. He sensed Dermot standing directly behind him, heard him breathing.

The thud of boots descending the stairs rebounded from the bare walls. The same trio that George had faced in the pub seated themselves facing him.

Carter reached into his jacket and placed a revolver on the tabletop. George recognised his own gun.

'The defendant will stand,' Carter intoned.

'Defendant? What the hell is going on here?'

Dermot grabbed him roughly by the collar, pulling him upright. 'Shut your damned mouth or I'll shut it for you,' he threatened.

'This tribunal is in session,' Carter announced. 'I will now read the indictment. The defendant, George Benson, stands accused of espionage and conspiring against the Irish nation.'

George's heart plummeted. He'd harboured the hope that his abduction might be some sort of test. A way to gauge his mettle, perhaps. He'd become increasingly confident about his assumed identity as Brendan Hogan. Thought he'd fooled them. How the devil did they uncover his deceit?

'Do you deny that your real name is George Benson?' Carter asked.

'I'm Brendan Hogan from Boston.'

Carter laughed, his companions joining in. 'You may as well drop the American accent, George. Oh, it sounds convincing enough. I'll grant you that. No doubt you congratulated yourself on fooling us Irish simpletons. But, you see, George, the joke is on you. Go on, guess how we found you out?'

'I'm Brendan Hogan,' George persisted doggedly, fighting the looming hopelessness he felt.

'Think back, George. That reception you attended at the Russian Embassy. Good night, was it? How were you and your companion announced? Miss Verity Mallard and Mr George Benson, that was it. How do I know? Well, that little string quartet in the corner. I'll bet you hardly noticed them, did you? The cello player is an old friend of mine from Dublin. He goes to the Bedford Arms once in a while. So, there he was, playing at the Russian Embassy, when in walks a man who's the image of that rich American standing drinks at the pub. Oh, he thinks, it's that Brendan Hogan, but then out comes the name George Benson.'

The game was up. George knew it.

'Who are you working for? Would it be the Special Branch? Or maybe it's Quilter. You know who I'm talking about, don't you, George?' Carter sat back, legs outstretched under the table. He took out his handkerchief and polished his pince-nez. 'Take your time, George. We're not going anywhere.'

George looked down at his feet.

Minutes passed in silence.

Carter replaced his spectacles and took out his pocket watch, placing it on the table.

The unnerving silence stretched out. George concentrated on breathing rhythmically, striving to suppress the rising tension he felt, clasping his bound hands tightly to keep himself from shaking.

Carter reached for his pocket watch and snapped it shut. 'Ten minutes. You've had your chance, George. Since you've chosen to say nothing in your defence, it only remains for me to pronounce sentence.'

George looked up sharply. 'Sentence? Listen here, Carter, or should I say O'Brien?' he called out defiantly, reverting to his normal accent. 'This is not a court. You're just a bunch of Irish thugs playing at soldiers. Whatever you're planning, you'd be wise to get out now before you're hunted down. Don't think the authorities aren't on to you. If I go missing, they'll know where to find you.'

He'd barely noticed Dermot in his peripheral vision when a vicious punch to his stomach had him doubled up and fighting for breath.

'The prisoner will remain silent while sentence is pronounced,' Carter exclaimed. 'Put that gag back, Dermot,' he commanded.

George's attempt to spit the gag out earned another crushing blow. He fought the urge to vomit. Dermot pulled him upright and forced him to face his accusers.

'The sentence of this tribunal is death,' Carter pronounced.

George glared at him.

'I had a very good friend. The best of men. The bravest of men,' Carter continued, his voice cracking with emotion. George listened uneasily, wondering where this was heading.

'You British put him to death. Just twenty, he was. I stood with his mother on a bleak winter morning outside the gates of Kilmainham Prison as they posted the notice of his execution. And I vowed to that poor woman and before God himself that I would avenge him.'

Carter paused, composing himself. 'They kept him in the condemned cell for seven days. Seven days of mental torture. Seven days hoping for a reprieve that never came. Then they marched him to the scaffold and murdered him. Seven days, George Benson, seven days to contemplate your miserable end. That's enough talk. Pat, Cormac, help Dermot to take him down to the cellar.'

The curly-headed duo rose from the table and gripped George's arms.

Chapter 24

Ambrose was in the best of spirits. Fortified by a hearty breakfast at the comfortable Paddington hotel he favoured on his occasional forays to the capital, he set out on foot for Montagu Square. His letter to Verity had warned her to expect him at 10 am. No doubt she'd invite him to stay for lunch, he thought. After that, he'd go on to the Russian Embassy.

Elsie answered his knock on the door. 'Good morning, Elsie,' Ambrose chirped, 'you're looking extremely well, if I may say so.'

Elsie stepped back. 'Go through to the drawing room, Mister Mallard,' she announced primly. Although he'd visited the house in Montagu Square on several occasions, Ambrose had never succeeded in eliciting anything other than the most formal of responses from Elsie. He saw it as a challenge. Reaching into his pocket, he withdrew a tin of Turkish Delight, hoping that a small token of friendship might soften the housekeeper's stiff demeanour.

She gazed expressionlessly at his outstretched hand. 'For you,' he said. For several moments, an embarrassing silence prevailed. Ambrose was on the point of returning the tin to his pocket when Elsie reached out hesitantly and took it. 'Thank you,' she whispered, spinning on her heel and hurrying away down the hall. Her face betrayed no hint of a smile, but her eyes told a different story.

The drawing room was unoccupied. Ambrose took a seat, expecting to hear Verity's footsteps in the hall at any moment. Minutes passed with only the ticking of the carriage clock on the mantelpiece to disturb the silence. It chimed the quarter hour. Still nothing. He rose and stationed himself at the window, observing the comings and goings in the street.

Ambrose gave a start at the sound of her voice.

'Hello, Ambrose.'

He turned round. Something wasn't right. Her greeting lacked the brisk confidence she habitually displayed. And her posture - the slumped shoulders, the downcast expression, spoke of a troubled mind.

'Verity. I say, are you quite well?'

'Well? Yes, of course I'm well,' Verity bristled. 'Sit down Ambrose, please.'

She took a seat facing him.

'How are things in Thorneycroft?' she asked after an awkward silence.

'Ah, things are very well. Very well indeed,' Ambrose replied, taking Mortimer's letter from his pocket.

He watched Verity's face as she opened the envelope and read its contents.

'Goodness gracious. Why, that's wonderful,' she exclaimed. 'How thrilling. The honeymoon wasn't wasted,' she added mischievously.

Ambrose wondered whether he'd misread her mood. This was more like the Verity he knew.

'They are both delighted, of course, and speaking of letters, yours was quite astonishing. Cherkasov. Here in London. How remarkable. A General?'

'Yes, and quite dashing, I must say. From our brief conversation, I gather that you and he were engaged in some clandestine adventure. You've never mentioned it before. What on earth were you up to, Ambrose?'

'Ah, that's a story for another day. I'm off to the Russian Embassy later. Perhaps I'll indulge your curiosity after I've met the fellow. And what of your other news? Young Jaqueline is here you wrote.'

Verity smiled. 'Yes, she's having the most marvellous time. Just remember Ambrose, that she's here as the daughter of my French cousin, Brigitte, as far as the world at large is concerned.'

Ambrose nodded.

'She's complaining of an upset stomach this morning, so I've kept her in bed. Come back tomorrow. I'm sure she'll be feeling better by then, and you can tell me all about your meeting with General Cherkasov.'

'Assuming I do meet him. I'm calling at the Russian Embassy on the off chance. Thought I'd surprise him. You also mentioned George Benson in your letter. Staying here, you said. Of course, it's none of my business really, but... why?'

A shadow seemed to pass across Verity's face. She became once more the worried soul he'd seen framed in the doorway.

'I shouldn't have mentioned it. It was a foolish oversight.'

'Oh, well, if there's something going on between you, you needn't elaborate. I'll be the soul of discretion, except…'

'Except what?'

'Except, I told Mortimer and Olivia about it. It never occurred to me that it might be a delicate matter.'

'Oh heavens. Ambrose, there's nothing going on between George and me. He'd laugh at the notion if he were here.'

'So what is this all about, Verity? You're troubled. It's perfectly obvious that something is amiss.'

***

'We're here, guv'nor,' the cabbie called out.

Ambrose remained lost in his thoughts, unaware that the hansom had reached its destination.

'Russian Embassy,' the driver shouted louder.

Ambrose stirred himself. Stepping stiffly on to the pavement and paying the fare. He stood in Chesham Place gazing dully at the embassy building, still striving to absorb what Verity had told him.

'George is missing,' she'd said nervously, rubbing her hands together in her lap. And then the whole tale had spilled out.

Ambrose winced at the mention of Quilter's name, recalling the way the Colonel had insinuated that he'd killed Bert Figgis that fateful night at Larkford Grange.

Militant Fenians. George impersonating an American sympathiser, and Verity even becoming involved. Ambrose heard her out in astonishment.

'He didn't come back last night, Ambrose. He went to meet them at a public house. Their leader calls himself

Captain Carter. They're planning something dreadful, some atrocity. George thought he could learn more about their plans. If they've discovered that he's working for Colonel Quilter, they won't hesitate to…' Verity choked on a sob. 'Oh dear, I shouldn't be telling you this,' she continued haltingly. 'I shouldn't involve you in this business, I know, but I have to tell someone. Am I being foolish, Ambrose? He could turn up at any moment, I suppose.'

'Not involve me? That would certainly be foolish, my dear. I count George as a friend. I admire him. After all, aren't the three of us comrades in arms after that Larkford Grange business?'

'Yes. Of course.'

'Very well. Then you must inform Quilter, without delay. He put George in danger. Therefore, he must take responsibility.'

Ambrose accompanied Verity to the nearest post office. The telegram she sent was terse –

GB MISSING. HELP. ADVISE SOONEST. VM.

Back at Montagu Square, they shared a bleak lunch, neither of them having any appetite to speak of. Ambrose offered to abandon his visit to the Russian Embassy.

'Nonsense, Ambrose. You must go. Come back here afterwards and tell me all about it.'

The embassy concierge took his card and asked him to take a seat. Ambrose hardly had a chance to take in the grandeur of the vestibule with its imperial trappings: an elaborate coat of arms with the black double-headed eagle at its centre, the white, blue and red of the massive State Flags suspended from the ceiling, and the life-sized portraits of the Tsar and Tsarina, when the concierge returned. One glance at the man accompanying him was enough. Though dressed in a dark civilian suit, there was no mistaking his military bearing and, despite the passage of time, Dmitri Cherkasov's features were instantly recognisable.

He came forward, grinning. 'What a wonderful surprise. Ambrose Mallard. The man who saved my life all those years ago.'

'When Verity wrote to tell me she'd met you here in London, I couldn't believe it. I simply had to come and see you for myself,' Ambrose replied, grasping Cherkasov's hand and shaking it vigorously. 'A General now, I gather.'

Cherkasov nodded. 'Embassies are not my preferred habitat. I am only here for a short time, then I must return to St. Petersburg.'

'Ah, not too soon, I hope. I thought we might have an opportunity to talk over old times.'

'And so we shall. Today, I fear that my time is not my own. How would the day after tomorrow suit? Come to dinner. As my guest. I insist. And bring Miss Mallard along. My conversation with her was all too brief. A charming lady.'

Chapter 25

'Stay there, Ambrose,' Verity commanded, shutting the door behind her and hastening to the hansom cab that had brought him back from the embassy to Montagu Square. She called out an address to the cabbie and seated herself next to Ambrose.

'Did you see General Cherkasov?'

'Yes, and he…'

'Never mind that now. Tell me about it later, after we've seen Quilter.'

'Oh, he's responded to your telegram?'

'Yes.'

Ambrose read her mood. They sat in brittle silence, barely aware of their surroundings as the cab threaded its way through the streets. Then, when the tension became almost unendurable, he felt her hand on his, light at first, then gripping him with a desperate ferocity.

The building off the Cromwell Road was suitably anonymous. Heavy dark blinds covered the ground-floor windows. At the front entrance was a small brass plate bearing the inscription:

B. R. Samson

Importer

Verity tugged at the bell-pull. The faintest of tinkles sounded within. She and Ambrose waited at the door, listening for the sound of footsteps. Abruptly, a small grille opened at eye level. 'State your business,' a harsh voice demanded.

'We're here to see Colonel Quilter.'

'Names.'

'Miss Verity Mallard and Mr Ambrose Mallard.'

The grille was slammed shut. A moment later, the door swung open, giving them a view of a sombre, dimly lit hallway and the ramrod straight figure holding the door open. Over six feet tall, with close cropped grey hair and a craggy face overlaid with deep frown lines, he pointed to the staircase halfway down the hall. 'First floor, second door off the landing,' he barked, shutting the door to the street.

To Verity's surprise, the room in which they found Colonel Quilter was almost homely, quite unlike the austere surroundings which she'd imagined. His desk faced a window overlooking the street, but the centre of the room contained four comfortably upholstered chairs ranged around a low mahogany table. The floor was covered with a large rug in an elaborate Persian design.

On either side of the fireplace, alcoves contained shelves filled with books and exotic *objects d'art*. What most caught her attention, however, was a large framed photograph of a family group, the Colonel in dress uniform stood next to a slender woman dressed in white, accompanied by three children, a boy and two girls ranging in age from ten to fifteen or thereabouts. The three of them looking confidently at the camera exuding youthful high spirits. But it was the woman that left the most striking impression. The face with its prominent cheekbones, flawless complexion and cool gaze marked her out as a great beauty.

Colonel Quilter rose from his desk. 'Miss Mallard, Verity, please take a seat,' he said gravely. 'Mr Mallard, I'm pleased to make your acquaintance again. Ambrose, isn't it? Please sit down.'

Ambrose thought back to the last time he'd faced the Colonel. Then, he'd been intimidated by being reminded of his rather murky past in India. Not that the Colonel knew the half of it, just enough to put Ambrose at a disadvantage.

'I'll get straight down to business,' the Colonel said. 'Much as it pains me to say it, we must assume that George Benson's true identity has been discovered by Carter and his associates, or at least they know that he is not a visiting American named Brendan Hogan.'

Verity had come with the intention of accusing Quilter of playing fast and loose with George's life. To vent her anger at the man. Wanting him to share in the pain that she felt. Needing someone to blame. But somewhere along the way from Montagu Square, her anger had burnt itself out. It was too exhausting to maintain. She realised that the only hope of saving George lay in cooperation, not confrontation.

'What now?' was her only response.

Colonel Quilter did his best to mask his surprise. He'd fully expected a furious broadside and had steeled himself to face its full force with humility, however alien that emotion was to him. He looked at her with a mixture of relief and admiration.

'Now, my focus is on moving heaven and earth to discover the whereabouts of Carter and his gang. My men have already raided the house in Greenland Road, where we believe Carter was living, and the premises in Camden High Street.'

Verity leaned forward. 'And what did you find?'

Quilter sighed. 'Precisely nothing. The house contained a bare amount of furniture but no personal items. No clothes and no papers or anything that might provide a clue as to Carter's present whereabouts. At Camden High Street we found only a room containing a desk and two chairs.'

Verity studied the Colonel's face and saw only dejection. 'So George could be anywhere in London, or somewhere outside London for that matter,' she said.

Quilter nodded.

'Surely there must be something you can do, some avenue of enquiry?'

'I've posted a watch on the public house, The Bedford Arms, but I can't imagine Carter would be fool enough to show himself there. George's abduction has forced me to show my hand. Carter will be in no doubt that George was working for me. I'm deeply sorry, Verity.'

Verity sat stony-faced. The slim hopes she'd nurtured that Quilter would have an answer, a way forward, shrivelled and died. 'Moving heaven and earth indeed?' she said caustically. 'It's hopeless then,' she added in a whisper.

'I don't believe it.' Verity and the Colonel turned to face Ambrose. 'It's not hopeless.' He insisted. 'There must be a chink in this fellow Carter's armour. Now then Colonel, think. Is there anyone or anything you haven't considered in all this?'

'No, I don't think so. Believe you me, I've done little else but run over all sorts of possibilities in my mind. These Fenians operate in small groups. The only name we know for sure is Carter's. George did mention someone called

William who asked him questions about Boston, but I doubt that he was a direct associate. But…'

'But what?'

Quilter hesitated. 'It may be nothing, so I urge you not to get your hopes up. The one other person that comes to mind is James Mulcahy. He's the one who befriended George at The Bedford Arms and brought him into Carter's orbit. But he's a dreamer. He's no stomach for action and Carter would never have him in his inner circle. I'm certain of that.'

'Then why mention the fellow?' Ambrose snapped.

'Because he's the only link we have. It's a long shot, but Carter might still have some use for Mulcahy. '

'So your men keep tabs on Mulcahy and there's a slim chance that he'll lead you to Carter?'

'Yes, Ambrose. But there's one fatal flaw in such a plan. The reason I involved George in this business was because there's a traitor within my organisation. I dare not use my own men.' Quilter shook his head in frustration.

'Hmm. Yes, Verity did explain that to me. We're stumped then,' Ambrose shrugged, glancing dejectedly at Verity.

Verity listened to the two men distractedly, her mind still numb with the hopelessness of the situation, until a glimmer of an idea brought her back to earth. 'How easily you men admit defeat,' she declared.

Their expressions, eyebrows arched in unison, struck her as quite comical.

'For heaven's sake, it's obvious, surely. Your men can't be trusted, Clarence, but we know who can?' Still, the penny hadn't dropped.

'The Cotton brothers,' she pronounced, stifling the urge to scream.

'Aha,' Ambrose exclaimed, slapping his knee. 'Of course. There you are, Colonel. Clarence, eh?' he added mischievously.

'I see. Very well. Where do I find them?' asked Quilter.

'You don't,' Verity insisted. 'They have no reason to trust you. Ambrose and I will deal with them.'

'But…'

'No buts, Clarence. My mind is made up.'

Chapter 26

Lensch shook the rain from his umbrella. A steady patter of raindrops dripped from the edge of the church portico under which he sheltered, but here and there shafts of sunlight found gaps in the clouds. Given the fickleness of the weather, he'd forsworn his favoured meeting place in St James's Park and instructed Riemann to meet him here instead.

Riemann's solid frame came into view, crossing the road, shoulders hunched and a cloth cap pulled well down. Lensch turned away and entered St Martin in the Fields. He heard Riemann's heavy tread following him as he led the way up to the gallery. Whereas the nave below was filled with a variety of folk, some seeking spiritual sustenance and others finding the church a convenient spot to shelter from the rain, the gallery was empty.

Lensch shuffled into one of the polished, dark wooden pews and waited for Riemann to join him. The two men sat, heads close together, as though in prayer.

'So, Riemann, you have found suitable premises?'

'I have, Major. I considered several places along the procession route. Only two give a clear line of sight, within range, but not too close.

The one I've chosen is a private house, a shabby tumbledown place. The old woman who owns it is in poor health, half-deaf. She only uses a few rooms. Most of the place is empty – apart from rats.'

'What did you tell her?'

'That I wanted to buy the place. She's not quite right in her mind. I don't think she understood. But I offered her twenty pounds to allow me access to make a survey. I'll need to come and go, I told her. And now, I've got this,' Riemann announced, producing a heavy iron key from his pocket. 'The shooting site will be up in the attic. I'll get it ready and take the Dutchman up the day before.'

'Are you sure this old lady won't cause problems? Ask awkward questions?'

'I doubt it. She just seemed mighty pleased with the money. I'll butter her up when I call there. Take her food and little gifts. Listen, Major, if she does get troublesome, there's no one that would miss her, if you get my meaning.'

Lensch dismissed Riemann and sat alone. Riemann's preparations for the Jubilee were proceeding to plan. He could report back to Eulenburg with confidence on that score.

He turned his mind to the matter of the Fenians. Carter's arrogant dismissal of Orpheus rankled. After all that Germany had done to help their cause, the man had the audacity to treat his ally with disdain. On the other hand, Lensch had to admit that in Carter's position, he'd have acted in the same way. He'd not risk jeopardising an operation to spare someone's feelings.

But he'd also have been more careful than Carter to cover his tracks. A ghost of a smile crossed his face as he recalled that morning's events. The address above the undertaker in Camden High Street was all he had to go on. The place where Orpheus met Carter from time to time.

His expectations were low. Carter would surely have cleared out of there and removed any incriminating information.

It was pure chance that he'd arrived when he did. He alighted from the hansom cab fifty yards away, allowing him to observe the place before approaching. Almost immediately, a cab drew up directly outside, disgorging three men. Lensch crossed the road and sat on a bench at an omnibus stop. Not given to strong emotions, he clinically analysed the plusses and minuses of the situation, thanking providence for the quirk of fate that had brought him there at that precise moment. A little earlier, and he could have been discovered in Carter's den by the men now making their way inside the premises. He'd no need to guess what their business was, for he recognised one of them from a photograph that Orpheus had given him. Colonel Clarence Quilter. Mingled with the relief he felt, however, was the frustration of knowing that Quilter and his men were engaged in searching the place. In the unlikely event that Carter had left some clue behind, it would be Quilter, not Lensch, who found it.

Worse still was the question of how Quilter knew of this place. That thought really worried him. It was the place set aside for meetings between Carter and Orpheus. Surely, there could only be two explanations. Either Quilter had discovered Orpheus's connection with Carter or Orpheus had turned traitor and betrayed Germany. He fought to clear his mind and concentrate on the scene in front of him.

When Quilter and his men emerged a mere ten minutes later, it seemed to Lensch that they'd discovered nothing. Quilter paced irritably up and down the pavement, muttering to his men until they boarded a cab and left the scene. The German watched until it became lost in the traffic, then crossed the road and entered the door next to the undertakers. He climbed the stairs and stepped nimbly past the glass doors of the secretarial agency, his footfalls masked by the clatter of typewriters. The corridor ahead turned through ninety degrees and ahead of him he saw the name Carter affixed to a half-open door.

A desk stood with its drawers open. Empty. A revolving leather chair stood next to it and a second chair of dark bentwood lay tipped over on the floor. That was all. Lensch felt under the drawers and looked underneath the desk to be thorough, but found nothing. He grunted and sat on the edge of the desk, reaching into his jacket pocket for his cigarette case.

Taking the smoke deep into his lungs, he brooded. There was no ashtray. Lensch was a fastidious man. He walked to the window and opened it, flicking a half inch of ash from the tip of his cigarette out into the enclosed yard below. He stood idly looking down at the grey cobbles beneath for a minute. There was not much to see, a couple of pieces of broken furniture lying against the back wall of the yard and...

Lensch was not built for rapid movement, but within forty seconds he'd traversed the corridor, descended the stairs and found the door to the yard. The rusty old brazier, which had caught his attention, stood in a corner close to the back wall of the building. He smoked the last of his cigarette as he crossed the yard and stood over the brazier. His eyes had not deceived him. There was something in there. Mostly ashes, but something more. He grimaced as he extended his gloved hand to take hold of a heavily singed notebook with a hard dark green cover. Most of it was reduced to ash, but the rest had somehow survived the flames. He shook it gently to detach the charred portion and slipped it into his jacket pocket.

The sound of the church organ brought von Lensch back to the present. He rose from his pew and headed for the stairs.

Chapter 27

George woke as a rat scuttled across the flagstones. He rubbed his eyes and spied its tail as it squeezed through the gap under the door of his cell. Not a cell by design, but a storeroom down in the warehouse basement. He took out his pocket watch and checked the time. Just over 24 hours he'd spent in there. They'd searched his pockets and taken everything from him. But Cormac had returned with his watch later.

'Captain Carter wants you to have this back,' he'd said with a gloating smile. 'D'ye want to know why?'

George took the watch in silence.

'Well, I'll tell you. He wants you to… feel the passage of time, as he put it. The time you have left, ticking away. Isn't that a grand thought? Tick, tick, tick.'

George got to his feet unsteadily. His ribs still ached from the punches he'd endured. After the sentencing, they'd dragged him away, down a rickety flight of steps. In the gloom of the basement, Dermot took the lead, holding an oil lamp aloft. They passed along a brick-lined corridor with heavy wooden doors at intervals. Near the end of the corridor, Dermot unlocked a door, standing to one side while Pat and Cormac shoved George inside.

The three of them became his jailers, taking turns to bring him a plate with half a small loaf with a hunk of cheese, and a tin mug of water. That had been his supper last evening and the same for breakfast. Since then, nothing. He looked at his watch again. Seven o'clock.

He'd experienced some grimly uncomfortable spots in his army days, but nothing as daunting and hopeless as this. Five paces from side to side and six from the door to the window. That was it. All he had was a threadbare blanket to wrap around himself at night and a bucket in the corner. He'd avoided using it as long as he could, but had to relieve himself eventually. The one saving grace was the window, set high in the wall. Barred and out of reach, it nevertheless admitted some daylight through its grimy panes.

Footsteps sounded in the corridor. He turned to face the door as it swung open. There were two of them: Pat and Dermot.

Dermot put his supper on the floor and picked up the old plate and mug.

'Time to get rid of that stinking mess,' Pat grunted. 'Pick that bucket up.'

George looked from Pat to the bucket and back again.

'If you'd rather spend the night with that thing overflowing, it's fine by me,' Pat said.

George took hold of the bucket's handle and lifted it carefully.

'Come on then,' Pat ordered, stepping back into the corridor and picking up the lamp he'd left outside.

George followed, treading slowly and deliberately to avoid spillage. 'Get a move on,' Dermot growled, bringing up the rear.

At the foot of the stairs, Pat turned into an open doorway. The room beyond was a little larger than

George's cell. It was empty save for a bench fixed to the far wall.

'Over there,' Pat pointed.

In the corner, George saw an opening, a hole six inches across with a brass tap protruding from the wall above it

George tilted the bucket carefully and emptied its contents into the hole. Pat turned the tap on for a few moments.

They took him back to his cell and Pat pushed him roughly inside. 'Now then,' he said. 'one more thing until we bid you good night.' He moved to the wall nearby and produced a stick of chalk, scratching seven vertical marks on the brickwork. 'See those. That's seven chalk marks for the seven days until we carry out your sentence.' He returned to the first mark and drew a diagonal line through it. 'Only six days to go now, though,' he added, grinning.

The door closed behind them.

George sat on his blanket and ate his meagre supper. Dusk gave way to night. In the darkness, he imagined the revenge he'd take if he ever emerged alive. A bullet through Carter's brain first. But most of all, he wanted to see the look in Quilter's eyes as he slowly choked the life out of him.

***

Joseph packed his valise. He'd not need much, just a change of clothes. It had been quite a day. He recalled the thunderous look on the headmaster's face when he said he was leaving forthwith.

'What? Today? Now? Without notice. Disgraceful. I've never heard the like. I'll tell you now, you'll never work as a teacher again, Maguire.'

Joseph had let him rant, marvelling at the deep purple flush spreading across his face. When he finally took a breath, Joseph said calmly, 'It's my father. The telegram from Father Coghlan said he's only got forty-eight hours. My mother collapsed with the shock of it. I'm all she's got, you see.'

The memory of the headmaster's slack-jawed expression made him chuckle as he closed the valise and took a last look around his bedroom.

All he'd said to Edna was that he was going back to Dublin. He had another story to tell if she asked why. But she just wished him a pleasant journey. Strange. He'd expected her to at least say that she'd miss him, or something like that, if only from politeness. But no. Oh well, never mind that. The time had come at last. He had his orders.

He padded softly downstairs to the front door and gripped the doorknob.

'Joseph,' Edna's voice was little more than a whisper.

He turned sheepishly.

She crossed the hall, wiping her hands nervously on her apron. 'I'm sorry if I was short with you earlier. I've enjoyed having you here. I really have, Joseph. But…'

'There's no need, Edna, I…'

'No Joseph. Hear me out, please. I'm not a fool. I know you're here for the cause. That Captain Carter and you. Those meetings you have in the front room. So, you needn't tell me you're going back to Dublin. You're off to do whatever it is that Carter called on you to do.'

'Edna, be careful now. It's none of your business. Don't go getting yourself involved in things that don't concern you.'

'Oh, but they do concern me. I'm as proudly Irish as you or that precious Captain. But do you know what you're getting into, Joseph? You're a fine young man with your life ahead of you. I wouldn't want to see you throw it all away.'

'If you really cared about the cause, you would not speak to me that way,' Joseph bristled, anxious to get on his way. 'Goodbye now, Edna.'

He didn't turn round.

Edna stood in the doorway until he reached Archway Road and turned the corner.

'God be with you,' she whispered.

Chapter 28

After they left Quilter's office, Verity prevailed on Ambrose to quit his hotel and move to Montagu Square. 'I need you close at hand, Ambrose. You can take George's room for now.'

She waited in the cab while he quickly packed his things and paid his bill. 'I'm sorry, Ambrose, but you won't have time for supper. We'll take your portmanteau to Montagu Square, then you must take the cab on to Covent Garden.'

'What? Eh?'

'To the Lamb and Flag. It's a public house. George mentioned that's where he would go to meet Alfie Cotton. You must go there tonight. I'll stay and tend to Jaqueline. You will go, won't you?'

***

The pub was packed when he got there. He pushed his way through the drinkers in the front bar. Alfie wasn't among them. The small back room was filled with a garrulous crowd engaged in a heated discussion about the relative merits of Spurs and Clapton Orient.

'Have you seen Alfie Cotton?' Ambrose asked one of them.

'Alfie? No, haven't seen him. Oi, anyone seen Alfie?' The man shouted out to be met by a general shaking of heads.

Ambrose was at a loss. He moved back into the front bar, thinking to find the landlord. The place was even more crowded than when he'd entered. He inched towards the bar, doing his best to avoid jostling the drinkers in his path and had almost reached it, when he stumbled over a small dog hidden in the forest of legs. Awkwardly striving to regain his balance, he cannoned into a man in the act of raising a full tankard of beer to his lips.

A hush descended as the fellow surveyed the dark stain of porter soaking into his waistcoat and the crotch of his trousers. Though shorter in stature than he, the man's broad shoulders and solid, muscular build put Ambrose on his guard.

'My dear chap, I'm so sorry. Please allow me to buy you another tankard of beer,' he offered.

The man put his half-empty tankard on the bar and slowly turned. Ambrose thought fleetingly of beating a hasty retreat, but the crowd of drinkers hemmed him in. No one spoke.

The man's face was expressionless. Somehow, it unnerved Ambrose more than a look of anger. His eyes narrowed and Ambrose gasped as the fellow's right hand clamped itself around his throat. He struggled to breathe, grasping the man's arm with both hands in a vain attempt to break his assailant's grip.

'P-please,' he stuttered, on the verge of losing consciousness. Blood pounded in his brain as his vision faltered.

'Here. I know you, don't I?' The man released his grip and Ambrose collapsed onto the grimy floorboards.

The man's face filled his field of vision. Strong arms lifted him to his feet.

'Well, I'm blowed. If it ain't Mister Mallard. Ambrose, ain't it?'

Ambrose gazed dully back, rubbing his throat. That voice. Yes, of course. 'Benny? Alfie's cousin? Benny the…'

'Ha. That's right. Benny the Bastard,' the man laughed. 'We showed em that night in Larkford Grange, didn't we, guv?'

Ambrose pictured the night when Benny and his cousins, Alfie and Dick Cotton, had helped to rescue Mary from the clutches of Anthony Spencer and his gang.

'Come on Ambrose, let's find you a seat so you can get your breath back,' Benny said, taking Ambrose gently by the arm. The crowd parted. Two men seated at a table in the corner of the bar looked up as Benny approached and quickly gave up their seats.

'Two pints over here,' Benny shouted over his shoulder.

He took a seat opposite Ambrose. 'Well, this is a right turn up and no mistake. Fancy you just 'appening to come in here,' he shook his head, grinning.

Ambrose managed a weak smile, continuing to massage his throat.

'I'm sorry I cut up rough.' Benny's grin became a look of concern. 'If I'd known it was you…'

Ambrose found his voice. 'No apologies necessary, old chap. Really, it's quite alright. You see, it wasn't simply a coincidence that I…' He paused as a barman placed two tankards on the table. 'I came here in the hope of finding

Alfie, you see, and it's a stroke of luck that I bumped into you.'

They both laughed.

'Can you take a message to him?'

'Yeah, course. What's it about?'

Ambrose watched Benny's good humour drain away as he outlined George's predicament. 'Can you ask him to come tomorrow?' Ambrose asked, giving Benny Verity's address.

'I'll get him there tomorrow or my name's not Benjamin Hopkins,' Benny replied, draining his tankard.

***

Alfie Cotton sat awkwardly, balancing a cup and saucer on his knee. His brother Dick and cousin Benny adopted similar poses sitting next to him on Verity's chesterfield.

'Thank you so much for coming so soon,' Verity said, sitting forward in her armchair. 'And all three of you. Are you really sure you can spare the time? I know it's asking a great deal.'

'Miss Mallard,' Alfie placed his cup and saucer on the side table at his elbow. 'There's no need to ask. We're here for George and it don't matter how much time it takes. If he's still in London, we'll find him and when we do, those Fenians better look out.'

'Look, Alfie,' Ambrose interjected, 'all we need from you is to find them. Colonel Quilter can do the rest.'

Alfie gave a thin smile. 'Quilter, eh? Well, I don't know about you, but I wouldn't trust that beggar any further than I could throw him. Now then, what's the plan? Where do we start?'

Verity resumed control. 'Trust him or not, he represents the Government. Let's not forget that this is not just about George. These Fenians are a threat to the state. Where do we start, you ask? With this man.'

Verity withdrew a photograph from her reticule and handed it to Alfie. 'That's James Mulcahy. Colonel Quilter obtained it from the Metropolitan Police.'

'Been in trouble with the rozzers, has he?' said Alfie. 'Doesn't look like he'd have it in him.'

'Arrested twice for being drunk and disorderly, I gather,' Verity explained. 'He's hardly a master criminal. But he likes to associate with the Irish republican fraternity, and he's a regular at the Bedford Arms. We need you to keep an eye on him. Follow him and see who he talks to. You already know what Carter looks like, but he's gone to ground. It's only a slim possibility, but maybe Mulcahy will lead us to Carter and, therefore, to George.'

Chapter 29

Bertie belched and patted his expansive stomach. It had been an hour since tea. The poached eggs and several slices of cake he'd devoured left him feeling bloated, but dinner was almost three hours away and no doubt he'd do it more than justice.

Alone in his study at Marlborough House, he gazed with satisfaction at the printer's proof of the official programme of the Royal Jubilee procession. The handsome document delighted him. Priced at one shilling, the proceeds would go to The Prince of Wales Hospital Fund for London.

He thumbed through its pages, pausing to study the map of the procession route wending its way from Buckingham Palace to St Paul's via Constitution Hill, Piccadilly, Pall Mall, Trafalgar Square, the Strand, Fleet Street and Ludgate Hill. Thence returning by crossing the Thames at London Bridge and along Borough High Street, St George's Circus, Westminster Bridge, Horse Guards and the Mall.

He imagined the thousands upon thousands of people lining the streets. Not just Londoners, but subjects from every corner of the nation and the Empire.

The order of the procession consumed his attention for fully twenty minutes. Page after page of the programme listed the participants in order of march. It was as though the Empire in miniature was on display to escort the monarch. At the head of the procession, Captain Oswald of the Life Guards, and the tallest man in the British Army, would have the honour of leading mounted troops of the Home forces: Dragoon Guards, Hussars and Lancers, in serried squadrons, and batteries of Royal Horse Artillery.

The Royal Family and members of the household would pass by the cheering crowds in a procession of sixteen carriages.

Next would come the Colonial Premiers from Australia, Canada, New Zealand, Rhodesia and South Africa, escorted by their own mounted troops and followed by cavalry of the Indian Army.

And then, at last, Her Majesty, the Queen Empress, in the state landau, with Bertie himself and the old Duke of Cambridge riding alongside her.

A glorious spectacle befitting a reign of sixty years.

***

Elsie cleared away the cups and saucers after the Cottons and Benny had gone. Verity waited for her to leave the room and turned to Ambrose.

'So now we wait. Heavens Ambrose, I feel so useless just sitting here hoping that something will turn up.'

'We've done all we can, my dear. Fretting will do nothing to help George. At least we have a plan of action. We must trust in Alfie.'

Verity said nothing, gazing vacantly into space.

'Ah, there is something I haven't told you,' Ambrose said abruptly.

'Yes?'

'My visit to Cherkasov. He's invited us to dinner at the embassy.'

'Really, when?'

'Tomorrow.'

'Oh. But how can we go out to dinner while George…'

'For heaven's sake. Our attending dinner with Cherkasov will hardly affect George's plight. Would you rather we sat here in gloomy contemplation? Come on, Verity, buck up. It's not like you to wallow in self-pity.'

He struck a chord. Verity gave him a hard look, then stood up. 'You're right, Ambrose. It is most unlike me. We will certainly take up his invitation. Now, the clouds are lifting. Let's stir ourselves and take Jaqueline for a walk in the park.'

***

Lensch placed his attaché case on the table. His hotel room was hardly suitable to examine the notebook he'd retrieved from the brazier.

In an office he'd commandeered at the German Embassy, he sat at a heavy mahogany desk with the notebook in front of him. Before being consigned to the flames, he estimated it would have measured some 20 cm by 12 cm. It retained its full thickness of 1.5 cm, but only a rough triangle, less than half its original size, had survived.

He'd bought a pair of tweezers and a small magnifying glass on his way from the hotel. With the aid of the tweezers and the penknife he habitually carried in his pocket, he bent over the notebook and set to work. Painstakingly, he teased the cover open and started separating the pages.

It was an awkward business. He concluded that It must have rained on the smouldering notebook, preventing its complete destruction but complicating the task of peeling its pages apart.

His frustration grew with each page. There was nothing. Just blank white paper streaked with ash. Ten, eleven, twelve half-burnt pages revealing nothing at all. A dull ache nagged in the small of his back. Discouraged, he sat up, arching his spine to relieve the discomfort, and reached for his cigarette case.

Lensch always maintained that smoking aided thinking. A third of his cigarette had burnt down, and he was exhaling a long plume of smoke when the idea struck him. Extinguishing his cigarette, he flipped the notebook over on its back and coaxed the penknife blade under the back cover. It was firmly stuck. He breathed heavily, applying all his concentration to the task. Bit by bit, the cover yielded.

Finally, he succeeded. His idea had been sound. The empty pages he'd first encountered must have been at the back of the notebook. He set to with renewed purpose. As the tweezers and knife did their work, fragments of writing appeared. Page after page. He resisted the urge to read the writing until he came upon blank pages again. Then he picked up his magnifying glass.

Passing through the embassy gates, he couldn't resist a triumphant twirl of his cane

Chapter 30

What had he expected? Joseph sat quietly at the table, mopping up the last of his soup with a crust. He'd felt a thrill of anticipation when he received his orders from Carter. And, though he'd never admit it, a laxity in his guts when he'd left Edna standing there in the doorway.

Whatever he'd been expecting, the reality of his surroundings lacked any sense of glory. Neither did his comrades match his concept of dedicated fighters for freedom.

His arrival at the warehouse had not been auspicious. 'Be there on the dot,' Carter had commanded, 'and wait at the gates.' A sudden downpour caught him in the open, two streets away from the warehouse. He could have sheltered in the doorway of a nearby pub, but that would make him late. The torrent didn't let up. Joseph put his head down and ran, gripping his valise and clamping his other hand onto the crown of his bowler. By the time he'd covered half the distance to the warehouse gates, the rain had found its way down the back of his neck and his tweed jacket clung heavily around his shoulders. His trousers and boots fared worse as he splashed through pavement puddles and murky rivulets flowing along the gutters.

Heedless by now of the clinging discomfort of his sodden clothes, he covered the final fifty yards, wheezing and grunting. The gates loomed above him. He leaned against the peeling green paintwork, gasping. Three minutes early, according to his wristwatch. He couldn't just wait there, exposed to the relentless downpour. A push confirmed that the gates were locked. He knocked, grazing his knuckles on the rough timbers. He kicked the gates, scuffing his shoe leather, harder and harder, then stopped to listen, hearing nothing beyond the drumming of the rain on the cobbles. Now, by his watch, the appointed time had passed. Why, in heaven's name, did Carter not open the gates?

Joseph turned around, scanning the street, looking for something – a brick, a cobblestone, anything solid to hammer against the gates. There was nothing. He turned back, almost crying in anger and frustration, at the instant the left-hand gate opened.

A scowling face, not Carter's, appeared, and a hand grabbed him roughly by the lapels, dragging him inside. The gates were slammed shut and Joseph found himself being marched across a courtyard to an open doorway.

'Hey, there's no need to push,' he protested.

His only answer was a sharp dig in the back.

That was three hours ago. Carter had shown him no sympathy. His wet clothes were draped over the back of a couple of chairs and set in front of a fireplace in one of the small rooms occupying one end of the first floor of the warehouse. The fire produced more smoke than heat, and Joseph stared dully at it as he chewed his crust. The indignity of sitting at the table dressed in his spare set of underwear was somewhat alleviated by the loan of an old overcoat that Carter had grudgingly given to him.

'There now, are you feeling better with that soup inside you?' the man sitting next to him asked. Joseph nodded, offering a weak smile to Cormac. Across the table sat Pat and next to him, the man who'd grabbed him at the gates. Dermot laughed, 'Mother of God, Joseph, you looked like a drowned rat, so you did. A picture of misery. Come on man, buck up, you're a New Immortal now, not a fussy schoolmaster.'

A New Immortal? Men like these? In Joseph's imagination, the fighters for the republican cause would be people like himself. Idealists and intellectuals. Nothing like these three rough-and-ready characters.

Carter sat at the head of the table puffing on a pipe. He'd said little to Joseph since his arrival. He took the pipe from his mouth and pointed the stem at him. 'You have a good night's sleep, my lad, because now you begin a new life. You wanted action, well now you'll get it. This place is our headquarters. This is where you'll learn to handle explosives. There, I said you'd get the chance, didn't I. These three will be your teachers. Just do as they tell you. The great day is not far off and until then you'll live, breathe and sleep here with us. Oh, and there's one thing more. You can take a turn at guarding our guest down in the basement.'

'Guest. What guest?'

Carter chuckled. 'You'll find out soon enough.'

***

His second night in the cell was an agony of wakefulness until fatigue finally claimed him. George dreamed of Effie and woke to the awful reality of his predicament. Mental anguish and physical discomfort tormented him equally.

The itchy stubble on his face, the friction of crumpled clothes against unwashed skin, and the mingled miasma of sweat and the contents of the bucket in the corner compounded his misery.

It took an effort of will to gain control over his emotions - to keep despair in check. If there was to be any hope of deliverance, he'd need a clear head.

It was Pat who brought his breakfast. The same bread and cheese, but staler. They didn't speak.

Physical and mental stimulation. That was it, he thought. By midday, he'd counted all the bricks in his cell, then repeated the exercise to see if the numbers agreed. They didn't. He thought back to his school days, trying to recall the names of his fellow pupils, with some success. Poems came next. *The Charge of the Light Brigade*, a favourite from his boyhood.

Half a league, half a league,
Half a league onward,
All in the valley of Death
Rode the six hundred.

The opening stanza came readily. A brief pause for thought, then the rest of the first verse followed. In fits and starts, verse two unfolded. Then his memory failed. There were snatches, something about sabres flashing, the jaws of death, and the mouth of hell, he could recall, but nothing more.

What else? Milton? He could envision his English teacher, Mister Matthews, declaiming *Lycidas* in front of the class, but he remembered not a single word. Finally, he settled on Wordsworth. To his delight, he had *I Wandered Lonely as a Cloud*, complete and word-perfect at the first attempt. He repeated the feat three times. Then he tried,

Composed upon Westminster Bridge. That was his true favourite. It took some effort, but he mastered it. There must be more, he thought, but they'll keep for tomorrow.

***

'Five hundred and twenty-five,' George whispered to himself. The number of circuits of his cell he'd completed. He looked up at the grime-smeared window above his head. Still quite light. Six minutes to seven, his pocket watch revealed. His stomach gurgled.

He sank onto his blanket, resting his head on his knees. What he'd give for a bath, or even just a bowl of water and a shave.

'Bejesus, I've smelled better pig sties, so I have.'

George didn't bother to raise his head at the sound of Cormac's voice.

'See, Joseph, this is what you're fighting against. Georgie here's a British spy. Look at him and think how the likes of him would put all our heads in a noose if he had his way. Ha, but here's the thing. It's him who'll be dancing a jig at the end of a rope. Come on and give him his dinner.'

George looked up. The man in the doorway hesitated, then crossed the room. Joseph, Cormac called him. Youngish chap, round-faced, clean-shaven, slicked black hair, and a diffident look. He offered George the plate and tin mug he held in his hands.

'Just put them on the floor, man. You're not his bloody servant,' Cormac ordered.

Joseph hesitated, then stepped back and deposited the items at George's feet.

'There you are, not so hard was it,' said Cormac dismissively. 'Now, it's mucking out time. Come on Georgie, get up off your arse and grab that bucket,' he added, prodding George with the toe of his boot.

George shuffled down the passage after Cormac and emptied his bucket into the drain. When he arrived back at his cell, Joseph still stood there. He turned as George appeared in the doorway and shuffled to one side, avoiding George's gaze.

'Come on then, Joseph, time for our own dinner,' Cormac said from the doorway. 'But first, there's this,' he added, holding up a stick of chalk.

Joseph took it and turned to the chalk marks on the wall, scribing a diagonal line through the second of them.

'Just five days left now, George,' Cormac gloated.

Chapter 31

Verity spent the entire day with Jaqueline. She felt guilty at the thought of leaving the child alone with only the servants for company while she and Ambrose attended the Russian Embassy. They lunched together at Fortnum's, followed by a visit to Hamleys. The look of amazement and joy on Jaqueline's face as she wandered through the vast toy emporium brought a lump to Verity's throat.

Jaqueline settled for a Steiff bear and a fascinating hand-painted toy theatre with movable scenery and a troupe of masked *commedia dell'arte* figurines in a wonderful array of colourful costumes. They were delivered that afternoon and Jaqueline offered no protest when asked if she would be happy to amuse herself until bedtime.

'Oh, no, *Maman*, I will not be alone, for I have all these new friends,' she said, hugging the bear and pointing to the theatre.

***

A liveried servant led them through the vestibule and along a brightly lit corridor hung with gilt mirrors and oil paintings. They turned a corner and proceeded along a narrower passage until he stopped at a door, opened it, and held out an arm to usher them inside.

An intimate setting greeted Verity and Ambrose. The room, illuminated in soft candlelight, contained a table set for dinner, and four chairs. Four? Verity had assumed that only she, Ambrose, and Cherkasov were dining.

'My dear Miss Mallard, how delightful to meet you again. I'm so glad you could come,' said Cherkasov, stepping out from her left. He bowed to kiss her hand and turned to welcome Ambrose. Rather than the full dress uniform he'd worn on the evening of the reception, he was in mess dress. It suited him, Verity thought.

'As you can see, there will be four of us for dinner,' Cherkasov continued. 'I believe that you and Miss Jesenska are already acquainted.'

From the opposite side of the room, Anna Jesenska materialised out of the shadows.

'Verity. How wonderful to see you again,' Anna said, bestowing a kiss on both her cheeks in the continental fashion. 'And you are Ambrose Mallard. I've heard so much about you from Dmitri, Anna pronounced, offering her hand. 'You are quite the adventurer, I understand.'

'*Enchanté*,' Ambrose bowed to kiss her hand with a flourish, finding her directness mildly disconcerting but damned alluring, nonetheless.

Verity thought back to the last time she had seen Anna. The night of the Embassy reception. It was Anna who introduced her to General Cherkasov and Verity had concluded that there was some personal connection between them, possibly a romantic one. But then she'd left with that other chap. What was the name again? Giles Temple-Swift, that was it.

'Ambrose and I will bore you both to distraction over dinner with tales of our adventures,' Cherkasov chuckled.

'Now, let us be seated. A glass of champagne.' He clicked his fingers to summon a servant to fill their glasses. 'And then you must try the caviar. The finest, Beluga.'

Boring it was not.

Cherkasov and Ambrose were back on that dusty plain. Young men on a knife edge, absorbed in the mechanics of loading, aiming, and firing. The rocks were at their back and the tribesmen advancing. The crackle of gunfire and the sharp tang of gunpowder filled their senses. Were they ever so gloriously alive?

The two women listened politely, spectators to an outpouring of martial sentiment as old as time. Cherkasov recounted the landslide and his flight from the tribesmen in sober terms, omitting the cutting down of the two unfortunate muleteers. Most of all, he talked of the relief and gratitude he felt at his deliverance.

In contrast, Ambrose indulged his fondness for florid language and dramatic turns of phrase, likening their action against the tribesmen to the heroism of the Spartans at Thermopylae. Not content to rely on words alone, he mimed aiming an imaginary rifle and bellowed, 'Boom! Boom!' as he squeezed its trigger. So absorbed was he that several minutes went by before he realised that Cherkasov had fallen silent, regarding him with affectionate amusement along with Verity and Anna.

'Oh,' he said sheepishly. 'Getting a bit carried away, was I?'

'Ambrose, you were magnificent,' Anna clapped her hands in appreciation.

'Ambrose has a talent for melodrama,' said Verity. 'What surprises me is that he's kept this remarkable tale to himself. You dark horse, Ambrose. What else have you been keeping secret?'

For once in his life, Ambrose hesitated to respond. He had no qualms about playing the black-sheep of the family. He enjoyed it. But he could hardly admit to the theft of expedition property. Being thought of as an amiable rogue was one thing, admitting to a base criminal act, quite another.

'My dear, the circumstance under which Dmitri and I were thrown together was the one instance of derring-do in an otherwise dull and worthy existence,' he inclined his head modestly.

Verity snorted. 'But…' she persisted.

'Ladies, Ambrose, if I may,' Cherkasov interrupted. 'A toast. To brothers in arms.'

'To brothers in arms.'

Cherkasov and Anna steered the conversation on to more conventional topics.

Dmitri satisfied Verity's curiosity about the court in St. Petersburg. Yes, the Winter Palace was every bit as grand as Verity imagined.

'I had the great honour of being presented to the Tsar and Tsarina only three months ago,' he declared.

'Hmm. What do you make of him?' asked Verity.

'Make of him? He is the Tsar. I would not presume to make anything of him, as you put it. I merely serve him.'

'He is an autocrat. Surely, as we stand at the threshold of a new century, absolute rule is nothing more than an anachronism,' Verity warmed to her theme. 'Do the Russian people not deserve a say as to how they are governed?'

Cherkasov inclined his head. 'Russia is not England. Our histories are quite different. We have a deep spiritual connection to the motherland, and the Tsar is the embodiment of that connection.'

Verity arched her eyebrows. 'Bravo, dear General, spoken like a true patriot. But you and I know that is a romantic fiction. Like it or not, there are forces at work throughout Europe. Social democracy is the future and if the Tsar stands in its way, it may sweep him aside.'

Cherkasov smiled and held up his hands. 'Have mercy, Miss Mallard. I bow before the force of your convictions. No doubt we could spend the whole evening sparring, but I propose a truce.'

'Oh Dmitri, just as I was enjoying our joust, you run up the white flag.'

'No, no, dear lady. I said a truce, not surrender,' Cherkasov laughed.

'At the risk of seeming frivolous, may I mention that Hedda Gabbler opens in one week's time?' Anna entered the conversation.

'Oh goodness, of course, the play. I really would love to see you and Mary performing. I must ask, Geo...' Verity stopped in mid-sentence.

'Do you mean Mr Benson? Why yes, of course, you must bring him along. I fear he may have thought me rude that night at the reception, departing as I did. Would he come, do you think, or does the theatre not interest him?'

Verity and Ambrose looked at one another in confusion.

'I'm sorry. Have I said something amiss?' Anna asked.

Verity blanched. 'Er, no, no, of course not, it's...'

Ambrose held up his hand. 'One moment please, Verity.' He turned to Cherkasov, 'Dmitri, back then, you asked a favour of me. Do you remember?'

'Yes, I remember. I asked you to keep our encounter secret. I had no right to do so, especially after you saved my life.'

'And I was happy to agree. I've kept the secret ever since. Now it is my turn to ask a favour of you.'

'Name it.'

'I won't be offended if you refuse. After all, you have your duty as an officer to consider.'

'My dear Ambrose, I can see that you and Verity are both troubled. If there is anything that I can do to help, I will be happy to do so. You have my word that anything you tell me will not go beyond this room. And you may also rely on Anna's discretion.'

'Thank you Dmitri. Verity, I think it's for the best. Tell them – about George.'

Haltingly, Verity unburdened herself. George's clandestine activities with the Fenians. His apparent acceptance as a republican sympathiser. The shock of his sudden disappearance and the grim realisation that he must have been abducted, all came out.

As she spoke, the spectre of Colonel Quilter's wrath and the possible consequences of divulging such information to anyone, let alone foreigners, weighed on her, but she pressed on. Bottling up her fears was more than she could bear.

'They have him. Somewhere, they have him. I feel so helpless.' she said despairingly.

Ambrose looked on, sharing Verity's pain, nodding encouragement when she found it difficult to continue. He also observed Dmitri and Anna. Gauging their reactions. Their faces were pictures of concern, but there was something more. Their frequent glances at one another, something in their eyes, gave the impression that they held secrets of their own.

Anna rose and placed her hands on Verity's shoulders to comfort her.

Cherkasov spoke softly to her in Russian.

Anna returned to her seat. 'Verity, Ambrose,' she began, 'you have placed your trust in us and we must now place our trust in you. This business that George Benson has become involved in, we are already aware of it.'

Verity jumped to her feet. 'What? You know about it? How? For heaven's sake, what is going on here?' she shouted, looking frantically at Anna and Cherkasov.

Ambrose interrupted before her agitation got the better of her.

'You will need to explain yourselves,' he said firmly.

Anna looked questioningly at Cherkasov. 'Go on,' he mouthed.

She took a deep breath. 'First of all, let me assure you that we knew nothing of George's involvement until you mentioned it, Verity. No, we are as shocked as you by that news. However, the existence of a Fenian plot here in London was already known to us. I will explain. You know me as an actress, and, of course, I am. But I have done many things in my life, unconventional things, things which might seem shocking to ordinary, respectable people. Cast your minds back to the night of the reception. The man I left with. I am his mistress.'

'Oh,' Verity blurted out, despite herself. She didn't think of herself as an ordinary, respectable person, but Anna's candour surprised her.

Anna smiled. 'To be clear, Giles Temple-Swift thinks of me as his mistress. But I am in no way kept by him, you understand. My motives are quite different.'

'Anna serves her country,' Cherkasov interjected.

'A spy,' said Ambrose. 'Is that it?'

'If you wish,' Anna conceded. 'Let's dispense with niceties. I am involved with him for one reason only. To discover information. Giles has an important position. A pillar of the establishment. Is that the correct English expression? He would not be the first man to let his guard down in the embrace of an attentive woman.'

'But what can this Temple-Swift fellow have to do with Fenians?' Ambrose asked.

'I can only tell you that I discovered some sheets of paper in his coat pocket. Scribbled notes really. It seems that he has been in contact with a leading Fenian, someone called… '

"Carter!" Verity exclaimed.

'Yes, that's right.'

'But why? Why would this pillar of the establishment, as you refer to him, consort with an enemy of the state?'

Anna shrugged. 'I found some notes that he had written. They mention a Captain Carter and plans to undertake a campaign of bombings. Look, the gist of what I read leads us to believe that Giles may somehow be in league with Carter.' Anna stopped, looking uncertainly at Cherkasov.

'I think we should leave it there,' Cherkasov pronounced. 'You will appreciate, Verity, that we are accountable to our masters. We have told you as much as we can.'

'But how does this help to find George? It tells us nothing other than that this Giles Temple-Swift could be playing some duplicitous game,' Verity protested. 'We must find out where George is being held.'

'There was mention of an address in Camden High Street,' Anna volunteered.

'Oh that. We know about that. He's not there. It's a dead end,' Verity snapped. 'Oh dear, that sounded ungrateful,' she added quickly. 'Do you mind me asking, are you still seeing this man?'

Anna nodded. 'Yes, I am still seeing him. And before you ask, I will inform you if anything comes to light that could help you find Mr Benson.'

***

It was hardly the evening that they'd expected. What had started so promisingly as a jolly reunion of two ageing men reliving the excitement of youth had taken a dark turn. Verity and Ambrose sat side by side, lost in their own thoughts as their cab rattled over the cobbles on their way back to Montagu Square.

Ambrose broke the silence. 'Should we tell Quilter about this Temple-Swift fellow?'

'I'm not sure. We don't really know what he's up to, do we? All Anna said was that she'd found some notes in his handwriting mentioning the Fenians. If he is up to something and Clarence Quilter goes charging in with his size tens, he could simply clam up or concoct some convincing tale.'

'Let me think it over. Perhaps Anna can find out more.'

At the embassy, Dmitri loosened his collar and blew a column of cigarette smoke towards the ceiling. 'Not quite the evening I'd been expecting,' he said in Russian.

'Perhaps we should have said nothing,' Anna mused.

'Perhaps,' answered Dmitri. 'However, now we can be sure that something serious is afoot. I've heard of this Colonel Quilter that Verity and George Benson are involved with. It means the British are taking this very seriously, but if these Irish revolutionaries are hell-bent on stirring up trouble again, it's all one to us. God knows we have enough trouble dealing with our home-grown enemies of the state. The question is why is Temple-Swift involved with them? He's an Englishman to the core, isn't he?'

'One who speaks German in his sleep,' Anna said.

'Really? What does he say?

'Nothing intelligible. He sometimes babbles in his dreams.'

'When are you next seeing him?'

'Tomorrow.'

Chapter 32

The Bedford Arms opened at ten thirty in the morning. Alfie took the first watch from when the doors opened until two o'clock, when his brother, Dick, took over.

Alfie went home for a slice of cold mutton pie and a mug of strong tea. He put his feet up in the front parlour and read the paper until a knock on the front door made him put it aside and shuffle to the window to see who it was.

'What yer got?' He let his caller in and shut the front door behind him.

'A few bits and pieces. 'Ouse in Wimbledon I've been keeping an eye on. Managed to slip inside the back door while the servant girl was 'anging out the washing. The old lady was snoring in the parlour so I nips up the stairs all quiet like and goes through her dressing table.'

Alfie led the way along the passage to the kitchen. 'Let's 'ave a butchers then,' he grunted.

His caller rummaged in the pockets of his grimy overcoat. Withdrawing one fistful and then another and spreading the contents on the kitchen table.

'There. Some nice pieces, ain't they? Fetch a bob or two, they will,' the man said eagerly.

Alfie extended an index finger, separating the items of jewellery into two piles, one much smaller than the other.

'Just grabbed 'em and stuffed 'em in your pockets, did you, Stan?'

'Well, I couldn't 'ang about could I.'

Well, see, this lot's just cheap stuff,' Alfie sniffed, pointing to the larger pile. 'Can't 'elp you with that. You may as well give it to your old mum.'

'Nah. Look. Them's diamonds,' Stan insisted, picking up a silver necklace set with stones.

'They're paste, me old china, and that's not silver neither.'

Stan looked crestfallen.

'Now then,' Alfie continued. 'These ain't too bad. The small pile in front of him contained a cameo brooch, a pendant with garnets and moonstones, two pairs of pearl earrings and a gold signet ring. I can take these off your 'ands. Let's say two quid the lot.'

Stan stared at him, slack-jawed. 'Two quid! Two lousy quid for that lot. I'll give you two quid alright,' he threatened, pounding the table.

'Keep your 'air on, Stan. Start any argy-bargy with me, and you can expect a visit from cousin Benny. You wouldn't like that one bit.'

Stan blinked. 'No need for that, Alfie. Can't you see yer way to giving me a bit more for 'em. Truth is, I'm behind with the rent. A few bob more?'

Alfie picked up the pendant and held it up to the light. Then he took a close look at one of the pairs of earrings. Stan followed his movements hopefully.

'Two pound seven and six. Take it or leave it,'

Stan grimaced, opening his mouth to complain but thinking better of it. He nodded and shuffled anxiously as Alfie laboriously counted out the money on the table.

'Nice doing business with you,' Alfie said to Stan's back as he closed the front door.

***

Dick glanced at his wristwatch. Five past six. 'Come on, Alfie,' he grumbled, stamping his foot to ease the pins and needles in his left leg. What a waste of time. From his vantage point on a bench across the street, he'd seen a steady stream of drinkers coming and going from the Bedford Arms. A couple of times, he'd strained his eyes, thinking that a new arrival might be Mulcahy, but a quick look at the photograph in his pocket confirmed that they were not his man.

If You Want to Know the Time, Ask a Policeman. Dick looked round as Alfie sauntered up, whistling the popular music hall tune.

'Ah, 'bout time too.'

Alfie took a seat next to him.

'Suppose you've been sitting with your feet up at 'ome?'

Alfie grinned. 'Nothing to report, then?'

'Nah. No sign of him.'

Alfie described Stan's visit with an air of satisfaction. 'Two pound seven and six, I gave him. Blimey, this is worth at least a tenner.' Dick looked at the brooch in Alfie's hand and grunted in agreement.

Dick got to his feet. 'I'll be getting along then.'

'Oi. Oi.' Alfie grabbed Dick's sleeve and pulled him back down.

'Eh?'

'Over there,' Alfie nodded towards the figure emerging from the door of the pub.

'Good Gawd. Didn't see him go in.' Dick reached into his pocket. 'It's him, ain't it?' he said, showing the photograph to Alfie.

'And you missed him going in?'

'Call of nature. Must 'ave been then. Couldn't use the lav in the pub. You said I had to stay outside. Popped along to an alley down the street. Couldn't have been more than two minutes, honest.'

'Never mind. I'll follow him. You get off 'ome.'

Chapter 33

He'd spent the morning with Cormac.

'You wanted to learn about explosives,' Cormac grinned, throwing a cardboard cylinder at him. He half-caught it, fumbled, then scrambled to close his fingers on it before it hit the ground. Cormac laughed. 'Bejesus, the last thing we need is a butterfingers.'

Joseph bit his tongue.

Cormac made several jokes at his expense, then turned serious.

'Alright my lad, it's not a game. Schoolmaster or not, don't forget that I'm the teacher now. That is real dynamite, and this here is a blasting cap. Keep em apart and you'll be as right as rain. But put them together and you've got an almighty explosion, so you have.'

Joseph listened and learned. He felt thrilled at the thought of action, of being a soldier for the cause, just like his granddaddy. A Dynamitard.

For men like Cormac, it seemed, the thought of maiming and killing came easily. The fellow boasted of being involved at the tail end of the Fenian bombing campaign a dozen years earlier.

'I was just a lad, of course, but we hit the House of Commons and the Tower of London, too.'

Lesson over, Joseph sat glumly watching Pat, Cormac and Dermot playing cribbage. The aimless waiting wore him down. Why hadn't he thought to bring a book or two with him? The prospect of an entire afternoon spent kicking his heels was more than he could bear.

He looked up as Carter entered.

'How's the prisoner doing, Dermot?'

'Oh, right enough, I suppose, for a man who's only got days to live. He's gone quiet on us.'

'Well, just don't let your guard down. That goes for all of you. Quiet or not, I don't want him giving any trouble.'

Dermot put his cards down. 'Why not get rid of him now, then? Save us all a lot of bother, if we just put a bullet through his head or string him up. Whatever way you want to finish him off. Me and the boys could go down there now, couldn't we, lads?'

'No. Sentence was passed by the court and the date of execution was set. We'll do this thing properly. Is that understood?'

Dermot shrugged. 'Aye.'

Carter approached, standing over Dermot and the others.

'Aye, what?'

'Aye, Captain.'

Carter waited until each of them said it, then spun on his heel. 'Joseph, with me. We're going on a reconnaissance.'

Fifteen feet below him, George Benson completed the six-hundredth circuit of his cell for the day.

The meagreness of his diet of bread and cheese was taking its toll. He willed himself to keep going, but fatigue and soreness in his calves and the soles of his feet compelled him to lean against the back wall of his cell. Just for a moment, he told himself, but it was no good. Limping, he retired to sit on his blanket.

Worse than his physical privation was the mental struggle. Taunted by the chalk marks - three of the seven were now scored through - he'd used his blanket to rub the chalk away. Scrubbing against the coarse brickwork until he'd worn a hole in the thin material. Although he tried his best, they remained dimly visible.

Pat and Cormac took great delight at chalking new marks when they brought him breakfast.

Recalling snatches of poetry was becoming too much of an effort. George's thoughts strayed to his past. Especially his childhood.

The river was his element. His earliest memories were of the Severn. The sight of it, sparkling in the sun, a stone's throw from the cottage door. Or dark and lifeless in the grip of winter, when he rubbed the frost from the inside of his bedroom window.

Consumption claimed Arnold Benson when George was but three years old. No memories of his father remained. Enid, his mother, remarried before his fifth birthday, and the man whose blood ran in George's veins was allowed to fade into the past.

'Why not let us change your name to Spalding?' she'd suggested on his tenth birthday. 'Jack would like that. We'd all have the same name then.'

He'd thought about it. He liked his step father well enough. But something held him back. His name was the only link he had with the shadowy figure who had given life to him.

His mother insisted that there were no photographs, but George found one hidden in the leaves of the family Bible, the only book in the cottage. Dressed in cricket whites, he sat with the other members of his team, proudly holding a silver cup. George couldn't tell where the photograph was taken or read the inscription on the cup. But the image of that beaming youthful face beneath a shock of dark hair was enough.

Jack was foreman of the flour mill when he married Enid. Ambitious, he used a small legacy to open a grocer's shop in the High Street. They left the cottage and set up home behind the shop. George hated it at first but grew to accept it.

'You'll go to the Grammar School,' Enid confided in him. 'Jack says the shop is doing well enough. He wants you to get an education. Says you've got a good brain, so you should use it, get a good start in life.'

George did well. He was always in the top three or four of his class. Jack let him work in the shop at weekends, trusting him to use the till and tally up the accounts. His brother came along when he was twelve. It seemed to take his parents by surprise. He hadn't complained when Jack and Enid focussed all their attention on the little boy, but the atmosphere at home changed.

Jack wanted him to spend more time working in the shop. His schoolwork took second place. Mr Tailor, his form master, expressed his dismay. 'You're not stupid, boy. So, what is it?'

George professed he'd try harder but sensed that his schooldays would soon be over.

Jack left Enid to break the news that, with yet another member of the family on the way, it was time for George 'to pull his weight', as she put it. 'You're almost fifteen. Most boys your age are already working'.

'I'll get you a job at the mill,' Jack told him. He tried it. Loathed it. But stuck it out for his mother's sake, handing over three-quarters of his wages every week. Then Jack started asking him to help out in the shop in the evenings and Saturday afternoons, too. He couldn't conceal his resentment.

Tommy Jenkins had been his first childhood friend. Their paths diverged when George moved from the cottage. While George attended the Grammar School, Tommy was apprenticed to his father, the local blacksmith.

In the space of three years, the weedy, freckled boy transformed into a solid mass of sinew and muscle. The diffidence of his childhood gave way to an easy confidence.

Their friendship was rekindled, and George spent what little free time he had with Tommy.

The funeral stuck in his memory. Not that there was anything remarkable about funerals. Even by that time, George was an old hand at them. His father's, of course, then Granny Stillman and Nan Benson within six months of one another. Uncle Jonathan fell in the river and drowned, and two of his young cousins succumbed to sickness. But this was the first funeral that wasn't a relative's.

Tommy's father, Cliff, dropped dead while fashioning new iron railings for the manse. The church was well attended by townsfolk and George sat near the back, watching Tommy all alone in the front pew. Cliff was the only kin he had. The vicar's wife went and sat with him when the service started, whispering words of comfort.

A group of Cliff's friends paid for the wake at the Black Lion. George shuffled in and stood nervously in a corner, trying to catch Tommy's eye. The lad was surrounded by mourners and looked bereft. George slipped outside after ten minutes and walked home.

Two weeks went by. George wanted to see his friend, but something held him back. He didn't know what he should say. The forge was closed, the front gate padlocked and shutters over the windows.

Finally, one evening, he summoned up the courage to go, only to run into Tommy coming the other way. George's mumbled attempts at expressing his condolences were brushed aside. 'No need for all that, Georgie. 'Tis over and done with now. Come along, I've got summat to tell you.'

Apart from the wake, he'd never been in a pub before. His stepfather was not a drinker. Other than a glass or two of sherry at Christmas, strong drink had no place in his household. Jack was partial to a pipe in the evenings, but Enid encouraged him to smoke it at the back door.

'Sit here.' Tommy indicated a table by the front window. George sat eyeing the occupants of the bar shyly. All men, except for the landlady. He recognised one or two of them, but the rest were strangers. Acutely conscious of his youth, he made himself sit upright as though to appear taller - and older. A couple of men standing nearby glanced at him and raised their glasses in mock salutation.

'Here you are.' Tommy put two tankards of foaming dark liquid on the table. George looked uncertainly at his drink.

'It's a pint of mild. Won't bite,' Tommy said, putting it to his lips.

George gripped the handle of his tankard. He lifted it carefully, eyeing the settling foam as it approached his mouth and sniffing its unfamiliar bitterness. It tasted as it smelled.

'Thanks.' George licked the foam from his lips.

'How've you been?'

'Alright. You? I was at the funeral.'

'Aye, saw you at the wake. You'd gone before I could speak to you, though.'

George nodded sheepishly. 'What you going to do now, then?'

Tommy took a long draught of his beer, looking at George over the rim, then wiped his mouth with the back of his hand. 'Dad left me the forge.'

'Ah, that's good. You'll be the new smithy then.'

Tommy grinned. 'Not me, Georgie boy. I've sold it.'

'Sold it?'

'Don't fancy spending the rest of my days slaving over hot coals. There's more to life than that. I'm leaving. Going down to Bristol.'

'What will you do there?'

'Dunno. But I'll have money in my pocket. I'll just see what comes along, I reckon.'

Money, thought George. *If I'd some money, I'd get out too. Away from the mill and Jack's bloody shop, too.*

'Come on, drink up. It's a celebration. Drinks are on me.' Tommy drained his beer and turned towards the bar.

George managed to finish his pint by the time Tommy returned, spilling the last drops down his shirt. He belched behind his hand, the sour beery taste filled his mouth. He swallowed it back, eyeing the fresh tankard in front of him warily.

Tommy was in fine form, recounting childhood pranks one minute, then leaning in close and confiding various amorous adventures with one or two of the town girls. George listened with a mixture of embarrassment and envy.

By the middle of his third pint, the growing disquiet in his stomach took an acute turn. Stumbling towards the door with a hand clamped over his mouth, he barely emerged onto the pavement before spraying the shoes of a passing gentleman with watery vomit.

The man's angry protest was in vain as George retched uncontrollably, leaning one hand on the pub wall for support. Rather than risk further exposure to the contents of George's stomach, the fellow hurried away, muttering fiercely.

Tommy helped him to get home. He walked him up and down outside the shop until George said he felt better.

'George, is that you?'

George's heart sank. His attempt to tiptoe quietly to his room was thwarted by the creaking third step.

Enid emerged from the back parlour.

'Where've you… oh, you've been sick. Look at your shirt. Oh, George, that's beer, I can smell it.'

'What's that?' Jack stood at Enid's side.

'You stink like a brewery, boy,' he thundered. 'Get to bed. I'll talk to you in the morning.'

George weathered Jack's righteous indignation the next day, despite nursing a frightful hangover. A whole pitcher of water had failed to slake his thirst, and the throbbing in his temple showed no sign of abating. He felt too ill to defend himself.

Jack read the riot act. 'Don't ask me to come and make excuses for you when you turn up at the mill, looking and smelling like that. Serve you right if they sack you. That's what I'd do if I was still foreman there.'

George nodded, muttered a few words of apology. But Jack wouldn't stop. On he went, over and over, piling on the humiliation. Only Enid's intercession to say that he'd be late for work enabled George to get to his feet and leave the room.

'Don't think you've heard the last of this,' Jack shouted after him.

The fresh air helped. He kept out of the foreman's way at the mill. By the lunch break, he'd made up his mind. He changed out of his overalls and slipped out of the gate.

The High Street was bustling. Market Day. George concealed himself at the entrance to an alleyway opposite the shop, waiting for the right moment. Jack liked to stand in the shop's entrance: showing off the produce stacked in boxes underneath the window to customers, chatting to acquaintances, or just watching the world go by. Elsie would mind the counter inside and keep an eye on the two children.

The sight of old Fred Armitage and his wife, walking along the pavement, raised George's hopes. Fred liked nothing better than a chinwag. He'd just spent ten minutes chatting with Pike, the butcher, and now he waved a cheery good day to Jack. George waited. Sure enough, the Armitages stopped to talk.

A loaded dray rumbled down the street. George used it as cover to cross the road. From the High Street, he turned right into Cowper Lane, then right again along a narrow path, stopping at the gate to Jack's back garden. He'd rehearsed what he'd say if his mother or Jack spotted him. 'Took ill, had to come away home. Came round the back in case I was sick coming through the shop.' It sounded lame, but it was all he could think of. What other reason could he give?

He cringed when the iron gate squeaked on its hinges and squeezed through rather than risk opening it wider. At the kitchen window, he pushed aside some strands of ivy. There was no one in there.

The familiar aroma of baking bread greeted him as he stepped through the back door. George listened, relieved to hear his mother's voice at the far end of the passage. "Runner beans are very good today, Mrs Tanner. Take some home for your tea."

The stairs were halfway along the passage. Just past the door to the parlour. George skirted the kitchen table and came to an abrupt halt at the sight of two bare feet. Timmy sat on the floor, half under the table, playing with a handful of toy soldiers. The tin guardsmen were the four-year-old's favourites, their red coats covered in dents and scratches.

George crouched down and grinned at the lad, putting a finger to his lips. 'Shh,' he mouthed. Timmy's blank face looked incuriously at him for an instant, then his attention returned to his toys.

George avoided the third step and made it to the landing. Taking comfort from the dim sound of his mother still chatting to Mrs Tanner, he slipped into his bedroom. Not his alone. Timmy's small bed took up a corner of the space.

Treading softly, he crossed to the window and eased the catch. He dared not lift the sash window more than an inch, just enough to hear Jack's voice from the street below. *God bless Fred Armitage*, he thought.

George reached under his jacket for the clean flour sack he'd purloined from the Mill. The only portmanteau the family possessed was in Jack and Enid's bedroom. He dared not look for that. It took only a couple of minutes to stuff a few clothes and his best boots into the sack. He'd concealed the money he'd saved from his work in one of those boots, tied up in a handkerchief. There wasn't much. He knew the exact amount. Two pounds, eighteen shillings and sixpence ha'penny.

'Bye now, Mrs Tanner.' Enid's voice floated along the passage as he stood at the foot of the stairs. 'I'd better go and see what our Timmy is up to.'

The rush of blood that propelled George through the kitchen, down the garden path and out into the back lane was also responsible for his split-second decision to grab a battered toffee tin from the dresser. He stuffed it under his arm, holding it tight against his body, feeling the weight of the coins within. There'd be no going back now.

In the space of twenty-four hours, George's life changed irrevocably. He'd reached a fork in the road and chosen a path that took him to Bristol with Tommy, and then through many a twist and turn to the army.

He'd seized the day then. Time to seize it again.

Chapter 34

Was it the oysters?

Well, the whiskey hadn't helped either, but James Mulcahy had a good head for alcohol. Or so he thought. At least on the top deck of the omnibus, he could feel the evening breeze on his face. He should have known better but, he'd enjoyed the craic too much to leave the pub earlier. He could have gone home and had a lie down, but now there was no time.

He flicked open his pocket watch. Ten minutes until his meeting with Henry Agnew. He'd met the publisher a week earlier at the offices of *The Shillelagh*. As an occasional contributor of poems, short stories and humorous pieces to that magazine, he'd considered himself fortunate to receive an invitation from the editor, Seamus Galloway, to attend a literary soirée.

Spotting Henry Agnew among the guests, Mulcahy prevailed on Seamus to introduce him. Emboldened by several glasses of champagne, he'd steered their conversation around to his manuscript of *The Broken Shamrock*, the tale of a young man's struggle from a Dublin slum to fame and fortune.

Agnew had been anything but encouraging. 'Why do you imagine that I would be interested in your book, Mr Mulcahy? I am inundated with manuscripts from unknown authors, who, for some unaccountable reason, consider themselves to be the next Henry James or Thomas Hardy.'

'Go on, Henry, give the man a chance.' Seamus put an arm around Agnew's shoulders. Gregarious and outspoken, with an irrepressible sense of humour, he had the knack of coaxing people to do him favours or at least humouring him. 'Can't do any harm. Perhaps James here is the next big thing. What do you say?' he persisted, playfully.

Henry Agnew took a card from his jacket pocket. 'Next Wednesday. Seven sharp at this address.'

James Mulcahy took the card. 'Would that be seven o'clock in the evening?'

Agnew gave him a withering look. 'Of course,' he said, turning on his heel.

Here was the stop. As the omnibus drew to a halt, James left his seat, gripping the leather satchel containing a copy of his manuscript, and followed some passengers down the stairs, oblivious of Alfie Cotton directly behind him.

In Moorgate, he looked around to get his bearings, then headed south, eyeing the street numbers until he found the right address.

On the second-floor landing, a glass panel bore the legend –

Agnew and Patterson
Publishers

James found himself in an anteroom. Several doors opened off it. All were shut.

'Mr Agnew's expecting me,' he said to the young man sitting at a desk inside. James looked down at the top of the fellow's head of slicked black hair. He was reading from a sheaf of papers and showed no sign of acknowledging James's presence, licking his thumb to turn a page and continuing to read.

Was the man deaf? He turned another page. James cleared his throat.

'Yes?' He still didn't raise his head.

'I have an appointment with Mr Agnew,' James pronounced, emphasising each word. 'Seven O'clock. Name's Mulcahey.'

'I that so?' The man looked up, lolling back in his chair.

Mulcahy swallowed. Was the fellow being deliberately rude? He was hardly more than a boy. His narrow, hollow-cheeked face was supported by a neck so spindly that his wing collar looked a couple of sizes too large.

'Yes,' said James, trying to contain his irritation. 'He invited me to bring my manuscript,' he added, patting the satchel.

'Mister Agnew's gone home.'

'Gone home? But…'

'Just leave your manuscript on the pile.'

'Eh?'

'There.' The whelp, as Mulcahy now thought of him, pointed to a small tower of papers sitting on the side of the desk. 'If we determine that your manuscript is worthy of further attention, we'll contact you. Could take a month or two.'

'But Mister Agnew gave me the impression that he would meet with me personally.'

A shrug of the shoulders was his only reply.

Mulcahy opened the satchel. On the point of adding his manuscript on the teetering pile of paper, he snorted, replaced it in the satchel and strode to the door, slamming it behind him.

Out on the street, he fumed silently, oblivious to the din of the traffic, and entirely unaware of Alfie loitering in a doorway ten paces away. Furious, he mentally rehearsed the scornful phrases that he'd use should he and Henry Agnew cross paths again. He considered returning in the morning and waylaying Agnew in his office. In the end, he realised that what he needed most was a drink.

Alfie kept him in view. Past the Bank of England, threading through the traffic near Mansion House and along King William Street, where a tavern took Mulcahy's fancy.

After buying an evening paper from the vendor outside, Alfie edged into the public bar in time to see Mulcahy order a large whiskey, down it in one gulp and order another. He found a space at the other end of the bar and ordered a bottle of brown ale, stealing an occasional glance at his target as he perused his *Evening Standard*. Crouched over his glass, Mulcahy stood muttering to himself. Something about his demeanour made the old man standing next to him move away and find a seat in the corner.

Four whiskeys was the count when Mulcahy detached himself from the bar, belched and shuffled a little unsteadily towards the door.

The shadows were lengthening as he emerged. The thought of those oysters came back to him as he belched again. A small voice within had urged caution when he ordered his fourth whiskey, but he'd ignored it. What he could not ignore, however, was the return of the queasiness he'd felt earlier on leaving the Bedford Arms.

Alfie left his newspaper on the bar and followed in Mulcahy's wake. He hovered in the doorway pretending to tie his shoelace, while Mulcahy turned first one way, then another before settling on continuing south along King William Street. Alfie lost him for a moment in the swirl of traffic at the junction with Cannon Street, but picked him out on Eastcheap. He threaded his way through a jam of cabs and delivery wagons, emerging on the pavement twenty feet behind his quarry.

Mulcahy had stopped, swaying slightly and shielding his eyes with his hand. What had he seen, Alfie wondered. Mulcahy started waving, then set off at an unsteady trot. What was that he was shouting?

'Captain! Oi there!' Mulcahy hollered over the din of the traffic.

Alfie quickened his pace. Passers-by looked askance at Mulcahy. One or two stopped and stared as he passed. Then Alfie fancied he could see who Mulcahy was calling to. Two men, one middle-aged, the other in his twenties, by Alfie's reckoning, turned and waited on the pavement.

Alfie saw words being exchanged. He walked casually in their direction.

The older man was not pleased. His aggressive posture and his gestures signalled his annoyance. His younger companion stood to one side, watching the exchange.

Alfie drew within earshot and slowed, pretending to search for something in his coat pockets.

'For God's sake, keep your voice down, you damned fool,' the older man hissed as Alfie approached.

'But Captain. I only wanted to say hello.' Mulcahy protested, swaying on his heels. 'This one of the Brotherhood?' he added, nodding at the younger man.

'Right, that's enough.' The older man took Mulcahy roughly by the elbow. 'Come away now.'

At the moment Alfie drew level with them, the three moved away. The older man practically frogmarching Mulcahy while the younger one followed close behind.

Alfie let them get twenty paces ahead and matched his pace to theirs. Anyone passing might have wondered why he sported such a broad grin. What had Verity said to him in her drawing room? 'It's only a slim possibility, but maybe Mulcahy will lead us to Carter and, therefore, to George.'

Mulcahy wasn't going quietly. Alfie couldn't hear his protests, but saw him try to tear himself free of Carter's grip. Unsuccessfully. Then, in an instant, the trio turned into a side street.

Idol Lane. Alfie risked a glance around the corner. The church of St Dunstan in the East lay at the end of the lane. Alfie had often passed by the building, but from the other direction on St Dunstan's Hill. The lane was cast in shade, but a street light halfway along the lane weakly illuminated the backs of the three men as they entered the churchyard.

He hesitated for a moment, anxious not to lose the trio but cautious of following them into the gloom. There was nothing for it. Treading as lightly as he could, Alfie hurried to the churchyard entrance, skirting the church until he found a gap in the railings.

His first thought was that he was under attack. The instant the gunshot sounded, he threw himself face down onto the gravel path, heart beating wildly. The echo of the shot merged with the fluttering wings of dozens of pigeons and the cawing of disgruntled crows.

'Don't know what came over me,' he admitted later. 'Should 'ave run a mile.'

The crunch of footsteps. Running, not walking, and going away across the churchyard encouraged him. His eyes adjusted to the gloom enough to make out the shapes of tombstones. He followed, hoping to catch sight of his quarry as they neared the street lights on St Dunstan's Hill, but a moment later, he hit the gravel again, stumbling over an object lying across the path. He knew before he hit the ground what the soft, yielding mass must be.

Alfie sat up and scrambled for the box of matches in his pocket. The flaring vesta cupped in his hand revealed James Mulcahy. The right side of his face was uppermost with a round, dark blemish at the temple. A pool of blood oozed across the gravel, from where the bullet had torn a gaping wound on exit. Next to the body, Mulcahey's satchel had spewed its contents. Pages of *The Broken Shamrock* blew around in the light evening breeze.

Any thoughts of attempting to pick up the trail of Mulcahy's killers evaporated with the sharp blasts of a police whistle. He blew out the match and ran.

***

'Calm yourself, man.' Carter hissed. 'Just keep walking. Forget those whistles. Just act normally.'

Joseph felt as though every eye in the street was watching him. Every second, he expected to hear the thud of police boots coming up behind them. Carter had given no warning, just pushed Mulcahey to the ground, put the muzzle of his revolver to the man's temple, and pulled the trigger. Jesus, the noise it made.

He walked in a daze at Carter's side, unaware of his surroundings until they reached the top of Tower Hill.

Everything had gone well until the moment Mulcahey had called out to them. What were the chances? Joseph hadn't met the man. He'd heard Cormac mention him disparagingly at the warehouse. Called him a drunken fool. Fool or not, to shoot the man down like a dog? He remembered when Carter had put him in his place back at Edna's, telling him how he'd killed that fellow in Cork. One of his own men. Mother of God, it was no idle boast.

'This is between you and me,' Carter told him when they arrived back at the warehouse gate. 'The others don't need to know. We'll tell them about our reconnaissance of the procession route, but that's all. Now pull yourself together. You're a soldier for the cause, so start acting like one or I'll have no use for you and you know what that means.'

Chapter 35

Anna peeled the counterpane back, shifting her body sideways until she lay at the edge of the mattress. Her bare skin gave up the warmth of her shared bed.

Her companion's rhythmic breathing continued undisturbed. Come the morning, he might well regret the copious amounts of champagne and claret he'd consumed over dinner, not to mention the scotch and soda for a nightcap, but for now it was the sedative effect of the alcohol that gave Anna the opportunity to slip away to her sitting room. It had been quite an evening. With only a matinee performance that day, she had the whole evening free. He'd come to her straight from Whitehall, in frock coat, top hat and carrying his attaché case. He swept her straight into the bedroom. Afterwards, she'd cooked dinner and indulged him in a second round of lovemaking before he fell asleep.

Sitting up, she felt for her discarded nightgown with her feet and stooped to pick it up. After manipulating the garment for a few moments to find a sleeve, she wound it around herself and stood up, allowing her eyes to adjust to the darkness. It made little difference. With one arm stretched out in front and the other at right angles, she edged step by step towards the door. Her left hand discovered a solid surface, the embossed wallpaper rippling under her fingers. Stepping crab-wise to her right, she maintained contact with the wallpaper until she found the door frame, then felt with her right hand for the handle.

Passing through, Anna took great care not to make a sound, one hand on the handle, the other along the doorjamb, until she felt the door touching it, then drawing it shut and slowly releasing the handle.

The sitting room smelled of stale cigarette smoke. Safely inside, she breathed deeply, relaxing her muscles. Here she had the advantage of some ambient light. Having earlier taken care to leave a chink in the curtains, a beam of light from the streetlamp outside provided all the illumination she required to walk to the sofa and reach for Giles's attaché case. That he should have brought it with him was more than she could have expected. The opportunity to rifle through it could not be denied.

Passing to the small kitchen of her rented apartment, Anna felt her way to the table and the oil lamp and box of matches she'd placed there in readiness, before they retired. While it would have been more convenient to examine the contents of the attaché case while sitting at the kitchen table, Anna could not run the risk of being discovered if he woke and came searching for her. Only the bathroom provided an assurance of privacy. Lighting the lamp, she slipped into the passage.

With the bathroom door securely bolted, she placed the lamp on a shelf above the wash-hand basin and sat on the closed toilet seat. Three manila departmental files revealed nothing of interest. Beneath them, she found a folded copy of The Times, several days old. She unfolded the newspaper and shook it briskly. Nothing fell out. That was it.

Her search of Giles's coat on an earlier occasion had produced immediate results in the shape of scraps of paper with some scrawled notes. Anna had committed the salient points to memory. A quantity of dynamite delivered to an address in Kilburn. The Irish Brotherhood, and something called the New Immortals. The name Carter and an address in Camden High Street, and the words that had especially triggered her interest –

Mainland bombing campaign – when and where?

Not a great deal to go on, but when Verity and Ambrose recounted the background to George's disappearance, it all fell into place. But what was Giles's game? Would he really be in league with his country's enemies? Perhaps it was the opposite. Maybe he was planning to thwart them.

Then there was that other intriguing reference:

Report to VL.

Who was VL?

Anna held the empty attaché case on her knee and prepared to replace its contents just as she'd found them. First the refolded newspaper, then, one by one, the manilla files. The last one slipped from her hand, sending the attaché case thudding onto the tiles. Anna froze, biting her lip. In her heightened nervous state, it sounded deafening, but surely it wouldn't have reached the bedroom?

Kneeling on the tiles. She turned the attaché case the right way up. Then she saw it. At the base of the case, a rectangle of leather had become detached, revealing a space half an inch deep. A false bottom. And from this space, a buff envelope had skittered across the bathroom floor.

Five minutes later, Anna slipped back into bed. Despite taking great care, the movement provoked a gruff snore from Giles. But to her immense relief, his breathing resumed the steady rhythm of a sound sleeper.

The attaché case was back on the sofa, its contents neatly replaced - save for the buff envelope.

Chapter 36

Sergeant Cooper leaned against the wall with his thumbs tucked into his belt. A creature of habit, half of him just wanted to be back home in bed. His shift had ended two hours ago. His other half gazed with satisfaction at the back of the suspect sitting at the table. He took his thumbs out and stood up straight as Inspector Tweed entered, giving the sergeant a cursory nod.

Tweed took a seat opposite the suspect, placing a notebook on the table and taking a fountain pen from his breast pocket. While some investigators liked to launch straight into an interrogation, Inspector Tweed favoured a different technique. Folding his hands in front of him, he locked eyes on the prisoner. It almost always worked. Tweed took great pride in his ability to out-stare suspects. He'd trained himself to do it.

The fellow stood it for a few minutes. Tried to stick it out, but capitulated pretty quickly. It wasn't a complete surrender, though; he leaned back in his chair with his eyes on the ceiling and whistled - *If You Want to Know the Time, Ask a Policeman.*

Sergeant Cooper's chuckle was quelled by Tweed darting a look in his direction.

'Name?' Tweed demanded.

'You know my name.'

'Don't bandy words with me. You've been arrested on suspicion of murder. I'd advise you to take care.'

'Alright. Alfred Sedgewick Cotton.'

The police were closer than Alfie realised when he heard their whistles and ran back up Idol Lane, hoping to reach Eastcheap and blend in with the passers-by. Ten yards short of his goal, his path was blocked by three policemen coming around the corner. With no opportunity to turn tail, he tried to brazen it out, tipping his bowler and wishing them a breezy 'good night' while edging past.

Sergeant Cooper's spade-like hand on his collar brought him to an abrupt halt.

'Not so fast. Where've you just come from then?' he said, shining his bull's eye lamp into Alfie's face.

'Oh, just down there,' Alfie glanced back down the lane.

'Down where that shot came from.'

'Oh. I heard a noise. Was that a shot?'

'Don't get clever with me, son. You're coming with us. Take him in hand you two,' Cooper instructed the two constables with him.

'But I've got to get 'ome to look after me old mum. Seventy-five she is, and not so well.' Alfie's protest fell on deaf ears as he was marched back along the lane with a constable gripping each arm.

The sergeant shone his lamp ahead of them, passing the church and arriving at the churchyard entrance.

'Now then, we'll have to search the area. Cuff him to the railings, Billings. Then take your lamp and go on down to the end of the lane. Owens, you come with me.'

Alfie watched Sergeant Cooper and Constable Owens pass into the churchyard, following the beams cast by their lanterns. A fruitless tug at the handcuffs only served to bruise his wrist. He knew it wouldn't take them long.

A shrill whistle blast brought Billings running back up the lane and into the churchyard.

Five minutes later, the sergeant and Billings emerged, leaving Owens to guard the scene. Without a word, Billings pushed Alfie roughly against the railings and went through his pockets. Finding only some loose change, a dirty handkerchief, and a box of matches, he turned to the sergeant and shook his head.

'Right then, it's down the station for you,' said Sergeant Cooper.

Alfie prided himself on keeping one step ahead of the rozzers. He had managed to avoid being charged with any offence, even though he'd been brought in for questioning on several occasions. This wasn't his normal patch, though, and being treated as a murder suspect was in a different league from fencing or petty theft.

Inspector Tweed pressed on. 'A man was shot dead in St Dunstan's churchyard tonight. You were apprehended trying to leave the area. So I ask myself, has Sergeant Cooper here caught the killer, or a witness who seems reluctant to help us with our enquiries?'

'I don't know nothin' about a murder.'

'So you say. You obviously heard the shot. If you weren't the killer, did you see who it was?'

Alfie shook his head.

'Perhaps a night in the cells will make you more co-operative. If not, I will charge you with murder tomorrow morning. Is that clear?' Inspector Tweed put his fountain pen back in his breast pocket and picked up his notebook, then pushed his chair back and stood up.

'Get Quilter.' Alfie said with a grin.

The Inspector hesitated briefly and sat back down.

Like a magic incantation, Alfie's words had an electrifying effect. Rather than facing the bare walls of a police cell he found himself sitting in Inspector Tweed's office with a cup of tea in front of him.

Colonel Quilter arrived in a little over an hour. For a man who was always impeccably turned out, the stubble on his face was testament to the haste with which he'd answered the inspector's message.

'Are you alright Mr Cotton?' were his first words.

Alfie nodded and took a sip of his tea. 'Right as rain, Colonel, thanks for asking. Don't know what I'm going to tell Miss Mallard.'

'Tell her? Do you imagine she'll be angry with you? Good God, man, you did everything that could be expected of you. You found Carter. You couldn't possibly have known things would turn out the way they did.'

'But now we'll never find George.'

'Colonel,' Inspector Tweed interjected. 'Could you tell me what you're talking about? Carter? Miss Mallard? George? Who are these people?'

'Anything I tell you must go no further. Is that understood?'

'But the Commissioner…?'

'You can leave the Commissioner to me.'

Chapter 37

Eulenburg's telegram came that morning. Lensch wasted no time in decoding it. He had Eulenburg's agreement and the money too.

Now he closed his eyes and turned his face to the sun, enjoying a few moments of satisfied reflection before Riemann joined him on his bench in St James's Park.

The movement of the bench underneath him as it adjusted to Riemann's weight disturbed his pleasant contemplation just as Big Ben sounded faintly in the distance. Eleven o'clock on the dot. It had been a busy two days since he'd examined the remains of Carter's notebook.

'A fine day, Riemann.'

'Yes, Major.'

'What do you have for me?'

'The Dutchman says yes.'

'How much did you offer?'

'One thousand. He settled for two.'

'Two thousand pounds on top of the five thousand for Operation Geck. He'll be a rich man. What did you make of the address?'

'It's a warehouse. Three floors. The main entrance is a gate leading into a courtyard. There's also a door from the street on the other side. Heavy timber affair. Locked. Probably bolted. We'll go over the main gate and find a way in from the courtyard. Ground floor windows have bars, but not the first floor. If we climb onto the coach house roof…'

'Any sign of the Fenians?'

'You said there were four of them.'

Lensch nodded. The wonderful stroke of luck in finding the remains of Carter's notebook had not only given him Carter's location but also identified members of his cell. Three initials cropped up: P, C, and D. Had the notebook not been burnt, he would have found the initial J as well. 'Three, besides Carter himself. There could be more, but the Fenians operate in small cells.'

'I saw two of them. They went out through the gate just after three o'clock yesterday afternoon. The description you gave me of Carter fitted one of them. I left not long after, to meet the Dutchman.'

Lensch took Riemann through the details of the operation. The time of entry. Weapons. Covering of tracks.

'Nothing must point to our involvement, Riemann. That is vital. No survivors. Understood?'

Riemann got to his feet. '*Jawohl.*'

***

Joseph was a shaken man. The image of Carter pulling the trigger, the sharp crack echoing around the gravestones, the splatter of blood and brains, played over and over in his mind. He held a hand out in front of him. The convulsive shaking he'd felt earlier had eased to a mild tremor. The worst thing about it, worse even than the act itself, was its cold-bloodedness. Carter had drawn his pistol, cocked it and shot Mulcahy in the space of a couple of heartbeats.

He remembered that time when Carter had threatened him. Put his revolver on the table and told him how he'd shot one of his own men. A bullet in the head. In the same breath, he'd boasted about killing three police informers in Ireland. And now Mulcahy.

The man who styled himself Captain Carter had killed five men, to Joseph's knowledge, and all of them Irishmen. How, in God's name, did that further the cause of Irish independence?

Why did Carter even need him? The other three, oafish though they appeared, seemed perfectly capable of carrying out the plan.

He'd played along as Carter briefed the others on the reconnaissance, saying nothing about Mulcahy. 'Well, lads, the day's not far off now. There are preparations going on all over the place.' Carter said with relish as they sat over a supper of greasy stew and brown bread. 'There's great big timber viewing stands going up along the procession route. We'll get everything in place the day before and set it all up in good time before the crowds get too thick. It's the perfect spot, just across the road from the Mansion House. Eat up now and we'll go out to the coach house.

The cobblestones in the yard were shiny and slick from a sudden sharp downpour. Carter led them to the coach house and swung open the double doors. Inside stood the cart that had carried George from the Bedford Arms. It was the conveyance standing next to it that drew everyone's attention.

'There it is,' Carter exclaimed.

The van looked brand new, its panels freshly painted in a shiny plum colour and on either side in gold lettering it bore the inscription:

Charles T Arrowfield

Cinematographer

Carter moved to the rear of the vehicle, opening the back door.

The others gathered round.

'See that,' Carter pointed.

'A camera, would that be?' Cormac squinted at the bulky wooden box standing atop a tripod.

'Aye, but not the sort you find in a photographer's studio. No, this camera takes moving pictures.' He stepped up into the van and crouched behind the contraption, looking through the eyepiece and turning a metal handle on the side.

'Dermot pushed Cormac to one side and stood in front of the camera, waving his arms about. 'Would you be taking a picture of us now, Captain?' he asked excitedly.

Carter stepped back down from the van. 'It's only for show, man. There's not a film in it. Now then, let's run through the plan again, shall we? Joseph, you're the only one who hasn't heard this before, so pay attention.'

Joseph moved closer. During Carter's reconnaissance, he'd only been told that somewhere on the Queen's Diamond Jubilee procession route, a cache of dynamite would be positioned in readiness to be detonated as the Queen's carriage reached the spot.

'We can thank one of the new wonders of the age for the cornerstone of our plan, lads. Moving pictures. The procession will be recorded for posterity through this invention,' Carter said, pointing to the camera. 'There will be cameras galore along the route. Aye, there'll be Gaumont and Lumière and a host of others, including our Mr Arrowfield.'

'What, you mean this fella is one of us?' Pat said, scratching his head.

Carter smiled. 'Not exactly. Mr Arrowfield has kindly allowed us to have the use of his camera and this fine van of his, as he is currently indisposed.'

'Indisposed, you say. You mean…'

'I mean, Pat, that he's taken his last picture.'

Dear God, thought Joseph. *Another one murdered.*

'Cormac, you'll be driving the van. Get it in position by midday the day before. Unhitch the horse and bring it back here. Pat and Dermot, you'll go with Cormac and stay with the van. We'll put some bedding in the back for you, right next to the box of dynamite. Nice and snug, eh?' Carter gave a humourless laugh.

Joseph listened uneasily. A whole crate of dynamite. The carnage would be unthinkable. Crowds of people, men, women and children. Rich and poor. Packed like sardines. The fight he'd always imagined, his fight, would be against the symbols of Ireland's oppressor. Barracks, law courts, government buildings. He'd no qualms about blowing the old Queen to smithereens, or the Prince of Wales. Soldiers and dignitaries were fair game, too. But scores of ordinary folk who'd just come for the spectacle? Where was the glory in that? Where was the justice?

'You're being very quiet there, Joseph.' Carter called out. 'Worried that I haven't got a job for you, are you?'

'Er, what do you want me to do?'

'Oh well, I've got the very thing. You'll be the cameraman. You even look the part. I can see you now pointing that thing as the Queen's carriage comes closer.'

'Christ, would you be blowing me up as well?'

'Not if you're quick on your feet. I'll be at the van. The other lads will already be on their way back here. It will be a short fuse, very short. Keep an eye out. I'll stand up and wave a Union Jack when the fuse is set. As soon as you see me, make for the van and keep walking. You'll have two minutes to get clear. I'll not wait for you.'

'But there'll be people all around me. It will look very odd. The cameraman leaving just when the Queen's carriage is coming.'

'Pretend you're having trouble with the camera. Make a fuss. Say you have to get some equipment from the van. You're supposed to be the intelligent one here. Improvise, man.'

Everyone's eyes were on him. Joseph's stomach churned. He couldn't trust himself to speak.

Pat nudged him sharply with his elbow.

Joseph swallowed. 'Yes. I'll improvise.'

'Right then, lads,' Carter closed the door of the van. 'Let's be getting back inside.'

Joseph turned away.

'Ah, no. I almost forgot. There's one more thing. Our friend down below - Georgie boy. I know I said his sentence was to be carried out seven days after I passed judgement, but I'd rather we just got on with it. We don't need distractions. I'm bringing the execution forward. Tomorrow morning.'

'Shall we string him up or shoot him?' Dermot piped up. 'I'll do it. Just tell me.'

'Now then, I was thinking about that. When he's taken down the corridor to slop out, just put a bullet through the back of his head while he's emptying the bucket. The sound won't carry from down there. I'd like to make more of a performance of the whole thing, but we need to keep our minds on the plan. The other thing is who will pull the trigger. I know you three have all dealt with enemies and traitors. So, won't this be a fine chance to blood Joseph?'

'What?' Joseph couldn't mask his alarm.

'No more games, Joseph. Time to get serious. Here, you can use his own gun,' Carter said, taking George's revolver from his coat pocket. 'Poetic justice. Cormac, you'll go with him, see he doesn't make a botch of it. Here, Joseph, take it.'

Joseph reached out and felt the weight of the dull grey metal on his palm. Carter clapped him on the shoulder. 'Away inside with you now. We'll have a wee glass of whiskey. Just think how proud your grandaddy would be of you.'

Chapter 38

George brooded. Seize the day, he'd told himself. Inaction would mean an ignominious death, better to take a chance. If his time was up, he'd go down fighting. At least he had no wife and children to worry about. Effie would be upset, but she'd get over it. Who else? Verity? He'd like to think she'd grieve for him, if only fleetingly. Shed a tear over his grave, perhaps?

He had the plan fresh in his mind. Not much of a plan, but it was all he had. The room at the end of the corridor where he went to slop out had seemed quite bare when he'd first been taken there, but in the corner by the door there was a broom, with thick hard bristles, and a shovel, propped against the wall.

He saw it unfolding in his mind's eye. There'd be two of them, of course. Cormac maybe, and perhaps that new young one, Joseph. Out of the cell they went and along the corridor. Poised to tip his bucket's contents into the drain, George turned and threw the stinking mess into Joseph's face. Cormac grunted and doubled up as the empty bucket was smashed into his stomach. Grabbing the broom and the shovel, George ran out into the corridor, slamming the door behind him and inserting the broom handle through the stout iron handle and across the door frame. With the shovel in his hands, he climbed the stairs to the floor above and then… the next part was hazy, but somehow he found his way into the yard and past the gate. With warm thoughts of freedom and hope, he nodded off.

When he awoke, it was not quite dark. George grunted and sat up. At his feet were a plate of bread and cheese and the tin cup of water. The bucket stood festering in the corner. His watch said nine twenty-five. Damnation. They'd been in and left him there sleeping. All that mental effort wasted. Well, not wasted. It would have to be tomorrow morning. Time was running out. He looked at the marks on the wall. Another line was scored through.

George forced the stale bread and cheese down, taking sips of water with each mouthful. He dozed fitfully, loath to fall into a deep sleep. He had to be ready this time. The faint sound of the key in the lock jolted him fully awake. Morning already? But it was dark.

George blinked as the door opened. A thin rectangle of light spread across the floor, widening gradually. It didn't feel right. Too tentative. The thought flashed through his mind that they'd come to take him to his execution. Creep in and drag him away before he was aware of what was going on. But it wasn't time yet. The marks on the wall showed it. He scrambled shakily to his feet.

The glare of the lantern hurt his eyes. Who was holding it? George put up a hand to shield himself.

'Shh.'

Did he hear right?

'What do you want?'

'It's me, Joseph. Keep your voice down.'

George could see him clearly now. Standing in the doorway, holding a lantern aloft in his left hand.

Joseph took a step forward. 'I've come to…'

George retreated.

Joseph's right hand went to his jacket pocket.

It had to be a gun. George's brain urged him to attack, but his legs reneged.

It was his gun. His British Bulldog.

Joseph brought the pistol up, level with George's heart – with the butt foremost.

'We're getting out of here. Both of us. Take the gun.'

George hesitated, wondering if this was an elaborate, cruel charade. Then he took the pistol from Joseph's trembling grip.

The journey along the passage seemed endless. At the foot of the stairs, Joseph whispered, 'I'm going to leave the lantern here. Stay close, hold on to my coat tail.'

The lantern's glow helped them to navigate the steps. At the top, Joseph waited with his hand on the handle of a heavy wooden door, listening.

'Not a sound now,' he whispered, easing the door ajar and stepping into the darkness. George might just as well have been a blind man, shuffling in Joseph's footsteps. Step. Stop and listen. Step. Stop.

Joseph moved by feel, fearing that he'd lose his way. As soon as Carter had ushered him and the others back inside from the yard, he knew what he had to do. He'd plotted the route from the cellar to the back door, looking round casually as he passed through the ground floor on his way upstairs to that wee whiskey that Carter had offered.

The hours that passed before everyone turned in were torture, seeing the others casting curious looks in his direction and trying to act normally. He joined in a game of cribbage to give himself something to do. Carter turned in first. He had a room of his own. He clapped Joseph on the shoulder as he passed. 'Good lad,' he grunted.

Joseph lay on his mattress in the corner, waiting for the others to finish playing cards, rigid with fearful anticipation. Cormac called out, 'sleep tight there, lad, I'll wake you good and early.' Joseph held the pistol to his chest, biding his time.

Now, despite all his fears and doubts, he'd done it. He felt George holding on to his coat and the man's breath on his neck. Smelt him too, the poor devil.

His eyes had adjusted to the darkness. No longer progressing by feel alone, he stepped forward with greater confidence. Misplaced confidence, as he found out when his toe struck a solid metal object. The resulting clang made his heart skip a beat. 'Sweet Jesus,' he muttered under his breath, standing stock still, pulse racing.

That damned coal scuttle. He'd forgotten that it stood by the back door. Satisfied, at last, that he hadn't woken his comrades, Joseph felt for the door. It was secured by bolts at the top and bottom. The upper bolt slid back easily. Stooping, he found the knob of the lower bolt and gently rotated it through ninety degrees before easing it sideways. It resisted stiffly until he put his shoulder to the door, pushing to counteract the friction.

George sniffed greedily at the cool, clean air as they crossed the threshold. Hardly daring to hope until now, he let go of Joseph's jacket and hurried across the yard to the gate, helping Joseph to lift the metal bar.

'Quick now, let's get clear of this place,' Joseph closed the gate behind them and broke into a run, heading for the nearest street corner. George trotted awkwardly after him, feeling the revolver in his jacket pocket slapping against his hip. Joseph stopped to allow George to catch up, then ran on again until they'd put a quarter of a mile between them and the warehouse.

With only the occasional streetlamp to aid him, George tried to get his bearings. The salty stench of the river announced the proximity of the Thames, then the pub on the corner clinched it. He was in Wapping.

After twenty minutes of intermittently running and walking through near deserted streets, they skirted the looming battlements of the Tower and came upon a cab rank by All Hallows Church.

George viewed the solitary cab as a drowning sailor might see a lifeboat. He looked uncertainly at Joseph. Until now, they'd hardly spoken a word to one-another.

'Where do you need to get to?' Joseph asked.

George hadn't thought that far ahead. His own rooms, or Montagu Square. He quickly patted his trouser pockets. Of course, his keys were on his bedside table at Verity's.

'Montagu Square. Damn, I've got no money.'

'Never mind that, I'll pay. We'll share the cab to Montagu Square and I'll take it on from there.'

They found the cabbie snoring on his box, with a blanket across his knees.

Joseph reached up and shook him repeatedly until the man reluctantly opened his eyes.

'Where to, guv?'

'Montagu Square first, then I'll tell you my final destination.'

The cabbie nodded, then caught sight of George. 'Don't carry no tramps. Lor, I can smell him from here.'

George knew how he must appear, clothes crumpled and stained and yes, he did stink.

'You'll get a gold sovereign for your trouble when we get to Montagu Square, that on top of your fare to wherever my companion is going.'

They climbed aboard while the cabbie muttered to himself.

George relaxed a little at the sound of the horse's hooves and the rumbling of the wheels on the road. Joseph sat rigidly by his side.

'Thank you.'

George waited. 'Thank you,' he repeated, touching Joseph's elbow.

'There's no need.'

'But, why?'

'It doesn't matter why.' Joseph turned his head away.

'It does to me.'

'Damn it, man. You're out of there. Isn't that enough? We're both out of that place. Now we go our separate ways and that's an end of it.'

They sat in brittle silence until the cab entered Portman Street. With Montagu Square approaching, George felt compelled to speak. 'I won't identify you. To the authorities, I mean.'

'Oh, right? Thanks.'

'What is Carter planning?'

Joseph snorted.

'Please.'

The cab turned into the square. 'The Jubilee.' Joseph said as it pulled up.

'I'll get you that sovereign,' George called to the cabbie as he climbed down and crossed the pavement.

'Please wake up,' he whispered to himself as he took hold of the door knocker, slamming it hard. He set his ear to the door and knocked again. In desperation, he raised the flap of the letterbox. 'It's George! Come to the door!' he yelled until he could do no more than croak.

The cab drew away, the cabbie's patience exhausted despite the dubious promise of a sovereign. George leaned with his head against the door, trying to summon the strength to renew his assault on the knocker. The sound of footsteps roused him.

He'd never forget the look on Verity's face, with Ambrose at her shoulder, or the way she didn't hesitate to embrace him despite his filthy condition. Her tears trickled through his matted beard as she drew him inside. She staggered under his weight when his legs gave way until Ambrose rushed forward to catch him.

Chapter 39

They propped their bicycles against the wall. With half an hour before first light, they stood together outside the warehouse gates, two figures in black with peaked caps pulled well down. Under their coats, each carried a C96 Mauser machine pistol with a ten round box magazine, in leather holsters across their chests, and sheathed stabbing knives attached to their belts.

The Dutchman placed his boot in Riemann's cupped hands and pulled himself up to grip the top of the gate. It was almost their undoing. The gate swung open with the Dutchman clinging to it and Riemann lost his balance, sprawling onto the cobblestones in the yard. He cursed and picked himself up. The metal bar used to secure the gate was lying at his feet.

He beckoned his companion. 'I hope to God they haven't cleared out.'

The Dutchman shrugged, pointing to the dark outline of the coach house. Riemann nodded. They moved in that direction.

Riemann peered into the gloom. Their success hinged on getting onto the roof of the coach house and somehow gaining entry to the warehouse through a first-floor window. There were two within reach of the apex of the coach house roof. Sash windows. With luck, they'd find one unlocked. Otherwise, he might need to use the jemmy tucked into his boot. Unless …

'Wait,' Riemann hissed.

'What?'

'Wait here. Don't move.'

He crossed the yard cautiously. The warehouse loomed above him, dark and ominous. His hand found the rough brick wall of the building and he sidled to his left, to where he thought the back door might be situated.

Brick gave way to timber. Riemann found the latch and pressed his thumb down. It rose with a metallic click. He pushed gently and met no resistance. His hunch had paid off. If the gate to the yard had been left unsecured, perhaps the same could be said for this door. But his relief was tempered by the growing conviction that the Fenians had gone.

'Well?' said the Dutchman when Riemann returned.

'I don't know. It doesn't feel right. Back door's not bolted.'

'They could be gone then.'

'Perhaps. But until we know, we assume they're in there. Come on. It will be getting light soon.'

Standing together inside the warehouse, they waited by the door for the first glow of light to reveal their surroundings. Darkness was ideal for cloaking their entry, but they needed enough light to navigate the interior and locate their quarry. First light, before the Fenians were awake with any luck, or at least still drowsy and slow to react.

Cormac grunted and turned over onto his back. The room was still dark, but he knew it must almost be daylight. He'd always had the knack of waking at a set time. 'It's like having an alarm clock in me head,' he'd say. *Best get it over with quick*, he thought, dragging on his trousers in the dark and feeling for his boots under the bed. *I'll bet Joseph's had hardly a wink all night. Still, he'll feel better when it's done. That's how I was the first time.*

'Right, my lad, time to do your duty,' he whispered, bending over Joseph's bed. 'Come on now,' Cormac reached out to shake Joseph's shoulder and felt instead the feather-filled plumpness of the pillow. He moved his hand along. Nothing but the roughness of an old horse blanket.

'Jesus,' he muttered. The Captain would go mad and Cormac knew he'd feel his wrath. He would be held responsible. His mind raced. Had Joseph buggered off? Or was he still in the warehouse, trying to build up his courage? He opened the door and poked his head out. It was getting light. The expanse of the first floor was empty.

'What's up Cormac?'

He looked round. 'Ah, Pat. I just went to wake Joseph. He isn't there.'

'Christ.'

'Shh, keep your voice down. I'm thinking he's here somewhere, just steeling himself, you know.'

'I'll wake Dermot and the Captain.'

'No. Don't be doing that. Not yet. Let's look for him first. If we can find him and get the job done, then no one needs to be any the wiser.' Cormac looked imploringly at his brother.

Pat hesitated, looking over at Dermot's bed in the far corner of the room. Reassured by the intermittent drone of Dermot's snores, he dressed quickly and joined Cormac at the door.

'He's not up here,' Cormac said, indicating the empty floor.

'Top floor?'

Cormac shook his head. 'Let's look downstairs first.'

Alerted by the squeaking of the floorboards above them, Riemann and the Dutchman moved from the door to crouch in the space under the stairs, unbuttoning their jackets to expose the Mausers resting in their holsters.

Cormac and Pat descended the staircase warily. Save for a few sticks of furniture, the ground floor was just a cavernous empty space.

'How about the yard?' Pat suggested.

'I'm for checking the cellar first,' Cormac replied.

'Why? D'ye think he's down there having a cosy chat with Benson about how he's about to blow his brains out?'

Cormac ignored his brother and strode to the door leading to the cellar. Framed in the doorway, he automatically reached inside for the lantern hanging from a hook inside. At the same time as his hand failed to make contact with the lantern, he saw its glow at the foot of the stairs. Muttering an oath, he padded stealthily down the steps.

Pat stood at the foot of the stairs from the first floor, wondering whether to follow Cormac or go out into the yard. His last thought was that he'd try the yard. The Dutchman's gloved hand clamped firmly over his mouth and nose, twisting his head to the left. He'd hardly felt the thrust of the wickedly pointed blade severing his carotid artery before unconsciousness eliminated all feeling. Death claimed him in ten seconds. The Dutchman avoided the immediate spurt of blood, then lowered the body to the floor, stepping away as a dark red puddle formed around it.

Riemann nodded towards the entrance to the cellar. The Dutchman raised a hand in acknowledgement and disappeared below, while Riemann retreated into the shadow beneath the staircase.

'Joseph. Joseph, man, are you down here?' Cormac kept his voice to a little above a whisper, leaving the steps and starting along the passage. A quick glance into the slopping-out room showed no sign of Joseph. Could Pat be right? Was the damned fool in with Benson?

He ran the twenty paces to the cell door. Reaching automatically for the key hanging on its nail outside, his hand met nothing but the bare nail head. Panicking now, Cormac looked stupidly at the door. The key was there in the lock.

'Oh no, Jesus, no,' his hand twisted the handle. Panic turned to terror at the sight of the empty cell. Spinning on his heel, Cormac darted back into the passage. 'Pat,' he screamed, 'he's gone. Get the Cap...'

Ten paces away, and robbed of the element of surprise, the Dutchman sheathed his knife.

The confusion fogging Cormac's brain cleared as adrenaline flooded his body. But his instinctive decision to throw his lantern at the intruder came too late. In a practised, fluid motion, the Dutchman drew his Mauser, aimed, and put two rounds between Cormac's eyes.

Stepping over the body, he glanced around the empty cell, then headed back along the passage.

Carter was in his room, dressed in shirtsleeves, combing his thinning strands of hair in an effort to conceal a spreading bald patch. He dropped the comb at the sound of Cormac's scream, punctuated by the crack, crack, of gunfire.

With his survival instincts at full stretch, he lifted his shoulder holster from the back of a chair and slipped it on, then put his jacket on over it.

Dermot was sitting on the edge of his bed in his vest and long johns, rubbing the sleep from his eyes, when he heard it. Seconds later, he was pounding down the stairs, barefoot, with a rifle in his hands. Halfway down, the sight of Pat's body arrested his headlong descent.

Riemann, concealed under the staircase, released his pistol's safety catch.

The open door to the cellar caught Dermot's attention. He took a tentative step downstairs, eyes fixed on the cellar doorway.

Readying to fire as soon as his target cleared the staircase, Riemann was caught off guard when Dermot leapt down the remaining stairs and ran for the cellar.

Framed in the doorway for an instant, Dermot was a sitting duck. The Dutchman, crouching on the steps below, fired a four-round burst, stepping back smartly as Dermot's body tumbled down, his rifle clattering alongside.

Riemann emerged, edging towards the cellar, pistol raised, covering the top of the staircase. Carter's first bullet missed his ear by a whisker. The second passed close enough to flick the hem of his overcoat. As he dived through the cellar door, a third round slammed into the doorpost.

Carter was already at the foot of the staircase. He fired again towards the cellar doorway, then put his head down and sprinted for the back door, leaping over Pat and wrenching it open.

Riemann sat on the steps, winded. The Dutchman pushed past him, reaching the back door in time to see

Carter three-quarters of the way to the open gate, crouching low. He held his breath to steady his aim, then dropped his arm. Carter was through.

He shook his head as Riemann joined him.

'We have to clear out. Now,' Riemann hissed.

Chapter 40

Dermot's crooked teeth were set in a demonic leer as he stood over George. Rough hands pulled him to his feet. They were all there. Pat and Cormac had hold of his arms. Carter stood by the wall, pointing at seven diagonal chalk marks, all scored through with a diagonal line. At his side, the young one, Joseph, stood with a rope looped over his arm. At a signal from Carter, he stepped forward and placed a noose over George's head. He thrashed around helplessly as they dragged him to the door. His screams died in his throat.

'George. You're safe, old man. Can you hear me, George? You're safe in Montagu Square.'

'Ambrose?'

'I'm here George. It's all over. Look, you're in Verity's house. Let's sit you up.'

'How long?'

'You arrived just after three. Good job I'm a light sleeper. The sight of you on the doorstep. I'll see those blackguards pay, if it's the last thing I do.'

'Verity. I must see Verity.'

'And so you shall, old chap. She's been here watching over you most of the time. I'll get her.'

George took stock of his surroundings. This wasn't the bedroom he'd occupied before. It was smaller. The roof sloped down, with a small window let into it. An attic room.

He let his mind wander. The beard was a physical reminder of his ordeal, along with a general soreness. But how wonderful to feel clean. He luxuriated in the fresh nightshirt and the smoothness of the bedsheets. Someone had stripped away his filthy clothes and washed him. He remembered nothing of it but felt a pang of disquiet at the thought that Verity might have had a hand in it.

'Hello, George,' a gentle voice intruded on his thoughts.

He turned his head.

'Verity…'

'You should rest.' George felt her cool fingers on his brow.

'No. Rest can wait. But there is something you can do for me.'

'Of course. What is it?'

'A cup of tea and get Quilter here.'

'I'll see to the tea. Clarence is already on his way.'

*****

Keen as he was to get rid of the beard, not least because of the number of silver threads it contained, George would not delay his meeting with the Colonel. Dressed in what was now his best suit, given that his previous favourite was beyond rescue and destined for the bonfire, he stood impatiently at the window.

Verity and Ambrose sat awkwardly at the drawing-room table. Desperate though they were to learn what had transpired, they respected George's wish to tell them all at the same time. 'I don't want to go over it again and again,' he insisted.

'At last.' George turned away from the window. 'I'll let him in.'

With a curt instruction to desist from asking questions, George recounted his ordeal. He kept nothing back, including the vile indignities of his predicament.

Quilter sat stony faced, taking notes.

Reaching the point where he'd arrived at Verity's door, George turned to the Colonel. 'You've got the address. There's four of them, Carter and the other three. They'll know I've gone by now. You'll have to move swiftly or they'll clear out. Perhaps they've already gone.'

Quilter closed his notebook and gave a thin smile, reaching into his breast pocket. 'I received this telegram shortly before I left home to come here. Shots were heard in Wapping shortly after dawn this morning. A stevedore on his way to work alerted a couple of local constables and showed them to a disused warehouse in the vicinity. There they discovered the bodies of three men in their twenties, one of whom is Dermot Kinsella, a known Fenian. Also found at the premises were several firearms and a conveyance containing a considerable quantity of dynamite.

George stared at the Colonel. 'Good God, there was dynamite there?'

'Somehow they'd acquired a van belonging to a cinematographer – moving pictures. There was enough dynamite in it to kill scores of people.'

Verity put her hand on Quilter's arm. 'You said three bodies. Men in their twenties.'

Quilter sighed. 'There was no sign of O'Brien – Carter.'

'Damn,' Ambrose slapped the table.

'Yes, it's a blow,' Quilter conceded. 'Nevertheless, this discovery has forestalled a calamity of incalculable proportions.

'Yes?' Verity and Ambrose spoke in unison.

'Papers discovered at the scene prove that their intention was to mount an attack on the Diamond Jubilee procession. These men planned to assassinate the Queen, members of the royal family, visiting dignitaries and anyone in range of the blast. A more dastardly act is hard to imagine.'

Verity blew out her cheeks. 'What now? When this gets out, it will cause a sensation.'

'It will go no further.'

Verity blinked. 'But…'

'At eleven o'clock this morning, I shall be attending a meeting at Marlborough House with the Prince of Wales and the Prime Minister. Not even the Home Secretary will be privy to this information. It is imperative that nothing should cast a shadow over the Jubilee. This is the Empire's last opportunity to show its love and gratitude to a sovereign who has reigned over us for sixty glorious years. We can thank God that the danger has been averted.

'And I need not remind the three of you that you cannot breathe a word of this. You will take the knowledge to your graves.'

Verity, George, and Ambrose looked at each other in dumb amazement.

Quilter broke the silence. 'You said there were four of them, George. But there was also a fifth. The man who helped you to escape. Who is he?'

'That man saved my life and put his own in jeopardy. I gave him my word that I would not betray him.'

'It's hardly a betrayal.' Quilter snapped. 'The man is an enemy of the state. It's your duty…'

George rose and leaned over the table, his face inches away from the Colonel's. 'Don't you dare talk to me about duty. I'm the one who's spent days in a bare cell, suffocating in the stench of my own filth, under sentence of death, while you sat in your office, enjoyed the company of your family and slept in the comfort of your own bed. Oh, don't worry, Colonel, I'll take the Jubilee plot to my grave and the identity of that man with it.'

Quilter blanched under the onslaught. As he opened his mouth to respond, George returned to the attack. 'Oh, and do you know what I thought about when I paced up and down in that cell? I thought of how much pleasure I'd get in breaking your scrawny neck, Clarence.' George pushed his seat back and stormed out of the drawing-room.

Colonel Quilter coughed and loosened his collar, his face now an angry shade of puce.

'Clarence, are you quite alright?'

'Ah… yes. Perhaps a glass of water.'

Verity filled a glass from a jug on the sideboard and placed it at the Colonel's elbow.

'A three-decker broadside, if ever there was one,' Ambrose quipped. 'Dare say I'd flare up a bit if I'd been through the same thing.'

Quilter put the glass down. 'I must be getting along.'

Verity shook her head. 'Your meeting is at eleven. You have plenty of time. Now, what about this man, Carter? A dangerous would-be assassin is at large in London. What do you propose to do about it?'

The Colonel opened his despatch case and placed his notebook inside. 'That need not concern you any further,' he said curtly.

Verity bristled. 'You forget that George told Carter that he was lodging at Montagu Square. A man who was about to murder George, is somewhere out there. Is there anything to suggest that he will not come here to finish the job? Put my mind at rest, Clarence, I'm all ears.'

'His description is being circulated. I could arrange to have a constable posted outside.'

'I see. Well, forgive me if I appear to be less than reassured.'

Quilter shrugged and rose to leave.

'One more question before you dash off to the Prince of Wales,' Ambrose leaned back casually in his chair. 'Who the devil killed these three Fenians? Assassinated the assassins as it were. How did they know where to find them when you had no clue?'

Quilter's footsteps retreated along the hall. He saw himself out.

'I could do with a stiff drink after that.'

Verity smiled. 'It's only ten-fifteen, Ambrose. A cup of tea will have to suffice. If Clarence hadn't left so abruptly, I would have mentioned it.'

'Tea?'

'No. Not that. I would have said something about Temple-Swift.'

'And reveal Anna Jesenska as a spy?'

'Hmm. Then again, do we owe her anything? We hardly know her.' Verity sensed a movement in the doorway. 'Oh, there you are, George. Quilter's gone. Come and sit back down while I order some tea,' she added, pressing the bell to summon Elsie.

They listened while George apologised for flying off the handle and persuaded him to recount again the dreadful events that he'd endured. He did so hesitantly, but felt a little better from talking about it.

Elsie's arrival with the tea interrupted them. When she'd left, George said, 'Carter's out there somewhere.'

Ambrose threw his hands up, 'but we have no way of finding him now.'

'What if he comes here?' Verity couldn't disguise her anguish at the thought.

'Then he'll do so at his peril. George and I are equal to the task of dealing with the fellow. Give him a taste of his own medicine, what?'

'For heaven's sake Ambrose, Jaqueline's here. Do you think for a moment that I would put her at risk? No, I've made up my mind. I'm taking her back to France.'

Chapter 41

Carter pushed his plate away and picked up the packet of cigarettes on the table. His pipe and tobacco pouch were back at the warehouse, so Woodbines would have to do. As the smoke filled his lungs, he contemplated his situation.

After his headlong rush across the yard and into the street, he'd concealed himself in a doorway fifty yards away with his finger on the trigger of the revolver in his pocket. Moments later, two men dressed in black emerged from the yard and mounted bicycles, riding away in the opposite direction. Carter wasted no time, walking purposefully but not so hurriedly as to draw attention to himself. By the time he heard police whistles, he was a quarter of a mile away.

A park bench was his first stop. His previous experience of desperate action had taught him that once the physical imperative of fight and flight had worn off, his body would react. Thank God it wasn't raining, he thought, as the morning sun helped to stem his shivers. The bench was his refuge until gradually the weakness in his legs and the trembling of his hands subsided.

Near St Paul's, he found a café and ordered breakfast. Normally a man of modest appetite, he'd eaten his way through fried eggs, several rashers of bacon, two pork sausages, fried bread, and mushrooms. A large mug of sweet strong tea steamed in front of him.

Little by little, Carter brought some order into the confusion of his thoughts. He called the questions milling around in his brain to order and started to deal with them, one by one.

The attackers? Quilter's men, surely. Who else could it be?

How did they know where to find him? Through Giles Temple-Swift? But he knew nothing about the warehouse.

What was it that Cormac had shouted out? *He's gone* – that's what it sounded like, but Carter couldn't be sure. Did he mean Benson was gone? But how the devil could he have escaped?

Pat was dead and Dermot. He'd seen that with his own eyes. Those first shots he heard must mean Cormac was dead, too. But what about Joseph? Could he be lying down there with him?

He went through it all again, with a growing feeling of unease. The conclusion was inescapable. Carter reached inside his overcoat, closing his hand over the chamber of his revolver. Two bullets remained. One for that lousy turncoat, Joseph Maguire, and the other for George Benson. He'd not escape a second time. First stop, Edna's place in Despard Road. With any luck, Joseph would go there. Then Montagu Square to find Benson.

***

Edna's sciatica had kept her awake. Somehow, she knew that the knock on the door was Joseph and she approached the door without qualms, shielding the candle in her hand. The hall clock said three twenty-five. Joseph looked dreadful, standing there shivering, with a haunted look in his eyes. 'I can't stay. Got to get to Dublin. Those clothes I left behind. I just need time to change and a quick feed. Oh, and there's that money of mine.'

'Mother of God, Joseph. You look like you've got the devil himself on your tail. Come into the kitchen and sit down. I'll make you a cup of tea.'

Edna added a dash of whiskey and put the cup and saucer on the table. 'What is it, Joseph?' she asked, sitting down next to him.

Joseph drank his tea in silence for a few moments.

'I'm in trouble, Edna. Awful trouble.'

'Are the police after you?'

'The police?' Joseph gave a mirthless laugh.

'Him then.'

He nodded. 'Carter, yes. Don't ask me why, Edna. But he'll come after me as soon as he knows…'

'You mean he'll come looking for you here?'

Joseph nodded. 'Bound to.'

'How long?'

Joseph looked nervously down the passage. 'I had a job to do, early, just after dawn. In a couple of hours, he'll know. They'll come after me.'

'They?'

'There's three others.'

'I see'. Edna shivered, drawing her dressing gown tighter around her. 'So, you want to get to Dublin?'

Joseph nodded. 'I can catch a train from Euston to Holyhead.'

'What makes you think you'll be safe in Dublin?'

Joseph shrugged. 'Look, I can't stay here. If you can just give me a bite to eat, I'll go up and change. The money I left will still be up there, won't it?'

Edna shifted in her seat. 'I took your clothes out of the wardrobe.'

'Eh?'

'Joseph, you walked out of here and said nothing about coming back. What was I supposed to do? I can't leave the room empty. I need the money. I've heard nothing from the Brotherhood. It's all very well being asked to support the cause, and I was happy having you here, but I have to earn a living. All I've got is the laundry I take in and that room to let out to lodgers. I've folded your clothes and put them in the box room.'

Joseph's shoulders slumped. 'Oh. I see. Of course, I understand. Thanks for looking after them.' Then the thought struck him. 'Do you mean to say that there's a lodger up there?' he hissed, pointing to the ceiling.

Edna reached over and patted his arm. 'I'll be putting a card in the newsagent's window later on. There's no one up there now.'

'Right. You had me going there for a minute. The money will be with the clothes then?'

Edna's silence unnerved him.

'The money, Edna. Where is it?'

'It's… it's safe.'

Joseph jumped to his feet, upsetting the cup and saucer.

Edna recoiled, putting her hands up to her face. 'It's in the savings bank,' she whispered through her fingers.

'Jesus!'

'I know, I know, but it was for safekeeping. I didn't want it lying around the place, not with another lodger coming into the house. Look, I'll show you.' Edna rose stiffly to her feet and shuffled over to the mantelpiece, picking up a japanned box and returning to the table with it. 'Here we are,' she said, lifting the lid and rummaging through the contents to produce a small blue booklet.

Joseph watched her open it and flick through a couple of pages. 'There you are. Deposit of forty-six pounds,' she flourished the bankbook in front of him. 'Safekeeping in the bank, for you,' she added defiantly.

Joseph collapsed onto his chair like a marionette with cut strings, shaking his head.

'I've got precisely one and threepence in my pocket after paying the cab that brought me, Edna. It was the money I left behind that I was counting on. That's why I had to come here.'

'But Joseph, you'll have the money. As soon as the bank…' Her voice trailed off.

'As soon as the bank opens, Edna, is that what you were going to say?'

Edna turned away, nodding, unable to look him in the face.

'When will it open?' Joseph said through gritted teeth.

'Ten,' a small voice responded.

'Dear God, I'm a dead man.'

All Edna could think of was to make another pot of tea. Anything to break the tension. Joseph sat stiffly at the table, gazing stupidly at the open bank book. Freed from his reproachful gaze, the mechanical act of making the tea gave her time to think.

'Joseph,' she ventured, setting the teapot on the table. 'If it wasn't for the money, you wouldn't have come here;

that's what you said. You'd have gone to Euston, wouldn't you?'

'Might have been a bit too early for the Holyhead train, but I could have found somewhere to lie low. There would always be a risk.'

'So when Carter comes after you, won't he be thinking that you might be making for Dublin? He might go to Euston rather than come here.'

'There's four of them, Edna. Why wouldn't two of them go to Euston and the other two come straight here? He'll come, Edna, I can feel it.'

Edna didn't argue. She'd acted for the best, but that made no difference to Joseph's predicament. She clasped his hand with both of hers.

Chapter 42

Although she'd been expecting it, the knock on the door gave Edna such a start that she almost dropped the pile of ironing in her hands. She put it down on the kitchen table, willing herself to control her palpitations.

The knocker sounded again, more insistently.

From the kitchen door, she could see down the hallway to the front door and the silhouette of the figure standing on the other side of the frosted glass.

'I'm coming,' she called, failing to disguise the quaver in her voice.

The clock in the passage struck the quarter hour as she unlocked the front door. Eight fifteen.

Without a word, Carter pushed past her.

'Hey, where do you think you're going?'

'Shut the door and go to the kitchen.' Carter turned to her, unbuttoning his coat. The sight of his pistol was all the urging she needed.

His boots pounded on the stairs. She listened to his footfalls going from room to room. In a minute he thudded back down, darting into the front parlour, then striding down the passage towards her.

'Where is he?'

Edna shook her head. 'Who…?'

The back of Carter's hand sent her staggering against the dresser.

'Joseph's time is up, Edna, and yours too, if you're hiding him. What's through there?' Carter pointed to the open doorway behind her.

'Just the pantry and the washhouse,' Edna blinked back tears, rubbing her swollen cheek, 'and the door to the backyard.'

Carter disappeared. She saw him through the window, peering around the small cobbled yard. In a moment, he was back.

'He's not here,' she whispered. 'I've not seen him. What's he done, for pity's sake?'

She flinched, imagining he was going to strike her again.

He took a seat at the kitchen table.

'Sit down, woman. I'll tell you what he did, alright.'

Edna's knees shook under the table while Carter recounted the raid on the warehouse.

'Thanks to that treacherous shite, three brave sons of Ireland are lying dead and a British spy has escaped. He deserves a thousand deaths for what he's done.' Carter grabbed her roughly by the wrist. 'So if you know anything about his whereabouts, you tell me now or by all that's holy, I'll choke the life out of you if I learn you've helped him.'

'I don't, please believe me.' Edna's voice cracked, tears filling her red-rimmed eyes and coursing down her cheeks.

Carter released his grip. 'Go and make some tea. I need time to think.'

Edna set the kettle to boil on the hob, relieved to be out of Carter's gaze and reach. Fishing in her apron for her handkerchief, she wiped the tears away. As he sat polishing his pince-nez, she considered the full import of what he'd said. He blamed the deaths of his men on Joseph, but Joseph had spoken to her as though they were alive. And what was that about a British spy? If what Carter said was true, what then? She'd be harbouring a traitor.

The kettle's whistling intruded on her thoughts. Turning the gas off, she reached for the tea caddy. Carter frightened the wits out of her. He'd snuff her out like a candle, if he thought she'd lied to him. What if she owned up? Gave up Joseph?

Carter replaced his spectacles and turned to look at her. It was then she knew for certain that he'd no intention of allowing her to live, whatever she said. She knew too much.

'Do you have a lantern?'

'What was that?'

'Are ye deaf, woman? I said, do you have a lantern?'

Edna felt her legs trembling again. 'Yes, in the pantry.'

'Get it.'

Standing on tiptoe in the pantry, she reached up for a small brass lantern standing on the top shelf. After blowing the dust off it, she placed it on the kitchen table and took a step back.

Carter picked it up and shook it, feeling the liquid movement of the kerosene inside. Edna looked on while he produced a matchbox from his pocket. As he concentrated on opening the lantern door and igniting the wick, she backed away until she felt the hard edge of the stove top against the small of her back.

'There now, that's a good strong light, so it is?' Carter spoke with his back to her, his hands around the base of the lantern. 'Don't you go thinking I've gone soft in the head, now, sitting here with a lantern while it's a bright sunny day?'

Edna's mouth felt bone dry.

'I'll tell you what. I could swear there's something different about this house.' He didn't look round. His tone was calm and measured. Somehow, it made it all the worse.

Edna dug her nails into her palms.

'That rug in the corner? Didn't I see that rug in the front parlour when I was last here?

Yes, I'm sure of it. Funny place to have a nice rug. Stuck in the corner of the kitchen like that. You're very quiet there, Edna.'

'Oh, I was just going to hang it on the line to give it a good beating. Get the dust out of it. I put it down there when you knocked on the door.' Edna hadn't fainted since she was a girl. That old feeling of nausea and light-headedness swept over her. If he turned round to look at her, she knew her knees would give way.

Carter went quiet.

Gradually, Edna felt the nausea pass. 'I'll finish making the tea, shall I?' Her voice came out half an octave too high.

'Not now, Edna. You stay right where you are.'

She'd never know how she managed to stifle a scream when he rose to his feet and shot her a glance of malevolent triumph before edging round the table and stooping to lift the edge of the rug.

Silently, Carter opened the trapdoor and shone the lantern into the void below, revealing a flight of wooden steps with a bare brick wall on one side and a rickety timber banister on the other.

At the far end of the cellar, Joseph crouched by the coal chute, holding a short-handled shovel. After Edna had persuaded him to take a bit of breakfast, he'd skulked down there. 'We can get through this,' she said. 'If we both keep our heads. When he comes to the door asking for you, I could either say you called here and then went away, or that I hadn't seen you at all. Would it make any difference either way?'

'Just say you haven't seen me.'

He should have taken his chances out on the street and arranged to meet Edna later when she had the money. Too late now. Rat in a trap. Just like Benson must have felt.

He had almost lost control of his bladder when he heard footsteps and muffled voices. How many of them were there? He imagined Edna cowering upstairs. Would her nerve hold? He doubted it.

Joseph moved to the foot of the stairs, straining to listen. He couldn't be sure, but it only sounded like two voices, mainly a dull murmur with an occasional harsh outburst. Carter, no doubt about it.

The whistling of the kettle gave him a start. He retreated to the coal heap. That's all there was down there. Before Edna closed the trapdoor, he'd looked around in the gloom. Nothing but bare walls. If Carter came down those steps, all he had to defend himself was a small shovel and lumps of coal.

Oh Jesus. The squeaking hinges of the trapdoor warned him a heartbeat before a dim shaft of daylight illuminated the staircase. A moment later came the bright glow of a lantern beam.

The staircase creaked under Carter's tread. He stopped three steps from the top. Joseph saw his legs encased in dark tweed.

'Joseph. I know you're there.'

One more step. Then another. Only Carter's head remained out of sight. Joseph could see the lantern in his left hand. In his right hand, Joseph saw the glint of gunmetal.

'It's all over. Be a man for once in your life. They're all dead because of you. I'll make it quick, which is more than you deserve.'

All dead?

Joseph launched himself. Halfway to the stairs, he heard the click of the hammer on Carter's pistol being drawn back, and ducked instinctively. His only hope lay in moving fast and hoping that Carter's aim would be off target, balanced awkwardly as he was with the lantern in one hand and his gun in the other. A mad notion flashed through his mind of smashing his shovel over Carter's head before a bullet tore through him.

Carter held his fire. Joseph came to a halt at the foot of the stairs. Blinking in the lantern light, he looked up at the muzzle of the revolver, dropped the shovel and shut his eyes.

The heavy iron frying pan cracked Carter's skull like an eggshell. Edna almost followed his body down the steps with the momentum of her wild swing, dropping the pan and managing to grab the handrail. Joseph teetered as Carter cannoned into his legs. The smashed lantern spilled flaming kerosene over the floor. Joseph stamped it out. Hot-blooded rage erupted in him. Taking up the shovel, he bent over Carter, smashing the already ruined head to a bloody pulp.

Chapter 43

'Must I go, Maman?'

Verity knew her sudden decision to take Jaqueline back to France would upset the child.

'*Chérie*. You know that you must go back to Montvalon. Are you not looking forward to seeing *tante* Claudette and your little friends?'

'But it is too soon. I like my friends here.'

Verity raised an eyebrow. 'Oh, do you mean the players in your little theatre? But you can take them with you.'

Jaqueline huffed and rolled her eyes. 'No. I mean funny old Monsieur Ambrose, and Elsie, and…'

'And who?'

'Monsieur Benson? Do you think he would be my friend?'

Verity knelt down and hugged her daughter. 'Of course, *chérie*. And you can see all of them again, next summer. There, won't that be something to look forward to?'

Jaqueline's eyes glistened.

'Begging your pardon, Miss. Post's just arrived.' Elsie stood in the doorway with a package and some letters in her hands.

Verity got to her feet. 'Would you have a little something in the kitchen? For Jaqueline.' she whispered, taking the mail from Elsie.

'Come along, Miss Jaqueline. I think I have a slice of sponge cake in the pantry.' Elsie took the girl's hand.

At her desk, Verity glanced quickly at the three envelopes in front of her. One from Olivia, she knew from the handwriting. The others, she guessed, were from journals to which she contributed articles. She turned to the package.

'Oh, am I interrupting?'

'No, of course not, George. Come on in. How do you feel this morning?'

'Quite my old self.'

'Just have a seat while I deal with this.' Verity held the package up and shook it. 'It's quite light. I wonder what it can be?'

'You weren't expecting a package then?'

'No, and it's curious that it only bears the street address. There's no name.'

Verity busied herself with a pair of scissors.

'Hmm. What's this? Something wrapped in cloth. I say, George, what do you make of this?'

'Make of what?' George stood and looked over Verity's shoulder.

Lying on a piece of flannel was a pair of pince-nez. Only one lens remained, and it was cracked.

Verity felt inside the partly open package. 'There's a sheet of paper here as well. What on earth does that mean?'

C is with D, P and C, in hell.
J

'It means you needn't hurry off to France with Jaqueline.' George picked up the pince-nez. 'These are

Carter's. The last time I saw him wearing them, he was sentencing me to death.'

'J?'

'Is the man who saved my life and brought me here. D, P and C are Dermot, Patrick, and Cormac, the men whose bodies were discovered at the warehouse.'

'How…?'

'How did Carter die? Your guess is as good as mine. But these pince-nez are definitely his.'

'I'll go and tell Jaqueline she can stay. She'll be thrilled.'

'I suppose we should inform Quilter.'

'Yes, I suppose so, George.'

Chapter 44

Orpheus was at a low ebb. Doubts had plagued him since his last meeting with Lensch. And now, his pleasant dalliance with Anna was nearing its end. Or at least that would be the sensible thing. When his wife returned in a week's time, he would have to quit the Traveller's Club and return home.

Still, it gave him a week.

He left his desk and moved to the window, looking out at Whitehall. Here was the heart of the British Empire, the centre of power. Its grand buildings exuding an elegant confidence, even on a day such as this, with pelting rain soaking their facades and an unseasonal biting wind from the west.

What use was he now? The plan for the Jubilee assassination was in Lensch's hands, and he, Orpheus, had no further part to play. Afterwards – who knew.

Victoria and her successor - dead. An empire in convulsions, shaken to its very roots. Two well-aimed shots and the course of world history irrevocably altered.

What had seemed a distant and madly exciting prospect when von Lensch had first broached it with him, now chilled him with awful foreboding at what it might unleash. Eulenburg's neat assumption that it would bring Britain and Germany together was all very well. But once the delicate balance of relations between the great powers was thrown into chaos, the consequences could not be foretold.

What irony. As a senior public official, he and his wife would have the privilege of watching the Jubilee procession from his office. Yet, he alone of those occupying the various official vantage points along Whitehall that day would know that the Queen would never reach them. Her carriage would pass beneath the firing point a little after 1pm if all went to plan. He wondered how long the dreadful news would take to reach Whitehall.

Reluctantly, he returned to his desk. An hour dealing with official papers was followed by a seemingly endless meeting with the Permanent Secretary. At 5.30 pm, he left for the club. The wind had eased, permitting him to raise his umbrella to ward off occasional flurries of rain. Promising himself an evening of rest and relaxation before his assignation with Anna, Orpheus left his attaché case behind, locked securely in his office. How it amused him that his Home Office colleagues had no inkling of what lay concealed in its false bottom.

He scowled when he thought back to his dinner with Lensch. The German had made it clear to him that he had no further part to play in Operation Geck, so who knew when he'd need that code book again? *Tomorrow, I'll put it in my bank vault*, he resolved.

Bathed, shaved, and with a hearty dinner inside him, Orpheus's mood had lifted considerably by the time he stepped into the waiting cab. He could leave Orpheus behind for the night and simply be Giles.

Anna had promised to leave the theatre promptly after the performance. 'I'll be waiting in my rooms for you at 11 pm. Take this key,' she said after their last tryst.

He took the stairs two at a time, imagining her reclining on her chaise longue with a bottle of champagne beside her.

'Anna,' he called out as he closed the apartment door behind him.

She appeared at the sitting-room door and skipped along the hallway towards him, lightly kissing his cheek.

'How was tonight's performance?' Giles pulled her to him.

'Another triumph, of course, my dear, thunderous applause and three curtain calls. Now then come through.' Anna detached herself from his embrace and led the way to the sitting room.

Giles blinked as he entered. He had happy memories of this room. On his previous visits, even in daylight, the curtains had been drawn, and the lights turned low, transforming it into a shadowy erotic cocoon. A fitting prelude to the bedroom.

Now everything stood out sharp and clear under the flaring gaslights. Two plump upholstered armchairs on either side of the fireplace. A large gilt mirror above the mantelpiece. A mahogany table with four matching chairs. Heavy velvet curtains drawn across the windows, and that chaise longue. Oh, and a screen with quaint Chinese scenes painted on it. Orpheus fondly thought of Anna emerging naked from behind it, as she did on their first romantic evening.

The champagne was on the table.

Anna advanced with two sparkling glasses. 'Sit down Giles and tell me about your day.'

'Good heaven's that's the last thing you'd want to hear about. Deadly dull as always. I'll only tell you if you come and sit on my knee.'

'Very well,' Anna smiled seductively, leading him to the chaise. 'Take off your coat.'

Orpheus put his glass down and slipped out of his coat, draping it over a dining chair.

Anna pushed him back onto the chaise and moved to sit beside him, draping her legs over his and clasping her hands behind his neck to draw his face to hers. She broke their kiss, to whisper in Orpheus's ear. He sat, bewitched, as she walked across the room and disappeared behind the screen with a coquettish look over her shoulder. Orpheus reached for his champagne. Stretching his legs and loosening his tie, he sat back, anticipating the revelation to come.

The rustle of clothing fed his ardour. In a few moments, her grey silk dress appeared, draped over the top of the screen. It went quiet. Orpheus strained his ears for any sound, imagining her undergarments dropping to the floor. He held his breath.

'You must close your eyes,' Anna called out.

Orpheus laughed. 'What on earth for? It's not as if I haven't seen you *au naturel* before.'

'Then you will not receive the surprise I have in store for you.'

'Surprise? I like the sound of that.'

'You must promise to shut your eyes. Tight shut now or I will put my dress back on.'

Anna's teasing stoked his sense of anticipation. He placed his champagne glass on the floor. 'They're shut,' he said hoarsely.

Anna's bare feet made no sound as she stepped across the carpet.

'Keep them shut, my darling,' she whispered as he felt her sitting next to him. An arm moved around his shoulders and her naked thigh pressed against his trousers. Her other arm took his right hand and placed it on her breast. Orpheus shivered. Her nose nuzzled his cheek. Having his eyes closed heightened his pleasure. What next?

'Your surprise is ready,' Anna murmured. 'You may open your eyes… now.'

A flash of intense light stabbed his eyeballs. He blinked - startled and disorientated. As the awful realisation dawned on him, his hand dropped from Anna's breast.

Anna was already on her feet. She joined Cherkasov behind the camera.

Giles groaned. One panel of the Chinese screen had been moved aside. He had no inkling that it had concealed a camera on a tripod, focussed on the chaise longue.

He fleetingly thought of making a rush for the camera and exposing the plate. The pistol in the man's hand dissuaded him.

The stark reality of his situation was horrifyingly clear to him. An elaborate hoax. A trick and he'd fallen for it.

Giles heard the rustle of clothing again as Anna ducked behind the screen and hurriedly dressed. He sized up the man in front of him. Fifty, maybe older, his grey eyes cold and unwavering. As tall as Orpheus himself and judging by the cut of his suit, he was no high street photographer. His pistol pointed at Giles's heart.

'Mr Temple-Swift, forgive me if I do not identify myself. Suffice to say that I am a representative of a foreign power. Not a cheap blackmailer, I can assure you.' Giles caught the hint of an accent. Polish? Russian perhaps?

Anna emerged fully clothed.

'Come and sit at the table, Giles. You look terribly pale. Shall I pour you another glass of champagne?'

He shook his head.

Anna took a seat. 'Come now,' she patted the chair next to her.

He joined her, dazed by the unreality of his situation.

Cherkasov sat opposite, his pistol still aimed at Giles.

'What do you want?'

'We will come to that in a moment. You are an interesting man, Mr Temple-Swift. Why don't I call you Giles? I feel I know so much about you. A high official in Her Majesty's Civil Service. A member of the Committee for Imperial Security, indeed.'

'How the devil do you know that?'

'Did you think that Anna was attracted to you for your looks and personality? She is an actress. She played a part and most successfully. We knew about your role at the Home Office from the outset and now we know a great deal more.'

Giles shifted uneasily in his seat. It made no sense. He'd not disclosed anything confidential to Anna, and she hadn't asked him suspicious questions.

'You look puzzled, Giles, and alarmed, too. Is the gun making you nervous?' Cherkasov put his pistol on the table. 'You don't look as though you're about to do something foolish. Very wise of you. Anna, tell Giles what you've discovered about him.'

'How is Carter, Giles?' Anna's question struck him like a slap to the face. 'Irish, isn't he?'

Giles swallowed.

'A bombing campaign, here in Great Britain. What is it to you, Giles? Are you trying to thwart it? Defending the country against these… what was the name? New Immortals, that's it.' Anna paused. 'Or could there be a different explanation?' She sounded genuinely curious, prodding him for an answer.

His clammy shirt stuck to his chest. Did they know about his links with Carter? *Bluff it out*, he thought, *say nothing*.

'Who is VL?'

The blood drained from Giles's face.

'Another Fenian, Giles? Or could there be some connection with this?' Anna crossed the room to a Davenport in the corner. Lifting the lid, she withdrew a buff envelope.

'Do you know what this envelope contains?' Anna placed it on the table.

'You had no business…'

The man interrupted. 'Let's dispense with this to and fro, shall we? As you know, the envelope contains a black leather-bound book. Show us, would you Anna?'

Anna slid the book onto the table.

'It's a German Code Book. Anna and I were worried that you might have discovered that it was missing, but your face tells me that it's the last thing you expected to be confronted with. Do you know, it would be a shame to let that champagne go flat. Anna, would you be so kind as to pour a glass for each of us?'

Desperate and close to panic, Giles eyed Cherkasov's revolver.

'Please, no heroics, Giles,' Cherkasov shook his head and covered the gun with his hand. 'Your best chance of emerging unscathed from this encounter is to co-operate. Ah, Anna, thank you,' he added, as she placed three glasses of champagne on the table.

Cherkasov took a sip and put his glass down, returning his attention to Giles. 'You have an affinity with Germany, don't you? I read your entry in Who's Who. Most impressive. Oxford then Heidelberg. A member of the Alpine Club. And what else? Ah, yes, your left ear bears the mark of a duelling sabre. But of course, you are half-German. Perfectly natural that you should take an interest in the place.'

He picked up the code book and flipped through the pages. 'Why did you decide to betray the country of your birth, Giles? Money? Surely you wouldn't be motivated by anything as grubby as that. Conviction then? Think the Kaiser is the man of the future, do you?'

Giles cleared his throat. 'Unless you mean to kill me, you will have to let me go at some point. Or do you intend to kidnap me, whisk me away to some dungeon? And why should you care whether my allegiances lie with Britain or Germany?'

Cherkasov brushed a speck of dust from his sleeve. 'If you prove to be of no use to us, we will kill you. Perhaps you think that I would not risk the noise of a pistol shot, but there are other ways.'

Giles had thought nothing of it when Anna stepped away from the table. Moments later, the silk scarf she'd looped over his head cut into his windpipe. The suddenness and brutality of the assault left him scrabbling ineffectually to release the pressure on his throat.

Cherkasov looked on, unmoved at the bulging eyes and scarlet hue of Anna's victim until Giles's hands fell to his sides. Then he nodded to Anna to release the pressure.

Giles spluttered. Hazily, he became aware of Anna holding a bottle of smelling salts under his nose. At first, he thought she'd crushed his Adam's apple, but he managed to swallow painfully.

'Please do not give Anna a reason to demonstrate again how essential it is that you co-operate with us,' Cherkasov warned. 'That was to leave you in no doubt that we are in deadly earnest. You will leave here tonight when you have told us what we need to know.

'If you fail to satisfy us, prints of the photograph I took will be sent to your wife and the Home Secretary. In addition, an anonymous letter will be sent to Colonel Quilter at the Home Office, accusing you of collaborating with Irish Republicans and Germany to harm Great Britain. Now then Giles, start talking.'

Chapter 45

A squirrel bounded across the path, disappearing into a tangle of ivy and bracken. The rustle of its progress through the undergrowth disturbed a mourner standing with bared head at the foot of a grave whose simple headstone showed none of the weathering of more established graves.

A gust of wind brought a brief flurry of pine needles with it. The man brushed them from his shoulders and stepped back, replacing his hat, and walking away.

As his footsteps receded, the squirrel emerged from the undergrowth, stopping briefly to look up at the headstone as though reading the inscription:

Sacred to the Memory of
IMOGEN ANNE QUILTER
BORN 22 AUGUST 1852
DIED 15 OCTOBER 1894
Safe in God's keeping

Near the entrance to Highgate Cemetery, Clarence Quilter settled himself on a bench. In the distance, a small group of mourners stood around an open grave as the priest in his surplice, a daub of white among funerary black, read the burial service.

Every month since her death of consumption, he came to honour his wife's memory. Alone, save for Christmas Eve, when his son Gerald and daughters, Harriet and Delia, stood by his side.

The two days since his acrimonious interview with Verity and George had aged him. His meeting with the Prince of Wales and the Prime Minister, the Marquess of Salisbury, turned out to be a bloody affair. Far from expressing satisfaction that a Fenian assassination plot had been averted, Bertie took Quilter to task.

'The leader of this gang of murderers remains at large, Colonel. What is being done to apprehend the blackguard?'

'His whereabouts are unknown at this stage, your Royal Highness, but I can assure you…'

'So you have no idea where this Carter fellow is? Who's to say that he's not outside this very house as we speak, waiting to take a pot shot at me or the Princess of Wales?'

'I shall, of course, ensure that Marlborough House is guarded, sir.'

'Pah, if you had done your job properly, Quilter, there would be no need to talk of such things.'

The Prince of Wales took a cigarette from a silver cigarette box at his elbow. Quilter waited nervously as Bertie set a match to it, simultaneously fixing the Colonel with a look of withering scorn. A plume of exhaled smoke blew in his direction.

'Damned bad business, Salisbury.'

'Indeed, sir, most regrettable.'

'And who the devil killed these three Fenians? Tell me that. You two gentlemen sit here saying that a great calamity has been averted, yet not only is the Fenian leader at large, but we also have an unknown assassin in our midst.'

Salisbury turned to Quilter. 'Well, Colonel, the ball is in your court. His Royal Highness has made it perfectly clear that nothing must be permitted to mar the Jubilee. You have only a few days to tidy up these loose ends.'

Quilter left Marlborough House in a trance with Salisbury's words ringing in his ears, imagining the uproar that would have resulted if he'd confessed that he also had an unidentified traitor in his organisation and that a second Fenian, George's saviour, was also at large.

***

The distant mourners filed past the grave, each casting a handful of soil on to the coffin.

Quilter reached into his overcoat and retrieved the note delivered to his office that morning. He'd left Montagu Square after his fractious meeting with Verity and George, vowing never to have anything further to do with them, believing the feeling to be mutual. He could hardly blame them. Now, this note had come addressed in Verity's hand.

Its arrival had interrupted him in the act of writing his resignation. He was a defeated man, devoid of ideas and hope. His one thought was to visit Imogen's grave. She'd begged him before she died to put duty aside to cast off the burden of service that he'd shouldered for so long. He'd go and tell her. Shed a tear. Then return and sign his resignation letter.

Gravel crunched as the mourners passed his bench on their way out of the cemetery, followed by the priest, who wished him a good morning. Quilter nodded and returned his attention to Verity's note.

Chapter 46

'Clarence. You came. I feared you might have decided to sever all contact with us.' Quilter allowed Verity to place his hat and coat on the hallstand.

'Goodness, you look positively haggard. Are you quite well?'

'Oh, a little tired. I've not been sleeping well.'

His voice was barely audible.

'Come on through,' Verity gently took him by the arm. 'No, not that way. We're in the dining room today.'

Quilter stopped in the doorway. 'Oh. I was expecting… who are these people?'

George and Ambrose sat at either end of the dining table. Between them, sitting side by side facing the door, were Dmitri Cherkasov and Anna Jesenska.

Cherkasov jumped up and approached. 'Colonel Quilter, I am honoured to make your acquaintance. I am General Dmitri Cherkasov of the Imperial Russian army.'

Quilter shook the proffered hand in a daze.

'General Cherkasov's companion is Miss Anna Jesenska, Clarence,' Verity whispered in his ear, leading him to a seat at the table. 'Can I get you anything?' she offered.

Quilter looked around the table, unable to mask his confusion. He turned to Verity. 'Get me anything? Yes, a large scotch. Then tell me what the devil is going on.'

'It could take some time,' George said as Verity bustled out to fetch a glass of scotch. 'You'll need to be patient. First there's these.'

Quilter reached for his monocle, then bent forward to inspect the objects George placed in front of him. The photograph of Carter that he'd supplied to Alfie lay next to a pair of shattered pince-nez. Despite their condition, Quilter matched them with those in the photograph. Next was the note from Joseph. Quilter studied it.

'Carter's dead?' he said, looking at George.

'Yes. And don't bother asking me who J is.'

'It's good news, isn't it?' Verity appeared with Quilter's scotch.

'Or an elaborate ruse.'

'You may choose to think whatever you wish, Clarence, but George is of the opinion that the note is genuine. I believe him and you would do well to do so too.'

Quilter downed half his scotch. 'Very well. Yes, it is good news. The Fenian threat would appear to be over. But that's not all, is it? Would someone kindly explain what General Cherkasov and Miss Jesenska are doing here?'

'Well, it's a little complicated…'

'If you would allow me, Verity,' Cherkasov interrupted. 'Colonel, although the Fenian threat is over, there remains a grave danger that an attack on the Diamond Jubilee procession will be carried out with the objective of assassinating both Queen Victoria and the Prince of Wales.'

All eyes turned on the Colonel. Only the ticking of a long-case clock in the corner broke the silence. He threw back the rest of the scotch. 'Please continue, General.'

'Somewhere along the procession route, a sharpshooter will be waiting.'

'For heaven's sake. Are you telling me that now we have a Fenian sharpshooter? So why not come out with it straight away instead of giving me all that rigmarole about the threat being over? Are you all hell bent on trying my patience?'

Verity, George, and Ambrose all started speaking at once until Cherkasov raised his voice, cutting through the clamour. 'Colonel, this has nothing to do with Fenians. This is the work of a foreign power. Germany is behind it.'

Quilter shook his head. 'I feel as though I'm trapped in a nightmare. Sitting here in London being told by a Russian general that Germany is plotting to shoot the Queen and the Prince of Wales.' He exhaled slowly and shrugged his shoulders. 'Please go on, General. Perhaps I'll wake up soon and find that it's all been a dream.'

'A German major by the name of Erich von Lensch is here in London, charged with organising the assassination.'

'Do you seriously expect me to believe that the Kaiser is planning to murder his grandmother and his uncle? It's no secret that the relationship between Wilhelm and the Prince of Wales has been strained from time to time, but this is preposterous.' Quilter stood up, looking furiously around the table. 'Verity, and you too George, is this your idea of some grotesque practical joke? I'll not stay to be made a fool of.'

'No Clarence,' Verity implored, clutching his sleeve. 'Please, please hear us out. It's not a joke. I've never been more serious about anything in my life.'

'Colonel, forgive me if I've been clumsy in explaining the situation,' Cherkasov came and stood in front of Colonel Quilter. 'We, around this table, may be all that stands between a glorious celebration of the Queen's reign and a catastrophe that could plunge our countries into war. This is not the Kaiser's doing. He knows nothing about it. The man behind it is Prince Philipp of Eulenburg, a man of much influence and serving presently as the German Ambassador to Austria.'

Cherkasov returned to his place at the table. Quilter hesitated, then sat down again.

'Assuming what you have just told me is correct, how does this concern Russia, General Cherkasov? I'm none the wiser as to why you and your companion, Miss Jesenska, are here.'

'Tell him, Anna.'

'The assassin will use a Russian rifle which will be left behind at the scene, together with items suggesting that Russia is behind the shooting. You see, Colonel, this plot is intended to create an unbridgeable rift between our two countries. And who will step into that rift but Germany? The prize will be a British/German alliance. A plan as audacious as it is ruthless.'

'Now, do you see why I asked you to come, Clarence?' Verity murmured.

'Dear God. How do they know all this, Verity, and how the devil are you and George connected with them?'

'Colonel,' George interjected. 'Those questions will have to wait. What matters now is what we do with this knowledge.'

'Do? All I have is an intimation from someone I've never met before, that a hugely improbable plot is afoot. Do you propose that I should march into the German embassy and attempt to apprehend this Major von Lensch? It's preposterous.' Quilter pounded the table with his fist. 'You have yet to convince me of anything. And if you think

I will go to the Prime Minister and the Prince of Wales and advise them to cancel the Jubilee on the strength of what I have just heard, you are hopelessly mistaken. What a…'

'Did you ever find out who killed those Fenians at the warehouse?' George's question cut across the highly charged atmosphere in the room.

Quilter twitched involuntarily. He was all at sea. His eyes betrayed him.

'You know how they met their death, don't you?' George persisted.

'Where is this leading?'

'Just answer, Clarence. You'll see where it's leading in a moment.'

'Two were shot. The third was knifed. An expert job, I'm informed.'

'Then Major von Lensch is behind it. He ordered their murder. And to save you asking why, I'll tell you. If the Fenians exploded their dynamite and blew up the Jubilee procession, the German assassination plan would be thwarted. Germany was quite happy to support the Irish until they became an obstacle to this grand plan of Eulenburg's. It sounds fantastic, but it's the truth. So, what are we going to do about it?'

Chapter 47

Orpheus poured another brandy. That morning, he'd sent a note to the Home Office informing the Permanent Secretary that he was suffering from an acute bout of influenza. He was back home in Hampstead, having no further need for the Traveller's Club. In a few days, his wife would be back. He needed time alone to think.

Putting a hand to his throat, he felt the weal raised by Anna's scarf. Swallowing was still painful, although the brandy helped.

He'd truly thought his time had come. Anna's transformation from lover to brutal tormentor shattered him.

He cursed his naïvety. But how could he possibly have foreseen such a turn of events? Consumed by emotions of betrayal, fear, and helplessness, Orpheus struggled to put his mind in order.

To be brought so low. To bargain for his life. To face the prospect of ruin and disgrace if he failed to co-operate. He'd told them all knew in the end. Everything: Operation Geck, his association with Carter, Eulenburg, Lensch, the need to eliminate the Fenians. Everything that he had knowledge of.

Still, they wanted more. 'Where is Lensch? What does he look like?'

He sang like a bird.

And still the questions came. 'Where will the shooting take place?'

But he didn't know. He thought he'd never convince them, panicking at the thought of Anna's silk scarf encircling his neck again.

'Find out,' they demanded.

The shame of it. The memory of breaking down and begging. Blubbering like a child. Saying over and over that Lensch had barred him from further involvement with the plot.

He thought of the contempt in Cherkasov's eyes and Anna's too when they finally released him - on condition that from now on, he was their creature. Free to continue his career. Free to work for the German Reich. But Russia would be his true master.

'Go,' Cherkasov said. 'And you'd better take this,' he added, handing the code book to Orpheus. 'We have taken a copy of course.'

***

'I thought the poor man would have a seizure. I never thought I would feel pity for Clarence, but he's a shadow of the man he was.' Verity returned to the dining room, having seen Colonel Quilter out.

'He's in an intolerable position. I'll grant you that. But he could have had the good grace to thank us. We're the only hope he has.' George got up to stretch his legs. 'What do you think, Ambrose? You've been unusually quiet.'

'I think that Colonel Quilter will blow his brains out if disaster befalls the Jubilee. He could never bear the dishonour.'

'Let us hope that no one's brains will be blown out,' Cherkasov looked around the room. 'We can only proceed as we have agreed this afternoon. We must focus our efforts entirely on observing Lensch in the hope that he will lead us to the sharpshooter. I can tell you that Lensch is staying at Brown's Hotel.'

'Very well, then it's you and me to find Alfie and Co. Ambrose,' George responded. 'We'll convene here again tomorrow.'

'Just one thing before we all go about our business,' Verity said as the others rose from the table. 'Can we be sure that Giles Temple-Swift is an innocent party? I still feel uncomfortable at not mentioning your discoveries about him to Colonel Quilter, Anna.'

'Oh, let me assure you that I've thought long and hard about the snippets of information I discovered, and both Dmitri and I are satisfied that he was not in league with the Fenians. On the contrary, his objective was to catch them. Incidentally, our liaison has ceased. He is of no further use to us, you see. Oh dear, I hope that doesn't sound too cold-blooded.'

Verity blinked. 'Um, well, we'll leave it at that then, shall we?'

Anna laughed. 'I see I've shocked you, Verity. A femme fatale with little in the way of moral scruples. Ah, well, I'll just have to live with the notoriety. Now, if you'll all excuse me, I must get ready for tonight's performance. You really must come along one evening. Mary is simply wonderful, you know.'

***

Wave after wave broke over the sand, advancing brashly and retreating with a sigh. Lensch contemplated the tidal rhythm for a few minutes, then made his way back to the promenade. Brighton fascinated him. He looked upon the sights and customs of the British seaside town with a condescending fondness. The piers, amusement halls, donkey rides, and Punch and Judy epitomised the wonderful eccentricity of the English at play.

Lensch also liked to play, but the innocent pursuits of the seaside were not what he sought. Miss Sadie Sweet, 'Swish' to her loyal clientele, the most celebrated purveyor of services to gentlemen with a penchant for discipline, had removed from her London establishment for a summer season in Brighton. She, and a whiff of sea air, were just what Lensch needed to clear his head before the concluding act of Operation Geck.

He'd left London after hearing Riemann's report of the raid on the warehouse.

No survivors. That was the order he'd given. At least Riemann had the good grace to apologise.

'The one who got away was Carter, you say?'

'Yes, Major. The three others are dead. But…'

'What, Riemann?'

'The one I saw with Carter earlier. Young one. He wasn't there.'

'So we have two Fenians unaccounted for.'

Lensch contained his annoyance. There was no turning back now. Operation Geck must go ahead, even with the uncomfortable knowledge that the two surviving Fenians might still pose a threat to the Jubilee.

'Listen Riemann, we must keep our minds on the task ahead. What's done is done. I will be away from London for five days. When I return, I will need your assurance that all is in readiness. Is that clear?'

Riemann nodded. 'Everything will be in place. I visited the house yesterday. The old lady grows frailer and more forgetful by the day. But I have a key, so it's of little consequence.'

Lensch dismissed him. Not only did the survival of the two Fenians worry him, but why had he seen nothing about the killings in the newspapers? Three men murdered and not a mention in the press. He briefly entertained the thought of telegraphing Eulenburg, but dismissed it. He had been entrusted with Operation Geck and it would be done. His next communication with Eulenburg would be to confirm its success.

He paced the length of the promenade. The sunshine had brought out the crowds. Couples and families passed by or sat on benches. A picture of simple contentment. The British at play.

No doubt, some of them would be in London for the Jubilee.

***

'Blimey, what now?' Alfie Cotton looked over his brother Dick's shoulder as George and Ambrose entered the back room of the Lamb and Flag.

'No more tangling with Fenians, Mister Benson. Heart's not up to it. That business with Mulcahy put years on me,' he protested.

George and Ambrose joined them at the table.

'Who said anything about Fenians?'

'So what is it, then? Nice little divorce case? Someone 'avin a bit of how's your father on the sly?' quipped Dick.

Alfie looked uneasily at Ambrose. 'No offence, Mr Mallard, but if you're here as well as Mr Benson, it looks like trouble.'

George turned to the three men drinking at the next table. 'Gentlemen, could I ask you to afford my colleagues and me some privacy?'

Their scowls were disarmed by the sight of the sovereign George flipped them. They shuffled out to the front bar.

'Not Fenians,' George whispered, 'Germans'.

Dick, who had just taken a mouthful of beer, spluttered and coughed violently. Ambrose slapped him on the back. 'Steady, old chap, can't have you choking.'

Alfie shook his head. 'This better be good, guv'nor.'

'Three times your usual rate, both of you, and we may need Benny.'

'Who's the moneybags client, then?'

'Never you mind.' George could just imagine the reaction if he'd said Russians.

Alfie grinned. 'So, who do you want us to keep tabs on this time?'

'A man named Major von Lensch. He's staying at Brown's.'

'Very nice digs too, so I'm told. Got a photo of this cove?'

'No. You'll have to use this,' George handed over a sketch Verity had produced based on the description Anna had gleaned from Orpheus. 'He's about five foot six.'

'How long do you want us on this job?'

'Seven days at the outside.'

'Righto. See, we was hoping to see the Jubilee.'

George nodded. 'One way or another, we'll need to have the job done by then. Right Alfie, it's you, me and Dick in shifts. I'll start tonight.'

Chapter 48

George drummed his fingers on the table, while Cherkasov, Verity and Ambrose took their seats at the dining table. Dispensing with pleasantries, he got straight to the point.

'There is still no sign of him. He's not been in or out of Brown's since we started watching the place.'

Two days of keeping watch on the hotel had produced nothing. Alfie, Dick and George, posing in a variety of guises: newspaper vendor, sandwich-board carrier, and even a distributor of religious tracts, had seen no sign of the major.

'Lying low in the hotel?' Verity ventured.

'Perhaps he's left. Decamped,' Ambrose suggested.

'Might you or your men have simply missed him?' Cherkasov asked. 'I don't mean to question your diligence or those of your colleagues, but it's possible is it not?'

'Well, General, if we suppose that in the course of a day a guest would emerge and return to the hotel at least once, then over two days there would be a minimum of four opportunities to spot him. That we should fail to do so on four separate occasions is not at all likely.' George responded evenly, despite the irritation he felt at having his competence questioned.

'No, I see your point. Of course.'

Verity patted George's sleeve. 'Can you not enquire of the hotel whether he is still staying there?'

'I've considered that. The danger of such a direct enquiry is that it might alert Lensch that someone is asking about him.'

Verity bit her lip. 'Well, what can we do? Does anyone have a suggestion?'

George turned to Cherkasov. 'Orpheus might know.'

'He said Lensch had ordered him to have no further involvement with this Operation Geck, as they call it. However…'

'Oh, bother, who's that at the door? I'll let Elsie deal with it. I told her we were not to be disturbed. 'Forgive me, Dmitri, you were saying?'

Everyone turned as the dining-room door opened and Elsie's head appeared.

'Beg pardon, Miss Mallard. It's Mister Cotton to see you. He says it's very important.'

Alfie hovered behind her, waving.

'Thank you Elsie. Do come in Alfie. And Elsie, we'll have tea in ten minutes,' Verity waved Alfie to a chair.

'What's so important, Alfie,' George asked.

Alfie looked around the table, nodding to Cherkasov and Ambrose. 'Thought you'd all like some good news. That Major von Lensch, he's been down in Brighton. No wonder we didn't see hide nor hair of him.'

'Brighton,' Ambrose exclaimed. 'What on earth would he be doing in Brighton?'

'Search me. Perhaps he's got a fancy woman down there,' Alfie grinned. 'The thing is, he's coming back tonight, back to the hotel.'

'Bravo, Mister Cotton,' Cherkasov clapped his hands together, 'how did you discover this?'

'Well, it was through my cousin Benny. His sister's youngest, Tommy, only turns out to be a porter at Brown's. Who'd have thought it?' Alfie shook his head in wonder at his revelation.

'Go on.' George prompted.

'Yes, well, I've just been round there to their 'ouse, 'aven't I. Cos Tommy's off duty, you see. Goes back for his evening shift at six and…'

'Yes, yes, Alfie,' George interjected. 'What exactly did Tommy tell you?'

'He said that he'd carried this German geezer's suitcase down to the cab for him last Wednesday. Was his name Lensch? I asks him. Yes, that was it. I hung around while he paid his bill and he says to the manager he'll be back next Sunday. Gave Tommy a bob for a tip.'

'Alfie, you're a marvel.' George reached for his wallet. 'Here's a quid for Tommy and ask him to let you know if he learns anything more about Lensch.'

'Already done that, guv'nor.'

'Would you care to stay for tea?' Verity asked.

'If it's all the same to you, Miss Mallard, I'll be getting along. I'll see my own way out.'

'Well, General,' George couldn't keep from grinning, 'we're back in business.'

'Yes. indeed and not a moment too soon. We have only four days until the Jubilee.'

Chapter 49

Dick yawned. He'd been observing Brown's since seven that morning, just in case Lensch came up from Brighton on an early train. Cabs came and went with no sign of the major and then at ten-fifteen, he saw him. Lensch stood waiting while the cabbie handed his suitcase to a hotel porter. Not young Tommy, Dick noted.

George joined him at noon. 'He's here guv. Arrived at quarter past ten. Still in the hotel. I'll leave you to it, shall I?'

'No, I'd like you to hang about, Dick. When Lensch comes out, it's a pound to a penny that he's going to meet someone. We'll both follow him and, if I'm right, you keep tailing Lensch afterwards and I'll follow whoever he meets up with.'

'What's this Lensch up to then, Mister Benson?'

'I can't tell you. Let's just say that he's up to no good.'

They didn't have long to wait. At twenty past twelve, Lensch's portly figure emerged. Verity's sketch proved to be an excellent likeness, although it flattered Lensch's girth. Dressed in a dark chesterfield overcoat with a black homburg and carrying a walking stick with a curved handle, he set off with a hint of a swagger along Albemarle Street.

George and Dick kept him in sight from the opposite side of the road, then hurriedly crossed when a gap in the traffic allowed.

Lensch showed no sign of being in a hurry. Walking with a measured pace, he stopped now and then to look in a shop window. George and Dick kept their distance, ducking into doorways or standing and pretending to have a conversation whenever Lensch halted.

Crossing Piccadilly, Lensch continued along St James's Street. Nearing St James's Palace, he consulted his pocket watch. Then, with a noticeable increase in pace, he hurried down Marlborough Road.

George and Dick spotted him crossing the Mall and entering St James's Park.

'Damnation.' George cursed as the passage of a troop of Life Guards along the Mall towards Buckingham Palace kept them waiting on the pavement. By the time the last pair of horses passed, there was no sign of the major.

They raced across to the park entrance and along the path leading to an iron suspension bridge spanning the lake.

'Which way Mr Benson?'

George knew the Park well. Paths encircled the lake to the east and the west. Lensch could have gone in either direction. He could even have passed straight through the park.

'This way.' George stepped onto the bridge. Out in the middle of the lake, they had a vantage point giving a view of the lakeside paths.

With Buckingham Palace in the distance, George scanned the western end of the lake. Two ladies with a pug on a lead. A family with two young girls throwing bread to the ducks and swans. A young man wearing a straw boater. No sign of Lensch.

'Could that be him?' George turned on his heel to join Dick on the other side of the bridge, looking towards Whitehall.

'Where?'

Dick pointed to a section of path on their left, immediately opposite Duck Island.

Lensch sat on a bench, resting his chin on his walking stick. As they watched, a tall bareheaded man approached and sat by the major's side.

George ambled towards Lensch and his companion. The other man was older, in his fifties, greying hair cropped very short, straight-backed and muscular, contrasting sharply with Lensch's tub-like torso and slouching posture. As George drew level, Lensch was speaking, his voice pitched low. Even had George heard him clearly, his only command of foreign languages amounted to a few words and phrases in Arabic from his army days.

The nearest vacant bench was ten yards away from the Germans. George occupied it, gazing out over the lake and turning his head occasionally in their direction as though following the movement of ducks busily criss-crossing the lake.

Meanwhile, Dick found a bench on the other side of Lensch and his companion.

***

Lensch was still puffing from his exertions when Riemann joined him. Lost in pleasant memories of his sojourn in Brighton, Lensch was taken aback when his watch showed a mere four minutes to his appointed meeting time.

'Did you have a pleasant journey, Major?' Lensch turned to look at Riemann. The impassive profile was the same as ever, but Riemann had never opened a conversation before.

'Thank you Riemann. Yes, since you ask? How was your visit to the house?'

Lensch kept his eyes on Riemann's face. Saw him swallow hard.

'Well?'

'I had a problem to deal with.'

'Out with it, Riemann.'

'I took the rifle with me, in its case, with the ammunition. The old lady was asleep in an armchair when I put my head round the door of the parlour. Snoring fit to wake the street. I went upstairs to the attic. Lord knows how she managed to climb the stairs. I was busy cleaning the rifle, you see, so I didn't know she was there until she starts jabbering and screaming, pointing at the rifle and threatening to get the police.'

'You said no one would miss her, Riemann. Have you killed her?'

'She saved me the trouble. Turned on her heel and started hobbling down stairs. She managed the first flight, but when she heard me coming after her, she tripped and tumbled down the next one. Broke her neck. I didn't have to lay a hand on her, Major.'

'Hmm. Better to have her out of the way. What about the body?'

'There's a large oak chest in her bedroom. I wrapped her tight in bed sheets and put her in.'

'Well, that will have to do. Let's hope the weather stays cool. Just three days now, Riemann. Tomorrow you will attend the embassy as usual?'

'Yes Major. I have taken leave of absence for the following day and the day of the Jubilee. The Dutchman will meet me at London Bridge. I'll take him to the house. Everything will be ready, Major. You have my word.'

Lensch nodded. He let his mind dwell on the possibilities a successful conclusion to Operation Geck would present. Advancement and glittering honours. Eulenburg's star would be in the ascendent and his with it.

A young boy clattering by with a hoop and stick shook him out of his daydream.

'You will meet me here at noon the day after the Jubilee, Riemann. Perhaps a quiet celebration might be in order. Good luck.'

Riemann got up without a word. The wound he'd suffered at Sedan pained him. He steeled himself, refusing to limp despite the French shrapnel still embedded in his thigh. This would be his last service to the Reich. He wanted nothing more than to retire to Cochem on the Moselle. His widowed sister had begged him to come and help her with the family's small holding and vineyard. Now, the time was right.

He straightened his shoulders and set off towards the Mall. Although it was Sunday, he stopped at the German Embassy at Carlton House Terrace to collect the cap he'd left on his desk.

***

'Here you are, Mister Riemann, a bottle of your usual.' The landlord of the Royal Oak placed a glass and a bottle of pale ale on the bar. 'Haven't seen you for a couple of days, Doris and I were wondering if you was alright. Feeling well, are you?'

'Ja, ja. Yes. I am well.' Riemann nodded and smiled, reaching into his pocket for his pipe and tobacco pouch.

George hadn't expected his quarry to emerge from the German Embassy after only ten minutes. Neither had he expected him to retrace his steps to St. James's Park. But this time he kept walking, through the park, then on into Westminster and Pimlico.

'What can I get for you, sir?' The landlord came down to the other end of the bar, where George was standing, wiping a glass with a tea towel.

'Pint of best bitter please.'

'New to the area, are you, sir? Haven't seen you in here before. It's mostly regulars in here, especially on a Sunday.' The barman asked pleasantly as he pulled George's pint.

'Just passing by.'

The landlord looked up as though waiting for George to confide something more. George avoided his gaze.

'That will be tuppence, please.'

George handed over two coppers and took his pint to a table in the corner.

The pub started to fill up. Riemann drained his pale ale and signalled to the landlord for another.

George made his pint last, wondering how long the German would stay. At least he now knew the fellow's name. The landlord called him Riemann.

His thoughts drifted to Effie. During the week since he'd escaped from the warehouse, she'd hardly crossed his mind. Try as he might to excuse himself, he'd behaved poorly. What must she be thinking? As soon as this Jubilee business was over, he'd call on her.'

'Afternoon.'

'Eh?' George glanced at the large, rotund, ruddy-faced man, with a fringe of dark hair surrounding his bald pate, lowering himself on to a seat at the next table.

'Good afternoon. Name's Braithwaite, Archie Braithwaite.' The man put his glass of beer down and extended a hand.

'Oh. George Benson.' The fellow's thick, sausage-like fingers gripped George's hand, squeezing hard. George absorbed the pressure for a moment, then squeezed back harder, showing no expression. Braithwaite grimaced. His grip relaxed.

George let go. From the corner of his eye, he saw Braithwaite surreptitiously flexing his fingers under the table. George lit a cigarette and returned his attention to Riemann.

He sensed Braithwaite staring at him, but kept his eyes on the German. After a few uncomfortable minutes, he heard a chair grating on the floorboards. Braithwaite shuffled past him and walked over to the bar, leaning across to have a whispered conversation with the landlord.

Riemann re-filled his pipe, showing no sign of leaving. George decided that it would be a good time to heed the call of his bladder. The gents' toilet was empty. When he'd finished, he stepped back from the urinal, buttoning his fly.

'This is a pub for locals.'

George turned.

'Stan the landlord, says you're not welcome. Doesn't like the look of you. Me and Harry here have come to give you the message.'

Archie Braithwaite stood in the doorway, hands on hips, grinning. His suit of loud brown and black checks reminded George of a bookmaker he'd seen at Goodwood. Behind him was a second man of similar height in a railway porter's uniform.

'Haven't finished my pint.'

'Listen to that, Harry. George wants to finish his pint.'

'Needs teachin' a lesson, Archie.'

'Yeah.' Archie took a step forward. Harry followed to stand at his side, rolling up his sleeves.

A moment's inattention was all it needed. While Harry fumbled with the button on his right cuff, George drove his boot into the porter's stomach. Archie threw a wild punch aiming for George's head, but only scored a faint glancing blow to his cheek.

George pressed home his assault on Harry, bent double, clutching his stomach. Seizing him by the collar, he spun the man round and smashed his head into the wall. Harry slid down the cracked white tiles, leaving a broad smear of blood.

Archie was on him before George could turn to face him. A fist connected with his right temple, knocking him to his knees. Archie laughed, then pummelled him with a right and left to the head. George crouched, taking the blows on the top of his skull.

Archie winced, stepping back and shaking his bruised knuckles. Unable to rise and get on an equal footing, George raised his head. There was only one avenue of attack open to him. As Archie raised his fist again. George flung himself forward with both hands, seizing Archie's testicles and squeezing with all his strength.

Archie got one vicious punch in, connecting with George's left eye, before a wave of hellish, excruciating pain enveloped his groin. Incapacitated by the agony pulsating in his abdomen and fighting for breath, Archie grunted and gurgled, fighting an urge to vomit. When George released his grip, Archie collapsed onto the grimy, urine-stained floor, drawing his legs up into the foetal position, moaning, eyes wide with pain and disbelief.

Harry was sitting with his back to the wall, blood dripping from his nose and mouth. He waved a hand in meek surrender when George looked in his direction.

All eyes turned on him as he re-entered the public bar. No one spoke as he walked to his table and downed the remains of his beer. He stared back defiantly, then marched to the door, sensing the eyes boring into his back. But one pair of eyes was missing. Riemann's stool at the bar was empty.

Chapter 50

Outside in the street, George cursed. The pub stood on the corner of Regency Street and Rutherford Road. There was no sign of Riemann in either. He couldn't have been gone long.

George trudged towards Horseferry Road, casting about more in hope than expectation. At the next corner, he stopped to look down Maunsel Street. The only sign of life was a group of children laughing and joking, occupying the whole pavement on his side of the road, some twenty yards away. He was about to turn away when one of them, a boy, detached himself and crossed the road. Seconds later the others followed, giving George a clear view down the street and there, crouching to stroke a thin black cat, was Riemann.

***

Colonel Quilter was the last to arrive. He'd come close to ignoring Verity's urgent entreaty to come to Montagu Square, having spent the past forty-eight hours in a fog of hopelessness and indecision. His resignation letter remained unsigned in his desk drawer. That afternoon he'd visited Tranter and Forsyth, his solicitors, to make some revisions to his will.

Verity smiled and led him to a seat at the dining table. He nodded to the others, George, Ambrose, General Cherkasov. The woman, Miss Jesenska, was absent, he noted. *What the devil?* His eyes narrowed at the sight of the three others sitting between George and Verity. They stared back nervously at him.

George stood and cleared his throat. 'Thank you all for coming at this late hour. I know that no one here needs reminding that time is short. The Jubilee procession is only three days away. General Cherkasov, you have already met Alfie. Let me introduce his two companions, Dick, Alfie's brother and their cousin Benny.'

Forewarned by Quilter's furious glare, George turned to the Colonel. 'I know, I know. The matter of the Jubilee and the threat posed to Her Majesty is highly confidential.'

'Not highly confidential, man. A state secret.'

'Then you decide. Either these men are permitted to help us and brought into our confidence, or you can explain to the Prime Minister how you failed to do everything in your power to protect the Queen and the Prince of Wales. You can do these three patriots the courtesy of treating them as honest, loyal, Englishmen, as devoted to the safety of the realm as you.'

'Dammit…'

'Clarence, look at me. You know George is right.' Verity said softly.

George's chest ached with tension in the ensuing silence.

'Yes.' Quilter's strained utterance broke the spell.

'Thank you,' Verity murmured.

'Yes, thank you,' George echoed.

'Today, I believe we may have found our sharpshooter.' George paused and held a hand up to quell the hubbub that his statement precipitated.

'Let me finish, please. Dick and I followed Lensch from his hotel this morning. In St James's Park, he met a man. Afterwards, that man made a brief visit to the German Embassy. I followed him from there to a pub in Pimlico. That's where I discovered his name. It's Riemann. Does that mean anything to you, Clarence, or you, Dmitri?'

Both men shook their heads.

'He's living at an address on Maunsel Street, off the Horseferry Road. A respectable lodging house, by the look of it.'

'Was Lensch with him?' Quilter interrupted.

'No, Lensch returned to Brown's after their meeting. Dick followed him.'

'Stayed outside for the rest of the afternoon, but he didn't come out again,' Dick elaborated.

Cherkasov leaned his elbows on the table. 'How can we be certain this Riemann is the sharpshooter?'

'I only said that we *may* have found the sharpshooter,' George replied. 'He certainly has a military bearing. A retired soldier, I'd guess. In his fifties. It's quite possible that he's not acting alone. But he's the one who receives Lensch's orders.'

'And you say that Riemann went into the German Embassy.'

'Yes, only for ten minutes. He was bareheaded in St James's Park, but he had a cap on his head when he came out.'

Quilter cleared his throat. 'If the Germans are behind this, why would Lensch and Riemann meet in the park rather than at the embassy? You're the source of this whole crazed notion, General. What do you make of it?'

'It seems that the assassination plot is not officially sanctioned by the German Government. If you recall, Colonel, I said that it is the brainchild of Prince Philipp of Eulenburg.'

Quilter shrugged, huffing in exasperation.

Verity rose and stood at George's side. 'Gentlemen, you can go around in circles speculating and arguing, to your heart's content. If Dmitri's concerns are well founded and I believe that they are, then we must do our utmost to prevent an attack on Her Majesty and the Prince of Wales. If it turns out that there really isn't a plot, then we can all breathe a sigh of relief. But we can't take the risk. Does anyone disagree?'

Verity waited. All was quiet. 'Very well. George, tell us what you propose.'

***

Thirty minutes later, the gathering dispersed. Quilter left first, without a goodbye. Alfie, Dick and Benny said their farewells and stepped out into the night. Colonel Cherkasov stopped at the dining-room door. 'One last thing, George. How did you come by the black eye?'

'A little misunderstanding with the Pimlico natives, General.' George attempted a wink, grimacing as he did so. 'Never fear, it had nothing to do with Riemann.'

Cherkasov nodded and turned to kiss Verity's hand. 'Good night and thank you,' he whispered.

Chapter 51

'The morning post has arrived, sir. Shall I put it in the study for you?'

'What?' Orpheus looked up from the copy of The Times he was reading at the breakfast table. 'No, leave it here, will you?'

The housemaid put two letters on the table and swiftly cleared the breakfast things away, returning with a silver letter opener.

Orpheus put his newspaper down. The first envelope contained a bill from his tailor. He glanced at it and put it aside. Poised to slit the second envelope, he sat back, staring at the address written in his wife's neat copperplate with her distinctive flourishes.

A letter? She was due to return from Sussex that afternoon. Why would she write to him, unless something was wrong? Hastily, he opened the envelope and extracted the contents.

He read it twice. His hand shook as he let it drop from his fingers on to the table.

It had all seemed so simple. Beatrice conveniently down in Sussex, leaving him free in London. Unsuspecting Beatrice, who'd showed no sign of concern, looking forward to a few weeks in the country with her parents and seven-year-old Florence.

A private detective agency? He'd never heard of Trenchard and Co. She'd enclosed a copy of their report. Times and places - each tryst with Anna, all meticulously recorded. When he arrived and when he left.

Beatrice's letter itself was terse. Given his shameful betrayal, she and Florence would remain in Sussex. The boys were to come to her at the end of their school term. She was taking advice from her father's solicitor and Giles could expect to hear from him in due course.

After the first wave of shock subsided, Orpheus couldn't help but marvel at the irony of his situation. Cherkasov and Anna held the threat over him of informing Beatrice of his infidelity, but at the same time she was acting on her own suspicions.

'Oh God,' he whispered as the full gravity of his circumstances dawned. All his hopes would be dashed if it became public. His career would be at an end. But not only his career. His masters in Germany would have no further use for him. Then there were the Russians. He was worthless to them as well. A liability, in fact. It was not only a matter of losing his marriage, reputation, and career. His life was at stake.

***

'Oh, there you are, Mr Benson.' Alfie made room on the bench. Waterloo Gardens offered the perfect observation point for keeping watch on the German Embassy.

In the distance, Big Ben struck ten.

'Morning Alfie. Just been over at Brown's with Dick and Ambrose. There's been no sign of Lensch so far.'

'All quiet here, too. I went straight down to Maunsell Gardens this morning and hung about on the corner till this geezer comes out at quarter to nine. Just like you described him, guv. I'd have picked him for a Prussian sort straightaway. Sets off at a quick march straight across the park like you said he would. He's been in there since.' Alfie nodded at the embassy building.

'Get off and have a cup of tea, Alfie. I'll take over until noon.'

***

Erich von Lensch emerged from Brown's at eleven thirty. In deference to the warm weather, he wore no overcoat and had exchanged his homburg for a straw boater. Breakfasted and freshly bathed, he felt a sense of calm. While it was true that his future hung on the success of Operation Geck, he'd done everything within his power to pave the way. Now it was up to Riemann and the Dutchman.

Determined to put any misgivings aside, Lensch embarked on a day of gentle indulgence.

Dick nudged Ambrose. 'He's on the move.'

'Eh?' Ambrose's daydream had him back at the Thorneycroft estate. 'Sorry old chap, just drifted off for a moment.'

'Come on,' Dick waited for an omnibus and a gig to pass, then swiftly crossed Albemarle Street. Ambrose hurried after, narrowly avoiding a hansom cab and falling in at Dick's side, puffing to catch his breath.

Something for Gudrun, thought Lensch. His wife would be expecting a gift when he returned to Berlin. He knew she resented not being asked to accompany him to London. He'd done his best to explain that it would not be possible. '*Liebchen*, there will be other times, I promise.' The accusation in her eyes warned him that a simple trinket would not suffice. He knew the very place.

'What do you think, Dick? Is he going to St. James's Park? Another meeting with that Riemann character?'

'Search me. But he's going in that direction alright. Hang on though, he's crossing the road.'

Lensch stood on the pavement, looking right and left, waiting for an opportunity to cross.

'Better keep walking,' Dick muttered. 'Don't want to look like we're following him.

Lensch found a gap in the traffic.

Unable to follow immediately, Dick and Ambrose kept pace with him until he reached Piccadilly and turned the corner.

'Damn this bloomin' traffic.' Dick took a chance. Weaving through a steady stream of vehicles, he made it to the other side and hurried to the corner.

Two minutes later, Ambrose caught up with him standing haplessly, craning his neck in a fruitless attempt to pick out Lensch from the throng of pedestrians.

'Lost him.'

'Sorry, old chap. Couldn't get across the road. Not as sprightly as I used to be. What should we do now?' Ambrose took out his handkerchief and dabbed his brow.

'Couldn't be helped, I suppose. I dunno. Might as well walk up as far as Piccadilly Circus. If we don't catch sight of him, we'll have to go back and wait at the hotel. Mr Benson won't be happy.'

***

'The perfect choice, if I may say so.' The tall, tail-coated assistant at Mappin and Webb clasped his hands together, smiling obsequiously as Lensch examined the necklace. Its two half-strands of pearls resting in his palms.

While the words were intended merely to flatter, they were nevertheless accurate. Lensch had no doubt that the necklace was precisely the right choice. He imagined Gudrun's delight as she opened the satin lined case and set eyes on it.

The sun dazzled him as he stepped out into the street with the gift nestled in the inside pocket of his jacket. Temporarily blinded, Lensch was almost toppled when a pedestrian bumped into him. With his eyesight still blurred, he tottered for a moment, until the man caught his sleeve and steadied him.

'Oops. Sorry, mister.'

Lensch blinked and focussed on the fellow. A young man over a head taller than he. A member of the working class by his dress.

'Ach. Clumsy fool.' Lensch detached his arm and waved the man away. Gathering his dignity, he walked briskly on.

'My word, Dick, I thought he was going to fall flat on his face. Not too pleased, was he?' Ambrose hurried over to Dick's side. 'At least we've found him again. Look, he's going into Burlington Arcade.'

Anxious not to follow too closely, they loitered for a moment in the portico. Lensch was slowly making his way up the arcade, stopping to look in some of the shop windows. Ambrose took the lead, with Dick following a few paces behind, anxious not to be recognised. He felt uncomfortably out of place in the exclusive shopping venue. And he looked it.

'Can I help you?' The tone was not friendly. Dick turned. Resplendent in top hat and frock coat, and with the build of a pugilist, the beadle cut an intimidating figure. Employed to police the arcade, the beadles were well known as guardians of seemly behaviour. Unfailingly courteous to those that belonged in such august surroundings, they were vigilant in discouraging the lower orders.

'What?'

'Do you have business here?' The beadle looked Dick up and down.

'I'm just walking through, minding me own business. No law against it, is there?'

The beadle scowled. 'Don't get funny with me. In this arcade, I am the law. And I see someone who's up to no good.'

'Is something amiss?' Ambrose appeared at Dick's side.

'Amiss, sir? No, I'm just telling this… person he's not wanted here?'

'Then you will need to explain yourself to me, my good man.' Ambrose affected his most patrician tone. 'I'm Sir Thomas Millewis and this young man is with me.' The name of a character in a detective story that Ambrose had recently read was the first thing that popped into his head.

The beadle pursed his lips. 'That's as may be, sir. But there's some as might say that a strapping young working fellow in the company of an older gent means…'

'How dare you? To imply that we're… it's a disgrace. I'll see to it that your employers hear of this.' Ambrose was genuinely shocked at the man's insinuation.

That the beadle was unmoved at his protest angered him all the more. The man simply shrugged, giving a half-smile.

'Come on, Dick, never mind this oaf.'

The beadle moved around them, standing with his arms spread, blocking them from advancing further into the arcade. Over his shoulder, they could see Lensch in the distance, near the far end. By now, a small crowd had gathered to watch their confrontation with the beadle. Red with embarrassment and anxious to get away, Ambrose retreated to Piccadilly with Dick close behind.

Chapter 52

The hall clock chimed midnight.

Elsie placed a tray of sandwiches on the dining table. On her way to the door, she sniffed and gave Verity a disapproving glance.

'Oh dear, Elsie is quite put out by these meetings of ours. I'll have to make it up to her after the dust settles.' Verity bustled about, handing out plates and napkins. 'Please help yourselves, everyone. Don't stand on ceremony. There are bottles of hock on the sideboard and beer for those that prefer it.'

She looked on while her guests milled about, filling plates and glasses. Not feeling hungry herself, she settled for a glass of wine.

George finished chewing his roast beef sandwich and rose to his feet.

'I'll get straight to the point. Today has been a disappointment. Despite our efforts, we're none the wiser.'

Cherkasov grimaced as George recounted how Ambrose and Dick had run foul of the Burlington Arcade beadle. 'Awfully sorry, Dmitri,' Ambrose apologised. 'We waited outside the hotel afterwards and he did turn up at five fifteen. He hadn't emerged again when we finally left to come here.'

'So, you don't know what he did after you lost him?'

'No. Mind you, he was carrying a couple of parcels. Could just have been shopping.'

'I wish I could report more success with Riemann,' George continued. 'He spent the day at the embassy, then went back to his lodgings. Stopped at the pub for half an hour. After my dust -up with the locals yesterday, I played it safe and stayed outside. He stayed home after that.' George paused, looking at the glum expressions around the table. 'Look, despite that, I want to say thank you for the work you've put in today. Alfie, Dick, Ambrose, you've all made a sterling effort.'

'Hear, hear,' Verity added.

'So we have one day left. It's now the twenty-first of June. Tomorrow is the day of the Jubilee.' Cherkasov picked up his glass and drained it.

George nodded. 'We're wasting time and effort in staking out Brown's Hotel. We should concentrate everything on Riemann. You say that there's one day left. That's right. It means that tomorrow Riemann must have everything in place. We will all work together. Where he goes, we all go. He must lead us to the place, somewhere along the procession route, where the shooting will take place.'

'All of us, George? asked Verity.

'I mean Alfie, Dick, Ambrose and myself. And, Benny, I'd like you to accompany us this time.'

'Happy to guv.' Benny grinned and winked at Alfie and Dick.

'So not all, then?' Verity raised an eyebrow.

'Well, I hadn't thought of General Cherkasov traipsing around London. Dmitri, what is your view?'

Cherkasov nodded. 'I think it's best to leave this to you and your associates, George. However, I expect you to inform me of developments. If you discover where the shooting is to take place, I must be told.'

'No role for the little woman, then?' All eyes turned to Verity.

George sighed. 'You can hardly stand around on street corners or follow Riemann into pubs or down dark alleys.'

'Well, that's a matter of opinion, but I do see your point. Shall I tell you what I think?'

George nodded.

'I propose that Dmitri and I wait here. When you have news, send one of your party back here. The question that arises is what are we to do with that information? Have you thought that far ahead, George? Finding the place is all very well, but then what?'

'Normally, I would say that Colonel Quilter would have to take action. But he seems to have washed his hands of the whole affair.'

'If he doesn't act, I will,' Cherkasov insisted.

'Understood, Dmitri, you can count on me as well. We'll have to stop them ourselves.' George reached for the pistol in his pocket and placed it on the table.

'And I.' Ambrose turned to Cherkasov. 'It will be like old times, eh, Dmitri?'

'We'll all be in it,' Alfie spoke up, with Dick and Benny nodding their agreement.

Chapter 53

'Think we've missed him?'

George thought it was all too likely.

'I'm starting to think so, Alfie.'

It had been a long day. With two men stationed at the top of Maunsel Street and one guarding the lane at the rear of Riemann's abode, George rotated his team every two hours, allowing two of them to take some rest at a café around the corner in the Horseferry road.

Six-fifteen. George snapped his pocket watch shut. He should let Verity and Dmitri know how things stood.

'I'm going round to Jackson's café. I'll send Ambrose back to Montagu Street. He can let Verity and the General know what's going on - or not going on, in this case. Benny can go and take over from Dick round the back. I'll give it another couple of hours, then we might as well call it a day.'

'Right you are, Mr Benson.' Alfie turned away. 'Oh, here's trouble.'

George hadn't noticed the two police constables bearing down on them. Just five paces away, he wondered whether they might pass by until one of them put a hand up to stop Alfie, and his companion beckoned George over.

'We've had reports of men loitering in this street,' the larger of the two constables said, planting his feet apart and hooking his thumbs into his belt.

'Really, constable. We're just passing through. Now you mention it though, there were a couple of shady looking characters at the far end.' George turned to point down the street. 'Hmm, can't see them now. Perhaps you might catch-up with them if you're quick.'

'Passing through, are you?' The second policeman moved closer, standing nose to nose with George. One hand resting on the handle of his truncheon.

'That's right. Just going to meet some friends at Jackson's café. Do you know it?'

The constable gave a humourless smile. 'What do you think, Ted?'

Ted put a hand on George's shoulder. 'I think these two should get on their way. Now then you two, get moving. If we see you back here, we'll run you in.'

George bumped into Alfie as the policeman gave him a hefty shove. 'Let's go,' he murmured.

The sound of voices across the street caught Riemann's attention. He watched the constables talking to two men, and sending them on their way. He waited for them to continue on their beat, but they stayed there, talking and sharing a joke. It was time for him to go. The presence of the police might mean nothing, but he'd rather not take any risks. Not now, at the eleventh hour. He'd have to leave through the back. Riemann stepped back from the attic window.

Dick had had enough. *Come on, Mister Benson*, he fretted, taking a last drag of his cigarette before stamping on the stub.

At the sound of a gate slamming shut, Dick instinctively drew back behind a hand cart parked at the side of the lane. Whistling, he pushed it along, nodding to the man striding towards him. Riemann inclined his head and passed by, avoiding eye contact.

Dick counted to ten, hearing Riemann's footsteps receding, then abandoned the handcart and turned to follow. The lane came out on the Horseferry Road. 'Turn right,' Dick muttered under his breath. That way would bring them in sight of the others - whoever was stationed on Maunsel Street. The café also lay in that direction.

'Shit,' he cursed as Riemann turned left, increasing his pace.

Dick hesitated. There was no one in sight. He thought of calling out but couldn't risk alerting Riemann. 'Bugger it,' he turned and hurried after the German.

Ten minutes later, Dick followed Riemann onto an omnibus.

***

'He wouldn't simply disappear.' George paced back and forth in Verity's dining room.

Two hours had passed since his ignominious return to Montagu Square. The grim atmosphere in the room persisted since he'd informed Cherkasov and Verity of his failure. They listened in stony-faced silence while he explained that after long hours, fruitlessly waiting for a sign of Riemann, the appearance of the police had left him with no option but to call of the observation.

The two constables still stood on the corner of Maunsell Street when he passed by after collecting Benny and Ambrose from Jackson's cafe. Alfie went on ahead to tell

310

Dick to stand down. His panicked reappearance with the news that his brother was nowhere to be seen set the seal on a thoroughly bad day.

Alfie nodded. 'Dick would never just go off of his own accord.'

'So, there is a possibility that Riemann departed through this back lane that Dick was watching and that he has gone off in pursuit without the opportunity to tell the rest of you what was happening,' Cherkasov observed dryly.

'It's the only possibility that I can think of,' George admitted.

'Then there's still hope.' Verity gave George a look of encouragement.

'Where there's life…' Ambrose quipped, sounding more cheerful than he felt. 'There, what did I tell you?'

Verity was already out in the hall as the knocker sounded a second time.

A few moments later, Dick looked nervously around the dining room table as every face turned expectantly in his direction.

'Couldn't half murder a beer.' The tension evaporated.

Alfie's guffaw set everyone laughing while Verity dashed off to the kitchen to find a bottle of ale.

'Thanks Miss Mallard.' Dick's hand shook as he poured.

'Take your time,' George waited for Dick to take a long draught, emptying half the glass.

'He went out the back, guv. Couldn't let you know, or I'd have lost him. I'm really sorry.' Dick suppressed a belch.

'No need to apologise. Go on.'

'Gets on a bus, doesn't he. Then off that and on to another one, and ends up at London Bridge. Well, I'm thinking, what now? There was people everywhere. Folk already grabbing spots for the procession tomorrow, crowds of them. You'd never credit it. I nearly lost him and then at the Southwark end I see him stop and talk to another bloke.'

'Aha. The plot thickens.' Ambrose slapped the table, earning a look of mild reproval from Verity.

Dick had another gulp of his beer, wiping his mouth with the back of his hand. 'Yeah, that's what I thought. Well, they only chatted for a minute and then off they go together.'

'What did this other man look like, Dick?' George asked.

'About my height, he was. He had this bushy black beard went halfway down his chest. I didn't get too close, but I'd recognise him again, alright. Anyway, I followed them. Straight down the procession route. There's flags and bunting and all sorts, and stands of seats. Rows and rows of them.'

'Did they stop anywhere or just keep walking?'

'There's a row of houses on Borough Road. They turn off up a lane, brings them round the back of these houses. Well, that's the funny thing, it's the backs that face the main road. The entrances are in the street behind.'

Cherkasov turned to George. 'They're using one of those houses as the firing point. It's just as I expected.'

'Yes, General, that must be it.' George breathed a sigh of relief. 'Which house did they go to, Dick?' As soon as he spoke, Dick's downcast expression warned that his relief was premature.

'You didn't see them enter a house?'

Dick turned to his brother. 'Of all the bad luck, Alfie. I only bumped into the King brothers.'

'Oh Gawd.' Alfie struck his forehead with the palm of his hand.

'The King brothers? Who the devil are the King brothers, Alfie?'

'Some south of the river toughs, Mr Benson. We've had a bit of a disagreement over a matter of business. They've taken into their heads that Dick and I owe them money. It's all nonsense, but there ain't no love lost between us.'

'Riemann and the other bloke were about twenty feet in front of me. I could see them clearly enough walking down the street. Then I pass these three blokes talking on the pavement and all of a sudden I feel someone grab me collar and spin me round.'

'You bumped into all three of them?' Alfie asked.

'Yes, it was Sammy as grabbed me. Then Reg and Freddie start pushing me around. *Where's our eighty quid?* they're yelling. I would have taken a right pasting if a couple of coalmen doing a delivery hadn't come to see what the trouble was. I took me chance and scarpered. Trouble is, I lost sight of Riemann and the other one. It's a long street so they can't have got to the far end. They just vanished.'

'You mean they must have entered one of the houses.'

'Yes, Mr Benson, but I don't know which one.'

'We can't just up sticks and head down to Borough Road. It's dark and we've got no idea what to do when we get there. We can hardly go along the street at night knocking on every door. That would just get us arrested for disturbing the peace.'

Despite a strong desire on the part of Alfie, Dick, Benny, and Ambrose to go storming down to south London, George, with Verity and Cherkasov's support, prevailed in persuading them to hold their horses.

'We'll set off in the morning,' George eyed Verity. 'Can they stay?'

'Yes, I don't know what on earth Elsie is going to say, but I'm sure she can rustle up some blankets and pillows. If you don't mind roughing it down here.'

Alfie, Dick and Benny nodded in agreement.

'Dmitri? Will you be going back to the embassy?'

'Yes, George. But I will join you tomorrow. When do you propose to get to Borough Road?'

George considered. 'I was thinking of setting off at first light, but if we get there too early and start knocking on doors, people may still be in bed. Let's say we arrive by eight o'clock.'

'That will give you five hours.' Verity brandished her copy of the official programme of the Royal Jubilee Procession. 'Her Majesty will leave Buckingham Palace at a quarter past eleven. The whole thing should take about three hours. There will be a service of thanksgiving at St Paul's, so the procession should reach Borough Road around one.'

Cherkasov cleared his throat. 'George, you speak of knocking on doors. Is that your plan, to go door to door simply knocking to see who answers? Won't that in itself look suspicious, a group of men gathering around each door?'

George grinned. 'I have an idea…'

Chapter 54

Verity opened the curtains.

The weather had been a subject of intense speculation for several days. Would the Jubilee procession be the glorious expression of the Empire's love and admiration for Queen Victoria that everyone hoped for, or would the weather turn it into a dismal, dispiriting, disappointment?

She viewed the overcast sky with trepidation. A superstitious person might take it as an omen. She turned towards the bed and gently shook its occupant. 'Jaqueline.' The girl moaned softly. '*Chérie*, it's time to wake up.' Jaqueline blinked. Verity shook her shoulder again and the little girl turned her head, clutching her bear from Hamleys.

'Maman?'

Verity sat on the bed, brushing Jaqueline's tousled hair from her eyes. 'Do you remember what today is?'

Jaqueline shook her head.

'Yes, you do. Today, we are going to see…'

The girl sat up. 'The Queen!'

The hectic events of the past few days had left Verity in a quandary. When she planned Jaqueline's visit, she'd had the Jubilee in mind. What a wonderful surprise it would be for her daughter to witness the grand procession. As fortune would have it, a wonderful view would be theirs without the bother of mingling with the crowds. Madame Claude, her dressmaker, had offered her most treasured customers a ringside seat from the first floor of her premises in the Strand.

It was only after she'd learned of Carter's demise that Verity told Jaqueline about the surprise. The little girl looked at her with bemusement, puzzled at the strange word her mother had used. 'Jub… Jub-ilee?'

Verity sat her down and showed her the Jubilee Programme with its wonderful illustrations of the regiments and dignitaries taking part in the grand parade. The child gazed in awe as Verity turned the pages, alighting eventually on a picture of the Royal carriage with Queen Victoria holding a parasol.

'Most of the night, Verity had wrestled with the question. How could she take Jaqueline to watch the procession, knowing that an assassin would be lying in wait? True, there was no risk to the child or herself in the Strand. But the thought of standing at Jaqueline's side, cheering and waving at the Royal party in the knowledge that they might be in mortal peril, tormented her. Should she call it off, pretend that she was unwell?

It was only when she woke at dawn after a short, fitful sleep that she decided to put her trust in providence. Matters were out of her hands. The child would have her surprise, and please God, all would be well.

George and the others had left earlier. Verity offered a silent prayer for them.

'Maman?' Jaqueline climbed out of bed and stood in the middle of the room with her hands on her hips. 'Who are they?'

'Who do you mean, dear?'

'The strange men. The ones you talk to in the dining room. I've heard them.'

'Ah, they are friends of Uncle George and Uncle Ambrose.'

'Oh. Are they good men?'

'Yes, darling, they are very good men.'

***

It was bedlam in the streets. George had never imagined that such a tide of humanity would wash across the streets of London. People everywhere. Some still lying in the parks, having stayed overnight to gain a place along the route. Others walking resolutely to take places reserved for them in the massive timber viewing stands erected at various points. And detachments of soldiers, sailors and police marching to take up their positions lining the procession route. Traffic was largely at a standstill and the procession route itself had been cordoned off since before dawn.

Time after time, they were forced to change direction and find themselves diverted from their chosen path. Alfie did his best, using his knowledge of back streets and alleyways to steer a way through the maze. It was a city transformed into a riot of red, white, and blue, with flags and bunting in profusion. They passed temporary constructions in the form of triumphal arches festooned in brightly coloured cloth and masses of flowers. Almost every building competed in displaying emblems and banners.

And the people too. Men, women and children proudly wearing rosettes or miniature Union flags pinned to their clothes.

The pickpockets of the metropolis were also out in droves, attracted by such an abundance of prey.

Ambrose had dropped behind, captivated by a dog cart weaving its way along the crowded street. The driver, dressed as John Bull, tipped his hat while his lady companion, splendidly attired as Britannia, complete with trident, shield and helmet, nodded graciously.

Turning to catch up with the others, Ambrose collided with a slight young man in a shabby grey suit, sending the fellow teetering and landing on his backside on the cobbles.

'My word, I'm so sorry, old chap, didn't see you there. Let me help you up.' Ambrose crouched to take the fellow's arm and help him to his feet. Oblivious to the waif-like young woman behind him, he felt nothing as she slid her small hand into the right-hand pocket of his jacket.'

'Oi, stop thief!'

Ambrose looked up at the sound of Alfie's voice. 'Eh? What's that? The waif brushed his arm, hurriedly withdrawing her hand. 'What the devil?' As Ambrose turned to face her, her accomplice shoved him hard in the back. In an instant, the pickpockets had merged into the crowd.

'Mister Mallard, are you alright?' It was Ambrose's turn to be helped to his feet. Alfie's attempt to lift him produced a wince of pain. 'Argh, my ankle.'

George, Dick and Benny gathered round.

'Blighters tried to rob me.'

'Did they take anything?' George brushed some dust from Ambrose's coat.

'Hmm,' Ambrose checked his pockets, 'no, nothing's missing.'

'Can you walk?'

Ambrose tried a step. The grimace on his face answered George's question.

'He could lean on my shoulder, guv.'

George shook his head. 'No Alfie, good of you to offer, but it would slow us down too much.'

'Don't mind about me. Just get going. I'll be alright. I'll hop back to Montagu Square if I have to,' Ambrose offered.

'I'll take him,' said Alfie. 'If we can get clear of these crowds, I'll put him in a cab. Time's getting on, Mister Benson. You lot get moving. I'll get along to Borough Road myself when I've seen to him.'

George consulted his watch. Alfie was right. At this rate, they'd be lucky to get there by ten thirty. 'Good luck.'

He nodded to Dick and Benny. 'Let's go.'

Chapter 55

Resplendent in his scarlet Field Marshal's uniform, Bertie surveyed the crowds outside Buckingham Palace. Hemmed in by rows of soldiers standing shoulder to shoulder lining the procession route, they revelled in patriotic outpourings of cheering and cries of 'God Save the Queen'. Outside the Palace gates, he spotted one of the cinematograph operators, bent over his apparatus.

The Queen was still at breakfast with her daughters. When he'd greeted her that morning, she'd embraced him warmly and whispered how invigorated she felt. 'How proud dear Albert would have been to witness the abiding love my subjects have for their monarch.'

Bertie cast a jaundiced eye at the sky, still overcast, but growing a little lighter, he fancied. Stepping away from the window, he retired to enjoy a last cigarette before proceedings commenced.

***

Erich von Lensch ran a finger around the stiff collar of his dress uniform. Low in the pecking order at the German Embassy, as a mere major, he was content to stay in the background. The Ambassador was surrounded by an entourage of diplomats and military men, recounting the private dinner that he had attended with Prince and

Princess Henry of Prussia, Kaiser Wilhelm's representatives at the Jubilee celebrations.

Later, the procession would pass by the embassy, along the Mall, returning Her Majesty to Buckingham Palace. Except, as only Lensch knew, the prized vantage point would never be witness to the Queen's triumphal return.

***

Orpheus sat in his Whitehall office. With his door closed to deter casual visitors, he gazed vacantly at the painting adorning the wall opposite. A landscape depicting a scene from antiquity by an undistinguished member of the Royal Academy. He'd paid scant attention to it until now. Framed by a ruined Grecian temple and a grove of tall trees, a group of diminutive figures sat in a circle, with sheep and cattle grazing in the foreground. In the middle distance, pastures and forests extended to a range of hazy hills.

Lost in contemplation and weighed down by dark thoughts, Orpheus looked wistfully at the canvas, wishing he could somehow enter the picture and disappear into those hills.

He tried to ignore the bustle of movement out in the corridor. Junior clerks, messengers, even the boiler men from the cellars, were all pressed into duty, putting the finishing touches to the Home Office's Jubilee decorations.

Soon, family members of senior civil servants would be admitted to take their places to view the procession. Orpheus had explained to colleagues that Beatrice was unaccountably detained in Sussex. 'You can imagine how disappointed she feels.'

Listlessly, he bent to open the bottom drawer of his desk and grasp the bottle of brandy he kept there. Pouring his third glass of the morning, he sat back and returned his attention to the painting.

***

Colonel Quilter sat stiffly upright at his desk. The family photograph that had aroused Verity's interest on the occasion that she and Ambrose had visited his office was placed squarely in front of him.

Three sealed white envelopes lay side by side in front of the photograph. The first contained his signed letter of resignation. Next was a personal letter to his son and daughters. And, finally, his last will and testament. The only other object on the polished walnut surface was his service revolver.

Even here in Hammersmith, the buzz of excited voices in the street, as people flocked eastwards toward the procession route, reminded him that, one way or another, his destiny would be decided before the day was out.

Chapter 56

London Bridge. At last.

George, Dick and Benny huddled together at the corner with Upper Thames Street, while a chaotic mass of humanity swirled around them. Peering across the sea of heads crowding the pavements on both sides of the bridge, George cursed himself for having come this far before crossing the Thames. Surely, Southwark Bridge would have been a better, less crowded option. London Bridge was on the procession route. Of course, it would be packed.

An old soldier drafted in to help steward the crowds and proudly displaying his campaign medals on his chest, vainly attempted to dissuade people from pushing their way into the crowd already occupying the bridge and jealously guarding their vantage points.

George pretended he hadn't heard him and edged his way forward, followed by Benny and Dick. Apologising to left and right and sidling through any small gaps that presented themselves, the trio eventually covered three quarters of the bridge span. Some made way for them without protest, others gave them dirty looks or voiced their displeasure.

Amid the general hubbub interspersed with snatches of patriotic songs and music hall ditties, George picked-up the sound of discordant male voices, indistinct at first but growing louder and coarser as George shuffled nearer.

He stepped into a small glade in the forest of Jubilee spectators, in the centre of which five young men dressed in the manner of city clerks stood singing and braying obscenities, each with a bottle of wine or beer in hand. Drunk and obnoxious, but thinking themselves the epitome of wit and jollity, their unseemly manner had prompted those around them to draw back as far as they could, given the press of people around them. Mothers pressed their hands over their children's ears while men called to the group to moderate their behaviour, producing a barrage of jibes and crude insults from the miscreants.

Despite the disgust he felt at such a boorish display, George suppressed his instinct to teach the louts a lesson. Time was his enemy. He must press on.

His attempt to edge around the group only served to attract their attention. 'Hey there you. Yes you, sneaking through there. Where do you think you're going?' The tallest to the group, who appeared to be their leader, stood in George's path brandishing a bottle of cheap champagne and swaying slightly.

'My companions and I would simply like to pass.'

'Ooh, listen to his lordship, *my companions and I would simply like to pass.*'

His friends roared with laughter, each of them mimicking George's words and prancing about, waving their bottles.

'Give him what for, Percy,' one of them shouted.

George put his hands up and smiled, stepping sideways to circumvent the fellow.

'Oh no, you don't.' Percy shoved George with his free hand. 'Come on lads, scrag him.'

Benny's knuckles caught Percy on the side of the jaw. George saw his eyeballs swivel upward as his knees gave way. Dick floored another lout with a straight jab, then both he and Benny confronted the remainder with raised fists. Faced with the prospect of a beating the three lads tried to back away.

Members of the crowd whistled and cheered, turning eagerly to watch.

'Come on. Let's go,' George urged.

To his right, he saw a flurry of movement, someone approaching from the southern end of the bridge. Police helmets, forcing a passage.

An inspector emerged, accompanied by a sergeant and three constables. 'Take those two,' the inspector ordered, pointing to Benny and Dick.

'Easy Benny, you too. Dick,' George called out, fearing that they would resist the officers.

'Take this one too,' the inspector instructed.

A constable with truncheon drawn took George by the arm and marched him away to the south bank, the crowd parting before them.

'You've arrested the wrong people,' George tried to attract the inspector's attention. 'Inspector, we are law-abiding citizens. Listen to me, will you?'

'Put them in the Black Maria, Sergeant. I'll deal with them later.' The Inspector walked away.

***

Bertie sat astride his horse, exchanging pleasantries with the Duke of Connaught, mounted alongside. In front of them, the State Landau, drawn by eight cream horses, stood ready to depart. Seated within were his wife, Alexandra, Princess of Wales, Princess Helena, the Queen's third daughter, and Her Majesty, Victoria, the Queen Empress.

At precisely 11.15 am, signalled by the firing of a gun in Hyde Park, the carriage moved out of Buckingham Palace. As though by royal command, the clouds dispersed to reveal a day of bright sunshine.

Taking its place in the midst of the vast procession, the royal carriage proceeded up Constitution Hill, accompanied by the tumultuous roar of the crowd.

***

George snapped his watch shut. The reverberations of the Hyde Park gun echoed in the distance.

'How long do you think they'll keep us here, guv?' Dick shuffled uneasily on the firm wooden bench of the Black Maria.

'I wish I knew.' George's attempts to find out when the inspector would return had been ignored. Sergeant Tanner, who stood outside with one of the constables, had not even turned his head.

'Damn it, we're running out of time,' George fretted.

'Good job they never searched us, though,' Benny grunted. 'I've still got this.' He patted his overcoat under which a short jemmy was concealed. 'And you've still got that pistol of yours, Mr Benson.'

Yes, thought George, and there'll be merry hell to pay if the inspector orders his men to search us when he comes back.

'Look, guv,' Benny leaned closer. 'There's only two rozzers out there. I could clock 'em both for you and we can scarper.'

George shook his head. But if they were delayed for much longer, he feared they would be forced to take desperate measures.

'Have they given any trouble, sergeant?'

'No, sir. No trouble.'

The inspector climbed up into the van and seated himself inside the back door.

'I'm Inspector Tweed. What are your names?'

George gave his name. Benny followed. The inspector held his hand up before Dick could follow suit.

'Benjamin Hopkins, did you say? Well, well, if it's not Benny the Bastard. What was it last time, Benny? Grievous bodily harm, wasn't it?'

'I done me time.'

Inspector Tweed grinned and turned to Dick.

'Dick… Richard Cotton.'

The inspector stared, open-mouthed. 'Cotton,' he echoed dully, shaking his head.

George seized the initiative. 'You're the inspector who interviewed Dick's brother, Alfie. He said it was an Inspector Tweed.'

'And how are you connected with Alfie Cotton?' Tweed asked warily.

'If I was to mention the name Quilter?'

'Oh God, not again.'

***

Back on the pavement, Benny clapped George on the shoulder. 'Put the wind up him that did, guv.'

George smiled. 'I thought he was going to keep us there while he got in touch with Colonel Quilter. Still, by then he knew we didn't start that fracas. There were enough witnesses to put him straight. He had to let us go, anyway. Let's get moving. Dick, you know the way. Lead on.'

Still hampered by the crowds, they eventually found their way to the spot where Dick had lost sight of Riemann and his associate.

'Alfie.' George pulled up short as he recognised the figure leaning on the railings of the nearest house.'

'Gawd, I'd almost given you up for lost. Been waiting here for ages wondering what could have 'appened. I got Mister Mallard a cab, then I nipped down here. Rotherhithe Bridge was pretty crowded. I expect London Bridge would have been impossible. What kept you?'

***

'When will we see the Queen, *Maman?*' Jaqueline looked up at her mother.

'Soon, Jaqueline.' The child's animation, as the bright ranks of soldiers rode by, had waned by the time the carriages, conveying royal personages from the wider royal family and representatives of European monarchies, passed under the windows of Madame Claude's establishment.

Verity consulted her programme. 'Yes. Listen, *chérie*. Can you hear? The cheering is getting louder? Look, here she comes.'

Jaqueline gave a squeak of excitement and started waving the small union flag Verity had bought her. Thousands of similar flags waved furiously in the street below.

'Aren't they lovely horses?' Verity's observation went unanswered. Jaqueline's attention being solely focused on the figure of the Queen.

Verity was intrigued. Hidden away for so long at Osborne, endlessly mourning Albert, the Queen had become a distant figure, rarely seen by her subjects. How would she react to such an overwhelming public occasion?

Sitting on her own at the back of the landau with the princesses, Alix and Helen, facing her, she sat upright holding a parasol aloft, smiling and bowing. Her enjoyment was obvious. Verity gave herself up to the emotion of the moment, waving and cheering madly.

Jaqueline screamed. 'She smiled at me. The Queen smiled at me,' hopping up and down and waving her flag with gusto.

And then it was over. The Queen passed on up the Strand toward the waiting magnificence of St Paul's Cathedral and the service of thanksgiving for her long, auspicious reign.

A cork popped.

Verity turned away from the window. As Madame Claude handed her a glass of champagne, her thoughts turned to George and the others, and the smile faded from her face.

Chapter 57

As George shamefacedly explained to Alfie the reason for their delayed arrival, a thought struck him.

'Dmitri. The General. He was to meet us here. Eight o'clock I said.'

'Oh, yes, well he's not a happy man I can tell you that.'

'You've seen him, Alfie?'

'He was 'anging about when I got here. Oh, he didn't get here by eight either. Took him 'til gone ten.'

'So where is he?'

He walked up and down the street a couple of times just in case he could get a glimpse of Riemann. Then he went round to Borough Road. Said something about trying to see if he could spot the firing point from down there. Wouldn't fancy his chances.'

'Neither would I. The crowds there are just as dense as they were on London Bridge.' George checked his watch. 'We can't wait. It's gone twelve. Ten past. We've got less than an hour.'

'I see you got the stuff.'

'Yes, there's flags, and rosettes, badges, paper streamers, figurines, all sorts.' George beckoned. 'Bring it over here, Dick.'

The tray of Jubilee themed trinkets that Dick held, supported by a cord around his neck, had been acquired at no little expense from a tout on Borough High Street. The fellow had been most reluctant to part with it, but the prospect of making twice its value in one transaction sent him on his way with a smile on his face.

This was George's clever idea. By posing as a tout, Dick could go from door to door without arousing suspicion. George and the others would observe from across the road, in the hope that Riemann or his associate would make an appearance.

'In heaven's name, what kept you?'

Cherkasov appeared at George's side, grim faced and perspiring with the exertion of pushing his way through the throng on Borough Road.

George explained.

Cherkasov fought to bring his agitation under control. 'Very well, we must make the best of the time that remains. I tried to view the backs of the houses from the main road, but I could see nothing to suggest a firing point. There are people at the windows. Just waving and cheering. There, do you hear, the head of the procession is approaching.'

'Alright. Dick, start with this one.'

Ten minutes later, Dick had only reached the third house along. There were fifteen more. At the first house, the man who came to the door was anxious to return to his back parlour. 'The procession's coming. I ain't got time to talk to you.' He started to shut the door, then hesitated. 'Here, give me two of them flags, will you?' Dick took his money and moved on.

The lady of the house next door was only too glad to inspect his wares. Unable to make up her mind, she rummaged through the tray. A cry of, 'come on Ma, you'll miss the soldiers,' drew her back inside without buying anything.

'It's taking too long,' George muttered to Cherkasov.

Dick wasted several minutes knocking fruitlessly on the door of the next house.

'Leave it, Dick. Next one,' George called out.

Cherkasov tapped him on the shoulder. 'Forgive me, George. I should have thought of it earlier.'

'What?' George failed to keep the irritation out of his voice.

'I said there were people standing at most of the windows.'

'Yes.'

'There was one house with no one. No people watching, leaning out of the windows. No flags draped over the windowsills.'

'Which one?'

Cherkasov pondered. 'I can't say exactly. Houses do not have numbers on their back walls. I would say that it was towards the far end, maybe ten houses along from here. I can't be sure.'

'Wait here.' George hurried across the road. 'Move along, Dick. Leave the next few houses, start from the seventh one along from here.'

'Oh, right you are, Mr Benson.' Dick moved on down the street, leaving a young lad at the house he'd just left bemused to find no one on the doorstep.

Nothing at the first house, although Dick could hear sounds of merriment within. Next door, a disgruntled housewife told him that her house was already awash with red, white, and blue.

Dick was struck by the shabbiness of the door to number twenty-four. It was not a well-to-do neighbourhood but even by the standards of its neighbours the flaking brown paint and signs of wood rot on the front door attested to a house badly in need of repair.

Dick banged hard with the knocker, half afraid that it would come away in his hand. He put his ear to the door. Nothing. He tried again and stood back. The rattling of a sticky sash window above made him look up. One of the two first-floor windows was opening. Dick craned his neck. The man wasted few words. 'Go away' was all Dick heard, followed by the window being slammed shut.

A glimpse was enough. The bullet head with its stubble of grey hair was plain to see.

Dick moved along the street until he was out of sight of number twenty-four. The others kept pace from the opposite side, then crossed to join him.

'What now?'

***

Victoria gave a silent prayer of thanks. Her fears that the weather would mar the Jubilee had proved unfounded. It was a glorious day. Her parasol provided welcome shade from the sun.

The thanksgiving service at St Paul's had affected her deeply. An occasion of both joy and solemnity. Conducted in the open air at the foot of the Cathedral steps, she received the prayers and benedictions of the Bishop of London and the Archbishop of Canterbury. A grand choir, five hundred-strong, sang the hymns, and a crowd of fifteen thousand, packed into the square, acclaimed their sovereign.

Now that the centrepiece of the Jubilee was behind her, she relaxed and gave herself over to the simple pleasure of receiving the acclamation of the people. Crossing the Thames, she entered the poorer quarters of the city.

On her right, keeping pace with her carriage, Bertie was preoccupied with his haemorrhoids. Of all the times to flare up. Gritting his teeth, he endured the unyielding saddle beneath him. His only consolation was the prospect of a large scotch and soda and a warm bath when this was all over.

***

The sound of cheering swelled as the crowds lining Borough Road anticipated the imminent arrival of Her Majesty.

George, Cherkasov and the Cottons waited anxiously two doors away from number twenty-four. Thankfully, the street was empty. Everyone in the district seemed to be occupied with the procession.

Benny stood at the front door. After glancing up and down the street, he leaned in and inserted his jemmy. In one slick movement, the lock gave way with a brief splintering crack.

The others hurried to join him, stepping gingerly into the hall and closing the door behind them

'Remember, Dmitri and I will take the lead. Alfie, you stay here. Dick, you follow Dmitri. Benny with me.' George took his pistol from his pocket and headed for the stairs. Cherkasov produced his own weapon, a Nagant M1895, seven shot revolver.

As George and Benny climbed the stairs, painstakingly testing each bare tread to avoid creaking timbers,

Cherkasov and Dick cautiously opened the door to the front parlour. Finding it unoccupied, they continued along the hall to the rear of the ground floor.

George held his breath. As his eyes drew level with the landing, a quick glimpse showed four closed doors giving on to the landing and a second flight of stairs.

Beckoning Dick to follow, George chose the door to the room where Riemann had appeared.

'Keep an eye on the stairs,' he mouthed. The brass handle turned with a pronounced squeak. George froze, listening for any sound within. With his pistol in his right hand, he pushed the door ajar. The rank, sweet, cloying odour made him gag. Dick turned his head, wrinkling his nose in disgust.

A threadbare rug, a filthy unkempt bed with an oak chest at its foot and a washstand were all it contained. A pair of ragged stained curtains hung at the window. George grimaced at the sight of a full chamber pot under the brass bedstead. But that didn't account for the smell.

Tiptoeing across the dusty floorboards, he stopped at the chest. A wave of foul air escaped as he lifted the top. George fought back the urge to retch and reached reluctantly for the sheet wrapped around the body that he knew it must conceal.

***

On the floor above, the Dutchman calmly went about his business.

During the previous evening, he'd prepared the firing point. Three attic rooms faced Borough Road. The window in the first room refused to budge. Rather than force it, he tried the second room. Its window opened with a little persuasion.

He turned to the two items he'd brought from downstairs. A battered bentwood chair and two cushions. With one cushion resting on the windowsill, he drew the chair up to the window and sat leaning forward, mimicking the action of aiming the rifle. Shaking his head, he reached for the second cushion and put it in the chair and resumed his firing posture.

'Now the rifle.' The Dutchman nodded to Riemann to open the long wooden case lying on the floor. Riemann lifted the Mosin-Nagant and handed it over. The Dutchman cradled it in his hands, testing its weight and feel and working the bolt.

'Cartridges.' Riemann handed the Dutchman a clip of five rounds and watched him load the magazine.

The Dutchman swivelled in his chair. Resting the rifle barrel on the cushion, he adopted the firing position, fitting the rifle snugly into his shoulder, and bringing the sights to bear on a hansom cab trundling slowly along Borough Road, in the dusk. He turned away.

'The telescopic sight.'

Riemann brought it and held the rifle steady while the Dutchman fitted the sight. Again, he took aim. An evening newspaper seller served as a target while he adjusted the focus.

Declaring himself satisfied, he stood back from the window and handed the rifle back to Riemann, who replaced it in its case ready for the next day.

It had been an uncomfortable night for the two of them, sleeping on two horsehair mattresses and eating a meagre supper of bread and German sausage washed down with a couple of bottles of warm beer. No matter, the Dutchman had endured much greater privations on the veld.

Now the time had come. His rehearsal the previous night had been in semi-darkness with little chance of being observed. In broad daylight and in bright sunshine, it was imperative to take the shots quickly, leaving the marksman exposed to view for the shortest possible time. True, the crowd, and the soldiers guarding the route, should be focused on the procession rather than a small attic window. All the more so, when the Queen herself came into view. However, success demanded that the gunman be exposed only for as long as it took to put a bullet through the substantial torso of the Prince of Wales and another through the sovereign herself.

He pictured the scene of devastating shock and confusion that would follow. Horror mingled with fear. Panic at the thought of more shooting. Anxious eyes looking frantically around to see where the shots had come from. By then, the rifle and cushion would be lying on the floor of the attic while the Dutchman and Riemann rushed down the stairs. In the space of thirty seconds, the two men would be outside, going their separate ways, while all around them the city descended into chaos and despair.

Crouched on his chair, the Dutchman waited with the rifle on his knee, ready to bring it to the aiming position. The cheering of the crowd became a roar.

Chapter 58

George let the sheet fall back. One look at the corpse's face was enough. 'Dead. Murdered?' he whispered to Dick. Cherkasov and Benny appeared in the doorway, signalling that they'd discovered no one on the ground floor.

Pausing only to show Dmitri and Benny his grim discovery, George ushered everyone back to the landing. Two minutes of stealthy searching confirmed that the other first-floor rooms were unoccupied.

With hand signals, he instructed Dick and Benny to wait on the landing. Dmitri was already halfway up the stairs to the attic by the time George followed.

George drew level with Dmitri at the head of the stairs. An attic room lay directly ahead of them with its door wide open. Padding silently to the entrance, they glanced inside. Turning away from the empty chamber, the faint, metallic, click-click of a rifle bolt broke the silence.

George reacted a mere second before Dmitri. All stealth abandoned, he raced to the door, pistol raised.

The Dutchman swung sideways at the thud of George's boots on the floorboards, dropping on one knee and aiming at the doorway.

George had no time to discover whether the old adage about a person's life passing before their eyes at the prospect of imminent death was true. All because of a rotten floorboard. Instead of a man framed in the doorway, the Dutchman saw a figure tottering clown-like across his field of vision. His shot went high, exactly where George's heart would have been if he'd stayed upright.

Working the bolt to extract the spent cartridge and load another, the Dutchman emerged, ready to finish the job. George scrambled to his knees, too slowly to bring his pistol to bear, staring directly into the muzzle of the Mosin-Nagant. It was fortunate he was kneeling, as two rounds from Cherkasov's pistol tore through the Dutchman's torso.

Concealed behind the door, Riemann thanked providence that he'd brought his machine pistol with him. It's not as though he was expecting trouble. Who? Why? How? A cascade of questions skittered through his mind. In true Prussian manner, he brought them to order. They'd keep for later. It didn't matter who was out there on the landing, why they'd come, or how they knew. His survival instinct took control.

Cherkasov stepped over the Dutchman's body and helped George to his feet. Their eyes met, flashing the same unspoken thought. Riemann!

The Prussian fired on the run. Holding the Mauser across his body, he sprayed a short burst, crossing the landing and thundering down the stairs. Benny braced himself on the bottom step, gripping the banister firmly with one hand and reaching for his jemmy. Two rounds took him in the chest a fraction of a second before Riemann crashed into him. Dick hit the floor, expecting a bullet.

Upstairs, Cherkasov stared at the blood smearing his palm. One of Riemann's shots had scored a shallow furrow in his scalp. George handed him a handkerchief and pushed past him to the stairs.

Riemann's boots thudded down the bottom flight. Alfie sprinted away along the passage, darting into the scullery and slamming the door behind him. By the time George reached Benny's side, Riemann had wrenched the front door open and taken to the street, buttoning his overcoat and hurrying away.

Cherkasov's cry to 'get after him,' died in his throat at the sight of the dark red puddle spreading from Benny's body.

Flat on his back with one hand still gripping his jemmy, Benny the Bastard gazed sightlessly up at George and Dick.

'Has Riemann gone?' Alfie's voice preceded him up the stairs.

'Oh, my Gawd. Not Benny.'

***

In Borough Road, the roar of the crowd moderated. Cheering and snatches of *Rule Britannia* and *God Save the Queen* still rippled through them, but the crescendo of noise, which reached its zenith as Her Majesty passed by, and which masked the sound of nearby gunshots, gradually subsided.

Chapter 59

Orpheus stood a little unsteadily, gazing down on Whitehall. The stately boardroom, which had been cleared of furniture, to accommodate the Home Office's senior civil servants and family members was filled with a noisy gaggle of spectators, enjoying the spectacle passing beneath them every bit as joyously, if a little more decorously, as the common herd out in the streets.

With the first murmurs of, 'here she comes,' the people surrounding him pressed closer to the windows. Orpheus backed away. Unnoticed, he retired to his office, collected his hat and coat, and made his way back to the cold, lonely confines of his house in Hampstead.

***

It took all George's persuasive powers to persuade Alfie and Dick to leave with him. 'Benny's beyond our help now. Go home, please. I'll inform Quilter when I get back to Montagu Square. One way or another, I'll make sure that you get to give Benny a decent burial.'

Cherkasov cleaned his wound as best he could. With George's handkerchief held in place by a ragged strip torn from a none too clean sheet and concealed under his hat, he assured George he would manage until he reached the embassy. 'I'll take this with me,' he said, holding the case containing the Dutchman's rifle under his arm.

***

Von Lensch was drowning. That's how it felt. Dimly aware of the procession passing along the Mall and the hum of conversation and commentary from the embassy dignitaries gathered to watch, he laboured to breathe, feeling the blood surging under the frantic beating of his heart and fearing that his legs might give way, he staggered to a seat at the back of the room.

***

Jaqueline hadn't stopped chattering since she'd arrived back at Montagu Square. Elsie received a minute-by-minute account of the parade, delivered breathlessly in a torrent of English and French.

Nodding encouragingly while preparing a plate of egg and cress sandwiches, she looked up as Verity entered the kitchen and stood leaning against the dresser, listening. Despite the mistress's smile, Elsie sensed the tension within. Something to do with Mister Ambrose limping up to the front door in the middle of the morning?

Verity brought Jaqueline away from Madam Claude's as soon as she could without giving offence to her hostess. Masking her surprise at seeing Ambrose sitting alone in her drawing room with his leg resting on a foot-stool, she'd listened to his account of a journey delayed by crowds, forced detours, and falling prey to pickpockets.

'Damned foolish of me, always managed to spot a pickpocket in Bombay. Had a sixth sense for them there.' Ambrose raised his head, listening to the mantle clock

342

sounding the half-hour. 'Twelve-thirty. Pray God they're in time.'

'Come, Jaqueline, you've told Elsie quite enough about the procession. Why don't we go out into the garden? It's such a lovely day, too nice to stay indoors.'

Had it been any other day, Verity could have thought of nothing more delightful than sitting in her garden with Jaqueline. Elsie brought them the sandwiches and a jug of delicious lemonade and Ambrose gamely hobbled outside with the aid of a walking stick, giving Jaqueline a reason to recount the morning's events all over again.

***

Jaqueline had long since tired of sitting still and was taking Marie-Louise, her imaginary friend, for a tour of the garden. Ambrose slept with his chin on his chest, occasionally mumbling in what Verity took to be some Indian dialect. Surely, if the worst had happened, she would know by now. The news of a royal assassination would reverberate throughout the city. A tidal wave of woe, flowing from street to street, neighbour to neighbour. A chorus of grief and disbelief and anger. But all was quiet. Jaqueline's voice and the droning of bumble bees around a buddleia were the only sounds. Perhaps Colonel Quilter's scornful dismissal of Dmitri's revelations about a German plot was justified. But von Lensch was real enough. And Riemann. And the mysterious bearded man.

A shadow fell over the table in front of her. 'Yes, Elsie?'

'It's me.'

'George!'

Verity wrapped her arms around him, looking anxiously into his eyes.

'It's alright,' he mouthed, not trusting himself to speak out loud.

Ambrose snorted and opened his eyes, and Jaqueline came running along the garden path.

'Jaqueline, please go and ask Elsie to make us all a cup of tea, will you?'

George kept his account short and to the point. A bitter sweet tale of triumph and loss. Verity brushed away a tear. 'Dear Benny.'

'I can't stay.'

'What? Why, George?'

'Quilter.'

Chapter 60

'Come in, Truscott.'

Sergeant Truscott, late of the Royal Marines, came to attention in front of Colonel Quilter's desk. 'The early edition of the evening paper, sir.'

'Thank you,' Quilter took the folded newspaper.

Truscott turned smartly on his heel and marched to the door, shutting it behind him. The presence of a pistol on Quilter's desk had not escaped him, but his was not to reason why.

The headline proclaimed the nation's undying loyalty to Her Majesty. Page after page recounted in the most florid of prose every detail of Her Majesty's triumphant Jubilee parade.

Scarlet and gold, azure and gold, purple and gold, emerald and gold, white and gold always a changing tumult of colours that seemed to list and gleam with a light of their own, and always blinding gold. It was enough. No eye could bear more gorgeousness, no more gorgeousness could be, unless princes are to clothe themselves in rainbows and the very sun. Gushed one correspondent.

When George was shown into his office thirty minutes later, the envelopes had been locked in Quilter's desk drawer and his pistol put away.

George ignored Quilter's offer of a chair. 'What you dismissed as a crazed notion came within a whisker of eliminating the sovereign and her heir.'

'I…'

'I haven't finished.' George gripped the edge of Quilter's desk. 'The assassin had his finger on the trigger. Dammit, man, it's your sworn duty to protect the sovereign, yet you've failed utterly. That this nation has not been plunged into the most unimaginable of crises is due to me, some salt of the earth Londoners, whom you seem to despise, and a Russian. Oh, and Verity Mallard, who possesses more spine and determination than a regiment of Colonel Quilters.'

'What happened?' Quilter asked in a hoarse whisper.

'A good man died. That's what happened.'

'Who… who died?'

'Benny. Benjamin Hopkins. A simple, brave soul who deserved better than to be shot down like a dog. No, don't say anything. Words of sympathy and regret mean nothing. The only thing you can do is make sure that his family are generously compensated for his sacrifice. I don't care how you make that happen, but I'll see you disgraced if you don't.'

Quilter nodded. Had he been minded to speak, the words wouldn't come. He looked dully at the scrap of paper George thrust at him.

'There's the address. You'll find the would-be assassin's body on the attic landing. Cherkasov shot him. It's thanks to him I'm standing here. Benny's lying on the first floor. And there's an old lady wrapped in a sheet in the front bedroom. Murdered I think.'

'The assassin was this man Riemann from the German Embassy?' Quilter spoke quietly, keeping his eyes on the paper.

'No. If you'd not distanced yourself from us, you'd be aware that Riemann had an associate. That's whose body you'll find. Riemann was there, but the other one was the sharpshooter.'

'I see. You say he was poised to shoot when you came upon him.'

George nodded. 'A Russian rifle with a telescopic sight. General Cherkasov took it away.'

'Hmm. I suppose I'd have done the same in his position. Do I take it that Riemann escaped?

George nodded.

There was no sign of Major von Lensch?'

'He's not the sort to get his hands dirty.'

Quilter's lame offer of a scotch produced a snort of derision. 'I'll send you my account.'

George saw himself out, brushing past Truscott on his way to the front door.

'Yes, sir,' the sergeant said a few moments later, in answer to Quilter's summons.

The Colonel pointed to the paper on his desk. 'We're going to this address. Right away.'

Chapter 61

'Are you quite settled back in your quarters now?' Verity asked.

In the week since the Jubilee, a semblance of normality had been restored. Ambrose was back in the familiar surroundings of Thorneycroft, mentioning to Mortimer and Olivia only that he'd met his Russian acquaintance and that an awkward fall had prevented him from witnessing the Jubilee procession.

Verity had given Elsie a well-deserved break, paying for her train ticket to visit her sister in Northampton. Sally, the parlour-maid, shouldered the housework while Verity herself turned her hand to cooking, with mixed results.

'Yes, back in the old routine,' George stretched his legs, settling into an armchair. 'I'm sorry I put you to all that trouble.'

'Fiddlesticks, George. No thanks necessary.' Verity passed a cup of tea to him. 'Even if it caused no end of trouble,' she added with a laugh. 'Is peace restored with Effie?'

George's rueful expression answered her question. 'Oh, I'm sorry.' George shook his head, the memory of how he'd approached Effie's shop two days after the Jubilee, with a gigantic box of chocolates under his arm only to spy her on the doorstep kissing a tall, well-dressed, moustachioed fellow, was still quite raw. Fortunately, they'd gone inside without seeing him.

'Well, here's something to cheer you up.' Verity put her cup down and went to the mantelpiece. 'Here we are. Courtesy of Mary. Two tickets to Hedda Gabbler. A box, no less. You must come. Just think, you'll see Anna.'

George pretended to ignore the twinkle in her eye. 'I'm quite cured of any thoughts I may have had in that direction.'

'But you'll come, won't you? Go on. Just say yes.'

George threw his hands up in mock surrender. 'I'll come.'

'Splendid. Now finish your tea and we'll take Jaqueline to the park.'

***

'I will report to the Prince of Wales that any loose ends arising from that Fenian business have been dealt with.'

Quilter nodded. He'd imagined that his interview with the prime minister would take place in more intimate surroundings. Instead, he found himself in the Cabinet room, sitting opposite Lord Salisbury, with the polished expanse of the Cabinet table stretching away on either side.

'Extraordinary business. All Fenians dead, you say, and a German assassin. A hair's breadth from calamity. Your country owes you a debt of gratitude, Colonel.'

'You're too kind, prime minister. I did no more than my duty.'

***

'Bravo. Bravo,' Verity was on her feet, clapping heartily the instant that the curtain came down. George joined her, glad

349

to stand after what seemed an interminable performance. His was a minority opinion. The crowd cheered and clapped through five curtain calls. Mary looked up between bows, beaming at her friends. Anna, the chief focus of the audience's adulation, maintained a dignified poise, as though it were no more than her due.

As the audience shuffled out, Mary appeared breathlessly in the box. 'Verity, George, did you like it? Wasn't Anna simply divine and Edward too?'

'You were all marvellous. And no false modesty, Mary. Your performance was a triumph. It almost made me want to resume my acting career, such as it was.' Verity turned to George. 'Wasn't Mary simply wonderful?'

'Yes, yes,' George nodded, uncertain what he should say next.

'Oh George,' Mary teased, 'there's no need to look so uncomfortable. I know it's not really your cup of tea, but thank you for coming along. Now then, do come backstage, both of you.'

Anna looked up from her dressing table. 'Verity,' she exclaimed, getting to her feet. 'And George too. It's such a pleasure to see you.'

'And in more normal circumstances,' she added in a whisper.

'Anna has agreed to join us for dinner.' Mary clapped her hands delightedly. 'And Edward insists on coming along.'

'Did I hear my name?' Edward Crawford struck a flamboyant attitude in the doorway.

Anna took them along the corridor to the stage door. 'I know a delightful little restaurant just a few minutes away. The chef is from Vienna.'

Outside, the glorious weather that graced the Jubilee had given way to blustery showers. Verity shivered and took George's arm. Mary did likewise on George's left.

Anna and Edward led their little procession along the narrow passage connecting the stage door to the bright lights of Leicester Square.

The intruder came from nowhere.

'Bitch. I'm ruined.' Swathed in a dark overcoat and with a scarf covering the lower half of his face, it was solely by his voice that Anna recognised Giles. Her handbag was the only defence she could muster against his knife thrust. The blade passed straight through the soft satin but stopped a half inch from her breast. Edward grabbed his arm with both hands but couldn't prevent Giles from wrenching his arm free.

'Giles!' Anna screamed. For a split second, the three of them stood frozen like some waxwork tableau, until the thud of George's boots broke the spell.

The Dutch-courage Giles had administered to himself beforehand spurred him to the end of the passage, throwing the knife aside and bursting into Leicester Square. Heedless of the crowds, he barged his way across the pavement. With the protests of a middle-aged gentleman he'd knocked over, and the sound of George's pursuit ringing in his ears, he darted around an omnibus, casting a hasty glance behind him.

Deftly avoiding a hansom cab coming in the other direction, he put on a spurt to get clear of a gig coming up behind at a fast clip. The change in the weather was his undoing. Failing to see a pile of squashed dung resting in the middle of a puddle, he skidded, flailing in a vain attempt to regain his balance. One of the horse's hoofs struck him square in the face as he fell sprawling on to the cobbles. The driver did his best to pull up, but not before a wheel passed over Giles's neck.

George stepped back, distancing himself from the hullabaloo. Traffic was at a standstill as curious bystanders gathered.

He found the others in a huddle at the entrance to the passage. In answer to their enquiring looks, he shook his head.

Mary stood shaking in Edward's arms. George could see that Edward was barely more composed himself.

Verity took Anna's arm. 'What on earth was that about?' she hissed. 'That was Giles, the man you played along as his mistress. You said he was no further use to you. I don't believe you, Anna, if that really is your name. I want the truth. What was Giles involved in?'

Anna smiled. 'Well, he certainly is no use to me now.' She paused, giving Verity an amused look. 'Giles Temple-Swift was a traitor to his country, Verity. He protected and helped those Fenians. But his real master was Lensch. He was a weak, vain man. He's served his purpose. I have no more to say on the matter. Do you know, I have quite lost my appetite.' Anna detached her arm and walked away.

Chapter 62

August 1897

'Yes, of course you can visit the stables, dear,' Oliva smiled down at Jaqueline. 'Ask Bernard to show you Tanglefoot.'

'She's besotted with horses,' Verity watched fondly as her daughter scampered from the room. 'I'll look out for a suitable pony when I take her back to Montvalon.'

'Ah, when will that be?'

'In a fortnight. I haven't broken the news to her yet. I'm dreading it. She's had such a happy time in London, but *c'est la vie*. Anyway, how are you, my dear? All well with the Mallard in waiting?'

'A little nausea in the mornings, but otherwise, I feel perfectly fine. Now, Mortimer promised he'd tear himself away from the estate office by noon at the latest. That gives us half an hour. Why don't I come up to the blue room and help you to unpack and settle in?'

Verity took Olivia's arm. During the three weeks that had elapsed since the Jubilee, she'd done her best to regain a sense of normality. A commission to write an article on the newly opened Tate Gallery for *The Englishwoman's Review* provided a welcome distraction.

Giles Temple-Swift's death had received some press coverage but was viewed as an unfortunate accident. Verity felt duty-bound to write a note to Colonel Quilter informing him of the actual circumstances and of Anna's revelations. A terse reply acknowledging her letter arrived by return of post.

Hedda Gabbler's run came to an end shortly after she and George attended. Mary and Edward called at Montagu Square the following day.

'Anna has left for the continent,' Mary told her. 'The last performances were quite an ordeal for both of us,' she said, exchanging glances with Edward, 'after that business with Giles.'

'Mind you, Anna behaved as though nothing had happened,' said Edward.

'Needless to say, we'll keep the whole matter to ourselves,' Mary added.

***

Then there was Benny's funeral. Verity attended with George.

While Benny's immediate relations only consisted of two sisters, it seemed that half the East End thought of him as family. Alfie and Dick and a small tribe of cousins, uncles and aunts flocked to Abney Park Cemetery with a wide cast of colourful characters from Whitechapel and surrounding boroughs.

***

'Aha, you've arrived.' Ambrose stood at the foot of the stairs. 'I insisted to Mortimer that I escort you to luncheon. Still hobbling a bit,' he added, waggling the walking stick in his right hand.

354

Verity leaned forward to accept a kiss on her cheek and took his arm.

'By the way,' he whispered, 'I haven't said a word to Mortimer or Olivia about the goings-on in London.'

'I should think not. You know it must remain a secret. You've not been tempted to, have you?'

'Not a bit. Soul of discretion.' Ambrose tapped the side of his nose. 'Got a bit of news for you. Dmitri sent me a letter. Appreciation and all that. He's back in St Petersburg.'

'Yes, he wrote to me as well.'

'Oh. Good of him.'

'Yes. He's invited me to go there.' The look on Ambrose's face was just what Verity had hoped for.

'Hey, you two, what's all that whispering? Cooking up some conspiracy, are you?' Mortimer's voice floated out from the dining room.

'Just discussing a mutual acquaintance, no one you know, Mortie.' Verity gave Ambrose a conspiratorial wink.

***

'Well, that brings you up to date on everything at Thorneycroft.' Mortimer pushed his empty dessert bowl aside. 'Oh, no, I almost forgot. The Jubilee.'

Verity gave a start, flashing a look of warning at Ambrose. 'The Jubilee?'

'Yes. It's all very well for you London dwellers, but we poor folk in the country could only read about it in the newspapers. However, thanks to the cinematograph, we can share in the spectacle.'

'Oh yes. There was a small army of men taking moving pictures on the day. Do you mean to say that you have seen a cinematograph film of the procession?'

'Not yet. Olivia and I will be hosting a showing of the Jubilee procession at Flaxminton Parish Hall tomorrow evening. Practically the whole village will be turning out. A Mister Downey is coming down from London with his projecting apparatus.'

****

'Quite a turnout,' Ambrose turned to Verity seated next to him.

'I don't think I've seen the Parish Hall so full.' Verity craned her neck. 'They're having to shut the doors now. I fancy, Mr Downey will have to give a second showing. Are you excited, *chérie*?' Jaqueline nodded enthusiastically.

Mortimer stood to welcome the audience and introduce Mr Downey, after which, the cinematographer gave a short exposition on the wonders of moving picture photography. 'I had the honour of filming the procession from a vantage point in Trafalgar Square,' he added. 'My colleagues were stationed at other locations such as St Paul's and Westminster and I have gathered together all our film to afford you as comprehensive a view as possible of the wonderful events of that day.'

The audience applauded, then an expectant hush descended on the Hall as the lights were dimmed and Mr Downey set his projector in motion.

Although she had witnessed the procession at first hand, Verity marvelled at the flickering images, bringing the entire spectacle alive again. The scene outside St Paul's Cathedral was especially poignant, with the shrunken figure of Her Majesty in her carriage, juxtaposed with the towering bulk of the cathedral and the massed ranks of the crowds in the stands surrounding the square.

The final scene shifted to Whitehall. It was when the Band of the Life Guards passed by that she saw him. In the gap between the Life Guards band and the next mounted formation, the camera focussed fleetingly on the crowd seated on the opposite side of the thoroughfare, under a large sign proclaiming *God Save The Queen.*

She caught her breath. A glimpse was all she had, but the saturnine features left an indelible image in her mind. The camera angle shifted, looking down the street to capture the length of the procession. Verity's concentration waned, her mind given over to that face. A face she had every reason to remember. The face of Anthony Spencer. The impresario turned devious criminal, who had so nearly been her nemesis.

Could she really be sure on the strength of a brief image? In a way, she hoped she was mistaken. Spencer had fled the country, and much as she might want him brought to justice, she took some comfort in the thought that he might be gone for good.

The camera angle changed once again. Squadrons of Hussars rode by. Verity concentrated, waiting for the last rank to pass.

'Yes!' her hand gripped Ambrose's arm. 'It's Anthony Spencer,' she hissed.

'What?'

'Spencer. On the screen. Oh, blast.' The Lancers, following the Hussars, obscured her view. 'After they've gone by,' she whispered, 'keep your eyes on the screen. It's him, I'm sure of it.'

Stifling an urge to scream, Verity willed the reel to move faster. 'Now!' she prodded Ambrose with her elbow.

'I'll be damned. It is him.'

Chapter 63

November 1897

'Welcome back, boys. Did you enjoy your half-term holiday?'

'Yes, sir.' A ragged, half-hearted chorus responded to Joseph's question.

'Very good. Then you will all be refreshed and ready for our next topic.'

Disregarding the inevitable *sotto voce* groans, Joseph applied his chalk to the blackboard with a flourish.

The Roman Empire

Joseph permitted himself a smile, recalling everything that had occurred since he'd last introduced that subject to a class of boys.

Settled in a new school, he committed himself to a new beginning. The cause remained dear to his heart, but now he recognised that he would serve it best by peaceful means. Employing the power of argument, and perseverance, was the way to Home Rule, however many setbacks must be overcome to achieve it. It required men with force of intellect rather than force of arms.

Tonight, when he went back to Edna's house, there'd be no envelope with half a playing card waiting for him.

Happily, the ground under the coal hole had been easy to dig. Edna had done her bit, bringing cups of tea while he shovelled, and bathing his blisters. An old curtain served for a shroud and Sean O'Brien, otherwise known as Captain Carter, was consigned to the earth. Edna ordered a fresh delivery of coal, and that was that.

***

Kaiser Wilhelm stretched his feet out towards the fire. 'It's good to see you back in Berlin, my dear friend.'

Philipp zu Eulenburg gave a simpering smile. 'All too short a visit, alas. But I could hardly return to Vienna without seeing you.'

Wilhelm reached out and patted his arm. 'I was only thinking the other day of that thought you expressed to me last year. How we and the British might enter into some form of alliance.'

Eulenburg's smile melted away. Where was Wilhelm going with this?

'Forgive me if I was a little slow on the uptake that day,' Wilhelm turned to him, grinning. 'I see now that it was merely a light-hearted jest on your part. If I'd not been so incensed about that British raid on the Boers, I would have known you were pulling my leg.'

Eulenburg sat forward in his seat. 'Ha, of course. A clumsy attempt at humour. The very idea.'

***

Von Lensch scratched at a mosquito bite on his neck, anxious to leave the heat and dust of the parade ground. The German Imperial Flag drooped on the flagpole, as lifeless as Erich felt. The triumphant return to Berlin of his imagination had turned out to be the cruellest of mirages.

As soon as the Jubilee procession passed by the German Embassy, he crept away, collected his luggage from Brown's and caught the first train for Harwich. He tried his best to disguise his despondency from Gudrun, but she could hardly fail to sense his downcast mood. He locked the pearls away in his bureau.

A meeting with Riemann in a dingy bierkeller filled in the details. A catastrophe. But how? There was only one conclusion. Orpheus must have betrayed him. He rehearsed what he would say to Eulenburg. God knows, he'd done his best. Why should he bear the blame for another's act of treachery? The opportunity never came.

Gudrun broke down in tears when he showed the letter, ordering him to his new post. 'You must go on your own. I'm staying in Berlin,' she cried, running from the room in floods of tears.

Kaiser-Wilhelmsland, German New Guinea. The end of the earth. Lensch gritted his teeth. His uniform clung to him in sweat-soaked patches. At last, the parade of his motley collection of soldiers was over. Mustering what little dignity he had left, he made for his quarters and the consolation of a bottle of schnapps.

***

Riemann gazed down from the vine terraces at the Mosel meandering through the valley. It had been a good grape harvest. Now, with Oktoberfest behind him, he looked forward to Christmas with his sister's family. His soldiering was all behind him. Guided by the weak sun's rays, he made his way home.

Historical Note

The Jameson Raid was a spectacular failure that gravely embarrassed the British government, further alienated the Boers, and exacerbated the already fractious relationship between Great Britain and Imperial Germany. Jameson himself can be said to have got off lightly. The Boer Government handed him over to the British and he was sentenced by a British Court to a prison term of fifteen months. His conspirators within the Transvaal were tried by the Boers for high treason, found guilty and sentenced to death by hanging. However, they were released within months on payment of substantial fines. Cecil Rhodes, the Prime Minister of Cape Colony, was implicated in supporting the raid and had to resign. Ultimately, Jameson prospered, becoming Prime Minister of the Cape Colony in 1904 and being awarded a baronetcy in 1911.

Kaiser Wilhelm's complicated relationships with his grandmother, Queen Victoria, and Bertie, Prince of Wales, is well documented. Highly sensitive to perceived snubs on the part of the Queen and her son, Wilhelm nursed a sense of grievance punctuated from time to time with expressions of love and admiration (at least to the Queen). To Wilhelm, Bertie was indeed that 'old peacock'.

Philipp, Prince of Eulenburg, became a figure of considerable influence in German foreign policy, stemming from his close friendship with Kaiser Wilhelm. A highly cultured man who wrote books and composed songs, he was also staunchly anti-Semitic and pursued a deep interest in the occult, which he shared with Wilhelm. Although married with eight children, Eulenburg indulged in affairs with both sexes. His homosexuality was ultimately his undoing. In an interesting parallel with the case of Oscar Wilde, allegations of homosexuality raised by Maximilian Harden, a crusading journalist, sparked a chain of events that saw Eulenburg arrested and put on trial for perjury in 1908. However, the trial was abandoned after he collapsed in court. His brilliant career and reputation in tatters, he died in 1921.

The Fenian plot to attack Queen Victoria's Diamond Jubilee is fiction. However, such a plot had indeed been hatched ten years earlier, which aimed to detonate a cache of explosives in Westminster Abbey when the Queen attended a Service of Thanksgiving during her Golden Jubilee celebrations. Inspired and financed by Clan-na-Gael, a group of militant Irish nationalists in the United States, a campaign of bombing was planned, led by an adventurer named Francis Millen. The plot never came to fruition. The British police became aware of it and steps were taken to shadow Millen and his co-conspirators. Ultimately, two Fenians, Thomas Callan and Michael Harkins, were convicted of possessing explosives and each sentenced to fifteen years of penal servitude.

However, there was more to this tale than a plot that failed. Francis Millen, who evaded capture and returned to the United States, turned out to be a double agent who had been an informer for the British for many years. Adding to the intrigue is the assertion by journalist Christy Campbell, in his book *Fenian Fire: The British Plot to Assassinate Queen Victoria*, that the whole business was an elaborate deception orchestrated by the British and sanctioned by the Prime Minister, Lord Salisbury. Not, of course, with the intention of harming the Queen, but of using the foiled plot to destroy the reputation of Charles Parnell, the parliamentary leader of the Irish cause, by implying falsely that he was implicated in it. A case of truth being stranger than fiction.

In 1840, Captain Arthur Connolly, of the 6th Bengal Light Cavalry, coined the term The Great Game, to describe the rivalry between the imperial powers of Russia and Great Britain for control in Central Asia. For almost the whole of the 19th century, enterprising men from both sides played cat and mouse, gathering intelligence and seeking to gain influence with a mishmash of regional powers across Persia, Afghanistan and the wild, mountainous badlands of the Pamirs and Karakorams. With Russian conquests in Central Asia bringing its armies ever closer to British India, the spectre of a Russian invasion spurred Britain to ever greater lengths to defend the *jewel in the crown* of its vast empire.

The mission in which Ambrose and Thakur Singh interpose themselves was indeed a major initiative on the part of the British to counter Russian influence with Yakub Beg, the Muslim ruler of that part of Central Asia known as Kashgaria. Although it was at first considered a success with grandiose promises of enduring friendship and a lucrative trading partnership, nothing was to come of it.

Acknowledgements

With thanks to Ian Hooper and all at Book Reality for making this book a reality.

About The Author

R J Williams was born in Aberystwyth in Wales and now lives in Perth, Western Australia.

After a busy career in information technology and management consulting, in the UK and Australia, retirement has given him the opportunity to indulge his interest in history and pursue his long-held ambition to become an author of historical novels.

He enjoys writing, cycling, travelling, and volunteering with Para Quad industries, who provide employment to people with disabilities.